RATTRAP

S. H. HAMILTON

CHAPTER 1

"Splat!"

Dexter Curtis pointed his index finger at the cornered rodent and simulated pulling the trigger. And then he stomped it dead viciously with one of his designer boots.

His companion cringed. "This place is a rattrap," his friend and teammate, Kevin Jones, muttered disgustedly. "Why in the hell did you bring me here, Dexter?"

"My personal trainer is in Miami," Curtis snapped back. "Got to get the good stuff somewhere." He flipped the rat over on its back with his foot. "You see what I did to that sucker? I pretended it was a pansy quarterback in a skirt."

"Don't ever drag me here again," Jones told his companion with the yellow towel wrapped around his head like a bandana. "And that 'good stuff' will get you suspended. Or kill you."

Another large rat scurried into a hole as the two large men in Steelers throw-back jerseys walked down the hall and out of the crack house.

"If you ever tell anybody we came here, dog, I'll kill *you*."

CHAPTER 2

Pittsburgh Tribune-Review reporter Jolyn Knowlton just listened and took mental notes as they reminisced about the good old days.

She and her editor, Stephen Winslow, and two other members of the staff had just left a retirement dinner. Jolyn had offered to provide transportation to the three men because they had expressed interest in obtaining the services of a designated driver. They wanted to celebrate with their retiring colleague without worrying about driving home. And she was the newest kid on the writer's block at the paper, due in part to the imminent departure of the guest of honor.

Jolyn had borrowed her father's Lincoln Navigator. It had so much more room than her ten year old Cavalier. And didn't stall.

Stephen Winslow sat in the front passenger seat.

His cell phone rang.

He listened.

"Okay, Ed, be right there," he finally said.

During the call Stephen's facial expression had changed from one of joviality to deep melancholy.

"What is it, Mr. Winslow?" Jolyn asked, concerned.

"That was Detective Ed Woods, a friend of mine. The Hansen little girl who disappeared four days ago? Possible abduction from her home while her parents slept? Her body has found in a dumpster. Chopped into pieces."

"Oh my dear God!" Jolyn blurted. "Why? *Why* is there so much evil in this world of ours?"

"Yes, Jolyn, *why?*"

He gave her driving directions.

After a few minutes Jolyn murmured softly and thoughtfully, "In order to defeat evil, you must understand the nature of evil." The exact words her lover Zeke had whispered as he lay dying in her arms.

Stephen glanced at her quizzically.

But the look on her face told him not to ask.

They rode the rest of the way to the crime scene in morbid silence.

CHAPTER 3

Ron Kingston, sports agent extraordinaire at least in his own mind, talked with Hank Gorton on the telephone.

He didn't trust the private dick but Gorton got the job done, although his methods sometimes even alarmed Kingston.

"Gorton, I want you to go to D.C. There is an honorable senator from Pennsylvania there who likes to slurp salami when his wife is not around. He's in the capitol to meet with several cabinet members. Get some pictures. I need his vote on a certain bill."

"Oh yeah, I heard about him. They call the guy 'Glory Hole Gary' behind his back. Pictures are a distinct possibility."

Next Kingston called Nathan Redmond, assassin for hire.

"Frankie Mancini—a hundred grand."

"Oh man, I like his songs. And I don't like to do the deed in Vegas. That's where I play."

"Another fifty. Tell him the bullet is from me before you put in his head. He's at the Stardust. I'm sure you can afford $59.95 for a ticket."

"What did he do, screw your wife?"

"Hell no, he's a fruit. I'd thank him profusely if he did the bitch. Then I wouldn't have to. The SEC is on my ass again. He ratted me out on some rather uh . . . questionable accounting practices I allegedly authorized for the cable company he's one of my partners in. Inflating subscription numbers, revenue, and cash flow? Now does that sound like yours truly? Obstruction of justice? I love justice—especially when I'm dispensing it."

"Fuck, I hate queers. I'm going to burn all of the cock sucker's CDs. Why did he squeal?"

"They had him by the balls so he went for a deal and gave me up. He don't like prison any better than you and I did, although he can get all the dick he wants. Must be the food."

"Yeah, the food sucks. You wouldn't believe what I had for dinner tonight."

"Do tell."

"A cute little dish named Maryanne. Sugar and spice and everything nice. Garlic, too."

"Redmond, I have to go now. Meeting with Nike about potential endorsements for my latest client, the Steelers number one draft pick. I'm going to make a fortune off this guy."

"Oh yeah, Dexter Curtis. You made a real coup, signing that dude. He kicks ass."

"Call me when Mancini is history."

"Consider that faggot snitch maggot bait."

CHAPTER 4

Harleys turned her on.

She always had a nice bike, starting with a little pink tricycle with streamers on the handlebars. Then she moved on to a red, white, and blue bicycle with training wheels.

Kim McConnell's brother Duane had taught her to ride a Harley. She learned on his old Panhead with the suicide clutch. Duane worked on Harleys for a living, when he wasn't in jail. He lent her the money to buy the used cobalt blue pearl XLH Sportster 883 Hugger. Perfect big girl's bike.

She liked to ride when she got depressed. Like now. The rainy, gloomy weather didn't help matters much.

Mirror, mirror on the wall.

She liked what she saw.

Black leather vest. Full collar, lapels and front zipper closure so one could display as much cleavage as one wanted, especially if one didn't wear a bra, which she didn't. Matching fancy fringed chaps with a front buckle and zippered sides. Braids hung from the waist. Open in both the front and back, but she had black panties on underneath. Chippewa seventeen inch lace-up motorcycle boots. Fingerless mesh gloves with leather palms. Bugz Tazar goggles with the silver lenses. EZ Rider helmet. Very worn Australian oilskin waterproof washed-back canvas duster she borrowed from her brother.

Kim rode and rode, enjoying the solitude and feeling the freedom. But she began to get a chill. It drizzled again.

Kim passed a little country bar that had a half dozen Harleys parked outside and a crooked sign over the door that said HOG HEAVEN. She did a U-turn and went back.

At first they couldn't tell she was a girl, not until she took off the helmet with the shield she had attached because of the rain. No other females were in the place. They stared.

"I love that Fatboy outside," she said, very friendly.

The biker who appeared to be the leader responded, "1993 custom built Fatboy. S & S rods and pistons, Edelbrock hand ported heads, Sifton 141 cam, PM four piston rear caliper, Merch performance case, Truett & Osborn flywheels, Dyna 2000 ignition and single fire— "

"You talk just like my brother," she interrupted. "The names of your Harleys like Panheads, Fatboys, and Knuckleheads are meant to correspond to the IQ of your typical biker dude," she joked. "Panhead—the motor cover looks like an upside down pan. Doh!"

"Get the pretty funny lady a beer on me," the leader demanded of the bartender. "Make hers a Molson Canadian Light and bring us another round."

"Hey, I like this!" she observed as she took a swig, and smiled. "Usually I drink Bud Light. Sometimes Miller Lite when I'm in the mood for wrestling with my girlfriend."

"Well, just look what these beers say on the back," the biker suggested. Yours says, 'Let's get me out of these wet clothes.' Mine says, 'I'm not wearing any underwear.' I'm *not* wearing any underwear. My man here, his says, 'Guess where my tattoo is.' I bet you got a tattoo, sweet meat."

"Yes, I do have a tattoo. But I am wearing underwear. Panties anyway."

Kim took off the wet duster. The vest's zipper was lowered far enough to almost see nipple.

"So let me see your tattoo, honey. I'd sure like to help you out of your wet clothes, and give you something to warm you up."

"I'm sure you would. My tattoo . . . is . . . uh . . . oh never mind."

"Do you know why Harleys are better than women?" he asked, leering lewdly.

"No, I'm afraid I don't."

"Harleys don't get headaches; if your Harley is too loose you can tighten it; if you get your Harley dirty, you don't have to apologize before you ride her again; you can ride your Harley as long as you want and it won't get sore."

She smirked, but didn't laugh.

The bikers ordered more beers and shots and they played several games of pool. Kim partnered with the leader and they won every game.

"You're good, honey, real good," he complimented, as he patted her on the behind.

She downed a double shot of Jim Beam.

"Yeah, I like pool."

"Hey, we're heading up to a biker rally outside of Toronto tomorrow. Come with us. I'd sure like to see you strut that sexy stuff of yours up there, babe."

"I can't. Classes. I'm a college student."

"They're having a strip tease contest and the finalists will be offered a job with one of the clubs the gangs run. You can make big money stripping, honey. You got a body that don't quit."

She laughed delightfully.

"Actually, I'm entering a wet T-shirt contest tomorrow night. A bet with my girlfriends."

Suddenly he reached for her vest and quickly unzipped it all the way. "Free them puppies!"

"Nice hooters!" one roared, as the others nodded approvingly.

She didn't make any effort to cover them.

"I think you like to show off those big brown eyes," the leader said as he tweaked a nipple gently, "don't you, honey? You like to cock tease. Do you know what's worse than a hurricane?"

"Uh . . ."

"A tit twister!"

"Ouch!" She slapped his hand away playfully.

"You got tits to die for, babe," he complimented, putting his hands under them and lifting them up.

"Hey thanks. Can you tell they're real? If you got it, flaunt it, I say. I like to ride topless on occasion and I don't mean without a helmet. Not that I want to cause an accident or anything so I pick my spots. My favorite little scene is pulling up to a gas station boobs bobbing and pumping my gas topless. Then I walk up to the door, stare curiously at the NO SHIRT-NO SHOES-NO SERVICE sign, put on my shirt and go inside any pay."

"I'd like to show you my other hog, darlin'. I think you'll like that one even better than the Fatboy outside." He grabbed his crotch.

"Nothing like feeling the vibration of a hog between your legs," she purred.

"You're not offended by what I said? It's not often a woman like you will give a guy like me the time of day."

"It's 6:45 PM," she replied matter-of-factly. "And what kind of woman like me do you mean? One with teeth?"

The leader's comrades roared. He looked serious.

"I could have my way with you if I wanted to, babe," the leader boasted. "I could screw you silly right on this pool table while my boys hold you down."

Kim didn't look upset.

She slipped off the vest and wiggled out of the chaps, standing in only the black panties.

"You must be a bang gang," she purred. "You won't rat on me and tell my daddy I'm a bad girl?"

"What happens in HOG HEAVEN stays in HOG HEAVEN, honey," the leader assured her quite solemnly.

"Then you can see my tattoo."

Kim slowly lowered the panties until they fell to her ankles and she kicked

9

them away.

CHAPTER 5

The Hummer hummed.

The training camp practice of the Pittsburgh Steelers at Saint Vincent College in Latrobe had just ended for the day under the scorching August sun and lung-sapping humidity. Dexter Curtis relished the boot-camp like atmosphere and frenzied antics of ex-linebacker head coach Bill Lowry. Dexter loved to hit. He lived to flip running backs like hamburgers and squash quarterbacks into mush. Coach Lowry reluctantly ordered Dexter to ease up on his teammates and save the slaughter for the first preseason game. The local sportswriters flocked around the rookie like flies on garbage. One called him a cross between Jack Lambert and Mean Joe Greene, but nastier than both hall-of-famers and members of the fabled "Steel Curtain" defense.

The day before training camp began Dexter Curtis, first round draft pick, had signed a multi-year contract. The team hoped the All American linebacker would fill the void left by the career ending spinal injury suffered by Donald Edwards in the Pro Bowl. Coach Lowry waxed ecstatic over the havoc Dexter wrecked in training camp. He could not be effectively blocked and played eons beyond intense. The offensive linemen trembled in consternation over his intimidating obsessive ferocity.

Curtis wanted to have a little fun and spend some of his new found fortune before the real football season began. One of the defensive linemen, Kevin Jones, had invited Dexter to spend some time at his condo in downtown Pittsburgh. Jones had graduated from Pitt and knew the city very well so he gave Dexter a tour. The Carnegie Science Center, the Phipps Conservatory and Botanical Gardens, a Gateway Clipper riverboat cruise, and much more. They partied all night at Kevin's favorite clubs and bars.

RATTRAP

Kevin and Dexter had become friends very quickly. They shared some of their personal histories. Dexter talked about his high school sweetheart, Juanita, who became his wife a year ago. She remained back home in Miami, pregnant with their first child. But Dexter clammed up when Kevin questioned him about his past brushes with the law that had made headlines.

"Those charges were dropped," was all Dexter would say.

Dexter parked the Hummer. He and Kevin got out and swaggered toward the entrance door of the bar.

"Hot white chicks in this place," Kevin predicted from past experience.

"Yeah man, I *need* some tight white ass," Dexter declared emphatically.

CHAPTER 7

Sweet cheeks.

Kim McConnell, soon to be a senior at Pitt, was a football cheerleader. Tall, long legs, strawberry blonde hair, pale and lightly freckled skin. An extraordinary beauty. And not lacking in the smarts department. She consistently made high honors.

Kevin Jones, a second year player with the Steelers, knew Kim. Not well, but they had occasionally shared pleasantries. Once they had been in the same speech class and she gave him some suggestions to overcome his fear of public speaking. He recognized her immediately in the bar, and sat on the unoccupied bar stool to her left.

"Hey Kevin," she greeted warmly, "how are you? Are the Steelers finally going to the Super Bowl this year?"

"You got that right, girl. Kim, meet our first round draft choice, Dexter Curtis." He stood at the bar next to Kevin. "He's the man," Kevin boasted confidently. "The difference. What we need to get over the big hump. Dexter teaches dogs how to be mean," Kevin joked. "Hey Dex, how about a little growl?"

"Woof, woof," Dexter muttered softly, and smacked his teammate playfully.

Kim and Dexter nodded at each other in polite acknowledgement. She jested, "I'm calling my bookie right now and putting my life's savings on the home team to win it all."

"You do that, Kim," Kevin retorted affably, "and you'll be wearing designer dresses instead of an old holy T-shirt and faded denim skirt. What's going on at this place tonight? A lot of pretty ladies are here. Incidentally, I can tell you're not wearing a bra. You better be careful a nipple doesn't poke through that little rip in your shirt."

"Wet T-shirt contest," Kim replied, a little embarrassed. "We cheerleaders made a little bet amongst ourselves. What are you doing in this honky-tonk, anyway?"

"Gary Randazzo, our center, is part owner of this here establishment. Didn't you notice all the Steelers pictures and memorabilia on the walls? Gary told us to stop by. Brew and wings on the house. Try the Steelers "DEEE-FENSE" ribs. They're broken. By the way, I predict you'll win the wet T-shirt contest, Kim," he offered with a smirk.

"Oh yeah? You should know, Kevin. Not that you've ever seen my boobs. But girls talk. I hear you get around. They both looked at Angie Covelli sitting at a table with some of the other cheerleaders. A rather voluptuous and deeply tanned, raven haired vixen of Greek and Italian heritage.

"Yes, I dated Angie. Until her parents met me. Kind of a *Guess Who's Coming to Dinner* thing that turned into a fiasco."

"She still talks about you, Kevin. As in crush and crushed. I think you broke her heart. Why don't you make her day and go over and chat her up?"

"I think I will, Kim." He got up from the bar stool and approached her. Angie gave him one of those sultry smiles that melt icebergs.

Dexter nursed a free beer. "Hey, Dexter, sit down," Kim said invitingly. "Tell me about Miami. That's where you went to school, right?"

She scrutinized him closely. About six-four, well over two hundred pounds. Ripped arms and abs displayed in the sleeveless bare-midriff shirt. Nice smile. Perfect bright white teeth. Shaved head. He had removed the Steelers cap once to scratch his shiny black dome.

"Yes indeed, Kim," he replied as he stretched out on the bar stool next to her. "Miami. What can I say? I love the weather. I haven't seen much snow. Just a few flakes here and there at games in the north, like Boston College."

Kim laughed gaily. "Get yourself a warm coat, a scarf, stocking hat, and boots. Brrr! Winter in Pittsburgh."

"Can't wait. I had hoped the Dolphins would draft me, but no such luck. But now I'm real glad the Steelers got me. Some of the players remind me of my home boys back in Miami. The Steelers have a nose tackle, Stump Davis, who just got out of prison for manslaughter. He caught his wife with the preacher. The preacher went to heaven and Stump's wife went to the hospital. Now Stump calls quarterbacks 'Reverend.' You should see him crush apples with one hand and rip the Pittsburgh phone book in half."

"Hey, you made that up! About the preacher."

Dexter laughed. "I just might become a preacher when my playing days are over."

"Oh really? My mother wanted me to attend a Christian college. I don't think so. What was your major at Miami, and your favorite courses?"

Dexter related that he had a Bachelor of Science Degree in Health Education

14

and his favorite course was "The Meaning of Leisure," and he also liked the exercise science classes.

Kim smiled knowingly. She told him that she majored in English and her favorite courses dealt with the study of the literature, context, and influence of British Romanticism. She wondered if that would interest Dexter much.

"Don Juan," she murmured.

"What? I didn't hear you."

"I said 'Don Juan,' Dexter."

"Who me?"

"Lord Byron. One of my favorite works. The poem's theme is that the abuses in society exist because of human flaws and negative tendencies. We deceive others because of our selfishness. Bryon equates the tendency in people to cheat to nature's everlasting changes. Society is obsessed with wealth and power and external beauty."

Dexter looked at her strangely. "Maybe I should take the class." He snickered. "I dig external beauty—yours. You are a stone cold fox."

"Thank you, Dexter." She could feel the blush. Or flush. "This semester I'm taking a class where the novels *Anna Karenina* and *Madame Bovary* are the focus of attention. I've already read them, of course. Several times."

"What are they about?"

"I would say that, briefly, the premise of both is that adultery leads to death."

Dexter snorted, and frowned. His sudden apparent discomfort prompted her to change the subject slightly.

"Did you know that Pitt was founded in 1787 as a small, private school, the Pittsburgh Academy, in a log cabin near the three rivers?" she asked.

"Did you know that the University of Miami actually is located in the city of Coral Gables?" he countered.

"Really? Pitt is actually located in Oakland."

"Huh?"

"The Oakland section of Pittsburgh. Your hat. Do you know what the logo represents?"

"Nope. Tell me."

"Don't they give you rookies an orientation or something?"

Kim informed him that the Steelmark logo consisting of a circle enclosing three hypocycloids and word "Steelers" on the team's helmets and other items was created by the then U.S. Steel Corporation to educate consumers about the importance of steel in their daily lives. She explained that the colors of the hypocycloids— yellow for coal, orange for ore, and blue for steel scrap— represented the three materials used to produce steel.

"And did you notice, Dexter, that the Steelers logo is only on one side of your helmets? Every other team has their logo on both sides."

"How interesting," he observed, amused by her seriousness. "Do you know what the 'Immaculate Reception' is?"

"My best guess is that it has something to do with sex."

That's what Kim had been thinking about—sex. She fidgeted and repeatedly crossed and uncrossed her legs as she talked with Dexter.

Kim began to talk about the Steelerettes, the NFL's first cheerleaders. She informed him the girls were students at Robert Morris Junior College, a school without a football team at the time.

"So you really like cheerleading I take it."

"Oh yeah. You'll have to come to a Pitt game and watch me shake it in my little blue with gold trim outfit."

"Love to."

Kevin came back over.

"Maria and I are going to leave," he announced with a wink at Dexter.

"Excuse me," Kim said, getting up, "I have to hit the girl's room."

As she walked off, Dexter glanced admiringly at her behind and groaned to Kevin, "Man, would you look at that tight little ass in that tight little skirt. Gonna git me some of that."

When Kim returned Maria and Kevin had left.

"Would you like to dance, Kim?" Dexter asked.

"To *Blue Eyes Crying in the Rain*? Sure I would."

Kim got up, took his arm, and led him to the dance floor.

Dexter held her at a distance as they moved slowly together.

"If I said you had a beautiful body, would you hold it against me?" Kim gibed. "Hey, dude, when people dance to this tune they like get a little closer. Are you afraid of me? I'm not a little doll that will break."

Dexter grinned. "No, Kim, I'm not afraid of you. And, you *are* a doll."

Their bodies pressed up against one another's. By the time the song ended she could feel the bulge in his pants.

They went back to the bar stools and had another drink. Dexter began to talk football.

The tips of Kim's nipples had become rigid and quite apparent through the tight T-shirt. Dexter's eyes fixated on her chest.

"Did you know that the sports bra came into being when two women sewed a couple of jockstraps together to create their own type of athletic supporter?"

"No, Kim, I didn't know that very interesting fact."

"Dexter, do you have a car?"

"Yeah, I drove. Just got a Hummer with my signing bonus."

"Let's go out to your Hummer and smoke some weed. I feel like getting a buzz. And I'm a little tense about doing this wet T-shirt thing. But I can't back out now or the girls will call me a wus. If I get stoned I won't care who soaks my shirt."

He looked somewhat reluctant.

"I don't . . . I . . . uh . . ."

"C'mon, Dexter, maybe I'll give you a hummer," she purred.

His apprehension quickly disappeared.

They got up and walked out.

Dexter had his arm around her waist.

His hand slipped lower.

"Sweet. You got a nice bum," he complimented. "You got a nice everything, Kim."

She put her hand on his taut behind and squeezed playfully.

CHAPTER 7

"This humdinger is a Hummer H2."

Dexter gave her the rundown. Six-liter V-8 rated 316 horsepower, 360 pounds of torque; full-time four-wheel drive that normally splits power 40% front, 60% rear and allows the driver to lock the center and rear differentials; and traction control that allows the selection of more or less wheel-spin to fit the surface conditions.

"You don't say," she said with a sigh, not very attentive.

"Let's get in the back," he suggested. "I had the regular seats taken out and put in something I can lay on. Just in case I get stranded somewhere in this desolate foreign country. That or get too trashed to drive. I never get lost in Miami."

The two got in the Hummer.

"Let's hear the sound system," Kim suggested. "That interests me more than the horsepower."

"You like hip-hop? I got 50 Cents' *Get Rich or Die Tryin'*. I play it over and over."

"Get rich? You got rich, didn't you, Dexter? I read about it in the papers. How many millions?"

"Enough millions to buy me a Hummer and whatever else I want."

Dexter stared at her with wanton lust.

Kim couldn't help but read the hungry expression on his face.

"Do you have any endorsement deals yet, Dexter?"

"Nike and McDonald's are talking to my agent."

"I like jazz. I see you have Norah Jones's *Come Away With Me*. Let's listen to that."

inched him slowly down her throat as far as she could. He started to squirm and groan as she moved up and down on him with her mouth and hands.

"Oh baby, that's good," he moaned. "You give great head, honey."

Kim paused momentarily to say, "Wait until the other girls hear I hooked up with the number one draft pick. And he's hung like a horse. And I gave him a hummer in his Hummer." She had a strange gleam in her eye. But then so did he.

Dexter spoke very softly. "You got me really ready, little white honey bunny. Now I'm going to spread your sweet cheeks and pack your crack with the big black wonder wand."

"No! I don't do anal!"

"You do now!"

He rolled her over on her stomach like a feather and propped up her behind with one hand, while he held her by the throat roughly with the other.

"Cute little tattoo, honey."

He licked it, and then bit it.

"Ouch! Please don't hurt me."

Curtis struggled to push his penis inside her.

"No, please, no!"

Norah Jones drowned out the screams.

CHAPTER 8

The terrible towel talked.

"Your semen and her blood are on the towel she took from your vehicle, Mr. Curtis," Detective Woods informed him.

The overweight and rumpled alcoholic detective had been on the force for more than twenty years. Close to collecting his pension, he didn't want to rock the boat at this stage in his career. But he had a daughter the alleged victim's age who had been raped by a gang of blacks.

Wood's daughter, Amanda, had been walking home from the library in the middle of the afternoon. She passed a house where they were hanging out on the front porch. They just surrounded Amanda and dragged her inside. And took turns.

The abortion devastated his daughter. More even than the brutal rape and loss of her virginity. It would have been his first grandchild.

The hospital used a rape kit furnished by the Sexual Assault Evidence Collection Program. Each kit contained detailed procedures for evidence collection and all the medical equipment necessary to conduct a thorough medical examination on a sexual assault victim. The rape kit administered to Amanda was sealed in plastic by hospital technicians, labeled with a case number by a detective, and stored in a refrigerator in the medical examiner's office. It mysteriously disappeared.

The gang-bangers got off, in more ways than one, the detective reflected bitterly.

"I didn't force her to do anything against her will," Curtis insisted adamantly.

"The girl says you did. There are bruises and lacerations in the area surrounding her anus. Her sphincter is badly damaged. There are marks on her buttocks. I wonder if they match your teeth."

"The girl said 'yes.' She wanted it. She begged. We got a little wild and crazy. Do you want to see the bite marks on my big black cock?"

Woods ignored the last remark. "Miss McConnell told me she said 'no' to anal sex. What makes you rich black studs think you can order up white chicks room service like chicken wings? This ain't KFC, buddy."

"My name's not Buddy, and I'm not your buddy."

"When I spoke to you the first time you said you didn't have sex with her. I think your *exact* words were, "I did *not* have sex with that woman!' But I can go back and listen to the tape again."

"What the fuck? I didn't know I was being taped. I'm not speaking to you any further, detective, without my attorney present. Got it?"

"Yeah, I got it."

Curtis got up and stormed angrily out of the police station.

"That guy has a problem people aren't talking about," Woods muttered to his fellow detective at the next desk.

Ed Woods had become disgusted with the criminal justice system which included, in his considered opinion, the lack of properly trained criminal investigators. Moreover, he felt the problem with society in general, and the justice system specifically, was that nobody wanted to be honest. He told his intimate friends that he couldn't find many people, other than privately and secretively, who were willing to be candid anymore. Too afraid of not being politically correct. Too apathetic.

Woods got up and went to the bathroom

He had a very stiff drink.

CHAPTER 9

Five hours later Dexter Curtis was arrested, booked, and released on $25,000 bond. He caught the first available flight home to Miami.

The damage control began immediately, initiated by his agent, Ron Kingston.

Kingston, a black former NBA player, represented several other NFL high draft picks and numerous other stars in professional sports. He had come a long way—NBA to prison to super agent.

"This is going to kill your pending endorsement deals, Dexter," the agent advised him. "And there goes my commission."

"I'm more worried about going to jail, Ron. And what my wife is going to say. I ain't talked to her yet. I'm afraid to."

"Yeah, the joint's no walk in the park. No matter how much money you have. We got you the best legal counsel available. A top criminal defense firm in New York. You heard what our people here said. Have a press conference. Admit you committed adultery. The cops do have your semen and her blood on that towel. They have a DNA sample from that previous incident. You had no choice but to admit you did the chick. How was she, anyway?"

"You saw the slut's picture plastered all over the internet already. A looker, man, a real looker. She screamed bloody murder when I reamed her butt hole. They all whine and cry but I never had one like that. Damn, man, you would have thought I was killing her."

"It might have been better if you did. Now she's telling the whole world and totally fucking up your life. Fucking white bitches. I never met one I could stand for half an hour. Dumb cunts. They beg for a ride on the teeter and then they think they own your black ass."

"No shit, man. I think what really pissed the chick off was that after I cornholed her she asked if I had a pen in the Hummer so she could give me her number. I told her not to bother. She flipped out. Hey, man, I got a wife. I don't need a problem."

"Well, you ended up with a problem. A big problem. And speaking of your wife, have her at your side at the news conference, supporting you big time."

"Just how do you propose that I accomplish that? The last time Juanita caught me porkin' some white snatch she pulled a gun on me."

"Yeah, and you took it away and pistol-whipped her. We had a helluva time whitewashing that one. This one is going to cost you even more."

"Fuck, man, there goes my signing bonus."

"At least you still have your salary—if you stay out of the slammer. Don't make our 'problem' any bigger than it is."

CHAPTER 10

"I am innocent."

Dexter Curtis said those words to everyone who would listen.

A few days after his arrest he held a news conference. His wife sat at his side, wearing a new diamond necklace with matching earrings and bracelets, and held her husband's hand.

"I am innocent," Dexter began, "of the allegations made against me by that woman. Yes, I had sex with her. I committed adultery. I have already asked Juanita and God to forgive me. I yielded to temptation. As we all do. We all fall short of the glory of God. But I did not force that woman. In fact, she seduced me. She offered me drugs, which I refused. It all will come out in the end. The truth will set you free. I have nothing more to say. Our legal system will resolve this matter if that is the direction this takes. My family and I need and appreciate the support and prayers we have received. I love my wife. She's a blessing and a piece of my heart. Thank you. I have no further comment at this time."

"Dexter, Dexter!" the reporters began to shout. He waved them off but didn't get up from his seat.

"I have a few comments," Juanita Curtis said into the microphone softly. "My husband made a mistake. He had consensual sex with a woman other than his wife. I have forgiven him. He has repented. God has forgiven him. I hope you will too. I stand with him to fight these false accusations. Dexter is a warm and caring person. He would never hurt anyone. I love him."

"Mrs. Curtis! Juanita!" the reporters cried.

"No questions!" Ron Kingston insisted brusquely as he took the microphone. He had been standing in the background.

Dexter Curtis was whisked away immediately for the airport. He flew to

New York to meet with lawyers that Kingston had hired to defend him if charges were filed, which seemed inevitable.

CHAPTER 11

Kim McConnell and her two best friends, Cassie Forrester and Alyssa Davis, watched the news conference intently.

"He's lying!" Kim blurted. "He raped me! The fucking nigger raped me!"

"Kim, what exactly happened?" Cassie asked. "You haven't told us."

"I didn't want to talk about it. Except to the cops and the people at the hospital. And then only because I had to. But now—"

"Tell us!" Alyssa begged.

"He asked if I wanted to walk outside and get some fresh air. It was very smoky in the bar. In the parking lot he pointed to his new Hummer. We walked over to it. He opened the rear door. Said he forgot his cell phone. He pushed me in. Before I knew what was happening he exposed himself and forced me down on it."

"Oh my God, Kim!" Alyssa exclaimed in horror.

"He's so strong," she continued. "His cock is so big. I choked and gagged. He didn't cum in my mouth, though. No, he said he wanted to pack my crack with his big black wonder wand. He said he did cheerleaders in the ass."

"And then he entered you anally?" Cassie asked.

"Yes. It was terrible! I felt like I was being ripped wide open. I never . . . it was . . . I can't..."

"Kim, you should take this asshole for everything he owns," Alyssa said coldly.

"I plan to. And I want to see his black ass in jail." She reached for her purse and searched for something. Finally she found the pipe."

"Kim! You said no more dope!" Cassie chastised angrily.

"This dulls the pain. It still hurts when I sit down. My dignity suffers even more." She lit the pipe.

"Somebody should do to that football player what he did to you, Kim," Alyssa commiserated.

"I will, I will." Kim's eyes glistened and her entire body trembled.

"He violated you, Kim," Alyssa snapped, "after you said 'no.' He raped you. The fucking nigger raped you."

"Yes, he did," she moaned, becoming hysterical.

"Men are so evil!" Cassie blurted.

"Yes, they are," Alyssa agreed angrily. "They just want to fuck you. Cum in you and all over you. And then they fuck over you."

"Let us make you feel better," Cassie urged, running her hand tentatively up Kim's skirt"

Alyssa sat on the other side of Kim and began to fondle her breasts.

"Oh . . . I . . . I'm . . . not . . . but . . . we shouldn't . . . I . . ."

The kisses smothered her and the gentle hands soothed her pain.

Lips on lips.

"I . . . ohhhh . . . I . . . ahhhh . . ."

Lips on lips.

"Sugar and spice and everything nice," Cassie whispered as she and Alyssa turned their girlfriend into a quivering and quaking inferno.

CHAPTER 12

Daddy's little girl?

Yeah, man, she look's like a sugar daddy's little girl—my little girl.

"What are you reading?" Dexter Curtis asked the extremely attractive woman sitting in the seat next to him on the plane.

"It's entitled *Daddy's Little Girl* by Mary Higgins Clark," she responded in a husky, sultry voice. He couldn't help but notice the long, lovely legs. The short skirt didn't hide much.

"Sounds like one of the stories you find on one of those websites featuring erotic literature. In the 'Incest' category.

"No, no. *Daddy's Little Girl* is a dark tale of a family shattered by crime. A fifteen-year-old girl's sister is murdered. The older sister's testimony leads to the conviction of the one she believes to be the killer. Years later he is set free and attempts to redeem his reputation. She wants to nail him to the cross again."

"I know about being nailed to the cross," he murmured.

"Should I call you Jesus? Yes, I guess you do know about being nailed to the cross. I know who you are, Dexter," she whispered, "despite the disguise. I watch a lot of news and read a lot of papers. My name is Sondra."

Dexter had donned a beard and dreadlocks for the flight.

He grimaced at her recognition.

But then he chuckled as he thought of the recent and premature retirement of the Dolphins star runner. Dicky Williamson had awesome dreadlocks before he got a haircut and a real job—world traveler—in search of the ultimate smoke. Dicky and Dexter had hung out in Miami and compared notes on marijuana masking agents.

"Well, Sondra, please don't tell. I don't really want to attract attention. I've had enough for awhile."

"Not to worry. My lips are sealed."

"Do you live in New York?"

"Yes."

"An actress? You are very pretty."

"Thank you. No, not an actress, exactly. I . . . uh . . . model for one of the top agencies. Just did a gig in Miami and I'm on my way home."

"I should have guessed model. Your hair and makeup are perfect. I love that platinum blonde color."

"Thank you. Why are you going to New York?"

"I'm meeting with the criminal defense firm that my agent hired to defend me if charges are filed."

"Oh. Do you think you will be charged?"

"Don't know. But the decision is imminent."

The two continued to chat amicably until the plane landed at JFK International Airport.

"When are you meeting with the lawyers?" Sondra asked as they departed the aircraft.

"Not until tomorrow morning."

"What are you going to do now?"

"I don't know. Are the Yankees or Mets playing at home? I'd like to maybe catch a ball game if I could."

"Just a second, I have a paper." She retrieved it from her bag and perused the sports page. "Florida is playing the Mets at Shea at 7:05."

"I know some guys on Florida. They'll get me tickets. Any chance you'd like to go with me?"

"No thanks. Baseball is boring."

Unless she ran on the field naked but for the body paint prominently displaying a website address. That little escapade earned her ten thousand dollars and a brief stay in jail. The casino that financed the endeavor liked the results and wanted her to do more advertising. And Howard Stern's people had contacted her about doing his show sometime in the same outfit she wore to the baseball game.

"Yeah, sometimes the action is rather slow. I could have played pro baseball, too. But football's my game—I love to hit—and hurt."

Sondra smiled knowingly.

"So what do *you* read, Dexter?"

"Not much. The Bible. The sports pages, especially when it's about me."

"Ah yes, the Bible. I saw the news conference on television with you and your wife. You said you are innocent. You said you asked your wife and God to forgive you. Your wife got jewelry. What did God get?"

He frowned dramatically, eyebrows raised.

"I am innocent. Do you think I have to rape women? I can have any bitch I want."

She could see the simmering anger.

"What are you going to do until game time?" she asked.

"Sightsee?"

"Would you like to get a hotel room? With me?"

"You . . . mean . . ."

"Sex? Yes. I mean sex."

Sondra suggested they go to the Radison Hotel, on 140th Street only a half mile from terminal nine. They walked. She had jogging shoes in her small bag and she put them on.

CHAPTER 13

They had just finished several hours of hot sex and they lay on the bed exhausted.

Sondra turned on the television with the remote.

A news conference had just begun on ESPN. The district attorney of Allegheny County, James Hawkins, spoke.

"That's the dude!" Dexter exclaimed excitedly. "The one who is handling the investigation of the accusations against me."

"My office has charged Dexter Curtis," Hawkins began, "with first degree felony assault. I'll quote directly from the document. 'Dexter Alexander Curtis, unlawfully, feloniously, and knowingly inflicted sexual intrusion or sexual penetration on the victim causing submission of the victim by means of sufficient consequence reasonably calculated to cause submission against victim's will. Further, the defendant caused submission of the victim through the actual application of physical force or physical violence.' I believe that my office can prove this case beyond a reasonable doubt. Mr. Curtis will be required to appear in Allegheny County court in the near future to formally hear the charges. Within sixty days from that appearance a judge will hear evidence at a preliminary hearing and decide whether to bring the case to trial. I have no further comment."

Dexter looked shocked although he had realized this was a definite possibility.

"How come they didn't tell you—about the charges?" Sondra asked.

"Don't know where I am I wouldn't think. I suppose they may have told my agent or wife or somebody."

"So did you?"

"Did I do what?"

"Feloniously sexually penetrate her?"

"Fuck no. She wanted it. I gave it to her."

Sondra had a strange expression on her face that he couldn't read. "Dexter, the afternoon delight you just had will cost you five thousand dollars."

"I knew you were a pro when you didn't squeal and squirm when I did you in the back door. You're a whore."

No, Sondra wasn't exactly a model. A high-priced call girl. She now knew that Dexter had indeed unlawfully violated the woman who accused him. Hurt her bad. Like he had hurt her. But she was used to it. Some of them liked to hurt her. But it was only her body. They couldn't mess with her mind.

"Who isn't a whore?" Sondra snapped sarcastically. "I'm a philosophical whore. I understand that there are various degrees of 'yes' and 'no.' Sometimes 'yes' and 'no' are a matter of perception. With me most things are 'yes.' As long as you ask first and pay for it. But you didn't ask, mister. That's a no-no. So *you* pay more."

Dexter dressed quickly, pulled out his wallet, and threw the money at Sondra still lying on the bed.

"I'll see you again, Dexter," she called tauntingly after him as he walked out the door.

What a flaming idiot, she thought. *Big dick, little brain.*

CHAPTER 14

We need the big spin, Ron Kingston concluded

He called Hank Gorton.

"Forget the senator for now. He'll still be getting his tonsils tickled when we get back to him."

Kingston elucidated. He wanted Gorton to dig up anything on Kim McConnell that might prove to be defamatory. It didn't have to be accurate. Just somewhat believable. Gorton promised to get right to work on the case, his zeal fueled by the promise of a fee three times his usual.

"Terrorize her," Kingston ordered. "Re-traumatize her. Dampen her enthusiasm for going to trial. And you make damn sure that Dexter Curtis isn't being bugged."

"The old 'nuts and sluts' defense, 'eh? Attack a woman's stability and drag in her past consensual relationships to at least cast a reasonable doubt as to consent."

"Exactly," Kingston concurred. "And if you get caught doing anything illegal I don't know you."

"I understand perfectly."

"Get some real nasty stuff on the internet. What's out there already is a little too tame. I want some really good shit."

Gorton hurriedly packed for his trip to Pittsburgh. The P.I. considered himself to be an expert in technical surveillance counter measures. And he had all the right equipment. The Box Broom device provided five of the most necessary sweep functions in one package. The R.F. probe "sniffed" the environment for hidden phone, room or body bugs, remote signals, computer, FAX or Telex transmitters, and even wide band frequency hopping or very low frequency "carrier current" signs. Auxiliary audio input allowed you to listen to telephones or lines for "hot mikes," hook-switch bypass and "infinity" bugs. Also unknown wires and cables could be tested for wired microphones. After a sweep, the alarm monitor guarded against new devices brought in, remote control activation, or someone tampering with the equipment. The twenty-four hour "evidence" recording output stored suspicious sounds on a cassette recorder.

The P.I. mulled over what hardware to take. He decided against a shotgun or the sniper rifle. Not that kind of operation. Of course he selected the .45 caliber Glock 21. His favorite handgun because of the unique combination of high magazine capacity, complete function reliability, and a true big bore caliber. He chose the TAC Thigh Rig and mounted the Roto Holster. The swivel joint permitted comfort while walking or driving. And he would be driving for more than a few hours. He also packed the Ruger Security Six .357 Magnum. That one always made a big impression.

Gorton used some of the drive time to talk with several of his associates involved in various aspects of private investigation. One happened to be an unparalleled computer guru. If there was anything about anybody on the web this dude could find it. Or plant something on the internet for propaganda or other purposes for others to find.

The smear tactics began immediately.

Gorton readily discovered that the McConnell woman had recently been hospitalized when she overdosed on pills after learning that her former boyfriend had cheated on her. The P.I. quickly tracked down the ex-boyfriend, Chuck Wooster. Chuckie said he had pictures. Gorton called the unscrupulous tabloid reporter he had done business with before. The lady jumped at his recommendation that she interview Chuckie.

CHAPTER 15

The tabloid reporter, Lydia Colvin, did smut journalism proud.

Soon a picture of the accuser appeared on the cover of the rag, *THE WHOLE TRUTH*. Disguised only by a black bandage covering her eyes. The front page headline read, "HER STORY: Cheerleader says football star is a rapist." The article reported that the star jock and the pretty young woman flirted with each other in a bar. They went out to his vehicle in the parking lot where he said he had various items he would autograph and give her, including one of the infamous yellow terrible towels.

Gorton wished Lydia would have said the girl wanted Curtis to write his name on her ass. He roared at his own joke. Yeah, she asked him to autograph her butt cheeks. After he gave it to her in the back door, she begging for it. She wanted him to write his name on her ass with cum.

The article mentioned that the girl had auditioned for a spot on *American Idol*. Supposedly she had been disqualified after she offered one of the judges some sort of bribe. But that could not be confirmed by reliable sources other than the judge himself, who soon thereafter had been fired for unspecified reasons. Being black, he cried discrimination. Gorton had tried to locate the judge, but with no luck so far.

Ms. Colvin quoted a former roommate who said that things that happened to the alleged victim in the past had a lot to do with what she said happened that night. Depression and suicidal ruminations were mentioned. "I caught her with a gun one night," the roommate said. "Where Kim got it I have no idea. She asked me if I wanted to play Russian roulette and kept sucking on the end of the barrel, simulating performing fellatio. I really thought she just might pull the trigger."

The article stated that several sources indicated the accuser often fantasized aloud about being sexually intimate with famous personalities. And, on occasion, she attempted to hook up with them. Sometimes successful, most of the time not. One unnamed young woman who did identify herself as a Pitt student took a class with Kim McConnell and said she overheard the professor joke with a colleague that Kim could suck a golf ball through a garden hose.

CHAPTER 16

Hank Gorton stopped at a fast-food restaurant off the interstate.

A skinny longhaired guy with tattoos prompted him to reflect on some of the cases he had worked. Most had been routine. Many divorce cases. But once in awhile a real winner came along. Like that rock star who allegedly murdered his girlfriend. According to her parents, anyway. But no body could be found and the police didn't have enough evidence to charge the group Death's Doorknob infamous bad boy drummer, Nicky Beloit. But Nicky liked to brag when he got stoned.

The P.I. found the body of the girlfriend, Sheryl Patterson. Thanks to illegal surveillance. It had been embalmed and rested in a very expensive coffin. Gorton deployed the hidden camera in the makeshift funeral parlor in the basement of Belloit's grandmother's house. A very old lady whose arthritic legs wouldn't permit her to traverse stairs any longer. She lived solely on the first floor of the huge old mansion.

Nicky had been having sex with his girlfriend. After she passed away. Gorton had heard of necrophilia but this was beyond even his comprehension, and he liked sick sex himself. The spaced-out drummer was more than happy to adequately compensate the private investigator in order to keep right on drumming his stone cold girlfriend. Especially when Gorton showed Nicky the pictures and threatened to sell them to the tabloids. "What spin would you put on this, Nicky?" Gorton inquired sarcastically—"Nicky Belloit, Death's Doorknob's drummer, stiffs the chicks. He finds his groupies in the morgue." Actually, Gorton suspected such publicity would have increased the drummer's popularity.

Unfortunately, Nicky soon overdosed on heroin and Gorton's little gold mine dried up. But the grieving parents gave him a nice bonus for the final resolution of their daughter's disappearance and the destruction of the evidence of the coffin caper.

The private dick mused to himself that Kim McConnell and Dexter Curtis apparently had a dispute over whether the light was red or green. He clucked dementedly, thinking of Sheryl Patterson and her lack of concern over what the little drummer boy did to her dead body. He snickered. Nicky could have made the case that Sheryl never said 'no.'

CHAPTER 17

Hank Gorton took a slight detour to Cleveland to pay a visit to Kim McConnell's father.

The father had been divorced from the girl's mother for many years. The father and daughter had not seen one another or spoken for more than a decade.

"Did Kim have a normal childhood?" Gorton asked him.

The man snorted, and spit off the front porch where they talked.

"Not hardly. My old lady married a real loser. He lived off her—the welfare, and my child support payments. He influenced her to prevent me from seeing my daughter. The guy beat my ex-wife. She told me. She'd call and whine about how she wanted to get back together with me. This is while the bitch is living with that stiff. But she still wouldn't let me see Kim. I think she was afraid Kim might tell me about the molestation. He finally croaked. A heart attack. I think it happened while he was sniffing Kim's panties, and she still was in them.

"What?" Gorton asked, shocked. Not much surprised him but this had headed in a direction he had not contemplated.

"Yeah, the old lady told me. Good old Tom took to dipping it in his stepdaughter, *my* daughter. If I would have known while he was still alive, he would have met his Maker even sooner. The ex walked in on Kim polishing Tom's knob one day when she came home early from work. And Kim didn't look like she was liking it. My old lady never said anything to anybody at the time. Too afraid of getting her ass kicked. So he kept doing Kim, until she got older, and threatened to tell the authorities."

"Kim has a new stepfather now. Do you think he's doing her too?"

"Nah, I doubt it. But who knows?"

"Thank you for the information, Mr. McConnell," Gorton said as he left.

"Oh, and here's a couple hundred for your candor. I'll be back in touch."

"Kim is a good girl," the father muttered as Gorton left.

CHAPTER 18

What are friends for.

Hank Gorton spent some time talking to Cassie Forrester and Alyssa Davis. Kim's two best friends had been interviewed on the major networks, telling what a wonderful person their friend is. The P.I. wanted to hear the rest of the story.

Gorton offered the two girls two hundred dollars each to answer a few questions. They took the money eagerly.

"Does Kim use drugs?" he asked.

"Uh . . . no . . . not at all," Cassie lied.

"Definitely not," Alyssa agreed warily.

"Has she had many lovers?" Gorton pressed on.

"Only a couple," Cassie responded. "Two or three in high school. Mostly she just hooked up. You know, hanging out. Then this guy named Chuck she met at Pitt. That's all I know about."

"Well, there's me," Alyssa offered. "And Cassie. We're her best girlfriends."

"Does she prefer to have sex with her boyfriends, or girlfriends?" the private dick asked, feigning innocence.

"She likes both," Alyssa answered too quickly. "Sometimes at the same time. We once did it at the beach with—"

"Shut up, Alyssa!" Cassie shouted. "That's all the questions you get to ask for two hundred bucks," she snarled at Gorton. "Get lost, dude."

"Very well, young ladies. I'll be talking to you again soon."

The girls had the television on while they talked with Gorton. He had heard one commentator say that this incident could help Dexter Curtis's street credibility. Another commentator countered that the American public will forgive many things. But rape isn't one of them. Especially the rape of a white woman by a black man.

But the slut raped him, he fantasized amusedly.

CHAPTER 19

Juanita Curtis sat in the kitchen of her luxurious home in Miami, talking with her mother.

"What did Dexter pay for your necklace, earrings, and bracelets?" the mother, Naomi Johnson, asked.

"Two million."

"Oh my God!"

"Yeah."

"The news said he commissioned the purchase of the jewelry ten days before the incident with that white trash."

"Bullshit!" Juanita laughed derisively.

"Are you going to divorce him?"

"No frigging way, Mama. Not now. That little white cock sucker ain't getting none of my money. Like I said in the news conference, I forgave Dexter and I love him. For now."

***

Coach Lowry made his weekly appearance on a local sports television program.

He gave a status report.

"I'm pleased with training camp so far. We look real good. It's Super Bowl or bust this year. And if we win it I'll run around the stadium in my jock strap. We had too many distractions last year. No more quarterback controversy. Our running backs have accepted the possibility of sharing time. It's that or you're gone."

"Coach! Coach!" the reporters beckoned. "What about Dexter Curtis?"

"I said before we began that I would take no questions on that matter. Are you guys frigging deaf and dumb? But let me say this. Dexter has assured me he is innocent of the allegations. The NFL and the Pittsburgh Steelers will take no action at this time. One is innocent until proven guilty in our great country. This woman is a gold-digger. Professional athletes are prime targets. The same thing happened to our star running back, didn't it? You know how that turned out. No doubt you heard about that dude at CNN. The woman who accused him of rape was also mentally ill. This news conference is over. And the next time I say don't ask—*don't ask.*"

The coach stormed off, his face very red, veins bulging from his neck.

***

Hank Gorton rested in his hotel room. His cell phone rang.

"What's up?" Ron Kingston asked.

"I sent a report to your Email."

"I read it. Good work. There are a couple more things I want you to pursue."

"Shoot."

"The District Attorney, James Hawkins. A little birdie told me the dude is gay."

"Gay? He's married. Beautiful wife and three kids, I think. He doesn't look queer to me."

"Oh? Like you can tell by how he looks? My sources tell me he likes to stick it in the glory holes in adult book stores on occasion. Check it out."

"You got it. Hey, maybe when our favorite fag senator is back home in Pittsburgh he's playing the district attorney's skin flute. What a spin we could put on that one."

"Yeah, talk about collusion. And that detective, Woods, he's a drunk. Get some good mud on him in case we need to say he screwed up evidence."

"Will do."

"And Gorton?"

"Yeah, Ron?"

"Get a gun that can't be traced. A revolver. Small caliber. Something a girl would shoot."

"I can do that. Why?"

"Never mind 'why.' Just do it."

"But—"

"I said never mind, Gorton."

Kingston hung up abruptly.

Why he asks? The bitch is suicidal. Sometimes one needs to help the inevitable along. Russian roulette, 'eh? Spin it.

CHAPTER 20

What is good and what is evil? Like 'yes' and 'no' sometimes a matter of perception.

That's what Sondra thought about as she spent the five thousand dollars Dexter Curtis had given her for services rendered. She made a substantial pharmaceutical investment with the money.

Sondra's preferred dealer had quite the inventory. K, E, STC, Adam, Lover's Speed, Stacy—names for Ecstasy, her personal favorite. People taking it sought euphoria, empathy, trust, heightened energy, and emotional warmth. He also had some Gamma Hydroxbutyrate—G, Liquid Ecstasy, Grievous Bodily Harm, Georgia Home Boy. People taking it sought relaxation, calm, and intoxication, similar to the effects of alcohol. And the dealer had Special K, also known as Super K and Vitamin K—Ketamine—more specifically Ketamine Hydrocloride. It gave one dreamy, floating sensations and hallucinations that made you like you are being removed from your body. Sondra sometimes liked to mix them up into her own special potion.

"Don't you want some crack, Sondra?" the dealer, Jimmy the Breeze, asked.

"Got some. And acid and weed. How about some 'tweakers'? I'm a little low."

Sondra purchased what she needed to stock her medicine cabinet. Her clients seemed to be more generous when stoned, whether they knowingly got trashed or not. And she herself could better tolerate the business of sex while "medicated" properly.

She checked her appointment book and sighed. Busy night.

***

Cabin fever drove her crazy.

Kim McConnell put on her mother's black wig, a halter top and skimpy shorts and snuck out of the house into the dark through a window facing the backyard. The slime camping outside never had a clue. Too busy drinking and partying.

The small tavern five blocks down the street was almost empty.

Three stereotypical drunks sat at the bar and two guys who had just got off second shift at a factory slumped at a small table. They looked beat and quickly worked on emptying a pitcher of beer.

Kim asked the bartender for a glass. "Do you mind if I join you?" she asked the two as she poured a glass. "The next pitcher is on me." They nodded. "What do you guys do?"

"Second shift at the factory at the end of Alden Street," one replied. "We just got off. Hotter than hell in that damn place. What do you do?"

She smiled coyly, and winked.

"Yeah, the other one asked again, "What *do* you do? Are you a hooker? We don't often see hookers like you in *this* place."

"No, I'm *not* a hooker," she responded, but didn't look angry. "I'm a college student—Pitt—a cheerleader."

They bought a round of shots.

Then another.

The two men got bolder.

One put his hand at her thigh, and started to slip his fingers up the edge of her shorts.

The other stared blatantly at her barely contained breasts in the halter top.

The three drunks on the bar stools staggered out one after the other.

"Last call boys and girl," the bartender announced.

One more round of shots. This time doubles.

"I *like* Jim Beam," Kim slurred.

The two men nodded.

"Is that your favorite?" one asked.

"No, my fav is Southern Comfort. Sweet. Like my pussy. So I've been told. Do you two guys like to eat pussy?"

They both looked startled.

"Well . . . uh . . . yeah . . . sure," one stammered.

Kim undid the halter top and freed her breasts.

"Yowsa! Nice hooters!" the other one cried.

The bartender approached the table, getting closer to better observe what had turned into a very interesting situation.

"Is there some place we can go?" she asked. "Do you guys want some?"

"I have a room upstairs," the bartender offered eagerly.

"Let's go," Kim replied, her face expressionless. "All three of you. But *no* anal."

"How much is this going to cost us?" one of the men asked, checking his wallet.

"Nothing. I told you I'm not a hooker. I'm a good girl. You can call this community service."

She giggled hysterically as they led her up the steps.

***

Nathan Redmond, in disguise, left the meeting at a Las Vegas hotel with the chief spokesman for the group promoting gay rights. They got in Redmond's rental car and went for a coffee and a private conversation.

Killing for money always fueled his lust for killing for pleasure. The Vegas entertainer who ratted on Kingston now had a bullet in his head and lay in a shallow grave off Route 372 near Pahrump, Nevada.

Redmond introduced himself at the meeting as Drew Brady, an international financier and a gay man who could never leave the closet for business reasons. He told Thomas Blaine, the head honcho, that he wanted to make a substantial anonymous contribution to the organization. He let Blaine have a peek at the stacks of crisp hundred dollar bills in his suitcase.

Sitting in the coffee shop, Drew said, "Thomas, I want you to use the money to carry on the fight against persecution of the gay community."

They talked about that persecution, now, and throughout history. Blaine seemed to be quite knowledgeable on the subject. He nauseated Redmond.

Blaine ranted on and on. He harped on how homosexuality was not inherently evil and the religious zealots who misconstrued the biblical message. He mentioned the Byzantine Emperor Justinian in the sixth century who ordered his Prefect to arrest any homosexual who refused to repent, and punish him. The punishment usually consisted of cutting off the convicted homosexual's testicles and thrusting a sharp reed through his penis. The victim then would be dragged naked through the streets for public humiliation and finally burned at the stake.

"Homophobia is a specific classifiable mental illness," Blaine insisted, "ranging from acute paranoia to mild anxiety. Physiological symptoms include an involuntary gag reflex and a shrinking effect in penis size when a homophobic looks at a naked male. I've reviewed as much research as I could find on the subject."

They left the coffee shop and Redmond pulled into the hotel parking lot where Blaine had said he left his car.

"Thank you so much for your generous donation, Drew. Can I do something for you?" He put his hand on Redmond's thigh, and moved it slowly to his zipper, waiting for a sign of approval.

"I'd rather get your rocks off first, Thomas."

"Only if you let me return the flavor," Blaine joked.

RATTRAP

Blaine slipped down his pants and boxers.
He had an erection.
Redmond pulled down his Dockers and briefs.
He didn't have an erection.
Redmond showed him the knife.
"Thomas, I am Justinian's Prefect."
Soon the killer did have an erection.

CHAPTER 21

Glass houses.

Jolyn Knowlton sat in her cubicle proofing the article on the newly opened emporium for hip hop furnishings. She wondered what she could say to make the custom Italian made glass sinks in the bathroom off the master bedroom more interesting. Glass had begun to bore her.

The phone call startled her. She had come in hours early for some quiet time. Caller I.D. told her who wanted to speak with her just as the sun rose.

"Good morning, Mr. Winslow."

"Please come into my office, Jolyn."

"Be right there."

Stephen Winslow had been managing editor of the *Pittsburgh Tribune-Review* for only a little over a year. He came from Boston and *The Globe* only because his wife wanted to return to her hometown to die. She had passed away six months ago.

"Joey, I've asked you not to call me Mr. Winslow. It's Stephen."

"And, Mr. Winslow, I've asked you not to call *me* Joey. It's Jolyn."

"Your father calls you Joey."

She grimaced.

"Yes, he does. I can't seem to break him of *that* bad habit. But then, he's been doing it for twenty-three years. What's your excuse?"

They both laughed lightly. Stephen Winslow had played football with David Knowlton at Pitt several decades ago.

"Why does he call you Joey?"

"He never told you? No, I suppose he wouldn't. He wanted a son. The doctors said my mother couldn't bear any more children after all the difficulty she had delivering me. So I became Joey. I hate it!"

"But you did play sports—basketball and softball in high school and college. How is your father, Jolyn?"

"Mr. Winslow, 'er I mean Stephen, you know very well how my father is. You played golf with him last week."

Now he laughed heartily. She smirked. He made her smile inside, but she usually tried to hide it.

"Yes, I did. And he trounced me as usual. And he says you usually put a whooping on him. I need a bigger handicap if I'm going to play you."

"You have a big handicap—you're a man."

They had badgered like this playfully on several previous occasions.

Stephen's face then turned very serious.

"Jolyn, I have a new assignment for you."

"Another article like the one about the Fort Pitt Bridge and Tunnel to be opened ahead of schedule? That was a thriller!"

"You're the rookie, Jolyn."

"Hey, I didn't mind at all covering the 'Ya Gotta Regatta' at Point State Park. I got to meet Lee Ann Womack. Did you know her song 'Lord, I Hope This Day is Good' was written by Dave Hanner of that local band?"

"No, I didn't know that."

"Don't you even read my stories? It was in there. And don't send me anywhere near the Chelsea Grille in Oakmont or any place like it. I loved the grilled swordfish served with cherry rice pilaf and honey grilled vegetables. But I kind of overdid it with three desserts."

"Chocolate no doubt."

"You should try the chocolate soufflé with warm raspberries and vanilla ice cream. I had two of those and then the roasted pear and fig with chocolate ice cream. Chocolate has a psychoactive effect you know. It increases endorphin levels like alcohol and some drugs. Chocolate lovers live longer. They did that study at Harvard."

"Yes, you told me. Several times. What did you do to your hair? It looks really nice."

"Thank you. It was getting too long to do much with. A volumetric haircut. Fusion color. Accent glossing."

"Well, I like it. Now, let's talk about your new assignment."

Jolyn had impressed Stephen immensely in the two months she had been with the paper. Just as he knew she would when he hired her. A beautiful young woman. Tall, leggy, and hair the color of which could best be described as scarlet, with or without the fusion color. Incredible energy. She always came in early and left late. The brightest of the bright. A diamond in the rough. But it was her eyes. Incredibly inquisitive and extraordinarily blue. Penetrating eyes. Sad eyes. He didn't know why. But he did know she had the most impressive resume he had ever scrutinized.

He recalled some of the specifics. B.A. in English from a small, private college. High honors. Concentration in news and magazine writing. Now enrolled in the graduate program. Thus far she had aced five courses: "Mass Communication Research and Methodology," "Law of Mass Communication," "Radio-Television Law and Regulation," "History of American Journalism and Mass Communications," and "Mass Communication Ethics." Between her undergraduate and graduate work she had traveled to the Middle East and taken a course at the Rothberg International School of the Hebrew University of Jerusalem. Something called "Media and Foreign Policy in the Middle East."

Stephen had given Jolyn a little test as he did all applicants. Write an article about this or that in one hour. She pulled out her laptop and did a five hundred word treatise on "Why I Love Chocolate." Perfect grammar and spelling and he still chuckled about what she composed. And then she really impressed him when she said that one day she eventually wanted to live in Hershey and told him a fascinating story he never heard before about how Milton Hershey screwed Fidel Castro.

"Don't think I'm not grateful, Stephen, for the work and mentoring you've given me. But I'd like to do something with a little more edge to it."

"What do you know about pro football?"

"Huh?"

"The Steelers."

"I don't really want to do sports. I mean, I will if you say so, but I . . . think—"

"Of course you don't want to do sports. You want to be an investigative reporter."

"Yes, I do."

"I'm assigning to you to this thing with Dexter Curtis, the Steelers player."

"Me?"

"Yes, *you.*"

"But Stephen, that's a huge story. You give that to me and you'll agitate every reporter in the newsroom with more seniority than me—which is all of them."

"Too bad. I want you to do it. Just a hunch of mine. And you can wear the miniskirts again."

He smiled.

She frowned dramatically.

Winslow had asked Jolyn to dress more conservatively in the newsroom and on assignment. He didn't say exactly why and she didn't ask. This day she wore a light beige pant suit and loafers. The day he spoke with her about her attire she had to admit the outfit she had donned was a little risqué. But the boutique she had been assigned to do a fashion piece about suggested she ascertain the quality of the merchandise by wearing it. Made sense to her.

"I can't tell you what this means to me, Stephen. Thank you."

"Don't thank me yet. I'll be watching your every move on this one."

"Everyone will be watching. Talk about *glass houses*."

"Yeah, forget about that article you are working on. I don't think I'll use it. Too much other stuff happening. Your copy on *this* assignment will certainly get the hatchet job from me, young lady. Please don't take it personal. I usually don't change much of your material. But this will be different."

"Whatever, boss."

"One caution, Jolyn."

"Yes, Stephen?"

"No anonymous sources. That's how *The New York Times* jeopardized its integrity. You know, the Jayson Blair scandal. I don't want any 'Holy Shit' journalism like *The Washington Post* started during the Watergate era and *The Times* adopted to compete. If your 'Deep Throat' won't permit him or herself to be identified, forget about it."

"I understand, Stephen. No fraud, plagiarism, or inaccuracies," she replied, her words dripping with sarcasm. "If I write that Dexter Curtis has a large penis—I have to prove it."

"Jolyn!"

"I'm sorry, I'm sorry. A professor of mine once accused me of plagiarism. That I copied some material he actually wrote. Fortunately for me, my computer proved me innocent."

Yes, that professor had been very upset when she rebuked his advances. There was some part of 'no' he didn't understand. He felt her up and she smashed his wire-rim glasses with the punch and gave him a black eye.

"Oh, I forgive your outburst, Jolyn, but—"

"Don't let it happen again?"

"Something like that, I guess."

"Yes, sir, *Mister* Winslow."

He couldn't help but return her smile.

"Stop it, Joey."

"I will. I saw that article in *THE WHOLE TRUTH* about the accuser. Her picture and that trash they wrote about her. Didn't you work at one of those tabloids in Boston before you came here? The *Globe*?" she joked.

"*The Boston Globe!*" he snapped back. "You read that crap? Those tabloids?"

"Hey, I pick them up at the supermarket. Can't resist. Headlines like 'Princess Diana was one hell of a shag' catch my eye."

Jolyn stood and leaned over Stephen's desk. She brushed her lips against his cheek esoterically. She knew why. He didn't.

"Please excuse my lack of professionalism," she murmured softly. "My father told me about your wife. How you met at that park and fell in love. He told me about the funeral. The wonderful words you spoke about her. I'm so sorry."

A single tear ran down her face.

53

He merely shrugged at her remarks.

"Stephen, one day I would like you to tell me what your emotions were during her illness and as she was dying. If you can. If you want to. I have a reason for asking."

Jolyn turned and walked from his office. She didn't hear him whisper, "Maybe. If you let me call you Joey."

CHAPTER 22

Emotions.

Back in her cubicle Jolyn pulled out a new yellow legal pad and printed the word "EMOTIONS" boldly at the top of the first page. Yes, emotions. She would not just report the facts regarding her new assignment. No, she would attempt to convey the emotions of the accused and the accuser throughout the traumatic ordeal both were about to embark upon. Perhaps even more traumatic than whatever had actually happened to precipitate the accusations.

Emotions. What do I know of emotions?

The tears flowed silently and fell on the tablet, soaking it.

Jolyn had been with three men, the first more a boy than a man. Her high school sweetheart. Then that other college professor in her sophomore year. Unfortunately, she had made a grave mistake on that weekend jaunt to Las Vegas. But what about Zeke? What were her emotions when she had been with him? She reminisced. Passion, ecstasy, joy, tenderness, sensuality, desire, melancholy, despair, grief. All those. And love. So intense but so brief.

Danny, the football star. They all wanted him but he wanted her. She gave it up. What was she thinking? Emotions? What had hers been? Not love. He treated her like a trophy. They never talked about anything that mattered.

That's what made Robert appealing at first. Sophisticated, intelligent, and well-spoken. Emotions. What had hers been? Not love, she understood later. Like Danny, he wanted to use her body. But Robert the Doctor of Psychology distracted her from realizing that fact with his intellectual jargon. Much older than she. More distinguished looking than handsome. As time went on he impressed her less and less. She matured. He just got stale. Not even a good lover. But she didn't have much of a measuring stick at the time.

Picking up the waste basket and putting it under her chin, Jolyn regurgitated.

After graduating from college in three years, Jolyn had decided to take a break. An extended vacation. Travel. See the world. Of all the places she wanted to visit, Israel topped the list. Her father objected vehemently. Too dangerous. But her mother had the final say. "David, she's a woman now. Let her go. I mean really let her go. She's not your little Joey anymore. Let the girl go." He acquiesced. But insisted that she do something besides bum around. So she enrolled in the Rothberg International School.

Jerusalem. God touched her there.

And so did Zeke. He touched her like she had never been touched before. In so many ways.

Upon arriving in the city she set off by herself to see everything. The Western Wall, the last remaining remnant of the Second Temple destroyed by the Romans in 70 CE, awed her. She loved to browse the quaint shops of Nahalat Shiva. She had breakfast at one of the many outdoor cafes each morning. Yad Vashem, Israel's most significant memorial to the six million Jews that perished in The Holocaust upset her tremendously. But she went back several times. And there she met Zeke, in the Hall of the Names.

His given name was actually Ezekiel. An American Jew investigating his heritage so he said. He seemed quite interested in the course she was taking, "Media and Foreign Policy in the Middle East." All about the role of the mass media in the decision making process in foreign affairs in Israel specifically and the Middle East generally. The double role of the media as a communication environment and negotiations channel.

Zeke. Tall, dark, and he *was* handsome. He looked like a young Warren Beatty in that old movie *Splendor in the Grass* she had watched on AMC one night as she studied for an exam. Jolyn always had the television or music on while she studied. For some strange reason the distraction improved her concentration. Zeke had a small apartment in Mea Shearim, an ultra orthodox Jewish neighborhood where time has stood still.

He gave her a much better tour of Jerusalem than she ever could have managed on her own. It happened for the first time one afternoon a week after they met when they had walked all over in the heat and came back to his apartment sticky and sweaty.

"Take a shower if you like, Jolyn. I'll give you a long shirt to wear while I wash your clothes. There's a washer and dryer in the basement the tenants share."

Jolyn luxuriated in the shower and lost track of time. She didn't hear Zeke come into the bathroom. He pulled back the shower curtain. He was naked. She couldn't help but stare. It was very impressive. What had her emotions been at that moment? Lust? Probably. She had not been with a man for a year. And never a man like this one.

"Hey girl," he said hopefully, "you're not the only one who needs a shower. Do you mind if I join you?"

"Uh . . . I guess so," she had stuttered, totally embarrassed, but yet excited. "I mean . . . uh . . . I guess you can . . . uh . . . come in with me. No funny business!"

"No, of course not," he agreed.

But then he washed her back. And that big thing poked her. She turned around and placed his soapy hands on her breasts.

"You are so lovely, Jolyn." She put more soap on her hands and began to wash him. Down there. "I'm sure you know where this might lead, Jolyn."

"To bed I hope." She had made up her mind. Her lust for him drowned out the guilt she felt—because of what she had done with Robert. *But is this the unforgivable sin?* she contemplated.

They rinsed off and Zeke carried her to the bedroom. He ravaged her body. But gently and passionately. She had never had an orgasm with a man. Until that afternoon. She couldn't begin to count how many.

Zeke had no regular job but plenty of spending money. "From my father," he had explained.

In the weeks that followed they couldn't keep their hands off one another. As they journeyed the streets of Jerusalem day after day Jolyn would occasionally drag him into an alley and lift her skirt for a quickie. She couldn't help it. Lust indeed. She hoped it would never fade. The exact moment it turned into love eluded her. But it happened.

Zeke confided in her more and more, but never completely she concluded. He began to talk extensively of the Israeli-Palestinian conflict and the militant groups Hamas and Islamic Jihad. He called them zealots who must be exterminated. His face turned dark and ominous as he spoke of them. Some mornings after all night lovemaking at his apartment she would find his side of the bed vacant. Her questions went unanswered. And then she found the pistol in his things and became even more concerned.

He taught her how to use the pistol expertly, a Jericho 941PS, the same gun prominently utilized by the Israeli Defense Forces and Israeli Police. She mentioned her previously somewhat limited experience with firearms. Their target practice led to other revelations. Zeke told her that he had been employed for a time with ISDS, an Israeli government approved company that provided security and counterterrorism training around the world.

"A young woman like you should know how to protect herself," he insisted, and proceeded to show her exactly how over the course of the next few weeks. "Besides, you want to become a journalist, so you say. Perhaps a war correspondent? Some major media outlets are now providing their people with antiterrorism training. One day you may end up in a real hot spot, not that where you are right now isn't, and you should know how to survive."

Jolyn particularly enjoyed rescue and escape simulations, the off-road driving instruction, and what he called *Krav Magrav*— unarmed protection exercises. The latter seemed to always evolve from martial arts to erotic wrestling.

They spent a considerable amount of time in the forested mountainous area just south and west of Jerusalem around villages such as Nes Harim, Ora, Beit Zayit and Sataf. He took her to wooded areas further south near the town of Beit Shemesh, the Park Britania forest, Eshtaol forest, Harel and the Beit Guvrin archaeological park.

Zeke had taken a one week class in Estonia taught by the Shadow Wolves. The Shadow Wolves—Native American trackers—had been commissioned to provide training in Baltic countries to national police, border guards, and customs on how to detect and track potential WDM smugglers who cross their borders.

Jolyn called their little games "playing Rambo" and found them quite stimulating. Zeke called her "the natural" and guessed that she had Native American blood.

He finally admitted when she wouldn't relent that he went after terrorists who were planning attacks because the Palestinian Authority had yet to do so. But he would not say anything more about the subject and made her promise not to ask.

And then what Jolyn feared the most happened.

She woke in the middle of the night.

Jolyn went out on the balcony to smoke one of his cigarettes which she rarely did unless extremely nervous.

She noticed the body about ten feet from the front door of the apartment complex.

Partially hidden from view by a tree.

The pool of blood.

Zeke had been stabbed numerous times. His throat had been slashed.

"Why, Zeke, why?" Jolyn had cried as she cradled his head.

He struggled to whisper, "In order to defeat evil, you must understand the nature of evil." And then he died in her arms.

Jolyn got her things and fled. She never told anyone about Zeke. What had her emotions been at that moment when she found his body?

The thought prompted her to pick up the waste basket again and spit vomit once more.

She got up from her chair, deciding to leave the newsroom before the working day even began for most.

"I'm going to the glass house," she said softly to the temporary who came in early to start the coffee.

"Why are you crying, Jolyn?" the temporary, an older woman named Rhonda, asked.

They had become friendly and Jolyn helped her out on occasion, with the computers and other things.

"Emotions," Jolyn whispered so softly.

"What, Jolyn? I didn't hear you."

"Rhonda, please tell Mr. Winslow a personal emergency is happening for me and I have to leave immediately. But I'll get in touch with him very soon."

"Okay, I sure will. You don't look well, Jolyn. Is there anything I can do?"

"No, Rhonda, I have to work this out myself, but thanks," Jolyn responded as she walked out the door. "Emotions," she whispered again.

So many emotions.

CHAPTER 23

A walk in the park.

After leaving the newsroom, Jolyn Knowlton ended up in Schenley Park. Sitting on a picnic table in the shade she began the story on her laptop.

Her editor, Stephen Winslow, had said to write the first article fast and keep it short. Not too much more than five hundred words. She could write more once she had the opportunity to do some legwork. And why did he smile so when he used the "legwork" she mused.

Jolyn made a phone call.

The mention of both her father's and Stephen Winslow's names put her in immediate touch with Matthew Norder, chancellor and chief executive officer of the University of Pittsburgh.

She explained what she wanted.

Chancellor Norder promised someone would get back to her regarding the matter as soon as possible.

About an hour later her cell phone rang.

Kim McConnell.

"I'm not talking to the press, as I'm sure you know, Ms. Knowlton. But Chancellor Norder himself asked me to speak with you. The university has been providing me with incredible support during my ordeal."

"Can I call you Kim and you call me, Jolyn?"

"Sure."

"I'm writing a story for the paper about your ordeal. I promise you only that I believe what will be published will be objective and fair. All I ask is that you give me permission to use your name."

Silence for a few moments.

"I guess so. What does it matter? My name is plastered all over the internet anyway. Go ahead. I think I'd rather see my name than 'that woman' or 'the alleged victim' or whatever. Go ahead."

"Thank you, Kim. Please send me a message indicating you give me permission to use your name." Jolyn gave her the Email address.

"Is that it?" Kim asked.

"Yes. Perhaps one day we can discuss your ordeal."

"Maybe. That would depend on what you say about me in your paper. I don't like being portrayed as a gold-digging slut. He raped me!"

Kim McConnell terminated the call brusquely.

The story seemed to write itself.

***

Emotionally speaking of rape case

By Jolyn Knowlton
Pittsburgh Tribune-Review

PITTSBURGH—McConnell vs. Curtis. I find myself watching ESPN more and more lately. Better than the soap operas. Yesterday I heard an ESPN commentator say, "The circus surrounding the Dexter Curtis case is swirling in emotion." Yes, it is. We don't know who is telling the truth. We may never know. But we can be certain that these two people are suffering emotionally. What were their emotions that night? What are their emotions now?

Anger? Is Dexter Curtis angry that Kim McConnell ratted on him? Whether he raped her or not she is primarily responsible for his adultery seeing the light of day. Anger is associated with violence, aggression, and disruptive behaviors. Was Dexter Curtis angry that night that he and Kim McConnell had sexual relations? Did anger possibly fuel violence and aggression on his part? What may have made him angry that night? Is he angry now? Is he angry on the football field? Does that anger carry over into his personal life?

Fear? Did Kim McConnell feel fear that night? If someone feels relatively in control of a threatening situation, a person might likely respond with anger. Without control, a person's reaction might likely be fear. Was Kim McConnell frightened that night, by what Dexter Curtis did and what she feared he might do? What does she fear now? That rape shield laws will not protect her from being victimized again, from a second unnecessary humiliation? It would appear the second victimization has begun with vigor. Obviously a sophisticated smear campaign has been launched against her. How far are these blood-suckers willing to go? They are playing hardball. Do offensive players fear Dexter Curtis? Do people in his personal life fear him?

Greed? Is Dexter Curtis concerned about his millionaire status? The legal proceedings alone could substantially lighten his wallet. Not to mention what Kim McConnell might be awarded in a civil verdict. To what extent will the accused and his entourage go to protect his career and bank account? And what about her? Is the possibility of financial gain motivating any of her actions?

Passion? Dexter Curtis and Kim McConnell had sex. Both admit that. Is passion a word that would accurately describe their intimate encounter? Does Dexter Curtis have a passion for football? My *Webster's New World Dictionary* defines "passion" as "intense emotional excitement, as rage, enthusiasm, lust, etc." Does Dexter Curtis rage on the football field? Does he rage off the field?"

Remorse? Are either Kim McConnell or Dexter Curtis sorry for whatever it is they did? Curtis expressed remorse for the adultery. Is his remorse for what he did or what it cost him? Two million for the jewelry and who knows how much for whatever else.

Shame? Should Kim McConnell be ashamed if she had sex with others before Dexter Curtis? Do you suppose that Dexter Curtis feels shame about his past sexual conquests? What about for cheating on his wife? Did he seem penitent in the news conference or more like somebody caught with his hand in the cookie jar?

Emotions, so many emotions. The facts of this case may not be known for many months. The judge issued a gag order restricting comments. We won't see any evidence until the preliminary hearing. And then probably not much. The district attorney will likely only reveal what he considers enough evidence to convince the judge the case should go to trial. Only at a trial, if one is held, will the facts be fully presented. Lacking facts, what will we be able to ascertain from the emotions of Kim McConnell and Dexter Curtis during a trial? Will their faces tell us a story? Their body language? Emotions are louder than words.

What do Kim McConnell and Dexter Curtis want, emotionally speaking? Justice? Revenge? Financial security? Notoriety? What? What lasting emotional damage will these two individuals suffer because of this incident and its repercussions?

Questions, so many questions.

Recently I covered the Motorola Women's Training Camp at St. Vincent's College. Over two hundred women from eighteen states participated in football drills led by former and current Steelers. Louie Lipps gave me some tips on catching passes and I gave him some tips on selling cars to women. Neither of us is telling.

Of course I just had to try the UPMC Steelers Experience. I did quite well in the "84 Lumber Thread the Nut" but forget about the "Kicking Nets." I think my feet are too big. Did you ever notice that most kickers have small feet? But what piqued my interest the most was the Steelers practice.

Coach Lowry has been talking it up that the defense has something to prove this year and how they need to play with a chip on their shoulders. He talks about closing the turnover ratio with the emphasis on taking the ball away. In the part of practice I watched the defense concentrated on stripping the football. Nobody was better at it that Dexter Curtis. And he looked angry. Raging. He trash talked and intimidated the offense with his animated gestures and screaming. And these were his teammates. I wonder what he'll do to the real opposition.

I deliberated about how much of the "anger" Dexter Curtis prominently displayed that afternoon in the sweltering sunshine is merely a motivational factor he employs only on the football field or if it is a part of his everyday personality pattern. Perhaps Kim McConnell knows.

Emotions, so many emotions.

***

After finishing the article Jolyn walked to an internet café called the Artist's Cup a few blocks from Schenley Park. She used a phone line to connect her own computer and checked her Email where she found the requested message from Kim McConnell. She then sent an Email to her editor with the article attached.

The menu looked appealing but the prices were exorbitant, at least to a junior staff writer. She decided to splurge anyway. A tropical fruit smoothie with chocolate flavored soy milk. A crispy oyster Caesar sandwich. Toasted ciabatta bread, garlic crusted gulf oysters, anchovy-garlic emulsion, aged goat cheese, shredded romaine lettuce. Garnished with Belgian white anchovies and roasted red pepper cayenne ketchup paired with Creole seasoned sweet potato fries. And it only cost sixteen dollars. She could only dream of the croque-monsieur with caviar. Thirty-five dollars. Unless? No, her editor wouldn't put this on the

63

expense account she didn't think.

As she ate Jolyn thought about who should she talk to first. The police certainly wouldn't tell her much. Or Dexter Curtis and his people. But Kim's friends might.

Her cell phone rang.

"I have information about the Dexter Curtis case that might interest you." Jolyn didn't recognize the voice and it seemed to be slightly muffled. "I heard you got the big assignment. For the paper."

"Who is this? How did you get my cell phone number? How did you know I got that assignment? It only happened a few hours ago."

"No matter. You might want to contact a woman in New York City named Sondra Lewis. You'll find an anonymous Email in your inbox with her address and directions. The woman flew back from Miami a couple days ago. She sat next to Dexter Curtis on the plane. Perhaps they talked."

Click.

Jolyn ordered a slice of chocolate fudge cake. She pondered the phone call as she savored the delicious dessert. Then she called her editor.

"Stephen, did you get my Email? Did you read my article?"

"Hey, you just sent it. But yes, I did get it and I did read it. It will be in tomorrow's edition. I didn't change a thing. Other than you misspelled one word. Shame, shame. Pay attention to spell check. But good job!"

"Thanks. You know, I just got the strangest phone call." She related the details.

"Jolyn," Stephen said after she finished, "I'd like you to go to New York City and talk to this woman. I'll authorize payment of your expenses. In fact, you head for the airport right now and call me when you get there. By then I'll have made a reservation for you."

"I'll have to go home and pack and—"

"Jolyn!" he interrupted. "Just go. Pick up anything you need there. Keep the receipts and the paper will reimburse you. And if you are going to get the top assignments you need to have a bag ready to go anywhere at anytime."

"I'm on my way to the airport, boss. But I need my favorite bear I sleep with, the Labatt Blue bear," she joked.

They both laughed as they hung up.

Jolyn reread her article.

I don't see any misspelled words.

CHAPTER 24

Milk and honey.

Jolyn listened to music on the flight to New York City as she scribbled notes on a tablet. It would have to be *Emotions* by Mariah Carey. She softly mimed the words. "I'm in love. I'm alive. Intoxicated. Flying high. It feels like a dream when you touch me tenderly. I don't know if it's real but I like the way I fell. Inside."

She couldn't help but recollect again the emotions she had felt with Zeke as she listened to the words of the song. Passion, ecstasy, joy, tenderness, sensuality, desire, melancholy, despair, grief. All those. And love. So intense but so brief.

Jolyn tried to pinpoint the exact moment when she fell in love with him. She tried to remember the first time she said she loved him. Yes, it had to be that time in the elevator. Now she was sure.

Zeke bought her flowers. From a street vendor as they walked along Sultan Suleiman Street in the old section of Jerusalem.

"Iris, Madonna lily, tulip, and hyacinth," he commented as she took the bouquet from his hand. "Beautiful flowers for a beautiful girl."

A block further she stopped and purchased fruit from another vendor. "Dates, avocado, guava, and mangos," she said as she gave the plastic bag to Zeke. "Eat fast," she suggested, "especially the avocado. I feel a moment coming on." And then she smiled that smile that melted icebergs and his heart. Hers already dripped like the gooey center of that molten chocolate fudge cake.

They didn't even make it back to his apartment. He put his arm around her as they walked and she smelled the flowers as he munched the fruit. As they passed the entrance of the Tulip Inn Jerusalem Golden Walls hotel, she paused and whispered, "Let's go in." They did. She led him to the elevator.

"Do you know someone here, Jolyn?" he asked, puzzled.

"Carnally? Not yet. You know, in the biblical sense. This nation Israel has an erotic effect on me. Either that, or you do, Zeke. Wasn't there a whole lot of phallic worship going on in Israel in Ezekiel's day? Hey, I went to Sunday school when I was a little girl."

"Yes . . . phallic worship . . . I . . . think so. In the temple even. Also . . . in the elevators."

"Yes, the elevators."

They got in and she pushed the buttons. All the buttons. Including "STOP."

"You know," she murmured, "I don't think you have kissed me today."

"Yes, I did. I surely did. You were half asleep. This morning when I came out of the shower. You screamed, 'No, not until I brush my teeth!' Don't you remember?"

"Yeah, that does sound vaguely familiar. But you still didn't kiss me."

"You wouldn't let me!"

"That's no excuse, dude!"

"I'm sorry, I'm sorry."

"Do I get a kiss now?"

Zeke moved closer and grazed her lips with his. Hands roamed her body gently, teasing. He kissed her again, like a brother.

"You're playing with me, Zeke. Now I'm going to play with you."

Jolyn began to bump and grind against him in the elevator. She knew he was getting bigger so she put her hand in his pants and felt him.

"Oh my God, Jolyn, you're hands are cold!"

"Yeah, baby, but my lips are warm."

She went down on her knees and unfastened his belt, unzipped him, pulled him out, and began to play. With her hands and with her mouth.

After ten minutes the security guard had solved the problem of the jammed elevator. He brought it back down to the first floor and opened the door.

Jolyn got up and walked out with Zeke in tow, wiping her chin with the bottom of her blouse. Two older couples waiting for the elevator gave the pair very irate looks.

"What can I say?" she asked loudly. "I love him! I love him!"

The two women smiled and jostled their husbands.

"*Chalab vedebash*," one of the women muttered in Hebrew.

"What does that mean?" Jolyn asked Zeke. "*Chalab vedebash* or whatever it was that she said?"

"It is the ancient art of seduction that literally means 'milk and honey.' How Delilah seduced Samson. Delilah learned 'all his heart' only after Samson was crazy with lust because of the milk and honey. She took his milk and gave him her honey. Got milk?" He laughed. "You missed a spot." He wiped off the gob above her lips with his handkerchief.

"I think we better go, Zeke. That security guard was kind of in shock there for awhile but let's not dally. Oh my God! Look at those closed circuit cameras! Somebody saw us . . . saw me . . ."

"I'm afraid so, Jolyn."

"Let's go to your apartment and finish this. Hurry! *Chalab vedebash,* you know. I had my milk and now you need some honey, Honey."

Fifteen minutes later they were naked and in his bed. Two hours later they cuddled and kissed and whispered.

"Jolyn, did you mean it when you told those people you love me?"

"Yes, I did. I really did."

"Why don't you tell me?"

"I love you, Zeke. I really do. So much. I want to be with you. Forever."

"I love you, Jolyn. I have from the first moment I saw you. I just couldn't tell you. Until I knew you felt the same way about me."

But then Zeke died. His life fluid in her mouth that day in the elevator. His life fluid pouring from the stab wound that night he lay outside the entrance to his apartment complex. All over her.

The sorrow. The anger. Hatred, even, directed towards those who savagely killed him.

But was it my fault?

Emotions. So many emotions.

CHAPTER 25

The super agent flipped.

He angrily heaved the paperweight, a figurine of the Heisman Trophy, against the wall.

Ron Kingston had just finished reading Jolyn Knowlton's article, "Emotionally speaking of rape case," in the *Pittsburgh Tribune-Review*. "Shit," he muttered, "Get me Hank Gorton on the damn phone!" he screamed at his secretary.

She did.

Within five minutes the private investigator was on hold to speak with Kingston.

"Gorton, did you read that article in today's *Pittsburgh Tribune-Review* that Knowlton bitch wrote?"

"Yeah. It . . . uh—"

"It sucked! That bullshit is all we need. She makes Dexter out to be some sort of vicious animal ranting and raving for blood. I want you to put the fear of God into that woman. Do you understand?"

"No . . . not exactly."

"Stalk her. Run her off the road. Find out what skeletons she has in *her* closet. Who has she been talking to? I want to know. We don't need this kind of crap in the papers. Do something to shut up her fat trap."

"That might not be easy, Ron."

"Get me the skinny on her."

"But—"

"I said do it."

"Right."

RATTRAP

"Right *now*, Gorton!"
Kingston slammed the phone down.

CHAPTER 26

Hank Gorton called Ron Kingston back several hours later.

"That Knowlton chick appears to be rather squeaky-clean, Ron. I don't know that there's much to work with to discredit her. But I tell you man, that bitch is a looker. From pictures, anyway."

"You didn't actually see her?"

"She took off to New York City."

"For what?"

"Damned if I know. My source at the paper had no idea. Maybe she took a little vacation."

"Don't be so fucking stupid, Gorton. It must be about Dexter. She wouldn't go on vacation now. This thing is too hot. Dexter met with that law firm in New York we hired to defend him a couple days ago. I'll talk to him. Find out if there is something he hasn't told me. Knowlton is up to something. That's all we need. *More* bullshit."

"What do you want me to do, Ron?"

"Talk to that dyke Lydia at *THE WHOLE TRUTH.* Have her make up some crap about the Knowlton bitch. It's not like she hasn't done it before." He snickered. "I read that stupid piece about Hillary Clinton screwing the alien. Far out shit. How about, 'Lead reporter on rape case is she-male' or something like that?"

"Will do, boss. Oh, I forgot. I talked to my guy in the Steelers front office. Our Ms. Knowlton requested a copy of Dexter's contract. They gave it to her."

"Now what in the hell does she want with that?"

"I have no clue, Ron."

"So it appears, Gorton. Now get in touch with that dyke and get me a shit stirring story that will make 'Little Miss Goodie Two Shoes' Knowlton wet her panties because she's so pissed." Kingston guffawed.

"She wears thongs."

"How the fuck would you know that?"

"My source at the paper said he lifted her skirt and bent her over. But I think he's lying. Wishful thinking. I don't know if she wears thongs. Not yet. But I'm going to put a camera in her bedroom while she's out of town. I wonder if she has a vibrator."

Kingston laughed again, this time lewdly. "Click, click. You finally got a good idea, Gorton. Of course I want to see the tape. We'll make a star out of that Knowlton pussy. Her snatch will be plastered all over the internet. Put a camera in her bathroom too."

"You got it, boss. Hey, maybe I could do the same to Kim McConnell."

"Forget it! Too many people watching her bloody ass. We'll just have to hope somebody comes across with some pictures of her doing a horse or some such thing. Did you sweep Dexter's place like I told you?"

"Yep. No bugs."

"Other than what he got from that McConnell slut. Now go give that bitch Knowlton a heart attack."

"Oh yeah, we'll make her squirm. And we'll watch."

Gorton sounded strange to Kingston. He hoped the P.I. didn't get too far out. He just didn't trust his judgment, or much else about him.

CHAPTER 27

Buggers.

District Attorney James Hawkins spent his lunch hour at Moe's News. He didn't particularly care for the reading material. But the buggers behind the walls could sure suck the chrome off a trailer hitch.

Hawkins didn't consider himself a homosexual, or even a bisexual. He had a wife and kids. No, he just liked to play king to the queens on occasion.

His wife didn't particularly care for giving head or getting it in the fanny. Just straight old knocking boots for her. So he indulged his fantasies elsewhere. Another man wasn't cheating he rationalized. No emotional attachment. Just sex. Glory days.

The P.I. filmed the D.A. as he left the adult book store.

CHAPTER 28

A morals clause.

Ron Kingston told his secretary to pull the contract from Dexter Curtis' file and bring it to him. He read the sections of it that interested him the most.

***

At the election of the Pittsburgh Steelers, this agreement may be terminated without penalty as described in paragraph C(2)(b), if any action of Dexter Curtis results in any of the following:

A. The conviction of Dexter Curtis of a felony or crime of moral turpitude; or

B. Comment about the Pittsburgh Steelers adverse to the image or financial interests of the Pittsburgh Steelers to local or national media, or any comment that the Pittsburgh Steelers abetted, encouraged, or condoned any such behavior outlined in paragraph A above.

In addition to above proscribed conduct, any action of a lewd, obscene or lascivious nature, any action violative of any state or federal criminal law, any public display or intoxicating use of a controlled substance, any display or brandishing of a firearm or other weapons, associating with persons engaged in any such conduct or making public comment reasonably perceived as condoning or supporting any such conduct, casting the Pittsburgh Steelers in a negative light or reflecting adversely on the public image of the Pittsburgh Steelers, may, at the election of the team, result in the termination of this Agreement without penalty as described in paragraph C(2)(b).

Dexter Curtis' warranty and covenant that no conduct engaged in prior to the date of execution of this Agreement would constitute a breach of this Agreement is material and valuable consideration without which the Pittsburgh Steelers would not have entered into this Agreement with Dexter Curtis, and evidence of breach of this warranty may, at the election of the Pittsburgh Steelers, result in the termination of this Agreement without penalty as described in paragraph C(2)(b).

Failure by the Pittsburgh Steelers to enforce the terms of this Agreement with respect to certain conduct of Dexter Curtis violative here of shall not operate as a waiver of the right to enforce the terms of this Agreement as a result of any subsequent conduct of Dexter Curtis violative of this paragraph.

***

Then Kingston called Dexter Curtis. "Dexter, have the Steelers management said anything to you about your contract? The morals clause?"

"Nope, not a word. Why, what does it say? Like I can remember. I didn't even really read the damn thing. You said it was okay. What's up with the contract?"

"Nothing. Never mind. I told you to grant interviews to the press but say nothing about the case. I haven't seen anything in the papers."

"I have a rough draft of a short article to appear in the *Pittsburgh Post-Gazette* tomorrow. The dude who wrote it let me review it. Looks good to me."

"FAX it to me. Right now. I didn't give you that machine to gather dust. Let me read it and I'll call you back in a few minutes. I have something else I want to talk to you about."

Curtis did as requested.

Kingston read the article.

***

In training camp Steelers linebacker Dexter Curtis wears a jersey with "GET MAD" on it instead of his name. Coach Lowry didn't bat an eye the first time he saw it. He likes angry linebackers. After all, he was one.

"All you need now is missing teeth," Coach Lowry was heard to say loudly, for the benefit of others.

"I plan to leave them in the butt of a few Lions, especially the

74

quarterback," Curtis countered just as loudly, making reference to the upcoming first preseason game.

Dexter Curtis is light years beyond aggressive. The smashing he gives running backs sends shivers up spines. When he makes contact, the ground shakes and teeth rattle.

Curtis, our first round draft pick, believes he is on the verge of a special season. For himself, but more importantly, for the team. "I'm the man," he says. "I'm going to have a big year. The team if going to have a big year. A Super Bowl year."

From the moment he arrived from the University of Miami, Dexter Curtis has impressed. He makes the big plays. He strikes fear in hearts. But he has a mellow side, too. No one spends more time signing every autograph. No one is more willing to talk to the media. He can't talk about his off-the-field troubles and the mainstream press doesn't ask, but he'll tell you for hours about his work with autistic children.

"I need to stay focused," Dexter says, "on the game. Keep my mind on the job. I refuse to get distracted by events in my personal life beyond my control. I can only try to challenge myself every day on the football field. Coach told me to take chances and make the big plays. That's exactly what I plan to do."

Pads cracked at Latrobe Memorial Stadium on that night of the first practice under the lights. A crowd estimated at 8,000 fell in love with our new linebacker. Our previously maligned defense stonewalled the offense. Fans chanted, "Dex wreck! Dex wreck!" over and over as he knocked down running backs like bowling pins. Rather than tackling them, it was more like he huffed and puffed and blew them all down.

Woe are the Detroit Lions. It may be a pre-season game but they are going to get a good look at the second coming of Lawrence Taylor, Dick Butkus, Ray Lewis, and Jack Lambert, all rolled into one.

Oh, and he plays a little offense too.

Offensive Coordinator Mike Mallory tells me a couple pass plays are in the works where Dexter runs tight end patterns. Can you imagine trying to tackle this incredible physical specimen when he has the ball in his hands and the end zone in his sights?

Hall of Fame, here comes Dexter Curtis.

***

Kingston called Curtis back.

"What's up with that bit about the autistic kids, Dex?"

"I made that shit up. Sounds good, 'eh?"

"Yeah." Kingston chuckled. "The article looks good, man. Seems you got this *Post-Gazette* reporter in your back pocket."

"No worries. But that bitch at the *Tribune-Review* scares me. I didn't like what she said."

"No, I didn't either. She's in New York City right now. Talking to someone. Who, Dexter? Did you hook up with somebody when you went to see the lawyers?"

"I . . . uh . . . I . . . I—"

"Dexter!"

"Okay, okay. I met some fucking whore on the plane. A hooker. We went to a hotel. I did her. That's all there is to that."

"Did you rough her up?"

"She didn't mind. She got paid. Very well paid."

"Damn, Dex! I told you to keep it in your pants."

"Shit happens. My old lady won't put out. She's too pissed about me butt-fucking that white trash. Besides, Juanita is in Miami and I'm here. I get lonely."

"Dexter, don't do anything else stupid. The heat is on. Lay low, for Christ's sake."

"That reporter chick, what's her name? Knowlton? I'm going to bend her over and pack her fudge. Snotty bitch. Damn good looking, though. I'll rip that red hair right off her fucking head while I'm giving her a doodie shoot."

"I'm taking care of her, Dexter. When I'm done she'll be begging for you to ram her dam and put her out of her misery."

"Promise, Ron?"

"I promise, Dex. I'll deliver her to you on a silver platter, butt up. If you behave for now."

"I'll fuck that bitch in the ass until she bleeds to death."

CHAPTER 29

Why are whores whores? she asked herself.

Am I a whore?

Is Kim McConnell a whore?

Sondra Lewis is a whore.

Is Dexter Curtis a whore?

Jolyn Knowlton called her editor, Stephen Winslow.

"Stephen, I talked to Sondra Lewis. She's a prostitute. Dexter Curtis had sex with her after they got off the plane. They went to a hotel. He hurt her. She thinks he hurt Kim McConnell."

"Will she be quoted directly and allow us to name her as a source?"

"Yes, I think so. Stephen, her story is compelling. I know some of it we couldn't print. But some of it we can. He went all wild and crazy on her. Like nothing she had ever experienced before. And she has been around the block a few times."

"What exactly did he do?"

"For one thing when he wanted anal intercourse and she tightened up her sphincter muscles and wouldn't let him enter her, he choked her and threatened to kill her. He didn't know she was a hooker at first."

"You believe her?"

"Yes, I do."

"Does she want money?"

"No, I asked about that. She wouldn't say exactly what she wants. Perhaps some sort of notion of revenge. I don't know. Perhaps she'll eventually tell me with a little probing."

"Write your compelling story."

"Oh, and I found something In Dexter Curtis's contract I can weave into the article."

"Good. I'll see you when you get back from Detroit.

"Yes, I'm sure."

Jolyn thought about Sondra Lewis, contemplating how a woman could spread her legs for money with no emotional connection to the person making the most intimate contact with her body. She would have to ask Sondra that very question. That might make interesting reading. *What emotions does a whore feel in the throes of someone else's passion?*

Disgust. Despondency. Depression.

How overwhelming they had been to Jolyn when she had stopped caring for Robert but had continued to have sex with him. And then one day she said 'no' but he had his way with her anyway.

Like Dexter Curtis took Kim McConnell. Yes, she believed that he violated the woman. But she couldn't let that color her judgment in reporting on the case. She would try to convey the emotions of a violated woman through the eyes of Sondra Lewis. It would be a catharsis for herself. Perhaps her own hell would fade.

If only I hadn't made that contract in Las Vegas, she thought miserably.

CHAPTER 30

Detective Ed Woods stopped by Kim McConnell's residence because something troubled him.

A hoard of reporters and other interested parties camped outside.

Kim's mother answered the door and asked him in. He said he wanted to speak to her daughter alone.

"Detective, why don't you arrest those scum suckers who hang out here and continually harass me?" Kim snarled. "For loitering or something."

"Unless they are trespassing on your property or violating some other law I can't do that."

"Shit. I have no privacy. I have no life."

"Miss McConnell, I have an important question to ask you. Those black panties you wore to the hospital the day after the alleged assault by Dexter Curtis . . ."

"Yes, detective? What about the panties?"

"They have been found to contain the semen of several different individuals—none of whom are Dexter Curtis."

"What? That's impossible!"

"No, it's a fact. And something Team Curtis will no doubt try to use against you. Did you have sexual contact with anyone else previous to Curtis, say within a few days of the alleged assault?"

"The 'alleged assault'? No, I didn't have 'sexual contact' with anyone. I can't explain the semen in my panties. You know, the night the fucking nigger raped me, I didn't even wear panties. I told you that before. Often I don't wear panties. My attorney advised me not to answer questions about my past sexual history."

"Miss McConnell, there has to be some— "
"Detective, please leave!"

CHAPTER 31

A grilling.

The Detroit Lions soundly whipped the Pittsburgh Steelers in the first preseason game.

No one on the Steelers played well. No one except Dexter Curtis. And he only played the first half. Two sacks and an interception. Thousands of fans traveled from Pittsburgh to the game in Detroit and wore "Free Dexter" jerseys. It appeared as though half the 58,735 fans at Ford Field that Saturday afternoon stood and cheered the linebacker as he ran onto the field. Even the opposition loved him, at least some of them. But then, Dexter had starred in high school in Detroit.

The preliminary hearing on the rape charge had been postponed and would likely be delayed even further pending rulings on motions by Curtis's lawyers. Presentation of the facts wouldn't happen for quite some time. Jolyn Knowlton knew that Dexter Curtis had but one defense: that his accuser is lying. Even more effort would be expended in the next several months to discredit Kim McConnell and those on her side. Life would be a living hell for the accuser.

Coach Lowry emerged into the press conference area, scowling. Two players accompanied him, Dexter Curtis and the third-string quarterback who scored the only Steelers touchdown on a bootleg.

"No, we didn't play very well," the coach began. "That's how I sum it up in a nutshell. Sluggish on both sides of the ball. They beat us at the line of scrimmage. We have a long ways to go and we recognize it. If this doesn't improve next week against Philadelphia, heads will roll. That's about all I have to say. Questions?"

"What about your defense, coach?"

"Except for Dexter, the first team looked like their feet were in cement."

Saliva ran from his mouth and he spit while he spoke.

"How would you evaluate the offense, coach? You moved the ball pretty well."

"We got field goals in the red zone in the first half. You got to put the ball across the goal line. The only one who did that was Benny here. Excellent execution on his part on the score."

"Is Benny moving up on the depth chart?"

"We'll let Dexter chase him next week in practice and see if he really wants to," the coach joked.

"Coach, you were very upset on the sidelines late in the first half. What happened?"

"Missed blocking assignment on that third-and-one. We should have had the first down but instead lost two yards. Don't blame the running back."

"Coach Lowry, you practically guaranteed a Super Bowl this year. You said you'd run around the field in a jock strap if it didn't happen. How do you feel about that now?"

"Almost naked. That's enough questions for me. We will be much better next week. Bet me. You can ask Dexter and Benny a few questions."

"Dexter, how did it feel to be back in Detroit, your hometown?"

"Great man, I love you Detroit! I hope Detroit wins the NFC and we meet in the Super Bowl."

"Dexter, what did you say to the Lion's quarterback after you sacked him and stood over him gesturing?"

"Eat dirt, girlie."

Everyone in the room guffawed.

"And their second string quarterback, what did you say to him after you chased him backwards fifteen yards, caught him, and flipped him down with one hand?"

"Did you see him bounce on the turf three times? I suggested to him that he wet his panties while I chased him. I could have crushed him, but I had mercy. It's only a preseason game. Hey, I like that dude. He called me God while he ran for his life. Actually, I think there was a suffix on that word." More laughter.

"What about the interception, Dexter?"

"The QB gave it away with his eyes. If I wouldn't have dove and hit the dirt I'd have scored a touchdown."

"Next week is Philadelphia. Do you have any message for their Pro Bowl quarterback?"

"Get a body double."

Snickers filled the room.

"Dexter, do you think you should voluntarily sit out until these rape allegations are resolved?" a female voice shouted from the back.

"Huh?"

"Sit out. Don't play."

"Why? I'm innocent!"

"Innocent? You raped a woman. You violated her. You had sex with her against her will. So some say."

"I'm innocent until proven guilty!" he screamed, losing control. "Who are those some who say?"

"Besides Kim McConnell? How about Sondra Lewis, a woman in New York City? You choked her and forced her. So she says."

"That bitch is a hooker! Who's gonna believe her, anyway?"

"So you admit you know her? Rather intimately, so she says. And this after you swore off adultery at the news conference as you held your wife's hand and looked her in the eye."

Dexter Curtis, speechless and recognizing his questioner, shook his fist menacingly.

"Coach Lowry, aren't you concerned that Mr. Curtis has violated the morals clause of his contract?" Jolyn Knowlton asked, changing the focus of her attention. "Among other things he has violated? Aren't you going to terminate his contract?"

"Get that woman out of here!" Coach Lowry roared.

Security personnel moved toward her quickly.

"Don't touch me!" she snapped. "See this press pass? I have the proper credentials."

"This news conference is over," the coach announced solemnly. "Blame it on the bimbo."

CHAPTER 32

Dirty tricks.

Hank Gorton, private investigator hired by Dexter Curtis's agent Ron Kingston, called his employer excitedly.

"Ron, wait until you see what I got. Wait until you see the tits on that Knowlton bitch. Holy shit!"

"So you got the cameras installed at her place."

"Yeah. She came back from New York, changed clothes quickly, re-packed her bag, and took off for Detroit."

"Yes, Detroit. I saw her performance at the news conference, the fucking bitch. I could strangle her."

"I'd like to choke her with my big fat dick. Man, that bitch is hot!"

"Did you get a shot of her snatch?"

"No. Fuck. When she changed her panties she had her back turned to the camera. Nice ass, though. I'd sure like to spread those cheeks with my one-eyed wonder worm."

"You didn't get her taking a pee?"

"She never hit the can. In and out of the place in fifteen minutes."

"Good work, Gorton. What you got is good enough. Put up her pics on that website you got that computer geek working on, 'Kim McConnell and Friends.' It's a fucking hoot. 'Lead reporter bares all' sounds good to me. She'll shit her panties."

"Oh, yeah. I sure hope we get some pics of her taking a dump and wiping her ass. And blowing her boyfriend. A chick that hot has to be getting and giving some."

"No! Gorton, you get those cameras the hell out of there! She'll know something is up the minute she gets wind of her titties all over the internet."

"Okay, okay, but man—"

"Gorton!"

"You got it, boss."

"And get that lesbo Lydia at *THE WHOLE TRUTH* to run it too. The Knowlton pics and a zipper opening article. Have her do a real good fish story."

"She'll have to cover her nipples with a black Band-Aid."

"Whatever happened to the she-male expose she was going to do on Knowlton?"

"Too far out she said. Worried about being sued I guess."

"Hillary Clinton didn't sue over the sex with the alien thing, did she?"

"She probably thought it referred to her once a year rendezvous with her husband."

"Funny, Gorton, funny. Now go get your shit out of the bitch's apartment."

CHAPTER 33

Hank Gorton returned to Jolyn Knowlton's apartment and retrieved his equipment.

He couldn't resist going through her dresser drawers.

Finding her lingerie, he took several pair of panties. And the ones she had discarded in the hamper as she changed quickly for the trip to Detroit.

"Funny, no condoms," he muttered amusedly as he looked through her medicinal products and makeup, "or vaginal lubricants."

***

Sondra Lewis lay dead on the floor of her penthouse in New York City.

The woman held the pharmaceutical supplies she had purchased with the money Dexter Curtis had given her. The prostitute had ingested enough illicit drugs to kill a football team.

Nathan Redmond called Ron Kingston as he admired his latest work.

"I did the whore. Drug overdose just might fly."

"Excellent, Redmond. This should dissuade a certain reporter from using that whore as a source, 'eh?"

"Dead whores don't talk."

"Oh yeah. Good work, Redmond, as usual."

Yes, he did do the whore. And she didn't even ask him to pay.

She only asked to live.

But he said no.

***

Having worked in her cubicle on her next article for the past hour, Jolyn went out into the bay for a cup of coffee. Several other reporters now had come in and she had seen Rhonda, the temporary, a half hour ago so she knew it was brewing.

Her editor, Stephen, saw her and beckoned frantically.

His look warned something serious had happened.

"What?" she blurted. "You didn't like what I asked at the news conference?"

"No, not that. I liked it. You know I liked it. You had it backed up with a source who granted written permission to be identified. What more could I want?"

"Then *what*? You look like your best friend died, Stephen."

"Take a deep breath and come over her to my computer screen, Jolyn."

She did.

"Oh, my God! That's . . . that's . . ."

"Yes, it's you."

"Yes! It is me! I . . . never . . . I . . ."

"But that definitely is you?"

"Of course it is. Can't you tell by the . . . uh . . ."

"You never posed for those pictures? For an old boyfriend or something?"

"No!" A tear ran down her cheek. "I'm not going to cry," she said firmly. "Someone planted a camera in my bedroom. Those pictures were taken last Friday."

"How can you tell?"

"See my earrings? I bought them on Thursday in New York City. I put them on Friday morning. After I had dressed. Then I got on the plane to come back here. I went to my apartment, changed, packed some fresh clothes, and headed back to the airport for Detroit."

"You are sure about this, Jolyn?"

"Absolutely positive."

"You have the receipt for the earrings?"

She rummaged around in her purse, found it, and showed it to him.

"I'm calling the police, Jolyn," Stephen said softly. "This is getting too dangerous. Go to your apartment and wait for them. Check for anything missing."

"I'm angry, Stephen, very angry. My privacy has been violated."

"Jolyn . . . I must say . . . you are stunning," Stephen said softly as he continued to stare at the computer screen.

She threw up her arms, turned, and stormed out of his office.

CHAPTER 34

What a whiff.

Hank Gorton had called Ron Kingston again. As he talked, he sniffed the panties he had taken from Jolyn Knowlton's hamper.

"More good news, boss."

"Spill it."

"I got my equipment out of that bitch's apartment." He put the panties over his head with the crotch in his face.

"You didn't call me for that, Gorton."

"The district attorney, that Hawkins? I got a dude who works for a male escort service who says they did anal."

"Do you believe him?"

"He got the Emails where they made arrangements to meet."

"Which one likes to get it up the butt?"

"The French Maid. He sent pics to Hawkins dressed in a little French maid outfit, bent over waiting for it, his own dick in his hand hard as a rock. Must be that Hawkins's old lady won't let him corn-hole her."

"Yes, that seems to be a major problem with our society today. Some girls just don't like to get it up the ass. Ask Dexter."

"Did he rape that McConnell chick?"

"Does it matter?"

"Not to me." He licked the crotch of the panties covering his face.

"Get pictures of the D.A. fucking the little French Maid queer in the ass."

"That is going to cost you a little more. Fucking with the powers that be."

"We are the powers that be. Five thousand now as a little bonus for your fine work. Five thousand more when you get the D.A. humping 'Frenchie' in the butt. That's more than a little more."

"Yeah, that'll do it. You know, that Knowlton bitch has one sweet smelling ass."

"And I'm *sure* you know that from personal experience, Gorton," Kingston snarled as he hung up.

CHAPTER 35

Other pictures that appeared on the website were even more revealing than those of Jolyn Knowlton. Like Kim McConnell and her ex-boyfriend, Chuckie Wooster, engaging in sex. An interview with Wooster accompanied the pictures.

Gorton laughed heartily when he read the ending.

"Kim is a slut. That's why we broke up. I caught her screwing some guy when I came home from work early one afternoon. She said it would never happen again. I forgave her.

"Two weeks later she had to work until midnight so she said. I went over to where she works about 11:00 PM to check up on her. I didn't want to spy on her, but she cheated on me so many times, even after we talked about marriage. I spotted her car in the parking lot and somebody in it. As I looked in, she pulled her mouth up off him as cum dribbled out of mouth and down her chin.

"I couldn't take her whoring around any more so I broke it off. Then she tried to kill herself. The woman is mentally ill, in my opinion. She is very, very sick. And she does drugs. Marijuana mostly, but she does cocaine too, when she can get it. Not to mention the prescription stuff. You name it, she's got it. A fix for everything under the sun."

***

Kim McConnell's friend, Allysa, saw the pictures and the interview on the internet first. She immediately called Kim.

"He's lying! He's lying!" Kim screamed over and over after she accessed the website.

Kim dropped the phone and rummaged around her room, searching for a bottle of pills.

CHAPTER 36

Detective Ed Woods knocked on the door to Jolyn Knowlton's apartment.

He took a quick swig of the Jack Daniels and put the small flask back in his jacket pocket. She opened the door far enough for him to display his badge. Then she unfastened the chain.

"Hello, Ms. Knowlton. I'm an admirer of yours."

"Please don't say from those pictures on the internet."

"No, not from those. Although I did see them. But not until your editor, Stephen Winslow, called me. Normally, a routine case like this would be assigned to one of the less experienced detectives. But I asked for this one. I wanted to meet you. I'm the detective who arrested Dexter Curtis."

"Yes, I know."

"And you know we can not discuss that case because of the gag order the judge issued."

"Yes."

Yes, that case. She reflected silently on the facts as she knew them. Kim McConnell, a cheerleader at Pitt, alleged that star linebacker, Dexter Curtis, raped her. The sex occurred in his Hummer parked at a bar. He admitted the sex, but said it was consensual, and confessed to adultery in a news conference. The D.A. charged him with first degree felony assault. The preliminary hearing had been postponed. A concerted propaganda campaign had been launched against the accuser to discredit her reputation. Now Jolyn herself had become a target.

"I understand, Detective Woods. I won't bring up matters pertaining to the case unless you do first."

"But if there is some connection between the Dexter Curtis case and what has happened to you—"

"Is that what *you* think happened?"

"I don't know," he responded too casually.

"Of course there is a connection!" she blurted, anger smoldering, ice cold intense blue eyes freezing him momentarily.

"You may well be right," he responded warily. "But proving it is another matter. Incidentally, I think you are one hell of a reporter."

"Oh? You read my article about the Fort Pitt Bridge and Tunnel being opened ahead of schedule?"

"You really put Dexter Curtis through the wringer at that news conference after the Detroit game."

"And because of that, naked pictures of me turn up on the internet. I have been violated. My privacy. My home has been broken into. Some of my personal things have been stolen. The intimate pictures were taken without my consent."

"Please give me a quick tour of your apartment, Ms. Knowlton."

She proceeded to do so.

He checked the front door and windows.

"I don't see any signs whatsoever of forced entry. Expert burglars have ways to get in without leaving a trace. I'll have a guy come over and check your place for bugs and cameras. But I doubt he'll find anything. Long gone I'd guess. I'll give you the name of a locksmith. He can fix up your place so no one can get in without breaking the door down. And that's a pretty sturdy door."

"Thank you, detective. That makes me breathe easier. That no one will be able to get in again."

"Do you have a gun, Ms. Knowlton."

"No, I don't."

"Are you familiar with weapons?"

"I am. My father and brothers are hunters. I mostly just shot at targets and their beer cans." She couldn't stifle a light laugh, fondly reminiscing about those days. "I did shoot Bambi's father once, but I don't care for venison, so what's the point?" She of course would not tell him about Zeke and the *other* training.

"How about with a handgun?"

"I'm not a bad shot. Need a little practice, though, I'm sure."

"You might want to consider purchasing a pistol. Something small and concealable. I'd recommend a Glock. I'll help you get a license quickly if you decide to do so."

"Do you think I'm in danger?"

"Who knows? Somebody wants to put a scare into you at the very least. Maybe it will get worse."

"Are you trying to scare me, detective?"

"I just want you to be careful. Let's go over what happened. Your editor, Mr. Winslow, gave me the rundown, but let's see if you have something more to add. You bought the earrings Thursday in New York City. Put them on Friday morning. Flew back to Pittsburgh that afternoon. Changed, repacked your bag, and returned to the airport to fly to Detroit. The pictures had to be taken Friday. How long were you here in your apartment?"

"Not more than twenty minutes. I can't think of anything to add to your account, detective."

"Tell me what's missing. Your place doesn't look disturbed."

Jolyn opened her lingerie drawer and held up a pair of red panties.

"Two white pair of panties just like these were taken out of this drawer. And the ones I had been wearing that day, again white, were taken out of my hamper. Why do they call them a pair of panties, anyway?"

"I wouldn't know, Ms. Knowlton. I don't wear panties. I wear briefs. And I don't know why lawyers call a forty page document a brief, either. When my daughter, Amanda, said she needed a training bra, I wondered what you train them to do."

Jolyn tittered, and smiled for the first time at Woods. But he didn't smile back and she wondered why. Suddenly he looked so sad.

"What's the matter?" she asked. "Don't you feel well, detective?"

He ignored her question. "So our perpetrator likes white panties. That doesn't narrow it down much for me. Is there any way your missing panties can be identified?"

"Good thing the perpetrator didn't take my Hipster Body by Victoria seamless stretch panties. Imported Tactel microdenier nylon/Lycra spandex. I have three pair." She held them up. "Teal, muslim, and glacial blue."

"Why is that such a good thing he didn't take those?"

"Because I wash these by hand. The missing panties, like the red ones, are Fruit of the Loom Fit for Me. There are three styles—your briefs, hi-cut, and bikini. Mine are bikini. See the label?"

"That's not much to go on, Ms. Knowlton. Even if I found the panties, it would be difficult to prove they are yours. Unless some DNA evidence could be found on the ones you wore. Did you . . . perhaps . . . you . . . ."

"Did I have sex with someone?"

"I had to . . . inquire."

"No. No sex. But there's probably semen on my panties now. From the pervert. But there's no need for DNA analysis, detective, should you ever find them. See this little laundry mark on the red ones? The white panties have the same mark."

"Very good. Maybe we'll get lucky and find your pervert. I assure you that this matter will be very high on my priority list. I'd like to get the wacko as much as you would."

"Detective Woods, have you been drinking? I smell liquor on your breath."

"I'm on medication."

Medicated with alcohol.

Woods had been a social drinker for years. The problem and the binges and the blackouts started after his daughter, Amanda, had been sexually violated.

Gang raped. Six months later he buried her. Perhaps those memories distorted his judgment on this Curtis case. He empathized with the McConnell girl, and believed her. At least about saying 'no' to anal sex. She had been ravaged. He saw the pictures. Few women would voluntarily submit themselves to being brutalized like that.

"Yes, I'm sure you are on medication, detective. What proof?"

"I'll call you if something develops, Ms. Knowlton."

"Incidentally, Detective Woods, I have a girlfriend who is a respected addictions counselor. Master of Science degree in Special Education with a concentration in Rehabilitation Sciences. Courses like 'Administering Rehabilitation Delivery Systems' and 'Intervention Strategies in Rehabilitation Sciences.' She also has a Certificate in Alcohol and Drug Counseling from Villanova. Courses like 'Interviewing and Counseling Techniques with Substance Abusers' and 'Advanced Group Counseling.' Nicole works for SAMHSA, the Substance Abuse and Mental Heath Services Administration."

"Why are you telling me this?"

"Denial," she whispered, barely audible.

"What?"

"Just making small talk."

"Goodbye, Ms. Knowlton."

He left. The flask was out of his jacket pocket as soon as she closed the door. After he departed, Jolyn deliberated on the fact that someone had violated her privacy, stolen her panties, and now was probably using them as a prop while pleasing himself. She wondered how many men masturbated as they reviewed the explicit pictures of her on the internet. As they zoomed in on her nipples and her lips, and her naked bum, fantasizing about sex with her.

Yes, maybe I will get a gun.

CHAPTER 37

Violated.

Sondra Lewis had a roommate, Diana Morrison, an airline stewardess and part-time call girl. She coordinated her other job with her flight schedule, setting up liaisons all over the world.

Diana found Sondra. Her body had been violated. Without her consent. With drugs. But Diana didn't know the how or why at that moment—just the what. She fainted when she discovered her best friend Sondra's corpse. Recovering a few minutes later, she called the police.

***

Alyssa Davis hurried to Kim McConnell's house after informing her friend about Chuckie Wooster and the pictures and interview. Kim's stepfather let her in the house.

"She's in her room as usual," he told Alyssa, motioning her to go on up.

Alyssa ran up the stairs and opened the door to Kim's room. Her stepfather had removed the lock.

"Kim! Wake up! Kim, Kim! Wake up!" She did. "Oh, thank God! I thought you might have . . . might . . ."

"No, Alyssa," Kim muttered groggily, "I didn't try to kill myself. I just took a couple pills to get some sleep."

"There's another interview with your ex-boyfriend on line. You better take a look."

Kim accessed the website in question and read parts of the second interview aloud. "Kim's favorite sexual activity is anal intercourse. I had never done it until we started dating.

"She explained to me, naïve on the subject of stern jobs, that the rectum has nerve endings similar to the vagina. Some women, like her, find stimulation of the anus with a penis incredibly pleasurable, if done right.

"Kim liked me to start with fingers, both in her vagina and rectum. The wall between them is so thin I could feel my own fingers pressing on each side. When she started barking I knew she was ready to get on her elbows and knees and get it up the heiny hole from behind.

"I didn't like it that much that way. But she begged and begged for it. Probably like she begged for it up the ass from Dexter Curtis. Can't say as I blame him. Anything to stop her whining, ya know?"

Kim started to sob.

"Did you really bark?" Alyssa asked, trying to lighten her friend's dark mood.

"Chuckie is such a lying little shit," Kim droned. "I wonder how much they're paying him."

"Kim, you told me you never did anal. Before Dexter Curtis raped you that way."

"That's the truth, Alyssa! But I don't know how the hell I can prove it. My ex-boyfriend sure trashed my credibility, now didn't he?"

"What exactly did Curtis do to you, Kim? You never really said."

Composing herself, she began solemnly, "He pushed me down in the back of his Hummer. The regular seats had been removed and he had like a mattress in there. "He . . . he . . ."

"C'mon, Kim, you'll feel better if you talk about it," Alyssa urged.

"Yeah, you're probably right. The cops I talked to looked at me like I was lying. I wore a short denim skirt that night. No panties. He pushed up the skirt. I couldn't fight him off. He had me on my side with his body forcing my top leg up to my chest. And then he pulled my cheeks apart with his hands and penetrated me. Once he got the head of his cock inside, he went wild, jamming it in me."

"Did it hurt?" Alyssa asked, beginning to cry because her friend did.

"Damn right it hurt! Bad. Real bad. He didn't care. The more I screamed and cried the more excited he got. The names he called me were almost as bad as the pain. He wiped the blood and cum off his cock with that yellow towel the cops have. After he finished with me, he dragged me out and yelled, 'Get lost, you stupid little white cunt.' The son of a bitch violated my body. Then he violated my dignity. But I had that towel in my hand when I ran off."

"Did he use a condom?"

"No Alyssa, no condom. No lube. Just pain. I didn't go to the hospital until the next day. The doctor who examined me said he had never seen a sphincter torn so badly. I told him I had been anally raped, after he kept badgering me about how I got that way. He called the cops and some crisis counselor.

Otherwise, I'm not sure I would have told. Now I almost wish I hadn't."

"The guy deserves to be punished, Kim. He should spend some time in the slammer. Getting it up his own ass. I heard that some tearing usually does occur with anal sex. That's why the HIV and AIDS."

"I probably should get tested."

"Have you told anyone else, besides the police, and now me, exactly what happened?"

Kim hadn't told anyone *exactly* what had happened. Not the police. Not Alyssa or Cassie, her best friends. She had flirted with Dexter Curtis and agreed to perform fellatio. In fact, she realized she initiated it. But when he demanded anal sex, she had said no. That didn't stop him. No, the word 'no' seemed to make him even more determined to ravage her virgin anus mercilessly.

"I told my brother," Kim admitted.

"Your brother? He's psycho. Still on parole, isn't he?"

"Yeah. He did forty-eight hours a couple weeks ago. His P.O. caught him in a bar."

"You don't think he'll go after Curtis, do you?"

"I think he just might."

Kim smirked.

I know he will.

***

Jolyn had decided to go grocery shopping. Sometimes baking cleared her mind. Why, she didn't know, but it seemed to work. She returned to her apartment and put away the food, leaving out only the ingredients for the chocolate mousse cake. Ten quarter-inch layers of light, not too sweet chocolate cake separated by quarter-inch layers of mousse made with Michel Chizel Chocolat Grand Amer. Frosted, of course, with more mousse. Puree some raspberries and guava, set with a little gelatin, and pipe onto the mousse in a swirl design, and then top if off with chocolate shavings.

The telephone interrupted her chocoholic cravings just as she was about to sample her sumptuous treat.

"I'm licking your panties," the deep voice grunted.

"What?" Jolyn snapped

"Your panties—the ones you wore and I watched you take off."

"You violated my privacy! You violated me!"

"No shit, Dick Tracy."

"You are evil. You *are* evil."

Jolyn threw the phone against the wall.

Followed by the plate of chocolate mousse cake.

CHAPTER 38

Early the next morning Jolyn Knowlton contacted Detective Ed Woods and told him about the obscene phone call.

"I'll put a trace on your phone," he offered. "Next time he calls keep him on the line, and get me on your cell phone. No doubt he's calling from a public phone. The only way to catch him is to keep him on the line until I find out where he is."

The detective slurred his words ever so slightly and Jolyn knew he had already had a few. But then, he seemed to always be drinking. She suspected he started his day with a shot of whiskey and ended his day in an alcoholic stupor.

"That sounds like a waste of time to me, putting a trace on my phone. How am I going to keep him on the line? He'll be suspicious. And he could call me at work."

"I'll put a trace on your phone at work, also. He likes your panties. Use your imagination."

"I'm not doing phone sex!"

"You want to nab the guy don't you? He did break into your apartment, take intimate pictures of you with a hidden camera, and had them posted on the internet. He stole your panties and is using them to satisfy some perverted fantasy. Did you forget already? And now he is making obscene calls. I suggest you ask your boss, Winslow, if I can put the trace on your work phone."

Yes, the loco lecher had violated her. Her privacy and her dignity. And now he wanted more Maybe she would give him move. More than he bargained for. Much more.

"I'm going to the office now. I'll ask Stephen. I'm sure he'll cooperate. Let's you and I make a deal. I'll keep the scum on the line. You catch him. And after you do, you talk to that girlfriend of mine, the addictions counselor."

The detective grunted irritably. Then he gave her his cell phone number. "Call me twenty-four/seven. I'll answer."

"Try and stay somewhat sober. I can see it now. You'll arrest the wacko weirdo for the panty raid on my place, and they'll arrest you for DUI when you transport him to the station."

"That's not funny, young lady."

"No, it's not."

General Telephone Company had installed a new model.

She flung it against the wall.

CHAPTER 39

Jolyn informed her editor of the phone call from the demented housebreaker and the discussion with Detective Woods. He readily agreed to the trace.

Their conversation moved on to other matters.

"Why do you suppose Dexter Curtis is not playing in any more preseason games?" she asked him.

"Coach Lowry said he slightly injured his back in practice and is having spasms. He wants to save him for the regular season, I guess. You're the lead reporter on this case. What do you think?"

"Curtis wasn't even on the sidelines for the last two games. Where has he been?"

"Tell me. Obviously you know something."

"New York City."

Jolyn told him about the other phone call—the muffled voice—that claimed Team Curtis had been in intense negotiations with Kim McConnell's lawyer. They met in New York because that's where the law firm representing Curtis was located. And they wanted to keep the meetings very hush-hush and distant from the scene of the crime. No revealing airline manifests. Dexter Curtis had been making the eight hour drive back and forth.

A possible civil settlement to the alleged victim was at issue. A figure in the vicinity of $2 million had been bantered about, according to the anonymous informant. The payoff, should it happen, would likely have the ultimate effect of short-circuiting the rape case against Curtis.

"Can you prove any of this, Jolyn?" Stephen asked after she finished.

"No. Not yet."

"You can't write it unless you can confirm it with reliable sources."

"I understand. I'm working on it."

"What's the latest with Sondra Lewis?"

"I have a few loose ends to tie up with her. Unanswered questions. But now I can't get in touch with her. Her phone just takes messages and she doesn't call back."

"I'm sure you saw Hawkins, the district attorney, in the press conference yesterday say that the arrest warrant on Curtis may be publicly released."

"Yes, but we won't know for sure for awhile. The judge gave the prosecution and the defense ten days to file possible appeals."

"Well, I guess we just wait. On pins and needles."

"Jolyn, remember that question you asked me?"

"Which one? I ask you a lot of questions. Let's see. I asked you if you were dating these days. You ignored me."

"The question about panties. Why they are called 'a pair of panties.' You wanted to know."

She laughed, rather deliciously he thought. "And you now know the answer. Tell me."

He did tell her. Words for nether garments historically have been plural, he explained. Panties, trousers, stockings, tights, breeches, knickers. Once upon a time such articles of clothing had been made in two parts, one for each leg, and then connected at the waist. Even after the advent of modern tailoring methods, the plural usage continued. Then he told her an amusing anecdote about the origin of the word pantaloons.

"What would I do without you, Stephen?"

Her smile made his heart flutter. He almost imagined, no it couldn't be. Why would a most beautiful and incredibly intelligent young woman pay him much attention. Not even a question. An improbability. No, an impossibility.

"Without me, you'd be managing editor," he joked, after contemplating the question for a moment.

"I'm sure. Actually, without you, I probably wouldn't have this job. I definitely wouldn't have this assignment."

"Speaking of that, when are you going to have a new story for me?"

"Why should we print what everybody else does? I'm holding off until we have something really, really big. An exclusive. Like catching Dexter Curtis with his pants down. Again."

"The tabloids are beating us to the punch."

"Is that the competition? Those rags aren't worth the paper they're printed on. That Lydia Colvin at THE WHOLE TRUTH had the unmitigated gall to call for my comment on her story on me."

"Yes, that 'Porn queen turns to reporting on sex' thing. Quite amusing."

"Be careful, Stephen, or I'll use the same words on you that I used on her."

He wished she would. Somehow the concept of this divine creature talking dirty appealed to him immensely. Perhaps he would ask her to tape the conversation if the pervert called again. No, he dismissed that idea because of the likelihood of being slapped smartly.

"Stephen, what in the world *are* you smirking like that about?"

"Oh . . . nothing."

"Tell me!"

"No!"

"Are you having a sexual fantasy about me?" she teased.

"Yeah, right." He wondered if she could read minds.

"You know Detective Woods. Why does he drink so much? I mean, the guy is an alcoholic."

Reluctantly, he told her. How the detective's daughter had been abducted in broad daylight while walking home from the library. How she had been dragged into the house and been brutally gang raped. Stephen had covered the trial. He became friendly with Ed Woods.

Stephen began to hang out in a sports bar that Woods frequented. Over time he learned more of the tragic story. The daughter became pregnant as a result of the activities of that terrible afternoon. She had an abortion that devastated her, more than even the rape itself, Woods confided in Stephen. Amanda committed suicide. Woods' wife soon after attempted suicide herself, but survived.

"No wonder he drinks. I could use a shot myself after that revelation. Do you . . . have . . ."

"Newspaper editors have a historical reputation to maintain." He pulled out a bottle of his desk drawer. "Scotch?"

"Whatever." Jolyn didn't even bother to wait until he poured her one. She just took the bottle from his hand and took a healthy swig. "I'd like to go home now. I don't feel well. Cramps and that sort of thing."

"Let's make a deal. I'll give you the rest of the day off on one condition."

"Oh, and what might that be?"

"You have dinner with me one evening in the near future."

She laughed lightly. "Stephen, you didn't have to give me the day off. All you had to do is ask."

"Really?"

"Really. But I have one condition."

"Oh, and what might that be?" he responded, mimicking her.

"Dinner at your place. You cook. I've heard all about your culinary capabilities."

"From who?"

"I don't disclose confidential sources." She winked. "I'll bring the dessert. And the wine. What do you like?"

"My mother told you. I see you gabbing with her every time she comes in. No doubt the dessert will be something chocolate. You decide on the wine."

"Your mother thinks a widower like you needs a wife to take care of him. Okay, I'm going now. Really, I need to lie down."

"Perhaps you should stop at Dairy Queen and get a Triple Chocolate Utopia. Creamy vanilla soft serve topped with cocoa fudge, chocolate chunks and chewy chocolate brownie pieces. That helps with the cramps. My mother told me."

"Thanks for the advice, doctor. I just might do that."

"I'll talk to you in the morning, Jolyn. I hope you feel better."

"You're a dear, Stephen."

Jolyn reached over his desk and kissed him on the cheek. The second time she had done that. This time seemed different. The look in those sad but brilliant and alluring blue eyes. He couldn't quite measure it. Some calamity in her life he conjectured.

CHAPTER 40

Let's make a deal.

Hank Gorton removed the gloves after he had mailed the envelope to the D.A., James Hawkins. The envelope contained pictures of Hawkins anally penetrating the male escort who had been bending Gorton's ear, for money. And bending over for Hawkins, for money. In the pictures the male escort wore a "Parlor Maid" outfit with a satin crop top, flared miniskirt, ruffle panty, headband, choker, leg garters, and lace gloves. Hawkins wore a shirt and tie, but no pants.

The computer printed note with the pictures said, "You might consider agreeing to reduce the criminal charges against a certain football player. Third degree assault as opposed to first degree sounds reasonable."

Gorton left the Post Office and stopped at the first phone booth he passed, and called Jolyn Knowlton.

"Hello?" she answered.

"Hi, honey. I'm wearing your panties. A little tight. Especially because my big cock is hard. You make it hard, honey."

"Would you like some more panties?" she inquired seductively.

"Jolyn covered the mouthpiece and quickly called Detective Woods on her cell phone. When he answered she said, "He's on the line," and terminated the call.

"Uh . . . uh . . . what?" Gorton stammered. "What did you say?"

"I asked if you would like some more of my panties."

"Yeah, baby. I could go for some more of your panties. Damn right I could. Especially after you wear them. Your ass smells good. And I like to lick the front."

Now her cell phone rang.

The screen indicated Stephen's number.

She covered the mouthpiece on the phone she spoke with the panty pervert on. "Stephen, I have the scumbag on the line. I can't talk now!"

"Sondra Lewis has been found dead in her apartment," Stephen said solemnly. "Drug overdose. Call me back when you can."

Jolyn wiped the tears swelling in her eyes, gritted her teeth, and went back to the other call. "How would you like some panties with me in them?"

"Huh?"

"So you liked those pictures of me, 'eh? Would you like to touch me? My breasts. Suck my nipples. Lick my hot, wet pussy."

"Yeah, baby, yeah! I knew you wanted it. You're some hot chick looking for a big fat dick. I'd be more than happy to oblige."

"Well, now, that's a definite possibility. Let's make a deal."

CHAPTER 41

"Detective Woods, what the hell do you mean you didn't arrest him? You saw the pervert in the phone booth still talking to me and you let him go?"

"Yes, I did, Ms. Knowlton. What did you say to him? He looked like he was slobbering."

"None of your damn business! You said to keep him on the line."

"That you did, my dear. That you did."

"Well, why isn't he in jail?"

"I know who he is—a rather unsavory private investigator. Now I need to find out exactly what he's up to, and who his employer might be."

"He's still on the loose, stalking me. That's what he's up to."

"I'll arrest him if you insist. But I guarantee you he'll be out on bail within a couple hours."

"Do it your way. I'll do it mine."

Jolyn hung up rudely.

She called her father.

He agreed to purchase a small pistol for her from his friend, the gun dealer. She didn't tell him about the stalker and the detective, not any more than he already knew, anyway. The fact that her father had seen naked pictures of her on the internet bothered him more than it did her, and it bothered her a lot. He said he'd have the Glock for her that evening.

"Would you like to have dinner with your mother and I tonight, Jolyn?"

"No thanks, Dad. I can't. I have a date. Some other time this week. Okay?"

"Sure. A date? With who?"

"Just a friend. A coworker. I'll talk to your later." They said goodbye.

Yes, she did have a date. With Stephen. When Jolyn called him back to talk about the fate of Sondra Lewis, he had asked her.

Jolyn wanted to say no.

But she said yes.

CHAPTER 42

"You look lovely, Jolyn," Stephen, awestruck, complimented as he opened the door.

Jolyn had selected one of her favorites, a candy apple red matte jersey dress. Mid-thigh, three-quarter sleeves, ruching and ruffle detail. Matching cross-strap stilettos.

"Thank you, Stephen," she replied self-consciously, knowing she blushed.

Stephen gave her a brief tour of his home. European style in a rustic décor. Tan leather and wood sofa, chairs, and ottomans. Earth colors on the walls. A mahogany topped accent table on a wrought iron base. Chunky baskets filled with blooming plants. Terra cotta pots and earthenware.

"Comfortable, but casually elegant," she observed, impressed.

"I totally changed everything after my wife died. Not that I didn't like how she did the interior decorating, it just reminded me too much of how much I miss her. If I didn't love this old house, I would have got rid of it too. My grandfather built it."

Finally he led her into the dining room. Wrought iron trestle table. Finished wood chairs with cushions. Ornate corner china cabinet, island server and hutch.

Stephen pulled out a chair for her. Not at one of the far ends. In the middle.

"I don't want us to have to shout," he said softly.

One dozen roses arranged with caspia and greens in a clear vase had been placed in the center of the table. White, pink, red, and yellow.

"The roses are beautiful, Stephen."

"They are for you, Jolyn. Beautiful flowers for a beautiful woman."

"Thank you," she gushed again.

"Actually, I have a rose garden. One of my favorite places in the world is

Longwood Gardens in Kennett Square. The property was once owned by Pierre S. du Pont. You can even go in winter and marvel over the indoor gardens under glass."

"My, my. A man of many talents. Chef Stephen, I smell sweet aromas coming from the kitchen."

"Are you hungry?"

"Simply famished."

Stephen went into the kitchen and brought out the appetizers. A trio of crepes: chicken and fresh peaches with a veloute sauce, escargot with lots of garlic and butter, and shrimp with fresh ginger and scallion and a ginger hollandaise.

"Do you mind if I say grace, Jolyn, or would you prefer I do it silently?"

"Let me, please."

He nodded. "Of course."

"Dear Lord, thank You for the blessings You have bestowed upon us. Thank You for this food of which we are about to partake. May it sustain us physically as You sustain us spiritually. We pray this in the name of Jesus. Amen."

"Amen. Do you attend church, Jolyn?"

Jolyn had just taken a bite of the escargot and made a strange face.

"Are you expecting vampires?"

"Huh?"

"The garlic. Allium Sativum. Since ancient times a charm against the powers of the evil ones."

"Is it too much?"

"No, no, absolutely delicious. Regarding your question, I do not attend church on a regular basis. Much to the chagrin of my mother. But I do believe in God, and the Bible. My own interpretation."

Yes, and she had just created a screen saver on her computer with two of the ten commandments.

Thou shalt not kill.

Thou shalt not commit adultery.

And she had highlighted "Thou shalt not commit adultery" on the screen.

"Then you won't mind if I ask you a Bible question. Jolyn, where did Jesus turn the water into wine?"

"Where in the Bible, or where geographically? The second chapter of John, the miracle at the wedding in Cana. Oh, I get it. That's a hint. I left the wine in your living room with my purse."

She got up and went to retrieve it. When she returned he had begun to make the classic Caesar salad, tableside.

"Taste this, and you'll never want to use that bottled dressing again, unless you don't like garlic, that is."

"Ah yes, Stephen, more garlic. Protection against the magic spell of witches. Are you afraid I may cast a spell upon you?" She winked, and poured the wine as he finished preparing the salad. "Do you have a coffee bean?"

"A coffee bean?"

"The cure for garlic breath. Seriously."

"I have several bags, actually. I grind my own." Stephen looked at the bottle and read the label, "Beringer White Zinfandel."

"Yes, I got it from my father's wine cellar. He insisted I take a bottle, so I took that because it's a big favorite in restaurants. I stopped by to get the gun."

"The gun?"

"Close your eyes."

"What?"

"I don't know you well enough to let you see what's between my legs."

"Huh?"

"Close your eyes!"

He did. Pulling her skirt up slightly, Jolyn pulled out the small pistol in the F.L.E.T.C.H. concealment holster strapped to the inside of her left thigh.

"Okay, Stephen, you can look now."

"It looks like a toy. It's so small."

"A .40 caliber toy. But it weighs less than twenty-seven ounces with a full magazine."

"I suppose it's a good idea, what with your apartment being broken into, and all. Provided you know how to use it properly."

"I do."

"Yes, I suspect you do. You look like the Annie Oakley gunslinger type. That dress doesn't fool anyone."

"If that's a compliment—thank you."

"We'll have to do some target practice some time. I have a Vietnam War Commemorative .45 that I have never fired. 24-karat gold plating. Well, it's time for the main course."

Stephen brought out the salmon roulade, stuffed with lobster, crab, and morels, baked in puff pastry and served with a wild mushroom and cognac cream sauce. On the side, some caramelized pearl onions and baby carrots with baby zucchini and fresh dill tossed in at the end.

"It's delicious! How did you know I love salmon?"

"Lucky guess. Actually, I noticed you eating a slice of salmon and a salad at your desk one day you brown bagged it for lunch."

"Salmon is extremely high in omega-3 and omega-6, EFAs that reduce inflammation in the body."

"What are EFAs?"

"Essential fatty acids. Inflammation causes cells to clog pores, leading to very bad things like acne and wrinkles."

"Pass me some more salmon, please."

"A salmon a day keeps Neutrogena anti-wrinkle cream away!"

"I'm afraid it's a little too late for me, but you have such a lovely complexion, Jolyn."

She took another large portion of the salmon, as she felt the flush in her face that he must have noticed.

"Oh, oh, it's getting rosy now," he quipped, enjoying her momentary discomfort.

They discussed a wide variety of subjects as they enjoyed the meal and each other's company immensely. She told him her idol was Ida Tarbell, investigative journalist par excellence. He told her his idol was his older brother, Nathan, a highly decorated naval boat commander who died in the Mekong Delta.

"Did you bring the dessert?" Stephen finally asked. "I didn't see it."

"No. I decided we'd skip the dessert, and dance and drink the rest of the wine instead."

"That's perfectly acceptable to me, but I suspect you forgot about the dessert."

Jolyn laughed delightfully.

"Yes, I did forget the dessert. I've been kind of distracted by recent events. And I'm afraid my temper has been getting the best of me. I threw a dish of chocolate mousse cake against the wall."

"Must be the red hair."

"Does that explain the smashed phones? The guy from GenTel must think I'm a wacko."

"Well, it's understandable you've been upset, under the circumstances."

He has such a calming effect on me.

"I promise I won't shoot when I'm mad."

"Shall we go into the living room? I'm holding you to the dancing part."

"Better make it something slow, then."

"This is one of my favorites—Aaron Neville—*Nature Boy.*"

"Yes, from *The Standards Album.* My father has that one."

"He and I always did have similar taste in music."

They sat on the sofa, drinking a glass of wine, listening to Neville's renditions of *Nature Boy* and *Who Will Buy* from the musical *Oliver!*

When *Danny Boy* began, Jolyn murmured, "I'll dance to that. I love that song." *But I didn't love Danny.*

"Me too." Stephen held her closely and expertly guided her around the hardwood floor of the living room.

"Quite the dancer too," she whispered in his ear.

Jolyn led him back to the sofa after the song ended.

"I haven't danced with anyone since my wife died," he confided, frowning.

"Would you like to tell me about your wife?" she asked. "I understand, Stephen, if you'd rather not."

Stephen talked for an hour about Caroline, their life together, the cancer, and what his emotions were during her illness. They both cried as he spoke of her final days.

He told Jolyn how they met, at that old amusement park on the lake, and pointed to the picture of her on the wall. "When she was your age," he said softly, with a sigh.

"Stephen, I told you before I had a reason for asking about the death of your wife—the day you gave me the Dexter Curtis story. You know I studied briefly at the Rothberg International School of the Hebrew University. I've never told anyone else this. I had a lover while I was in Jerusalem. I found him in a pool of blood and he died in my arms."

Teary and sobbing, Jolyn told him of her emotions when she discovered her only true love's body. *Thou shalt not commit adultery. Adultery is death. Death of the soul. But is it the unpardonable sin?*

They held one another tightly for what seemed like hours, but it had to be only a few brief minutes.

"I'm so sorry," Stephen whispered several times as he brushed her hair with his hand.

"Did you ever commit adultery, Stephen?" Jolyn asked suddenly.

"What?"

"Did you ever cheat on your wife?"

Taken aback, he grimaced.

"Yes, once. It just happened. I met a woman at a newspaper editor's conference in Miami. We had a brief affair. I always regretted it, especially while my wife lay dying."

"Well, it's getting late, Stephen. I better go. It's been a wonderful evening. A superb dinner, stimulating conversation."

"But I made you cry."

"No, I made me cry.

Jolyn rose to leave.

"Shall we do this again?"

"There's just one little problem that concerns me."

"That you work for me?"

"That too. I could become rather . . . oh . . . what's the right word? Problematical perhaps. You did give me a top assignment. One I'm not sure I deserved."

"We already discussed my reasons for that, Jolyn."

"Yes we did. I'd like a rain check on another date. I'll ask you next time, and I think there will be one."

Jolyn kissed him delicately on the lips.

And then she left.

Stephen went to the wall and took down the picture of his late wife.

"I love you, Caroline, always. I'll do as you asked. Never will I forget you but I will move on. You made me promise I wouldn't remain alone. See you in heaven."

He kissed the picture.

CHAPTER 43

Dexter Curtis prowled the streets of Oakmont in his Hummer.

Looking for love in all the wrong places.

One hooker strutting at the old abandoned gas station at the corner of Allegheny Avenue and Hulton Road caught his eye and he pulled over. Young Hispanic chick dressed in not much of anything. They talked through the open passenger side window.

"What's your name, baby?" Dexter inquired.

"Rose."

"Sure it is. My name's Dick. And mine needs some attention."

"You came to the right place, honey. Fifty bucks for a blow job. That's all I do. No intercourse. I'm married."

"Well, we wouldn't want you to cheat on your husband, now would we? Get in, Rose."

She did.

He found a secluded spot in an alley. Rose quickly unzipped Dexter.

"My God you're big!" she squealed.

"I bet you say that to all the guys."

"Yeah, but I *mean* it this time."

She started to give him head.

After a few minutes he muttered rather unexcitedly. "You're good, baby, real good."

He was hard but didn't otherwise seem very excited.

"I love to suck cock, honey, I love the taste of cum. Down my throat. All over my face."

"Hey, baby, let's get in the back," he suggested. "I'm too cramped in the front."

"Sure, honey. You're a big boy in more ways than one."

She giggled.

They moved.

He offered her a drink of the Jim Beam in the paper bag and a few hits off the joint.

"Hey, honey," she purred, "it's real comfortable in the rear. Do you want to cum in my mouth now? The clock's running."

"No, baby, not in your mouth. Let's see just how comfortable it is in the rear—yours."

"Huh?"

"I'm going to fuck you in your sweet little ass."

"No! I don't do *that*! Just blow jobs. I told you."

"You do *that* now."

She tried to get out but he grabbed her roughly and pushed her down, lifted up her short skirt, and pulled down her panties.

"No! No!" she screamed in panic.

"Oh my fucking God!" he blurted.

Rose had a penis.

CHAPTER 44

Kim McConnell's brother Duane disassembled and cleaned his Intratec TEC AB-10.

He had stripped off the Field & Stream one-piece camouflage coveralls and kicked off the Wolverine Sports Tracker boots and his socks. Sitting naked, he gave his favorite weapon loving attention.

The 9mm caliber, single-action semi-automatic firearm had been based on the Swedish KG-99 submachine gun, he recalled. The magazine held thirty-two rounds of ammunition. Duane laughed. When the District of Columbia enacted a law in 1991 imposing strict liability for shootings with IntraTec's TEC-9 assault-style pistol, the company "mockingly" renamed it the TEC-DC9. The TEC-DC9 was the gun used in the Columbine High School shootings in Colorado. After the 1994 ban, Intratec changed the name again, this time to the TEC AB-10. AB stood for "after ban" but it was largely the same gun.

Duane had fired the entire clip in Dexter Curtis's direction. Unfortunately, he had heard on the news reports that others had suffered a fate worse than Curtis. His sister's rapist ran, he reflected, and ran fast. He caught one in the butt. Just like the bastard Curtis had given his sister Kim one in the butt, against her will.

Kim's friend Alyssa told Duane what had really happened with his sister and the football player. She told under duress. Alyssa didn't want to talk, but after he threatened to cut off her nipples with the hunting knife, she relented.

Duane finished with the TEC AB-10. Thinking about putting a bullet in his sister's rapist's ass gave him a hard-on. He fetched the pictures of Alyssa in nothing but spiked heels. She had very willingly agreed to pose and then serviced him with her mouth. "You tell my sister or anybody else and I'll be back with the knife," he had warned her.

He grinned about Alyssa.

And spit venom about Dexter Curtis.

Next time I'll blowup your ass, motherfucker.

CHAPTER 45

Jolyn Knowlton called Stephen Sunday morning. Right after her first glimpse of CNN.

"Stephen, Dexter Curtis got shot last night!"

"Yes, Jolyn, I know. He's in serious condition at UMPC St. Margaret's Hospital after suffering a gunshot wound in the . . . uh . . . backside. But apparently the injury is not life-threatening."

"What exactly happened, do you know?"

Stephen informed her that Curtis had been hanging out in the parking lot of a bar called Reggie's Fat City in Oakmont in the early morning hours. A drive-by shooting around 2:00 A.M. Six people wounded. One man died. Two women among the victims. Well, one was a woman. The other was a transvestite hooker named William Ortiz, also known as Rose. "She" took two bullets in the abdomen and when they went to remove them they found a big surprise.

"Rose was Dexter's new girlfriend," Stephen deadpanned.

"Where did you get *that* information?"

"I have my sources. Confidential, of course."

"Of course." *Yes, and so do I—an anonymous muffled voice.*

"The bullet entered his left buttocks and is lodged in his right thigh. They don't think it hit any vital organs."

"Stephen, I don't want to write the story. Not unless it has something to do with the woman Curtis raped, Kim McConnell."

"Allegedly raped."

"Whatever. So Team Curtis has subpoenaed her to appear at the preliminary hearing I heard somebody say."

"Yes, so I understand."

"And her attorney responded with a petition requesting that a videotape of her statement be permitted in lieu of an actual personal appearance. I have no problem with you not wanting to write the shooting story. I'll have one of our regular sports reporters do this thing, with my help, since I already have the skinny."

"Skinny?"

"You know, the lowdown, the scoop."

"Yes, the scoop. But I'm still the lead reporter on the rape case?"

"Certainly. But I'd rather you didn't attend any more Steelers press conferences. I don't think the coach likes you." He snickered.

Jolyn recalled the look on Coach Lowry's face when she asked Dexter Curtis at the press conference after the first preseason game if he thought he should voluntarily sit out until the rape allegations were resolved. Then the coach turned red and the veins popped out in his neck when she mentioned Sondra Lewis to Curtis. Coach Lowry had roared, "Get that woman out of here!" as his mute number one draft choice shook his fist menacingly at her.

"What's so funny?" Stephen asked.

Jolyn could only shake her head.

"I'm happy you find me so amusing. When *are you* going to write another article on the rape case, by the way? I've kind of been anxiously awaiting something new."

"I told you I don't want to do a rehash of what everybody else is doing."

She explained that she was expecting the autopsy report on Sondra Lewis to be made available soon. That hopefully would shed more light on the cause of the woman's death. Jolyn worried that if Team Curtis and others portrayed Sondra as a drug addict whore who overdosed, using what the woman revealed about her liaison with Curtis wouldn't have much credibility.

Poor Sondra, I liked her, Jolyn thought to herself. The woman had met Curtis on a flight to New York City on her way home from Miami, and he going to meet with his attorneys. Right after he held his wife's hand on television and confessed to adultery and nothing else. Sondra played Dexter Curtis for money. He took more than his money's worth from her. Now she lay in a grave, after having been dissected to determine the proximate cause of her death. *Drug overdose? Maybe. But I don't think she either accidentally or intentionally killed herself.*

"Yes, credibility is essential," Stephen agreed. "Incidentally, I hear there is some rumbling in the D.A.'s office about possibly reducing the charges from rape to third degree assault."

"I wonder what that's all about."

Yes, she did think that was odd. The D.A. had initially seemed so intent on prosecuting Dexter to the full extent of the law.

"I'm looking into it, Jolyn."

Stephen had been. Detective Woods told him under an oath of secrecy that he had searched the renegade private investigator Gorton's hotel room and found some very incriminating although illegally obtained evidence. Some of it implicated District Attorney James Hawkins in some rather unsavory activities.

"Now why do I think you're not telling me everything, Stephen?"

He shrugged and changed the subject.

"Have you received any obscene phone calls lately?" he asked her.

"Yes, but I just hang up, as instructed to by Detective Woods. He has the perpetrator under surveillance but doesn't want to arrest him yet. I wish he would. The guy is creepy."

"How is your new little gun?"

Jolyn touched the small Glock pistol she now had holstered behind her back, concealed very well by the blazer she wore over her shirt.

"I did a little target practice yesterday."

"What are you going to do today? Martial arts?"

"Oh yeah. Have the Steelers issued a statement about the latest Dexter Curtis incident?"

"The usual noncommittal spiel. Would you like to have dinner with me?"

"I'm going to my parents. I promised my father. But thank you again for dinner the other night. I had wonderful time. The salmon was delicious. And so was the company."

Too wonderful, Jolyn reminisced.

She hung up without waiting for a goodbye.

CHAPTER 46

Kim McConnell played with the Colt Anaconda .44 caliber revolver she had taken from her stepfather's nightstand.

The sun had just set as she lay on the bed in her room, the only place she felt safe these days, and looked out the window. The lights were off.

She recalled what her stepfather had said about the revolver. "This is by far the best method of home protection. Unlike a semi-automatic pistol which can jam at inopportune times, the revolver is totally reliable. If you properly clean and maintain it, of course."

Kim had put on her blue with gold trim Pitt cheerleader outfit. In the past two years the squad had finished fifth and third at the National Collegiate Cheerleading Championships. This year they had been pegged for first.

But Kim wouldn't be there.

She quit.

And then she dropped out of school entirely.

The scrutiny and pressure had proved to be just too intense.

She caressed the blue steel and then put the long barrel of the revolver in her mouth.

Kim pulled it out.

Then she sang.

"Dad a dad a da-da. Fight, Pitt, fight! Pitt must win today! Rah! Rah! Rah! Dad a dad a da-da. Fight, Pitt, fight!"

She sucked on the barrel of the revolver again.

"Suck, suck, suck. My life sucks."

I can't stand this.

Kim pulled the trigger.

Her stepfather heard the gunshots outside where he had just taken the dog for a walk in the backyard.

CHAPTER 47

Detective Ed Woods had placed the deranged private investigator who had broken into Jolyn Knowlton's apartment under his own personal surveillance.

He didn't notify his superiors because he didn't want any leaks. No, he didn't want Gorton to find out that he was on to him. Not yet, anyway.

Woods reviewed in his mind the sequence of events that led to him sniffing out Gorton as the culprit. The pervert's panty fetish did him in.

At this very moment Woods sat in his car in the parking lot outside Gorton's hotel. Watching. Waiting. Waiting for him to come out.

Finally the man made an appearance and got into his rental car. Woods wondered if Gorton had any inkling that he had been caught with his hand in the cookie jar.

Woods followed in his 1987 Chrysler New Yorker. He drove the old black car because he thought it to be less conspicuous than the unmarked police car assigned to him, or his red Dodge Ram. It began to overheat. The gauge ran all the way up. Steam began to rise from under the hood. It stalled out and he managed to get it off to the side of the road.

Gorton drove to Jolyn Knowlton's apartment again. Her car was not parked in its usual place. Now he waited, having made up his mind to confront her, anonymously. She had been hanging up on him. He'd fix the snotty bitch.

Jolyn showed up about midnight, after having had dinner with her parents and then stopping to visit a girlfriend.

Gorton hid behind a truck a few spaces from where the woman parked. He had shorted out the lights in the parking lot.

Just as she got out of her car, he pulled the mask with the eyes, nose, and mouth cut out over his face, approached her silently, and pushed her roughly to the ground.

"Get up, bitch!" he demanded.

Jolyn struggled to her feet.

"Take off your panties."

"Wha . . . what?"

"You heard me. Take your fucking panties off, you bitch!"

He pointed the Ruger Security Six .357 Magnum at her head. Gorton chose that weapon rather than his favorite Glock because he wanted to make a bigger impression at the right moment.

"Oh, recognize my voice, 'eh? How come no more phone sex, baby? Yeah, I took the panties from your apartment. I put the hidden camera in your bedroom and made sure your tits and ass got plastered all over the internet. Too bad I didn't get a shot of your pussy. Though I did get a nice whiff of it from the panties you took off that day. But I want to see your pussy now."

"But . . . you can't . . . you—"

"Yes, I can. Now get those damn panties off!"

"You are evil," she sputtered, "you *are* evil."

Jolyn reached under her HaleBob black silk skirt with snap trim and slipped the ice blue shimmer briefs down. She hadn't bothered with stockings or pantyhose. The panties fell to her ankles and she kicked them toward her assailant.

"Lift that skirt up, bitch, and let me see your little love box."

Very slowly, she did.

"Nice nookie, darlin'! I love that neatly trimmed patch of red hair. I'd lick your goober for you, but I don't have the time at the moment. Let me see your tits. Again. Now!"

Jolyn complied reluctantly, unbuttoning her Dockers white button-down shirt and unfastening the front close of the racerback bra that matched her panties.

"Free those puppies! Hurry up!" he roared. She did. "You got some nifty knockers, sweet meat. So . . . do you like them touched? Are they sensitive? Softly? Gently? So lightly that the fingers barely disturb the fine hairs, just enough to send a shiver down your spine, and to set your entire body a-prickle with goose bumps? Show me how you like it."

Jolyn rolled the tip of her left nipple very gently with the forefinger and thumb of her right hand, as she briefly considered making a run for it.

"This is how I like it," she said softly. The tip quickly became erect. Once the tips were aroused, she like to have them sucked, rather vigorously, but she wasn't about to ask this pervert if he wanted to get milk.

"Play with your pussy with your other hand!" he demanded.

"But . . . I . . . uh . . . I—"

"What? Not in the mood to masturbate? I bet you masturbated while we talked dirty on the phone. I did—right in your panties."

"I . . . don't . . . I—"

"Do it, bitch!" He waved the gun menacingly in her face. She began to do as he commanded. "Stick your fingers in it."

The man in the mask retrieved the camera from the bag he carried.

"Wha . . . what . . . are you . . . going . . . to—"

"You like my Canon XL1s? Cost me over four grand. C'mon, honey, play with that pussy. I bet you're real wet now, 'eh?"

He began to film.

In a few minutes he finished and put the camera back in the case.

"I *really* like these light blue ones."

"Ice blue," she muttered disgustedly.

Gorton had picked up the panties from the ground. Now he began to lick the crotch enthusiastically.

"See you and your juicy pussy on the internet soon, pretty lady."

He guffawed and turned to walk away.

But then he remembered. Kingston wanted Knowlton's fingerprints on an untraceable gun. What for he had no idea.

"Uh . . . one more thing. Here."

Jolyn never moved.

"Take it, bitch!"

Hesitantly she took the pistol.

Then she aimed it at him.

Click.

"Of course it's not loaded," she spat.

"Of course." Gorton yanked the pistol from her hand by the barrel and put it in a plastic bag.

Then he turned once again and began to walk away.

Jolyn reached behind herself and slipped the small Glock out of the holster behind her back, feeling so fortunate she had not strapped it to her thigh this time.

She pointed it at his back.

"Hey you!" she screamed.

He turned around to face her.

"What the fuck?" He blurted.

"This one *has* bullets."

Jolyn fired a shot in the dark.

CHAPTER 48

Kim McConnell's stepfather ran up to her bedroom after hearing the gunshots, fearing the worst.

The nineteen-inch Panasonic television had been blown into bits and pieces.

"Kim, wha . . . what happened?"

Her step-father slowly removed the huge Colt Anaconda .44 caliber revolver from her right hand.

"Oh, Dad," she sobbed, "Dexter Curtis was on some TV show, talking about being shot."

Kim called her stepfather Dad at her mother's request. But then, she had called the other one Daddy—the one who molested her.

"What did he say, Kim?"

"Some trash about how hard this all has been on his family— the *false* rape allegations and now the shooting. *His* poor family? He lay in that hospital bed and everyone felt sorry for him. What about me? And he has a new tattoo—of the 27th Psalm. What a joke."

"Honey, I told you over and over not to watch television. It just upsets you. But you are probably going to have to testify in court, sooner or later. We may be able to just show that videotape of you at the preliminary hearing, and pictures of your injuries. Our people filed a motion to deny a request from the defense lawyers to make you appear in person, because compelling your presence would cause anxiety and intimidation."

"Yeah, yeah," she snapped sarcastically, "but those pictures of my injuries are so awful, Daddy." Kim sounded like a little child. "I'm not sure I want to go through with it. I don't think I can. I'm having second thoughts. I mean, there are even people offering to commit murder—my murder. And they're going to say

I'm a whore."

Sam Green reflected on what progress had been made with respect to negotiations. Meetings between the two sides had taken place in New York, but nothing close to a settlement had been reached. He didn't tell his stepdaughter that Team Curtis had threatened to file a multi-million lawsuit against her for extortion and defamation, and inhibiting Dexter Curtis' ability to earn money as a professional football player.

"Honey, I think it might be a good idea if you get away for awhile," Sam said soothingly. "There is too much pressure here. At least until the preliminary hearing, and you likely will not even have to come back for that."

"Yes, Daddy, I think you might be right."

"Kim, no matter what Curtis and his henchmen do, the truth will win out. You will be vindicated, and that rapist will go to jail." *In any event, we will make a lot of money,* he surmised, thinking of the recent $1 million award to a young woman who claimed in a lawsuit she was raped by a former Notre Dame football player. Kim would likely get more, much more, in a civil suit or preferably, an out-of-court settlement.

"Yes, Daddy, I think so too. I should go away. It's just so painful to deal with all this."

"Think about where you'd like to go."

"I will, Daddy."

Her childlike demeanor reminded him of what she had related about her real father. Those had been the happy days Kim said. When she sat on his lap and he read her *Winnie the Pooh*, again and again. Her favorite toy as a toddler was My Little Pony. She still had those ponies, and now held one in her left hand. The Rainbow Dash Pony with the purple, orange, and green hair. She had begged her father to buy it for her, and he always had great difficulty refusing her anything. Daddy's little girl.

Sam kissed Kim on the cheek, and took the revolver to lock it in the gun cabinet so she couldn't take it again. No, he certainly didn't want Kim killing herself. No profit in that.

Kim took several more pills and tried to sleep.

But the memories of her first stepfather haunted her.

How he relentlessly forced her to perform fellatio and engage in his perverted fantasies.

How her mother caught them.

But her mother did nothing about it for years.

He didn't stop until she herself threatened to tell. But she never did tell because of the humiliation that would follow. Humiliation like what she now felt because she told on Dexter Curtis.

Her first stepfather was dead now.

But Dexter Curtis wasn't.

Kim got the pipe and smoked dope until she passed out.

CHAPTER 49

Jolyn had pondered whether she could use the small Glock the moment her father had given it to her.

Can I shoot to kill?

Thou shalt not kill.

The question ran through her mind again as she reflected on the traumatic and disgusting incident.

The masked assailant had hid in the dark parking lot, after he killed the lights, and confronted her with a gun. He forced her to take her panties off. He made her lift up her skirt and show him. He wanted to see her breasts then, and demanded she masturbate as he pointed the gun at her. She had no choice. He filmed her. As he left, she pulled her own gun. But she intentionally fired over his head.

Jolyn called Detective Ed Woods and told him what had happened.

"Are you going to arrest him now?" she demanded.

"Why?" the detective asked, after contemplating what she had reported. "Can you identify him in a lineup?"

"No! I told you he wore a mask."

"If I arrest him, like I told you before, he'll be out on bail within an hour. You haven't given me any more evidence than I had previously. If I talk to webmasters who put the pictures on the web, they will just tell me the pictures came from an anonymous source. I doubt I'd discover otherwise even if I subpoena records."

"Wonderful. Pictures of my privates and me playing with them will soon be plastered all over the internet."

"Yes, I'm afraid so. But I suggest we keep this latest incident under wraps.

Your stalker will wonder why it wasn't reported to the police. Perhaps he will become even bolder."

"I should have put a bullet in him."

Jolyn hung up, very upset.

In his foot, anyway.

She began to shake uncontrollably, and to cry silently.

CHAPTER 50

Coach Bill Lowry addressed the media in his weekly press conference and gave a summary of the loss to the Eagles.

No one seemed very interested. They wanted to hear about Dexter Curtis.

"I'm going to make a statement about the Dexter Curtis shooting," the coach finally said. "But I will not take any questions regarding the matter. I'm limited in what I can say by league policy on these situations. Is that reporter from the *Tribune-Review* here? Knowlton?"

"No!" a voice from the crowd shouted.

The coach recognized him as one of the regular sports writers for the paper.

"Good," he responded icily. "Dexter was an innocent bystander. I have talked to him several times about the incident. We are waiting for a more complete medical evaluation, but hopefully he will fully recover and be playing again soon. Of course, he is disappointed about not being in there butting heads, but his health is of the utmost importance right now. That's it on this issue."

"Coach?" a voice called from the group of reporters.

"Yes, Stan?"

"As I'm sure you're aware, Dexter Curtis's name has surfaced in another matter. He and his agent Ron Kingston and their ghostwriter have been sued for defamation by Diana Fausnaught, a former assistant trainer at the University of Miami. Because of what they said in that book, *Hurricane Homeboy*."

"Sure I read and heard about it, Stan. That has to do with a civil matter and nothing to do with the Pittsburgh Steelers."

"The lady says while she examined his knee, he pulled down his shorts and sat on her head and face. The deposition actually says, 'It was the gluteus maximus, the rectum, the testicles and the area in between the testicles. And all

130

that was on my face when I pushed him up. To get leverage, I took my head out to push him up and off.' Coach, do you think Dexter Curtis is becoming too much of a distraction? Are you having second thoughts about making him your number one draft pick? Do you think he should play at all this year, what with the rape charge, and now this other?"

"Stan," the coach growled, "I respect you so I won't bite your head off. You're not a cheap shot artist like that certain female reporter from the *Tribune-Review*. That book and the suit pertain to Dexter's time at Miami. I only know what I read and heard in the media. So I have no comment on the subject. None. Dexter has not been found guilty of anything. Now, let's talk about the game we just played with the Eagles, or our next game with the Cowboys."

The reporter nodded. The coach fielded about a dozen questions and the press conference ended.

CHAPTER 51

Aldo Martinez visited his friend, William Ortiz, at UMPC St. Margaret's Hospital.

They hugged and wept.

"Finally," Aldo muttered, "they let me in to see you, Rose."

Well, I was in intensive care, and you're not technically a member of my immediate family."

"I *am* your significant other."

"But *they* have their rules."

"What the hell *were* you doing outside that bar, Reggie's Fat City, in Oakmont?"

"Meeting Dexter Curtis. I heard he hangs there. A couple nights before he picked me up hooking at the corner of Allegheny Avenue and Hannon Road. I told him I just did blow jobs but he wanted to shag my bung hole. I said 'no' but he tried anyway. Then he couldn't help but . . . uh . . . notice my penis. He went totally fricking wild! Beat the shit out of me. I didn't know who he was until a day later, when I saw him talking in some interview on TV about his rape case. I tried to hook up with him at the bar to score some easy scratch. Then somebody started shooting."

"This is all too crazy, Rose. You remember when I told you some dude said he'd pay me big money to film another dude doing my heiny hole? I got all dolled up in my 'Parlor Maid' outfit. The one with the satin crop top, flared miniskirt, ruffle panty, and garters. I'm sure I looked more like a 'Mexican' maid," Aldo said with a giggle, "but that didn't stop the district attorney from digging in my dirt hole. I recognized him from pictures in the paper. Some fat slob named Gorton put me up to it. I had our buddy Frankie at the DMV trace his license plate. He paid me good, but now I'm having second thoughts. I mean, *you* got shot! There are some strange things happening here."

"We got to milk this thing, Aldo. There may never be another opportunity for us to make a big score. Maybe we can get our nest egg. I can have sexual reassignment surgery like we talked about and we can get married."

Rose began to cry at the thought of the surgery he wanted so desperately. *I just want to be normal,* he begged a higher power silently. By nine years old, William Garcia, born as a boy, knew his gender was wrong and started to dress in girl's clothing. He could no longer face the possibility that he would have to spend his entire lifetime in the wrong body. He had to legally become a female or he did not want to continue living. His parents paid for the electrolysis and psychiatric therapy, but could not afford $17,000 for the surgery. He and Aldo had no income other than what they derived from sexual liaisons, and that money barely kept them in food and rent.

Aldo began to cry at the sight of his Rose crying.

"What do you think we should do?" Aldo asked, stifling his tears and sniffling.

"There is this reporter at the *Tribune-Review*, Jolyn Knowlton, who we should talk to. Not really tell her anything. Just drop a few hints. And then we'll let Curtis and this Gorton dude know we just might spill our guts to the chick. You know, threaten to tell Curtis likes hookers. After he gave that hypocritical speech about being so sorry he cheated on his wife. And that Gorton is possibly blackmailing the district attorney."

CHAPTER 52

Hank Gorton called Ron Kingston.

"Ya know, Ron, I'm having second thoughts about my fee for services rendered. I think you owe me a little more. Damn, I thought for sure that Knowlton bitch was going to shoot me. Gutless, I guess. Lucky for me." He snickered. "I should have frisked her. Next time."

As he spoke, Gorton sniffed the most recent pair of panties he had obtained from Jolyn Knowlton. A new scent. He figured it for fear. The P.I. was surprised the incident apparently wasn't reported to the police. He had heard nothing about it. *She's scared shitless,* he surmised.

"Gorton, you'll get more fucking money," Kingston responded angrily. "But you'll have to do something for it. What, I'm not sure yet, but I'll think of something."

"Hey, I got her fingerprints on the gun. So how about wiring me a couple grand. I . . . uh . . . I'm running a little low on play money. Incidental expenses, ya know?"

"Stay away from the strip joints and lap dances. Your check is in the mail. And don't fuck with me, Gorton. I'll have your head on a platter. Like John the Baptist."

"Oh, you're into the Bible now, too, huh? Like Dexter and his new tattoo? You're scaring me, Ronny. Don't forget I know in whose closet to look for the skeletons."

"Fuck you, Gorton."

"No, fuck you, Ron. You and your homeboy, Curtis."

"Are we still doing business or not, Gorton?"

"Sure we are, Ron. Send me some funny money."

"It's on the way."

"Thanks, boss," he snarled sarcastically.

Dumb fucking Uncle Tom, Gorton said to himself as he hung up.

CHAPTER 53

The editor read the Email from his "star" reporter.

"Stephen, I'm having serious second thoughts about being an investigative reporter. The hunted becomes the hunter, especially when you are dealing with very powerful people. And they take no prisoners. Ask the late Sondra Lewis. I have decided to resign from the paper. I'll be at the office tomorrow morning to clean out my desk. Jolyn."

***

Kim McConnell called her friend, Alyssa Davis.

"Girlfriend, I'm going away for awhile. Liked we talked about. Cassis is going with me. I would have asked you, but I know you can't get off work."

"For the best, Kim—you going away."

"I want you to do something for me."

"Anything, Kim. Just you name it."

"The marijuana and the pipe are in my hope chest, under the red photo album. Dexter Curtis likes to smoke weed. Maybe the dope will get caught with the dope."

"I get the picture, Kim. You can count on me. But he's not doing me in the back door."

"Yeah, well don't tell *him* that. Lead him on. Be the prick tease that you know you are."

They both giggled.

"He'll just have to settle for a blow job," Alyssa said boldly. *Like your brother did*, she thought but didn't say. The recollection of Duane and the tip of the knife pressed against her nipple made her shiver.

"Well, he didn't settle for a blow job with me. I'm having second thoughts about all this legal business. The nigger rapes me and I get painted as the harlot. It's just not fair."

"I'll make him squirm, Kim—in more ways than one."

CHAPTER 54

Game boy.

Jolyn and Stephen made their way to Heintz Field for the season opener against the Ravens.

Winslow parked his car at the PPG garage on Third Avenue and they took the route across the Roberto Clemente Bridge on foot.

Stephen had persuaded Jolyn to take a paid leave of absence for two weeks rather than resign. She had reluctantly agreed. Those two weeks had passed.

Only one major event had occurred in the Curtis case in those two weeks. District Attorney James Hawkins had suddenly resigned. He cited health reasons but no specifics had been forthcoming. Stephen seemed to know more about the matter than he had been telling Jolyn.

"So, Jolyn, how do you see the game?" he asked as they walked.

She thought about the last Steelers news conference. Coach Lowry's words echoed in her mind.

The real season begins this Sunday against Baltimore. Our first goal is to take it one game at a time. Concentrate totally on this week's opponent, and hopefully win. Our second goal is to finish first in the AFC North. That will put us in the Super Bowl tournament. Baltimore is our first obstacle, and a formidable one. Yes, they have a rookie quarterback, but he looks like he'll be a good one. They have a running back who should lead the league in rushing or come close. And they have that all-world linebacker and an incredibly intense defense. I know you want to ask about Dexter Curtis. Don't. He has made a rather miraculous recovery. I can't wait until he gets back to full speed. But he won't play against Baltimore. Dexter is going to be one of the best, a future member of the Hall of Fame. Ask Mean Joe Greene. I heard him say Dexter is better than any linebacker who ever wore the black and gold—and that's before he has even played one regular season down. Now, let's talk about our game this Sunday. Let's talk about the Ravens versus the Steelers. My job will not be through until I get the fifth Super Bowl ring here in Pittsburgh.

"I'll be watching Dexter Curtis of course," she finally said.

"He's not playing."

"No, but he'll be the focus of attention, as usual."

"Think so? We'll see. What's your prediction on the outcome of the game?"

"Steelers by at least two touchdowns. They didn't look all that good in the preseason, but the Ravens do have that rookie quarterback. It's going to take him awhile to be productive. Maybe a few games . . . maybe most or all of the season. The Steelers will win this one, but the Ravens will take the division. I predict this is going to be a disastrous season for "our" team."

"Now isn't that just a far-out in left field prediction," Stephen retorted, wondering if she was joking.

The two passed security at the Heintz field gates as officers checked for prohibited coolers, backpacks, and large purses, bigger than eight-and-a-half inches by eleven inches. An officer inspected Jolyn's Gap polka-dot knit hobo bag.

"What do you suppose he was looking for?" she asked Stephen.

"A thermos? Obviously he didn't find your little pistol or you would still be answering questions."

"It's strapped to my leg. I know you peeked that night we had dinner at your place and I pulled it from the F.L.E.T.C.H. concealment holster on the inside of my left thigh."

"I did not peek! Did you wear those red panties today?"

"Shut up you snot!"

They got to the field and they prowled the sidelines, press passes pinned to their jackets.

Jolyn wore sunglasses and a Steelers cap with her long red hair pinned under it. She doubted anyone would recognize her, especially Dexter Curtis. She got as close to him as she could without being obvious, or for him being able to read the name on her press pass. He talked loudly about putting a hurt on the Ravens, attempting to fire up his fellow linebackers, especially his replacement Calvin Haynes.

The yellow "terrible towels" waved in the stands. Jolyn thought of the semen and bloodstained towel produced by Kim McConnell after she reported to the police that Curtis had anally raped her.

"Stephen, how did this 'terrible towel' business begin? They have been around as long as I can remember."

"Actually, it did begin before you were born, by a few years."

He explained it was the brainchild of television commentator Myron Cope intended to involve the fans, which it surely did. Not only that, but it could be used to wipe seats clean, worn as a muffler against the cold, or draped over one's head if it rained.

Or to clean off the blood and semen, Jolyn reflected solemnly.

Stephen laughed, himself dwelling on the origination of the towel gimmick. And then he told her that before the towel the powers that be had considered black masks with the gold lettering "Whatever it takes," which was the coach at the time Chuck Noll's motto. But wiser minds prevailed and the yellow towel became famous.

Even more famous now, Jolyn surmised silently, *now that it contains the evidence of Dexter Curtis's crime.*

Just before the game started, Dexter Curtis walked onto the field in street clothes to join his teammates. The Ravens all-pro linebacker and emotional leader Rick Louis sauntered up to him. They began to argue heatedly.

"I wonder what that's all about."

"Don't know, Jolyn, but we'll probably find out after the game."

The contest turned out to be a blowout. Pittsburgh contained Baltimore's star running back, and the Ravens rookie quarterback couldn't muster much of a passing attack.

Jolyn, becoming disinterested in the game, engaged Stephen in conversation.

"So what do you think of Dexter's tattoo?" she asked her editor.

Curtis wore a sleeveless Steelers sweatshirt. His biceps bulged prominently. But the tattoo on his right arm stood out even more.

"You tell me first," he suggested. "What's your take on the new ink?"

"Well, you have a crown over his wife Juanita's name. Then angel wings and a reference to Psalm 27. The name Juanita means consecrated to God, according to what Curtis said in an interview."

"I suppose you can quote Psalm 27," Stephen commented wistfully, recalling their previous biblical conversations.

"A few verses. 'When the wicked came up against me to eat up my flesh, My enemies and foes they stumbled and fell.' That's verse 2. 'Deliver me not over unto the will of mine enemies: For false witnesses are risen up against me, and such as breathe out cruelty.' That's verse 13."

"So what do you think Dexter's tattoo is trying to tell us, Jolyn?"

"Probably that people like us are cannibals who create a feeding frenzy to slander and destroy him. It's a symbolic declaration."

The game ended in a 34-15 victory for Pittsburgh. Jolyn proposed they stop somewhere to eat and watch the post-game report.

"Is this a date?" he inquired.

"No, I don't think so. This is business, not pleasure. I want to hear what the coach and the players have to say about the big win."

Stephen drove to one of his favorite places—The Church Brew Works on the corner of 36th Street and Liberty, a block past the Iron City Brewery. He told her the entire story, although she was already familiar with some of it. The cornerstone of the church had been laid in 1902. It served as a spiritual sanctuary to its members through two world wars, and a more tangible godsend through the depression and the flood of 1936. But the mills closing down took its toll and the Diocese of Pittsburgh finally shut down the parish in 1993. Three years later The Church Brew Works reopened the doors.

"You can get drunk if you like, Jolyn," Stephen jested, "I'm driving."

"Say what? So you can take advantage of me? Well, 1 Timothy 5:23 does say, 'Drink no longer water, but use a little wine for thy stomach's sake and thine often infirmities' now doesn't it?" Jolyn asked with a smile as she marveled over the establishment. She had never actually been inside before.

Stephen pointed out that the original pews had been modified and converted into booth seating. The top of the bar was built out of planks salvaged from shortening of the pews.

"One of the confessionals remains intact behind the bar," Stephen mentioned.

"Oh, do you think I need to go to confession?" she inquired glibly.

"That's not for me to say," he responded, "but you can talk to me about anything, you know. The confessional now contains merchandise for sale."

"Kind of like the sale of indulgences hundreds of years ago, which prompted Martin Luther to set the wheels of the Reformation in motion."

"Whatever you say, Jolyn." He raised his eyebrows overly dramatically.

"Hey, let's eat. I'm starving. You have a recommendation?"

The waiter approached and asked if they wanted a beverage. Jolyn looked at Stephen for guidance.

"The lady will have a Pious Monk Dunkel and I'd like a Pipe Organ Pale Ale." The young man nodded and turned and walked away.

"Pious Monk Dunkel?" she asked, raising her eyebrows even more emphatically than he had done.

"Quite appropriate, no? Considering that I'm probably going to soon hear a lecture on popes and protestants. I think you'll like this dark style lager. It's surprisingly mellow."

"I should have ordered myself—an IC Light. But I would like your advice on the dinner entrees."

"Your mention of we cannibals made me hungry for red meat. Let us dine ravishingly on the Shogun Filet—known as Wagyu or Kobe beef, this is the finest steak available. Comes direct from the Morgan Ranch, whose Wagyu graze deep in the heart of the Nebraskan Sand Hills."

"You have convinced me, sir. And I'd like the Conscous Salad."

"Good choice—chilled marinated Israeli couscous, baby greens and spinach, marinated artichokes and pine nut crusted chevre cheese, finished with a red pepper vinaigrette. Why, I guess I'll have one too. Perhaps you developed a taste for conscous during your stay in Israel?"

"Perhaps."

Jolyn reminisced briefly about her dead lover Zeke. A single tear drooled from one sad blue eye. She had been celibate since she held his lifeless body in her arms that night. *Thou shalt not commit adultery.*

Their drinks arrived and Stephen informed the waiter of their selections.

"Not bad," Jolyn observed, taking a sip of the lager. "It has a delightful clean and roasty aroma. Low on the hop bitterness level."

"Glad you approve. Mine is heavier on the hops, but the caramel malt flavor balances its profile quite nicely. Only the best English hops—East Kent Goldings."

"Hush now, Stephen," she requested. "I want to watch the sports report. We missed the post-game press conference." She stared at one of the large screen televisions, straining to hear.

"You could have been in the locker room and at the press conference," he gibed.

"Yeah, right," she snapped. "It seems to me that you requested that I stay away from that kind of thing."

"Only for your own protection, Jolyn. I was afraid the coach might sic the linebackers on you for a sack after you stirred things up at that one press conference."

"I didn't even get warmed up. The coach kicked me out."

Stephen laughed. "You made his face as red as your hair, Jolyn."

"Be quiet! They're talking about what happened with Dexter Curtis and Rick Louis."

The two television reporters discussed an incident between the two linebackers of the opposing teams. Louis came up to Curtis before the game and imitated Dexter's trademark leg kick he had named "the boot" to celebrate big plays. Curtis took exception. They had words. Then Louis did it again during the game when he sacked the Steelers quarterback. After the game Dexter went to the Ravens bus and called out Louis, who got off the bus. Witnesses said they shouted loudly at each other.

A clip of an interview with Dexter after the game in the locker room was shown. Curtis, in a diatribe mixed liberally with obscenities, said Louis disrespected him.

"Sounds like they were just talking trash to each other, like many of them do," Stephen concluded.

"Maybe. But if looks could kill . . ."

"That's how Curtis looked at you at the press conference when you brought up his liaison with Sondra Lewis, after he swore off adultery."

"Doesn't it, though? And coincidentally, I'm sure you recall Ray Louis beat a murder rap a couple years ago. What's up with these linebackers?"

Jolyn didn't wait for an answer. She got up and picked up her purse.

"Where are you off to?"

"The powder room."

As soon as she returned the waiter brought their salads and then their entrees. Jolyn said grace. They ate in silence for awhile. Jolyn gorged and Stephen mostly nibbled and watched her amusedly.

"This is delicious!" she complimented.

"Didn't I tell you so?"

"Yes, Stephen, so you did. But you didn't tell me what's up with this overly aggressive and hostile behavior on the part of NFL linebackers."

"Steroids?"

"What?"

"Steroids. There is another Dexter Curtis story about to break. I gave it to Randy. You said no Curtis stories for you unless they involve Kim McConnell and the alleged rape. Didn't you?"

"Yes, I said that."

"Besides, you have been on a leave of absence."

Stephen proceeded to tell her that Dexter Curtis's personal trainer while at Miami, Hector DelMonte, and three others would be indicted in the next few days on charges of money laundering and giving steroids and other drugs to scores of elite athletes. Those to be charged allegedly gave athletes anabolic steroids, a liquid "designer" drug called THG and the prescription drugs EPO and modafinil without prescriptions.

Hank Gorton sat in a booth directly across the dining room.

He stared at them.

The man pulled out something and appeared to be sniffing whatever it was.

Jolyn noticed him.

"What is that guy doing?" she asked Stephen. "The one in the green blazer. Other than watch us," she muttered.

"Oh, I think he's drinking a pitcher of Bell Tower Brown Ale—I can tell by the dark ruby hue—and playing a GameBoy. 'Max Payne' I would guess."

"And what is 'Max Payne' I wonder, Mr. Winslow?"

"Max Payne and his quest for vengeance."

Stephen explained that Max is a New York homicide detective seeking retribution for the murder of his wife and daughter. Drug dealers ordered the hit on his family. When the detective seeks to dethrone the drug empire, the tables are turned and they frame him for the murder of a friend.

"Sounds like fun," she mumbled sarcastically. "And you play it too, I suppose?"

"No, but I do have to use the men's room."

He got up and left the table.

Soon Jolyn's cell phone rang.

She answered it.

The muffled anonymous voice.

The voice terminated the call after about thirty seconds, Jolyn not having said anything.

"So how does the saga of Max Payne end?" she asked upon Stephen's return.

"Depends on how effectively you use 'Bullet Time' I guess. That's the ability to slow the action such that you can dodge bullets. But the power is limited and diminishes each time you use it."

"That's no handkerchief," she observed.

"Say what?"

"Stephen, I wonder how effectively that gentleman who is playing with my panties can dodge bullets."

Stephen's jaw fell. He couldn't hide the alarm.

"You recognize him?"

"No, but I *do* recognize my panties."

Jolyn got up from her seat and strode defiantly toward the man.

CHAPTER 55

Stephen Winslow had paid the check at The Church Brew Works as quickly as he could.

By that time Jolyn had hailed a cab and headed for her apartment.

He knocked on her door.

She opened it slowly, peeking through the crack, the chain still fastened.

"I'm *very* angry with you, Stephen!" she blurted.

"So I gathered. Detective Woods told me who your stalker is, but I swore not to tell you."

"Don't worry, you didn't."

"No?"

"No? That phone call I got at dinner? My own personal 'Deep Throat.' A disguised voice. I haven't a clue who it is—now. I suspected perhaps it might be you. But you were with me. That voice told me about Sondra Lewis and Dexter Curtis. What's in the bag?"

"Dessert. You didn't stay for dessert."

She forced a smile.

"Something chocolate?"

He nodded hopefully.

"Well, I suppose . . ." she conceded. "Come in. For a little while."

Jolyn kicked off her Bebe open-toe pumps and gave him a tour of her apartment.

"I picked up the rugs," she admitted, "because I love the feel of the wood on my bare feet." She smiled coyly. "That's why I don't like to wear stockings or pantyhose."

"Aren't you going to show me your bedroom?" he inquired, a twinkle in his eye. "I'd like to see the scene of the crime."

"What? You want to see my panties?"

"Sure I do."

"Promise not to think I'm coming on to you?"

"Sure I do."

"Why not? You've already seen me naked on the internet."

"That's what I say—why not?"

Jolyn snarled dramatically, then smiled demurely.

She lifted up her skirt displaying the Esprit Hawaiiana black, red, and green flower-patterned boy shorts.

"New style. I trashed my panty drawer. Threw them all away. *He* touched them. Do you like these?"

"Uh . . . why . . . uh . . . yes . . . I . . . uh . . . do," he stammered. "*Very* colorful."

Stephen followed Jolyn into her bedroom.

He admired the antique walnut bedroom suite, running his fingers over the intricate carvings of winged griffins, fruit, and flowers of the top crest.

"This furniture belonged to my great aunt and uncle," she explained. "Well over a hundred years old."

Jolyn opened the top right-hand dresser drawer and held up the contents.

"I . . . uh . . . like the white lacy ones."

"Wonderbra Love it Lace girl's boy shorts."

"Do tell."

"So what's in the bag, Stephen?"

"The Church Brew Works homemade double chocolate mousse cake and malted ice cream, with almonds and peanuts."

Jolyn led Stephen into the kitchen and she fetched dishes, glasses, silverware, and a bottle of Kahlua.

They sat in the high-back wrought iron bar stools and pulled up to the glass-topped bistro table.

Stephen poured them each a small dose of the Kahlua.

"To good health," he toasted, clicking her glass.

"I hope a certain someone chokes on the next pair of panties he steals and no one is around to do the Heimlich maneuver."

"Do you know some of the more infamous drinks made with this stuff, the second largest selling liqueur worldwide?" he asked.

"Mudslide is one. I can't think of any others at the moment. Detective Woods might know. He likes his booze. I'm not much of a drinker. Are you?"

"Moosemilk, Smith and Wesson, Paralyzer, French Dream, and Dirty Banana are a few others. Bars can be a very good place to gather information. Especially when you're buying potential sources drinks. What did you say to the guy who fell in love with your panties, if I may ask?"

"I said, 'You are evil. You *are* evil.' Then I snatched them out of his grubby paws."

"He looked shocked. You looked very . . . upset."

"*Really*? Well, my little pistol didn't appear to faze him much. He continued to follow me. I doubt my facial expression is going to give him nightmares. But now he knows I know who he is. At least what he looks like. Detective Woods will spill the beans on him to me after this latest development. What a demented, perverted psycho. The sick bastard preys on unsuspecting women. I certainly doubt I'm his first victim."

"Don't hold back."

"So Woods told you about this wacko? Probably after you loosened him up with the booze. He has a serious drinking problem. I offered to get him some help."

Stephen nodded. "The detective thought it best if I didn't tell you. He wanted to track this guy back to whoever hired him."

"Unfortunately, Detective Woods must have suffered some sort of lapse. He's supposed to be following the perp."

"He asked me to keep an eye on you today. Said he had pressing personal business."

Yes, the detective did have an important matter to attend to. It had been awhile since he visited the grave of his daughter, Amanda. He needed to talk with her.

"I told Woods I'd see you safely back to your apartment. The perp won't bother you here—he knows you have a gun."

Yes, she reflected, *and he knows I won't shoot him unless I have no other choice. Either that or he thinks I have real bad aim.*

They finished the dessert.

"The mousse was quite good. But you'll have to try my Mousse au Chocolat a la menthe some time."

"I'd love to, Jolyn." *But I'd rather taste you,* he thought, not being able to hold back a smirk, knowing it bordered on lascivious.

"What's that look on your face all about?" she inquired.

"I'll never tell."

"You're a pervert, too. Do you want to watch television, Stephen? CNN, of course. A reporter has to keep up with current events, you know. I didn't even get a chance to read my Sunday papers today."

"Sure. The news sounds good to me."

Jolyn took Stephen by the hand to the living room.

"You have very warm hands," he commented. "Some women have hands that feel like small dead fish."

"No wonder you can't get a date. You're *so* rude. Your hands feel strong, but gentle."

Jolyn turned on the forty-two inch widescreen flat panel LCD high-definition television.

Stephen surveyed the art on the wall. Replicas of William Blake's work.

"Nice TV, Jolyn. Great picture."

"You really wanted to comment about the art. So what's your favorite? I just put these up."

"Blake can equally portray the softness of love or the darkness of evil. I rather like *Possession*."

You would. My favorite is *Satan, Sin, and Death*. The TV is my only luxury acquisition. Cost more than my car."

"Well, your Cavalier is ten years old."

"When it quits running I'll buy another one a little newer. I'd like a Lincoln Navigator like my father's. Hint, hint. How about a nice big raise so I can afford one?"

They sat on the l-shaped leather sectional sofa.

Stephen couldn't help but see the yellow legal pads filled with handwritten notes and a pile of folders lying on the coffee table.

"Looks like you're working on something."

"Research."

"Oh. On what?"

"Sexual assault cases involving athletes."

"So tell me about it. May I have a look?"

"Go ahead. My scribbling may be a little difficult to decipher."

He began to peruse her notes and files. Jolyn gave him an overview. All about hundreds of sexual assault allegations against athletes in the past decade. She offered the conclusion that sports personalities fare much better at trial than defendants from the general population. More than two-thirds of the athletes were never charged, saw the charges dropped, or were acquitted. The opposite is true in the case of the general population she maintained.

"And just why do you suppose that is?" he asked.

"Pressure on the victim not to press charges against a celebrity, the financial resources of the athlete to hire the best legal representation available, the tendency to believe a celebrity defendant over an accuser unknown to jurors, to name a few."

"But the opposite side of the coin is that athletes can be a target for false accusations."

"Unfortunately, yes. But maybe these athletes should steer clear of bars and strip clubs. An incident looking for a place to happen."

"You just left a bar, Jolyn."

"Yeah, and I wonder what Dexter Curtis is up to right about now."

"Probably looking for love in all the wrong places. I do know what he'll be doing tomorrow night."

"Oh really? And what's that?"

"When you went off to powder your pretty nose I went up to the bar to say hello to a guy I know. A pile of flyers caught my attention." He paused.

"Flyers about what?"

Stephen took the folded paper from his pocket and handed it to Jolyn.

She read that Steelers linebacker Dexter Curtis and defensive end Kevin Jones would be featured guests of The Church Brew Works and radio station WEAE for MONDAY NIGHT MAYHEM IN THE BAR. On-air personality Jake Bell would be interviewing the players and fans. Trivia contests, give-a-ways, and drink and food specials galor.

"Hey, maybe I should don a wig and glasses and surprise Dexter," Jolyn offered with a sly grin.

"You wouldn't."

"Are you ordering me not to?"

"Not exactly. I doubt I can keep you from hanging out in bars if that's your predilection. No more than the Steelers can keep players from doing likewise."

"But this time Dexter will be on a public relations mission for the team. Unlike the night he met Kim McConnell or the night he got shot."

"So *what about* Dexter Curtis and Kim McConnell?"

"Where there's smoke there's fire. How come I haven't received the autopsy report on Sondra Lewis yet? Is there anyone in New York you can call to speed things up."

"Maybe."

"Thou shalt not commit adultery," she said softly.

"What?"

"CNN. Aren't you listening?"

"No. Actually, I'm hanging on your every word."

"Well, quit staring at me like that. You're making me nervous."

"That's not staring—it's flirting. I've been reading these books. It's been a long time for me. You know, flirting."

"You don't need to flirt, Stephen. I've seen how the women at the office, especially the single ones, fawn over you."

"I never noticed."

"Yeah, right. Now hush for a minute. I want to hear this. They are talking on CNN about the controversy in Georgia regarding the five thousand pound monument displaying the Ten Commandments in the rotunda of the State Judicial Building."

"Violates the First Amendment principle of separation of church and state, so some say."

"Yes, so some say."

"So what's your take on the issue, Jolyn?"

"I don't like to debate 'religious' issues. It's an exercise in futility. Various denominations can't even agree on what are the Ten Commandments. Calvinist and fundamentalist Protestants have one version and Catholics, Lutherans, and Episcopalians have another."

"What do you think about gay marriage?"

"Why? Do you have a boyfriend, Stephen?"

She erupted in laughter and squeezed his arm playfully, and then brushed imaginary lint off his shirt.

"Funny, Jolyn, funny."

"Which reminds me—William Ortiz, also known as Rose, wants to talk to me about Dexter Curtis. But not until Ortiz is released from the hospital. He sent me an Email to the address listed in my articles."

"Wonder what he—or is that she—wants."

"Yes, I wonder."

Jolyn crossed her legs in the direction of Stephen.

She has the most exquisite feet and ankles I have ever seen, he mused silently.

A knock at the door interrupted his pleasurable observations.

Jolyn let Detective Woods in.

She had called him as soon as she got back to her apartment.

"Hello, Stephen," Woods greeted when Jolyn led him to the living room.

"You asked me to 'watch' her," Stephen responded.

The two men laughed.

Jolyn shot them both an icy blue glare.

"I can't stay but a minute. My wife's in the car. Just wanted to let you know I've decided to arrest Gorton."

"How is your wife, Ed?"

"Missing Amanda," he utter ruefully. "Like me. We talked to Amanda today. At her gravesite. I can find my own way out."

Detective Woods left, pulling his flask from his jacket pocket as soon as he got out the door.

CHAPTER 56

"I'll bet you're glad Woods is going to arrest him," Stephen said after the detective left.

"That pervert *belongs* in jail."

A news segment about a *USA TODAY* reporter who just resigned came on CNN. The foreign correspondent allegedly misled editors. He invented witnesses to corroborate his stories so they said.

"That guy was a finalist for a Pulitzer Prize a couple years ago," Stephen murmured, shaking his head. "He traveled the world and put his life in jeopardy in war-torn lands."

"I met him briefly once. In Jerusalem. He spoke to a group of students at Rothberg about attacks on Palestinians by Jewish settlers in the West Bank."

Jolyn began to cry softly, as her mind drifted to her dead lover Zeke once more. Stephen moved closer on the sofa and put his arm around her.

She flinched slightly, sensing from his body language what might come next.

"You are a beautiful creature, Jolyn."

Stephen took a sniff of her hair, inhaling deeply. The tip of his nose touched her scalp. He touched the rim of her ear with his lips in a kind of brushing motion.

Jolyn drew her head away. He returned to her lovely long red hair, lingering luxuriously.

She sighed as he turned his attention to her ears and nibbled and sucked on the lobes.

His lips moved to the nape of her neck.

Stephen slowly nuzzled along to the corner of her luscious mouth. Suddenly he felt her stiffen her shoulders under his arms.

He felt her quiver as he rubbed his fingers seductively across her lips.

Jolyn parted her lips slightly.

Stephen kissed her, a soul kiss.

The two gently caressed each other's tongues.

She closed her eyes.

He detached his lips from hers and raised them to her closed eyelids. First one, then the other. Then he traced her nose with his tongue, and back to her lips.

Jolyn let him ease her down slowly on her back on the sofa.

"Oh Stephen, I . . ."

"You are so lovely, Jolyn," he whispered, pressing his body upon hers, becoming frenzied in his passion.

"Stephen . . ."

"I want you, Jolyn. I want you so much."

"But . . . you . . . but . . ."

Stephen ran his hands up under the bottom of Jolyn's loose sweatshirt. She hadn't bothered with a bra. He began to tease her hardened nipples.

Jolyn moaned deliciously.

Then he pushed up her skirt around her waist.

Stephen's lips licked and kissed the inside of her thighs. He made heart-shaped designs on her legs with the tip of his tongue.

But she froze when he got to the edge of her panties and started to slowly slip them down with his teeth.

"Stephen, no! I can't. Please don't."

Jolyn wriggled free from under him.

"I'm sorry, Jolyn."

"No, it was my fault. You better go."

The words of the sixth, or perhaps the seventh depending on your denomination, commandment echoed over and over in her mind.

Thou shalt not commit adultery.

Jolyn rose, rearranged her clothing, and strode toward the door.

Stephen followed reluctantly.

"I'll see you tomorrow, Stephen, at the office."

"Are we . . . do we . . . uh . . ."

"No, we don't have a problem. My doing as much as yours. But I can't go any further. And I don't want a repeat performance. Not now. The temptation is too great."

"I don't understand."

"I don't expect you to. Maybe one day you will. Good night, Stephen."

Jolyn kissed him sweetly on the cheek.

Stephen shook his head in confusion as he walked to his car.

After he left she stared at Blake's *Satan, Sin, and Death*

RATTRAP

It spoke to her.

CHAPTER 57

"Ron, that Knowlton bitch knows I'm the one who broke into her apartment."

"Now, how in the hell would she know that, Gorton? Unless you got stupid."

"I don't know. I followed her and that editor Winslow to a restaurant after the game. Keeping tabs on her, ya know? Like you said. She approached me and . . . uh . . . accused me."

"That's all?"

"Yeah. Then she stormed out of the place."

Kingston knew Gorton lied. He knew because one of his sources informed him that Detective Ed Woods had been snooping around. Asking questions about a possible connection between himself and the private investigator.

"Well, no harm done, I guess. But lay low for awhile. At least with respect to her. Go to Chicago. I have a little job for you there. Very financially rewarding. Be at the Pump Room of the Omni Ambassador East around 8:00 PM. I'll have someone meet you and fill you in on the assignment."

"Sounds good, boss. Those Bull Shots at the Pump Room are great for the Windy City chill. One more thing . . ."

"Yeah, what's that Gorton?"

"That stupid little homo I paid for the butt fucking pictures with the D.A. is barking for more money. He's threatening to spill his guts to the press, especially that bitch, Knowlton. I know Hawkins resigned, but still . . ."

"Does the faggot know your name or anything?"

"Nope."

"Good. I'll take care of that one myself, since you will be occupied elsewhere."

"Oh, and talk about a coincidence—the homo has a girlfriend—a chick with a dick. Name of William Ortiz, also known as Rose. Name sound familiar?"

"No, not off hand."

"This Rose got shot in that bar parking lot along with Dexter and the others."

"Sounds like more than a coincidence."

"Yeah, don't it though."

"I'll take care of him, or her, too. I don't want you hanging around now that Knowlton has seen your face."

"I don't think she knows my name. How could she?"

Because you're an idiot, asshole. You fucked up. Now I have to deal with it.

"Maybe not, but let's play it safe. Give the gun with Knowlton's fingerprints on it to the guy in Chicago."

"Will do, boss. I still don't understand why you didn't want me to have her latest porno pics put up on that website."

"Strategy, Gorton, strategy. The incident strangely didn't make the news or the papers. Maybe she didn't report it to the police. Rather embarrassing, telling the cops a masked gunman made you masturbate while he filmed you. And no proof if the pictures aren't published. We'll save those pictures for just the right moment."

"Yeah, we should use the pictures when her engagement announcement appears in the *Tribune-Review*."

"Oh, is she getting married?"

"I heard a rumor she *is* married. Hitched up with some professor a couple years ago. But I couldn't find this professor or any record of a marriage license. I thought maybe I could get some dirt on her through this professor, but he seems to have just up and vanished."

"Well, get your ass to Chicago. Knowlton is no longer your concern."

Kingston rang off with Gorton.

Stupid motherfucker.

He made a phone call.

"Tomorrow Gorton will be in Chicago at the Omni Ambassador East in the Pump Room around 8:00 PM. The fucktard has become a liability. And he's not telling me everything about him and this reporter Knowlton. He did something to give himself away."

"I told you not to hire that dumb ass," the deep voice responded.

"Well, you don't do surveillance."

"Too damn boring."

"Gorton is going to give you a revolver. It has fingerprints on it. Don't mess them up. I have several possibilities in mind."

"Whose fingerprints are on it? Just curious."

"That reporter—Knowlton."

155

"Interesting. So what about Gorton? You want the silent treatment?" the deep voice asked.

"Yes, the permanent type—the Windy City shot and chill."

CHAPTER 58

Nathan Redmond had executed twenty-three men in the past five years, and two women. Murder for hire. But there had been others—the ones he did for his own personal pleasure.

The assassin accepted assignments only from a select group of clients whom he respected for one reason or another. He had met Ron Kingston in prison. Kingston provided him with the legal and financial resources that helped him get out of the joint earlier than anticipated. Redmond somewhat trusted Kingston because he was as cold and ruthless as himself. They understood each other.

Almost six years ago, after a decade in prison, Redmond's lawyers hired by Kingston discovered police notes that showed a witness had been coached by police on how to testify. And that another witness had been paid thousands of dollars for work on the case. Both former comrades of Redmond's in crime had denied being coached or paid. Prosecutors had not informed the court or Redmond's attorneys that the men lied. The new trial resulted in a hung jury. A deal was negotiated where the charges were reduced to manslaughter, Redmond plead guilty, and was sentenced to time served.

The killer had made too many mistakes before his stint in the penitentiary where he found willing tutors. In retrospect he thought he might owe a debt of gratitude—for his prison education—to his two former associates who had been given immunity to testify against him. He had no intentions of getting caught again. The two rats had mysteriously disappeared shortly after his release. He chortled.

Redmond's current modus operandi for contract murder was simple. He didn't like to deviate much from what had proven so successful.

Operate totally alone.

Untraceable gun.

Disguise.

Put a bullet in the victim's head.

Make it look like a robbery.

Plant the body in a shallow grave in a wooded area off an interstate or other major highway. That or, depending on the circumstances, cremate the body in his very own facilities. He did that only if the client insisted that the body never be found.

Only in the case of the two women he contracted to terminate did make arrangements for the demise of the target other than a bullet in the head at the request of the client. And that cost a whole lot more.

Besides Kingston, some of his clients included drug dealers and organized crime figures he had also met behind bars.

Most of the bodies had been found within a few weeks. One the next day. Several had yet to be discovered. That didn't concern the killer. What did is that he had never become a suspect in any of the murders. He always disassembled the weapon and discarded the various parts in different places.

Redmond surveyed his cache of disposable handguns. Hungarian Model GKK semiautomatic .45 ACP pistol. U.S.A Model I1462NJSP Army Special .38 revolver. Czech Model CZ-27 semiautomatic .32 ACP pistol. British Mark IV revolver, converted to .45 ACP. Spanish Model 600 semiautomatic 9mm Parabellum pistol. He decided on the Japanese Type 14 Nambu semiautomatic pistol and machined off the numbers and markings.

He got in his BMW-745Li for the drive from Detroit to Chicago. He intended to go to O'Hare and obtain a rental vehicle under one of his aliases. Then purchase a good shovel at a hardware store.

CHAPTER 59

Make him squirm.

She had promised Kim.

Alyssa Davis settled on a white strapless chiffon top with a built-in bra and a lavender satin bias-cut skirt. White satin sandals with bows. She borrowed her mother's butterscotch ASA by Tony of Beverly wig with long cascading curls.

When she walked in The Church Brew Works she immediately saw that Jake Bell of WEAE had begun to interview Dexter Curtis and Kevin Jones. She summoned a drink from a bartender and got as close as she could.

Curtis looked directly and menacingly into the camera and snarled, "Rick Louis, I'm going to get you."

"I take it you don't like that guy?" Bell asked coquettishly.

"He's a jerk. If he runs through our pre-game stretching line again the next time we play them I'll knock him on his ass. I just wish he played a little offense like that bigmouth dude on the Raiders."

"What you have here is two teams who plain don't like each other," Kevin Jones added.

"Yeah," Dexter blurted, "and Louis is a criminal. He just got lucky. And maybe that running back won't be so lucky."

"What do you mean by that, Dexter?" Bell asked. "About the running back."

"Never mind. But I'll bet you a bundle he ends up in the slammer."

"What about this Sunday, Dexter, and the game at Kansas City? Are you going to play?"

"Tomorrow is our day off and the doctors will examine me. If they give the green light I'll be going at it full speed in pads at practice on Wednesday."

Several of the fans asked questions for a few minutes and the interview ended. Curtis and Jones sat at a table and signed autographs. They shared a pitcher of Bell Tower Brown Ale and Dexter had a rather large glass of whiskey on the side.

Alyssa stood in line.

Finally she got her turn.

But no, Alyssa didn't ask for autographs.

She handed Dexter Curtis a slip of paper with something written on it.

He looked her over thoroughly, very impressed.

"What's the note say, Dexter?" Kevin asked him.

Dexter chuckled.

"Well?" Kevin inquired again.

"It says, 'I love anal.' Really."

"Sure it does."

Dexter showed it to his teammate.

Kevin scowled.

"You better keep it in your pants, Dexter. I think you got enough trouble already."

"Did you take a good look at that fox? I'm going to at least talk to her."

The two players finished signing autographs. Dexter got up from the table and sauntered over to the bar where Alyssa sat on a stool, surrounded by several admirers.

No place for him to sit.

He motioned for her to follow him.

"Let's take a walk outside," he suggested. "It's crowded in here. I want to talk to you about your literary masterpiece." He held up her note and grinned lewdly. She looked at him demurely, but smirked noticeably.

"Is that your Hummer?" she asked outside in the parking lot.

"Yeah. Shall we sit it in and chat?"

"Sure we should."

Once inside the vehicle, Alyssa looked a little apprehensive.

"What's wrong?"

"I'm nervous, Dexter. You intimidate me a little. What with being a star football player and all. My name is Jennifer. Jenny. I'm a student at Carnegie Mellon. Computer science major. And I have an important exam first thing in the morning. So I have to leave soon."

"No reason to be nervous, Jenny. I'm a very friendly person. You are a very attractive young lady. Probably very intelligent."

"Thanks, Dexter." She smiled seductively. "Oh my, I'm kind of embarrassed about that note. But I wanted to get your attention."

"You did, Jenny. You really did. But do you really love anal?"

"Uh ... well ... I ..."

"C'mon spit it out, girl!"

He couldn't help but laugh at her naïve facial expression.

"Do you mind if I smoke?" she asked.

"No, I guess not."

Alyssa reached into her purse. She held up the plastic bag and small rasta leaf pipe.

"I mean smoke this," she purred. "It relaxes me when I'm very nervous."

"If it's good shit I'll take a hit myself, Jenny."

"It's better than good."

Alyssa fired up the pipe and they shared a bowl silently.

"So tell me about your love of anal sex, Jenny," Dexter encouraged.

Alyssa filled the pipe again.

I love anal if it's another girl with a strap-on. Men don't ring my bell. Yeah, I'll tell him a story.

"Chicks dig the long ball," she purred.

"Huh?"

"I got gang-banged by some black studs. At my request. I wanted it. I wanted it bad."

She told him the story.

How one day she noticed four black dudes playing basketball at a park. Older guys. In their thirties she had guessed. There were two nice cars parked nearby that had to be theirs. A Lincoln Navigator and a Cadillac something or other sedan. Both looked new or close to it.

She stopped and started to talk to them when they took a break. They seemed nice. They were polite. She wore shorts and a halter top. The dudes stared as inconspicuously as they could. She introduced herself and they did likewise.

Alyssa said she finally got up the nerve and asked, "Would you gentlemen like some white pussy?" She figured she might as well be blunt and get right to the point.

Three of them seemed nice, anyway. But one of them talked that ghetto jive. They all screamed "Yes!" in unison but then the rude dude added, "Yeah baby, white chicks dig the big fat long black dick. We get requests to do horny white snatch like you all the time."

Another one, Joe he said his name was, asked, "How much is it going to cost us? For some white pussy?"

"Oh, probably a twelve-pack of Miller Lite," Alyssa had responded.

They bought the beer and took her to a cheap hotel.

"Are you an exotic dancer?" Joe had asked as she tossed her halter top and then wriggled seductively out of her shorts, and then her panties.

In ten minutes they had her moaning and groaning. She lay on top of one doing sixty-nine. That big black cock pumped in and out of her mouth deeper and deeper. Two of the others lay on each side of her. She stroked one's cock with her left hand and the other's with her right hand.

161

But what Joe did interested her the most. He kissed her ass. He started with a light flicking, licking around the center. Gently he pushed at the hole. Then he held his tongue rigid and pushed firmly inside.

Joe used his hands to gently massage the area right around the opening. "Relax, honey, I'm going to use my finger now," he said as he put lube on the middle finger of his left hand and slowly pushed it inside her.

Soon she felt something bigger—much bigger. Ever so slowly Joe pushed it further and further inside her. Alyssa said she begged for more. "Oh Joe . . . ahh . . . ohh . . . that hurts . . . but no . . . no . . . don't stop. Fuck my ass, Joe! Harder! Oh yeah, oh yeah!"

And then she screamed incredibly loud like a stuck pig and collapsed on the floor on her back as her body convulsed in ecstasy. Joe stroked his cock a few times after she pulled away from him and shot a huge load all over her face and breasts.

After a few minutes she got up on all fours and started barking like a dog. Well, maybe more like a puppy wanting to be petted. Another took his turn. Soon another. And then the last.

Alyssa paused and looked at Dexter expectantly. He said nothing so she continued.

Finally she lost consciousness. Joe performed CPR while one of the others dialed 911. When the EMTs arrived she still was a little groggy but otherwise seemed fine.

"What happened, miss?" one of the EMTs had asked her.

"I just got lightheaded and fainted I think," she had replied shakily.

"Do you have any idea why?" he queried.

"The long ball," she whispered.

"Huh?" he had muttered.

"Multiple orgasms," she had said, louder.

He nodded knowingly, glancing jealously at four huge black cocks still looking eager for action.

Alyssa smiled gloriously, waiting for Dexter to say something.

"Did that *really* happen, Jenny? Or is it just a fantasy of yours? I make dreams come true."

"I have to go now, Dexter. Like I said, big exam tomorrow. Bad time of month for me, anyway. But I would like to see you again."

"You're going to take off on me after that story you just told me? I have a raging hard-on."

"Well . . . I . . . I . . ."

"You got to take care of my problem, baby."

"Okay, I'll give you a little special surprise. Close your eyes, please."

He did.

Oh well, she thought, *if the cops are going to find his saliva on the pipe I guess I'll have to put my saliva on his cock. Not the first time I ever swallowed spunk to get what I want.*

Alyssa tossed the pipe and bag on the floor in the back seat. Then she unzipped him and struggled to get his huge, bulging penis out of his pants.

CHAPTER 60

Gorton.

You're a dead man.

Nathan Redmond readily spotted Hank Gorton slumping on a bar stool in the Pump Room of the Omni Ambassador East.

Gorton definitely looked intoxicated.

This will be even easier than usual, the assassin concluded to himself, silently and gratefully. His last hit had been a little more difficult. Somehow the whore bitch knew he intended to off her, one way or another. She didn't want to cooperate. But eventually she did and drank it. "Drink it, or I'll cut out your liver and eat it," he had threatened. She believed him.

"I'm Larry Andrews," Redmond announced as he offered his hand to what he figured for a fat, stupid slob. An easy mark. "Emissary from Ron Kingston and Mr. Maloney, my boss. I'm going to drive you to meet Mr. Maloney, where he will explain your . . . objective."

"O-kay An-drew-s-s-s," Gorton slurred. "But let me finish this Bull Shit . . .'er Shot first. Do you by chance know the best strip clubs around here? I could use a little action, ya know?"

"Sure. After we take care of business, we'll party with some exotic dancers. I know *all* the hot spots."

Redmond ordered a Diet Pepsi and told Gorton about the Admiral Theatre on W. Lawrence Avenue, the hundred or so table dancers, and the Las Vegas-style revue. The mark listened to the descriptions of several of the entertainers, and drooled.

"So tell me, Andrews, what's this job?" Gorton asked as he rubbed his crotch.

"Mr. Mahoney always instructs me not to discuss such matters and stick to my job—transportation. But believe me, Gorton, your bjective is . . . a real looker. You will be engaging in surveillance. Your pal Kingston told Mr. Mahoney you are the best."

"Yeah, that's me—the best. You wouldn't believe the snatch I caught on film in my last caper. So what's the story on this 'real looker' of yours?"

"Well, I'll just tell you this—she's Mr. Mahoney's main squeeze—a model. He thinks she's doing this black dude who is the lead singer at a nightclub she frequents."

"Fucking niggers."

"Yeah. Are you ready to go?"

Gorton downed the drink. "How far?"

"Not too far. We have to get on I-94 for awhile. About an hour or so to Mr. Maloney's place. He lives in a frigging mansion in the sticks. Wait until you see this place. Five frigging bathrooms."

The two got in the rental car.

"Do you have the gun, Gorton?" Redmond asked. "You were supposed to bring it and give it to me."

The fat man removed the plastic bag containing the weapon from his jacket pocket and gave it to his companion.

Gorton soon nodded off.

After about forty-five minutes of driving, Redmond pulled off onto the berm on I-94.

Gorton stirred and opened his eyes. "Where are you going?" he asked as the driver got out of the car.

"I got to take a piss."

Redmond didn't want blood and brains splattered all over the rental car. He planned to take it back, after wiping it down for fingerprints and such. He knew Gorton would eventually get out of the car. Either to relieve himself or to look for his companion, wondering what took so long.

Gorton finally became impatient and did get out. He wandered into the edge of the woods. Unzipping his pants, he began to urinate.

"Andrews, where the hell are you?" he called.

"Right here."

Redmond waited until the fat man zipped up and then put a bullet in his head.

"What a stiff," the killer muttered as he dragged the heavy body further into the woods.

The killer guffawed maniacally as he dug.

He took Gorton's wallet and Rolex, kicked him into the shallow grave, and covered the body with dirt.

RATTRAP

***

Dexter Curtis sauntered back in The Church Brew Works.

Alyssa Davis took the tire iron from her trunk and shattered the Hummer's right tail light. Then she drove hurriedly out of the parking lot.

She stopped at the first public phone booth she spotted outside of a gas station. Kim McConnell had given her Detective Woods number.

The detective answered on the second ring.

"Dexter Curtis's Hummer is parked in the lot of The Church Brew Works on Liberty Avenue, a block from Iron City Brewing. His vehicle has a broken tail light and there is a bag of grass and a pipe on the floor of the back seat. You will find his DNA on the pipe. He's inside and probably legally drunk."

She hung up.

CHAPTER 61

About a dozen reporters crowded into *Tribune-Review* editor Stephen Winslow's office. The weekly Tuesday press conference at noon with Steelers coach Bill Lowry would begin in a few minutes.

Most of them had heard the news that Dexter Curtis had been arrested in the early morning hours and charged with DUI and possession of marijuana.

"How exactly did he get busted?" Jolyn asked the group, having only caught a snippet of the incident on the radio driving to work.

"Stopped by a cop for driving his Hummer like a speedball and having a broken tail light," Stephen replied. "That led to the field sobriety test, breathalyzer, and search of the vehicle."

"Is he in jail?"

"No, Jolyn," he got released on his own recognizance a couple hours ago, with the assistance of his lawyers, of course."

Coach Lowry came to the table and addressed the media.

"I haven't spoken to Dexter Curtis yet. He didn't snow up for his appointment with the doctors this morning. Therefore he will not be permitted to practice at full speed this week and will not be activated for the game with the Chiefs on Sunday. I don't have any further comment on the subject of his arrest early this morning at the moment. Let's talk football. We played pretty well on both sides of the ball against Baltimore. But it's a sixteen game schedule. It's not a sprint, it's a marathon. Kansas City has a potent offense, especially at home. After the game on Sunday we'll have a better idea of just how good we are."

The coach went on to talk more about the past game with the Ravens and the next game with the Chiefs. Reporters asked questions, but nothing about Dexter Curtis.

Jolyn shrugged irritably. "We have a reporter there. Where's the tough questions?" She glared at Stephen.

"I told him not to," her editor responded, "or else we'd have another reporter blackballed. What would you have asked, Jolyn?"

"Hey coach, are you sorry yet you drafted this fatal distraction?"

Stephen laughed and a few of the others smirked and chuckled.

The other reporters slowly filed out of the office. All but Jolyn.

"So do you think he'll get suspended?" she asked Stephen.

"I doubt it unless there have been other incidents we don't know about. He'll just get a slap on the wrist and be required to comply with phase one of the NFL's substance abuse policy. Only repeat offenders get suspended, for booze and marijuana anyway. Ephedra is a different matter—automatic four game suspension for the first offense. But it's all hush-hush for the most part. The NFL won't permit much information to be released."

"He could be tied to steroids too, after what you told me the other night. When's that story going to hit the fan?"

"Any day now. Speaking of the other night, where do you and I stand with respect to that?"

"It never happened."

"I see."

"No, you don't. But perhaps one day you will."

"Hope so. I got you your autopsy report on Sondra Lewis. She died from acute opiate toxicity." He paused.

"Go on."

"Overdose of cocaine and heroin, with the emphasis on the latter. I believe they call that particular deadly mixture a speedball."

"How did the drugs enter her system?"

"Taken orally. Probably with a soft drink since there was no alcohol in her system. The coroner ruled accidental death due to self-inflicted ingestion of controlled substances. The heroin found on the coffee table was seventy-two percent pure, in contrast to the typical street heroin which is fifteen to thirty percent pure. A glass on the table contained the residue of the speedball. Only her fingerprints were found on the glass. The coroner believes she didn't know how potent the drugs were according to the report."

"Can I read the report?"

"Here—it's all yours. So I guess this means you won't . . . use the rest of the information she gave you?"

"Not unless someone can prove there is more to the story of her death than what you just told me. This makes me look somewhat like a fool after what I said at that press conference about Sondra Lewis and Dexter Curtis. I mean, using a drug addict prostitute as a source?"

"But now we have Curtis linked to drugs, too."

"Birds of a feather . . ."

"Jolyn, please don't disclose any of the autopsy information to anyone for any reason. Not yet. The report has not been released for public consumption. Have you talked to Detective Woods about your panty thief?"

"I talked to him Sunday night. He called me back yesterday afternoon and informed me that Gorton took a flight to Chicago. Yes, Woods told me the guy's name and that he is a private investigator. Either Woods doesn't know who Gorton is working for or he won't tell me. Not that I can't guess. Maybe I should hire my own private investigator."

"You can afford that? On your salary?"

"I'm an heiress, didn't you know?"

"No, I didn't."

The anonymous voice had called yesterday morning telling her where to find $25,000, money to assist her in the investigation of the Curtis matter. And use it she would.

"I'll be out of the office for the rest of the day, Stephen. I have an appointment with William Ortiz, the transvestite hooker who got shot that night along with Dexter Curtis. This Ortiz just got released from the hospital. I told you he wanted to talk to me."

"Fine. You do that, Jolyn. One day soon you are going to have to produce another article on the Dexter Curtis/Kim McConnell matter. That or I'll have to give you other assignments. Some of the other reporters are grumbling about your lack of production."

Jolyn frowned and turned and walked out of his office.

CHAPTER 62

Ron Kingston listened to his telephone messages.

"The job is done."

He recognized the voice.

Kingston called Dexter Curtis.

"Dexter, come to Miami," he ordered, "now. You're going to be suspended for four games. No point in you hanging around Pittsburgh. You won't be permitted to have any contact with the team during your suspension. Spend some time with your family. And the press is much friendlier around these parts." He thought of Jolyn Knowlton and what she might say about this latest incident, if so inclined. He would have to find someone else to harass her if she caused any more problems.

Curtis reluctantly agreed.

They hung up.

The super agent reflected on his relationship with Dexter.

Kingston knew he had to plug the hole in the dam, and quickly. The lucrative endorsement deals for which the agent would have received his cut had already slipped away. Now the contract could be in jeopardy. He needed to talk finances with Dexter, among other things. Lawyers, private investigators, and exterminators ran up the tab. But Dexter knew nothing of the latter.

He called Redmond who had stayed in Chicago overnight at a hotel.

"There's two queers in Pittsburgh that need to get offed," Kingston announced irritably.

"Same fee as the last one," the killer for hire responded in his typical monotone. "Two for the price of one this time. I don't like funny boys."

"Call me when you get to Pittsburgh and I'll give you the details."
"Right, but I'm not going to hurry. It might be a day or two."
"Okay, but don't take too long."

CHAPTER 63

Nathan Redmond had slept for another hour, showered, returned the rental car to O'Hare, and ditched the theatrical wig and beard and moustache. He had many others and didn't like to wear the same face twice.

Eastbound on I-95, headed back to Detroit for a brief stop, Redmond saw visions, exit after exit.

Visions of sex and death.

Time for some random killing for recreational purposes, he mused.

Killing that fat private dick had been too easy. Didn't satisfy his lust for death. But then, that one was for money. The next one would be for fun. The next one would be soon—very, very, soon.

Redmond decided to stop and eat at a truck stop off the interstate. Hadn't had much but snacks in the past day or so. He liked truck stop food for some strange reason. Not as well as his own cooking, though. But then he selected the choicest cuts. The killer laughed hysterically.

As he ate the greasy burgers and fries and washed the food down with black coffee he noticed a young, very attractive woman talking to a table of truck drivers next to him. At first he thought she might be a hooker, but no, too good looking and not dressed in typical attire for that particular profession. She wore a loose sweatshirt, very tight pair of jeans, and light denim jacket. Blonde hair and pigtails. Cute, but not enough skin showing for his taste. *Maybe I can change that,* he considered lecherously.

The girl asked if the drivers were going east. They shook their heads indicating not.

"Miss?" Redmond interrupted as she walked from their table and past him.

"Yes?"

"Do you need a ride east?"

She looked him over carefully. He prided himself on his trust invoking appearance and demeanor. Without the disguises, anyway. Most women, even the young ones, usually considered him rather handsome and sexually appealing.

"Well . . . I . . ."

"Please sit down for a minute, miss. Would you like a cup of coffee? Something to eat?"

"Coffee. I didn't come here to eat."

He summoned the waitress.

"Where are you headed—east?"

"New York City. I'm a struggling actress, you might say. Had a gig in L.A., then one in Chicago, and now I'm auditioning for a part in a Broadway play in a week."

"So you hitch rides with truck drivers?"

"Yeah." She smiled. "They seem rather safe. I won't stand on the highway and thumb. Meeting them in a truck stop first gives me a chance to check them out."

"You don't look poor—like you couldn't afford go by bus, train, or plane."

"Oh, I could I suppose. But I'd rather save what little money I have for other things, like a place to sleep and food when I get to the Big Apple."

"I'm going to make a quick stop in Detroit at my business and then I'm heading directly for Pittsburgh. My name is Nathan Redmond. I'm a funeral director." He handed her a business card. "I could drop you at a truck stop right off I-80 outside of Pittsburgh if you like."

"Sure, that sounds good, Mr. Redmond. I'm not going to make any progress in this place any time soon. Kind of empty at the moment. My name is Roxanne Peterson."

She drained her coffee. He had already finished his.

"Well, Roxanne, let's be on our way."

They rose and he paid the check.

"Nice wheels, Mr. Redmond," she complimented as they got in his car.

Once inside the vehicle, he gave her all the details.

"Brand spanking new BMW-745Li. Talk about high tech, you need to be a computer geek to navigate this thing. Most automotive experts conclude that the BMW-7 series are the most technologically advanced vehicles in the world."

"I like the small shark fin on the roof."

He laughed, and then she did. *Splendid smile*, he thought. *Great body. What I can see of it looks delicious. I think I just might cook her.*

"Check this out," he said, "by simply touching a button on the steering wheel . . ."

A computer-generated voice responded, prompting him to respond in turn. He dialed a preset phone number and then demonstrated how the voice command worked.

Roxanne critiqued, "It looks like the inside of a modern, contemporary European home, rather than European automobile. I do like this non-gloss, light brown wood mixed with silver matte accents."

"Tell me how much you like the ride once we really get going. This car has an active roll stabilization system that uses electronic sensors to manage the behavior of the split anti-roll bars. The aluminum frame provides extreme rigidity which allows the entire suspension system to perform to perfection. It's amazingly flat on the curves."

The speedometer read almost a hundred miles an hour.

"You're a speedball," she joked glibly. "It seems to me, Mr. Redmond, that you *have* really got going."

He grimaced slightly at her use of the word speedball.

"Speedball?" he asked, mustering mock confusion.

"Name of a paintball game, for one thing. In an open field rather than the woods—so spectators can watch. Also there is group that is kind of the darling of the New York underground scene called Speedball something or other. Can't remember. I heard them once."

"Isn't speedball some sort of illegal drug?"

"Oh, that too—cocaine and heroin. Not that I've ever tried one. I say 'no' to drugs."

But you will try one, my dear, yes you will.

"I'm not too worried about the speed," he commented. He pointed at the equipment. "Radar detector and laser jammer."

"Oh, do you often break the law, Mr. Redmond?" she kidded, becoming very relaxed with him.

"Sure, I kill people. It's good for my funeral business. And would you please call me Nathan? It's not like I'm old enough to be your father."

"How old are you, Nathan?"

"Thirty-six."

"My father is forty-seven."

"How old are you?"

"Twenty-two. Well, in three weeks I will be."

I don't think you're going to see another birthday, my dear.

"Have you been to New York before, Roxanne?"

"Born and raised in Charlotte, North Carolina. Can you tell? I worked hard at losing the accent. Attended Columbia for two years, and then a year at Julliard. And now a little over a year on the road trying to make it in the real world."

He glanced over at her. Too bad she'd never win an Oscar. Not that she didn't have the looks for it. But a bit on the dumb blonde side.

"You are a very lovely and intelligent young woman, Roxanne. That is glaringly obvious. My first impression is that one day you will be a star."

She blushed.

"Thank you, Nathan. I hope you're right!"

"Sure I'm right. Why don't you take a little nap? You look tired."

"I am. Think I will. Got music, Nathan? Something soothing and relaxing, yet stimulating?"

He played Dave Brubeck's *The Gates of Justice.* A cantata based on biblical and Hebrew liturgical texts, and quotations from the Rev. Martin Luther King and the Jewish sage Hillel. It amalgamated Brubeck's distinctive jazz language with Hebraic modes and African-American spirituals.

"I like this. Powerful and dramatic."

She closed her eyes.

Soon you will be sleeping forever, my dear.

CHAPTER 64

Rose got quite agitated.

The man hadn't got back to him about the money.

Little did Rose, whose birth certificate read William Garcia Ortiz, know that Hank Gorton had begun to be eaten by maggots. The guy didn't return Rose's numerous messages left on his voice mail. And now Rose had to meet with that reporter, Knowlton.

Because of his injuries Rose didn't want to struggle out of the house unless absolutely necessary. So he invited the reporter to stop by some time that afternoon.

Jolyn Knowlton rang the doorbell to the old ranch house about thirty miles north of Pittsburgh about half past four. The home sat back off the road several hundred yards and was surrounded on three sides by woods.

Rose's significant other, Aldo Martinez, let Jolyn in.

They introduced themselves and Aldo led her into the living room where Rose reclined on a couch with his head propped with pillows.

"Hi, Miss Knowlton," Rose greeted as she approached.

"Hello . . . uh . . ."

"I'd prefer you address me as Rose, as opposed to William or Mr. Ortiz."

"That's fine . . . Rose. Please call me Jolyn."

She did have to admit he looked like a woman at first glance—a very attractive woman. She could almost fool anyone. At least until the moment of truth.

"Please pull up a chair, Miss Knowlton."

Jolyn did. Aldo went back to his work in the kitchen. She glanced around the room, noticing the lack of anything on the walls, or plants and the like. Just basic furniture.

"Aldo is renovating and decorating our new home, little by little," Rose remarked. "Well, as you can tell it's not exactly new, except for us. We wanted to get out of the city. Kind of like the country. Except for the varmints."

"I saw the Havahart live traps outside. Squirrels?"

"Rats. We're trying to trap some rats. Live traps instead of poison or snap traps because of Suzette."

The toy poodle cuddled up contentedly to Rose on the couch.

"Oh. Well, I hope you trap the rats."

Verses of Robert Browning's *The Pied Piper of Hamelin* came suddenly to mind:

Rats!
They fought the dogs and killed the cats,
And bit the babies in the cradles,
And ate the cheeses out of the vats,
And licked the soup from the cooks' own ladles,
Split open the keep of salted sprats,
Made nests inside men's Sunday hats,
And even spoiled the women's chats,
By drowning their speaking
With shrieking and squeaking
In fifty different sharps and flats.

Rose's voice interrupted Jolyn's musings about her own rats—the human kind.

"So far Aldo has remodeled the bathroom and kitchen, his favorite room. Quite the cook, Aldo is."

"Yes, I can smell exquisite aromas I assume are coming from the kitchen. Speaking of bathrooms, do you mind if I use yours?"

He pointed. "First door on your left."

The walls were painted a deep fiery red and matching shades for the candle sconces were trimmed in tasseled braid. A coordinating, Venetian inspired red silk brocade was used to make a skirt under the modern looking sink to hide the plumbing and create a storage spot for extra tissue rolls. An antique armoire and a bamboo étagère did double-duty as storage for towels and many more bath products than her own bathroom contained. She laughed when she noticed the rubber toys.

"I just love your powder room," Jolyn complimented upon returning to the living room. You don't have a hidden camera in there, do you?"

"Of course not!" he replied indignantly. "Why would you ask that?"

"I'm kidding, I'm kidding. So you wanted to talk to me, Rose?"

Rose stared at Jolyn's hands.

"What *is* that nail enamel? It looks so perfect—no chips."

Jolyn laughed lightly.

"ColorStay REVLON, 'Berry Reliable.' Would you like to try some?" Rose nodded. "Here, you can have the rest of this color." Jolyn reached into her purse and offered it. "I'm going to try 'Endless Pink' next. This stuff is good for over a week."

"Thank you, Miss Knowlton."

"You're welcome, Rose. And would you please call me Jolyn like I said?"

Rose looked puzzled. "Do you think that the media has the right to intrude into the lives of others, Jolyn?"

Now Jolyn appeared a little confused. "Yes and no. I have a long answer, and a short one. The short one is that I personally have my own code of conduct. Kind of like the golden rule. I will tell you this, Rose—with respect to you—I will not report anything for which you do not give me permission. On that I give you my word."

"Okay, but I'm not sure at this moment about how much I want to tell you."

"Rose, you got shot that night in the parking lot along with the others, including Dexter Curtis. That's a matter of record."

"It is. But then there is the rest of the story."

"Oh?"

"Indeed. I could make your ears burn."

"But *will* you?"

"That *is* the question, isn't it?"

Jolyn thought momentarily of another person who had confided in her about Dexter Curtis. Poor Sondra.

"Rose, let's not play games. I know you are a transsexual and a prostitute. You have a record, several arrests for solicitation. One for possession of crack cocaine."

Rose frowned. "I'm clean—after three rehabs."

"And what I can only suspect," Jolyn continued, "is that you have had some sort of relationship with Dexter Curtis, centering either on drugs or sex."

Rose nodded.

Just then Aldo entered the living room with two plates and two bottles of spring water.

"Try some of my casereccia," he offered.

They did. Jolyn prayed silently before indulging, including a blessing for Rose and Aldo. She had an ominous intuition about them.

Soon Aldo joined them with his own dish.

"This is simply delicious, Aldo," Jolyn complimented. "You'll have to give me the recipe!"

Aldo smiled gloriously. A tablet and pen lay on the coffee table. He began to scribble.

Finally he handed the paper to Jolyn. "Can you read it?"

"Yes, I think so. Sourdough bread, casereccia, cherry tomatoes, arugula, chopped shallot, garlic, hot red pepper flakes, freshly grated Parmigiano-Reggiano cheese, extra-virgin olive oil. I can do that. Thanks!" *That's me, extra-virgin. At least these days. Thou shalt not commit adultery.*

"You're quite welcome."

Rose gazed at Aldo lovingly. He moved closer and they held hands.

"Aldo, tell Jolyn what your connection to this thing with Dexter Curtis is. Just what we talked about." Rose stared at Jolyn. "Off the record. Your word?"

Jolyn shook her head in affirmation.

"I provided someone with . . . uh . . . pictures of myself and a person in the district attorney's office engaging in certain sexual acts. That someone I believe is working for Curtis somehow. I can't prove that, but that's how I figure it. The dude I gave the pictures to appeared rather . . . unscrupulous . . . and dangerous. And he had this weird looking large scar on his neck. Like someone slashed his throat or something. Maybe a vampire got him." He chuckled.

"What?" Jolyn blurted.

"I said I provided— "

"No, no," Jolyn interrupted. "I heard that. The scar—I know this guy. Heavyset, about six-two. Furry eyebrows, balding but trying to hide it, large slightly crooked nose, a chipped front tooth."

Aldo nodded. "That's the dude."

"What you have here is a recipe for disaster. You could be in danger," she warned.

"What do you mean, Jolyn?" Aldo asked.

Jolyn told them about the surreptitious filming of her in various stages of undress and how the pictures ended up on the internet. How then Gorton confronted her with a gun and made her do those things. She told them as much of the story as was necessary to shake them up.

"And Rose," Jolyn concluded, "I believe that you got shot because someone was after Dexter Curtis. You two have a rattrap of another kind—rattrap—a word which also means a difficult entangling situation."

Aldo and Rose both looked shocked.

A Bible sat underneath the coffee table. Jolyn picked it up and began leafing through it.

"Jesus said nothing about homosexuality, you know," Aldo commented sternly. "Do you suppose if Rose has sexual reassignment surgery that God will bless our marriage?"

Rose explained he had been born in the wrong body and didn't want to continue living unless he could legally become a female. Jolyn listened attentively as he talked about the electrolysis, hormone treatments, breast implants, and psychiatric therapy.

But Jesus had much to say about adultery, she thought but didn't say. *"For the wages of sin is death." Romans 6:23. The way of adultery is a one-way street to the gates of hell. That's what the ministers of fire say.*

"May God bless you both, if that is His will," Jolyn spoke. "I have to go. But, please, *please* call me if you want to talk more."

CHAPTER 65

Roxanne Peterson slept peacefully in the passenger seat of Nathan Redmond's luxurious BMW until he reached his place of business.

He shook her gently.

"Wake up, Roxanne. We're here."

She focused and yawned.

"Wow, this place is huge!"

"Brand new building. I purchased three funeral homes within a five mile radius of this place. Consolidation—economies of scale—that sort of thing. The smaller, independent family-owned operations can no longer compete favorably with the big, national death care chains. Eventually, I will close those three funeral homes. Right now we just do cremations here. Those other places I bought don't have the equipment. I'm going to Pittsburgh to negotiate a deal for a similar consolidation. C'mon, I'll give you a tour. I bet you'd like that."

He smiled, amused by her grimace.

"Are there bodies inside?"

"No—no bodies. The funeral directors have a service at their facility and then bring the deceased here in a hearse followed by the family and friends. Nothing scheduled for today. There's a forty-eight hour legally mandated waiting period, so I know in advance."

They went into the building, Redmond tugging the reluctant young woman by the arm. It looked similar to some funeral homes she had been inside, but much larger.

Suddenly the young woman laughed.

"What's so funny?"

Roxanne told him about the time she entered a very small funeral home and somehow managed to find herself standing in front of the casket of the wrong person. She never imagined such a tiny place had more than one "customer" and didn't notice any posting of the person's name or anything.

"A real moment," she admitted, "but you had to be there to understand how *totally* embarrassing. Actually I never met the deceased, but I should have wondered when I didn't see my co-worker his daughter or recognize anyone."

He sniggered.

"Let me assure you, Roxanne, such things don't happen in *my* establishments. The bodies are all properly identified for your viewing pleasure."

"Well good, because I almost wet my pants when some old dude walked up to me at the casket and asked, 'How did you know Jim?' I thought I was praying over somebody named Frank."

"Funny story, Roxanne."

Roxanne surveyed the plethora of Bible quotations on the walls and read aloud, ". . . the day of one's death is better than the day of one's birth, Ecclesiastes 7:1" and ". . . prefer rather to be absent from the body and to be at home with the Lord, 2 Corinthians 5:8."

"I utilize those verses to reassure people about death. Do you fear death, Roxanne?"

"I . . . uh . . . I . . ."

"Did you ever witness a cremation, Roxanne?"

"No. And I'm not sure I want to."

"I'll show you the equipment. You must have some curiosity about the process. Most do. Cremations are becoming more and more popular compared to burials."

Redmond led her to the room.

This very pretty innocent looking girl reminded him of one of his early conquests, a coed at the University of South Carolina in Columbia. *The first one I ate*, he fondly remembered.

He demonstrated how the container was automatically loaded into the front of the Enter-Tek Cremation System and the remains were removed from the rear. She looked bored as he raved about the unique draft control and air distribution system for optimum performance and environmental control.

"How long does it take . . . to . . . ?"

"It would take about an hour to cremate your body."

"Oh really?"

"Perhaps you'd like to be cremated when you pass away," he offered, a statement rather than a question."

Roxanne shrugged, beginning to look queasy. "Well, I guess it doesn't make much difference what happens to your body after you die."

"I can tell this interests you *immensely*," he said somewhat sarcastically. *You'd pay more a little more attention if you realized you're next.*

"Coincidentally, I purchased this equipment from Matthews Cremation Group of Pittsburgh. Let me get some papers and we'll head for Pittsburgh."

Redmond motioned for her to follow him up the stairs to the second floor.

"I'm living here until I finalize the consolidation."

He took her into the kitchen and proudly presented the rich dark-green ubatuba granite countertops, custom maple cabinetry with black accents, professional-grade Thermador range, apron front sink, Sub-Zero refrigerator, and ceramic backsplash with matching stainless accents. He pointed to the warming drawer on top of the range.

"Wow, nice kitchen!"

"My favorite room. Love to cook. I make a terrific Guekhakhte Leber."

"A what?"

"Traditional Jewish dish—liver pate."

"Are you Jewish?"

"My culinary habits are. The Jews of the Old Testament ate people you know."

"They did?"

"Yes indeed. Didn't you ever read Jeremiah 19:9? 'And I will cause them to eat the flesh of their sons and the flesh of their daughters, and they shall eat every one the flesh of his friend...' It's God's will."

Roxanne grimaced.

Redmond showed her his collection of German high carbon steel alloy butcher knives. He pointed the largest—the one with the twelve-inch blade—at her, the tip against the material of her loose sweatshirt.

Roxanne flinched.

"Please don't do that," she said softly.

"Maybe I'll eat *you*, Roxanne."

"I don't do oral sex with somebody I just met."

The sudden intense coldness of his eyes frightened her tremendously.

He pulled her sweatshirt out from her body by the neck and cut the material quickly down the middle with the sharp knife. Then he cut her bra with a quick flick.

"Nice. You have lovely breasts. I am going to eat you, Roxanne. Your liver is in my recipe for Guekhakhte Leber. Yes, I'm going to eat you. But first . . ."

The scream stuck in her throat.

Roxanne knew at that moment this man would have his way with her flesh, one way or another.

Now he looked like the Grim Reaper.

"Drink this," he demanded, pushing the glass in her face with his left hand, as he circled her nipple with the butcher knife held in his right hand.

"I . . . I . . ."

He drew breast blood.

"Quickly, please," he suggested, smiling the smile of death.

Roxanne reluctantly took the glass and drained it.

"I'll do whatever you want," she pleaded. "*Anything*. Please don't hurt me."

"I'll bet you're a real tiger when you're stoned out of your mind, Little Miss Pigtails."

"I said I'd do *anything*," she moaned, and began to weep.

She unbuttoned her jeans and slipped them off.

Then her white cotton panties.

"Yes, you *will* do *anything*," he agreed smugly. "Do you like to be eaten?"

"About . . . what I said . . . the oral sex . . . I . . . you can . . . I will . . . whatever you want . . . ."

"Get down on your knees."

Roxanne did.

She prayed.

CHAPTER 66

Over the falls.
 In a barrel.
 Maybe that's how I should kill myself.
That's what Kim McConnell thought about as she took Exit #53 to US 190 North and headed toward the Peace Bridge.

Cassie Forrester slept in the backseat of the car. Kim had suggested to her mother and stepfather that Cassie accompany her. She didn't want to be alone. They all had mutually decided on Niagra Falls as a location. Not that far away where Kim couldn't readily return for any legally required court appearances.

They had visited Kim's father in Cleveland before heading to the Falls. Kim hadn't seen him for a dozen years. It had been Kim's first stepfather, Tom, who thwarted any relationship with her real father. Tom, the one who molested her for years.

I'm glad he's dead, Kim now reflected as she woke Cassie as they approached Customs. *I wish Dexter Curtis was dead. I wish whoever shot him had better aim.*

Customs was a breeze. She then drove north on Queen Elizabeth Way and exited on Highway 420 to Niagra Falls. Then she turned left on Stanley Avenue, made several more turns according to her map, and found Simcoe Street and the Maid of the Mist Bed and Breakfast.

"So what's on the agenda?" Cassie asked.

"Sightsee, of course. Find the hot spots at night. Get laid."

The proprietor, a large and obviously Native American man named Maxwell Whitefeather, led the two young women to the honeymoon suite.

"You know," he commented wryly, "I think you are the first two girls who stayed in the suite. All the rest have been couples."

"Well, this *is* your best accommodations, and that's what we wanted," Kim responded. She had made the reservation under phony names. "Here's the money for a week, although we may stay longer than that." He took the cash. Her stepfather had gladly "financed" her vacation, looking forward to the day they hit pay dirt with a settlement.

Maxwell led them to the suite and chatted up a storm. He elaborated on the Maid of the Mist tales, the central theme of his establishment, and the legend of the Thunder Beings. There were several different versions of the story that had originated with the Iroquois but had been adulterated by the white man for financial reasons. The Thunder Beings had been in absentia for a long time but then appeared once again to intervene on behalf of a beautiful young woman who was plagued by a snake sent in a spell cast by an old witch. The snake crawled unseen under the girl's dress and bit a succession of her lovers, causing their untimely demise.

I wish the snake would bite some of my previous lovers, Kim mused as Maxwell rambled, *especially that lying shit Chuckie. I bet he got paid good.*

The distraught woman decided to take her own life because she could not cope with the tragedies and took her canoe down the rapids and plunged over the edge of the Falls. But the Thunder Beings caught her canoe and gently lowered it into the water and returned the girl to her people.

Another version of the legend was that the Iroquois sacrificed a maiden to the Falls to appease a wicked serpent. They sent her over the Falls in a white canoe decorated with flowers. The maiden was to be the sexual plaything of the Thunder Beings for the next year. To be sacrificed in such a manner was considered to be a great honor.

Sacrificed to the Thunder Beings. I like that, Kim surmised, and then requested, "Tell us about people who have jumped the falls, Maxwell."

"Intending to kill themselves, or not? I don't think the authorities like to publicize the suicides. Nor does the business community. They say at least seventeen people have gone over the falls as a publicity stunt, since Annie Taylor first did it in 1901. Ten survived. Last year a guy took the one hundred eighty-foot plunge into the churning cauldron of Horseshoe Falls perhaps intending to end it all. But he miraculously didn't. The first to jump Horsehoe Falls without any sort of safety device. The park police charged him with performing an illegal stunt. No one has ever survived a trip over the narrower and rockier American Falls, with or without a barrel or some such thing."

"What are you singing?" Cassie questioned.

"The lyrics to *Over the Falls* by Primas, the *Brown Album.* "

"You're scaring me, Kim."

"I'm scaring myself."

"Would you really jump?"

"I want to meet the Thunder Beings, don't you, Cassie?"

"I have a better idea."

"Oh?"

"You go jump over the falls if you want. I'm going to jump in the Jacuzzi."

CHAPTER 67

Hot spots.

Nathan Redmond loaded Roxanne Peterson's butchered carcass in the Enter-Tek Cremation System.   .

Yes, just about an hour, he figured. *Just long enough for my dinner.*

He went back upstairs to the kitchen and went to work.

Wash liver and peel off the skin. Chop it into small pieces and fry it in oil until cooked. Grind liver pieces with a soaked in water white bread slice. Fry finely chopped onion until light brown and add it with salt, pepper, and melted fat to mince. Stir thoroughly.

Ready!

He served it to himself in a deep plate decorated with slices of hardboiled eggs and chopped greens

And then he began to eat her liver.

Other delicacies and prime cuts he had wrapped and placed in the freezer portion of the Sub-Zero refrigerator.   .

His cell phone rang.

Kingston.

"Aren't you in Pittsburgh yet, Redmond?"

"Soon, Ron. I can't talk now—have a young lady over for dinner."

"Call me when you get to Pittsburgh. My source in the D.A.'s office tells me our alleged rape victim may have flown the coop. I want to know where she is and what she's doing. The bitch—our football player got set up and busted for drugs—I wonder by *who*. She just might have to wind up like some of our other friends. And I want those two queers shut up permanently."

"Right. Call you when I get there."

188

Redmond terminated the call.

"Quite the piece of meat," he uttered amusedly to himself as he returned to her liver. "In more ways than one."

***

Cassie steamed.

Bubbles, millions of bubbles.

She lounged in the emerald-hued Jacuzzi spa when Kim woke from her nap.

"Hey, c'mon in," Cassie implored. "If this doesn't make you feel better, not much will. I love this waterfall. You can adjust it from a trickle to a full cascade."

A few minutes later they both luxuriated in the millions of swirling bubbles.

"It is *hot* in here!" Kim exclaimed, sensitive to the temperature of the water.

"Mostly because of your naked body."

"Yeah, right. You turned it up full blast, Cassie."

"Because I'm going to cook you and eat you. We haven't made love in so long. And we *are* in the honeymoon suite."

"I'm done, stick a fork in me."

Kim rose and stood in front of her girlfriend.

Cassie began to tease Kim's hot spot with her tongue.

CHAPTER 68

Dexter Curtis found his home boys as soon as he got to Miami.

He loved Miami, especially the night life. He liked to mingle with celebrities at places like Prive, B.E.D., and Mynt when in town. He liked the concept at B.E.D. where you lie about, get waited on hand and foot and can even get it on behind billowy white curtains.

He and his home boys watched the Hurricanes crush East Carolina at the Orange Bowl. Nate Brown and P.J. Washington had played on defense with Curtis the previous year at Miami. Both, though good players, didn't have sufficient talent to make the NFL.

"Man, I miss it, the hitting, the excitement," Nate complained.

"Yeah, man, me too," P.J. agreed. "And the cheerleaders. I don't get any of that sweet meat now that I'm not playing."

After the game they headed for the Rumi chic eatery and nightclub in South Beach. Nate claimed the place had been packed with incredibly hot chicks lately.

A sizable crowd clamored outside in line to get in.

One of the humorless, imperturbable door staff immediately recognized Curtis and waved him up to the front.

"Hey Dex, come right on in, man," the doorman chimed. "Good to see you, man." They embraced.

Curtis and his two friends found seats at an internally lit cocktail table at the mezzanine bar. The ceiling appeared as an amber canopy because of the overlapping Plexiglas panels back lit by gelled neon.

The three ordered several rounds of drinks and bantered back and forth, waiting for the action to pick up, which it always did.

"So what's up with the rape thing?" Nate asked.

"You can't rape the willing," Dexter replied with a somewhat alcohol induced smirk. "Gold diggin' slut. I can get whoever I want. I took her to another level and she decided to let the whole world know, looking for the big payout."

"The babes are startin' to roll in," P.J. observed approvingly.

"Yeah, man, got to pick me one," Dexter countered.

"How about that tall bitch in the leather miniskirt with the fringes?" Nate suggested.

"Yeah, man, I pick that one," Dexter concurred. "Before the night is done I'm going to bend her over, lift up that skirt, and stick it right up her ass."

"Yeah, man!" Nate encouraged.

"Give her the good old doodie shoot," P.J. added enthusiasticall·.

***

Majority owner of the Pittsburgh Steelers, Jeremiah Jones, summoned the coach into his office.

"Bill," Jones began solemnly, "we're on the hot spot here. Didn't I strongly recommend we take that quarterback rather than Curtis in the draft?"

"Yes, that you did, Jeremiah, that you did. But it's a little early for second guessing I think."

"But no, you had to have the linebacker. You have this thing for linebackers. So *you* got *your* linebacker. Curtis has brought the team the kind of unwanted attention and adverse publicity we don't need."

"I think he's just been at the wrong place at the wrong time, Jeremiah. He's basically a good guy—and a great player. We'll get him turned in the right direction."

"I hope so, Bill, I hope so. For your sake. I'm expecting a strong effort against Kansas City, with or without your star number one draft pick. I'm expecting a Super Bowl year."

"I guarantee it, Jeremiah."

"And how about winning it this time."

***

Kim gave Cassie an informative lecture as they took in the glory and beauty of American Falls. She went back five hundred million years. Eventually she got to about 12,000 years ago, when the last glaciers melted away from the Niagra area.

"Mother Nature's orgasm," Kim murmured.

"As good as the one I gave you?" Cassie inquired coyly.

At Horseshoe Falls, Kim elaborated on the fact that the Niagra River wasn't really a river but instead a strait connecting Lake Ontario and Lake Erie. She explained how the massive amount of water that makes up the Great Lakes leads to evaporation that moderates air temperature in the winter and inhibits cloud formation in the summer.

"Kim?"

"Yes, Cassie?"

"I'm getting bored with sightseeing."

"Well, I could fucking jump and really entertain you!"

"No thanks. Let's hit the casinos."

"Yeah, we can play some blackjack."

"Hey Kim, didn't you already *play* the black jack?"

"Oh yeah, girlfriend. But I didn't get my settlement yet. So we'll have to win some money tonight. That or put out for profit."

"Right on! Let's go find some hot spots."

CHAPTER 69

The defense looked weak.

Kansas City pounded the Steelers.

Dexter Curtis and Ron Kingston watched the game at a private club in Miami, along with a few friends of each.

"Your team sucks, Dexter," Kingston observed. "The defense is piss poor."

"Yeah, without me."

"You'd be playing if you hadn't been busted."

"I got set up. That chick hit on me, ask Kevin."

"Ask who?"

"My teammate, Kevin Jones. He'll tell you. Then the bitch planted the dope and pipe in my Hummer."

"You said that before. But you have no proof. Why would this woman do such a thing?"

But Kingston suspected he knew the answer.

"Hey man, who knows. Maybe she did drop the stuff by accident. But it was hers, not mine."

"Well, you got caught with the dope and were legally drunk while driving. No defense for that."

"Hey man, so I like a little moota and nail once in awhile. You know, a doobie, some wheat."

"You do the smoke but here's the joke: now you're going to be suspended."

"Fuck."

"Fucked is more like it. The worst part is you're not going to get paid. At a time when your bills for the lawyers and related matters are mounting. Well, maybe that's *not* the worst part. The worst part may be that you're fucking up

193

your credibility with all this bullshit. Your rape trial is going to come down to *your* word against *her* word."

"Fuck."

"You're just lucky the chick is so stupid she wore panties with some other dude's cum in them to the emergency room the next day. Maybe our lawyers can get her past sexual history admitted into evidence."

The score ended 41-20.

Dexter Curtis's name came up several times, as the announcers wrapped up the telecast.

"Dexter, how is your wife?" Kingston asked.

"She's so ticked off she won't even talk to me, Ron, let only fuck me. I don't really want to be in Miami."

"Well, I sure as hell don't want you in Pittsburgh right now—or Detroit. Definitely not Detroit. It's just one thing after another with you Dexter. Now that business about you being *paid* to go to high school has surfaced again. You *have* to keep a low profile."

Dexter Curtis name had recently been erased from the Michigan High School Athletics Association record books. His elite private school team had been urged to forfeit two state titles. A Miami booster had paid Curtis while he attended high school, according to the association, with the intention that he would become a Hurricane.

"They're making me a target. I talked to the headmaster. He says he has been given no credible evidence that I violated my amateur status. He says the school will fight to keep the championships. It's just political bullshit."

"Think about hard time, Dexter. Think about never playing a down in a regular season NFL game. Think about being poor—like when you were a kid. Think about the rats in the tenement in Detroit where you lived. Rats, Dexter, big rats."

"Fuck. I hate rats—rats like that McConnell bitch. I just gave it to her like she wanted it, and then she rats me out." He snickered. "You know, Ron, she has a cute little butterfly tattoo on her butt. She tattooed her ass—so did I. What's the big deal?"

"I should hire a bodyguard for you, Dexter. Somebody to keep an eye on you."

"Yeah, well make it a chick. One who likes to take it up the ass."

Curtis guffawed.

Kingston couldn't help but break a smile.

"Dexter, I think we need to counteract your lack of a defense for sticking it up that McConnell chick's ass with a strong offense."

"How so?"

"I wonder who she had sex with just before and just after you did her. I wonder."

"Probably a whole fucking football team."

RATTRAP

Now Kingston roared.

***

The Knowlton family sat in the living room watching the post-game conference on the local Pittsburgh station telecasting the game. Stephen Winslow, Jolyn's editor and David Knowlton's old friend, had been invited to join them for dinner and a football game.

Jolyn had reluctantly agreed to attend church with her parents. Stephen met them at the Knowlton's house afterwards.

Coach Lowry addressed the media after the game. He dwelled on the special teams and breakdowns on the Steelers kick coverage. Then he lamented the four turnovers. He passed off the Chiefs running success with, "They have the best back in the game in my opinion. Nobody stops him much, especially from scoring." Then he commented briefly on the upcoming game with the Bengals.

The coach was asked about Dexter Curtis's status for the Cincinnati game. "We need somebody to stop the run, *unlike* against the Chiefs," the reporter complained. The coach replied he would comment on the linebacker's status at his weekly news conference on Tuesday. He fielded other questions and then got up and strode off.

"Hey Dave, remember way back when—when the Steelers had those five shutouts in one season?" Stephen asked.

"Like I'd forget 1976. We sat in the stands for two of those shutouts, against the Chargers and the Bucs. The only forgettable part of that season was that we lost to the Raiders in the AFC Championship."

"Do you two think the Steelers are sorry yet they took Curtis as their first draft pick?" Jolyn asked.

"Sure, somewhat," her father replied. "Too early to tell. If Curtis has a great career and we win some Super Bowls, many will forget all this other business."

"But if he goes to prison for rape . . ."

The others merely nodded at Jolyn's remark.

Stephen broke the silence of a few minutes. "In retrospect the worst draft mistake the Steelers *ever* made was when they didn't take Dan Marino in 1983."

"Yeah," David Knowlton agreed, "we had the twenty-first pick in the first round and took a defensive lineman, Gabriel Rivera from Texas Tech. Miami took Marino with the twenty-seventh pick."

"Gabe Rivera, now there's a tragic story," Stephen said with a sigh. "Had a rather mediocre rookie season and then got crippled in an auto accident."

"Stephen, remember that bowl game against Georgia in Marino's junior year at Pitt?"

"Oh yeah, Dave. Touchdown pass on fourth down with under a minute left in the game."

195

"What about that 1974 Steelers draft, Stephen? Four Hall of Famers—Lynn Swann, Jack Lambert, John Stallworth, and Mike Webster."

"Best ever, by *anybody*. But the key was still drafting Bradshaw as the number one pick overall in the draft a few years before that. You've got to have the quarterback. Too bad we didn't take a quarterback this past draft. No, we got a lemon it looks like—and his name is Dexter Curtis."

"Would you two quit talking about things I'm not old enough to remember?" Jolyn asked irritably. "What about Terry Bradshaw and his Depression Tour?"

"His what?" her mother asked.

Jolyn explained. Bradshaw had been diagnosed with clinical depression about five years ago. Now he led a national campaign sponsored by a drug maker. His message emphasized it's a mistake to suffer in silence and shame.

"Mom, did you know that major depressive disorder is the leading cause of disability in the United States?"

"No, I didn't."

"Would you like to hear my evaluation of selective serotonin reuptake inhibitors versus tricyclic medications as effective antidepressants?"

"Why sure we would, Joey," her father patronized.

"I told you *not* to call me that, at least not in front of others!" she blurted. "Tricyclic drugs can be fatal in overdoses. Suicidal tendencies are a symptom of depression. Doesn't make much good sense to me to give a person talking or thinking suicide a loaded gun. Now does it?"

Jolyn looked very upset.

"Perhaps you need anger management therapy," Stephen joked.

If looks could kill.

"Why the interest in major depressive disorder, Jolyn?" her mother asked.

"Kim McConnell. Just one of her problems according to some. It might explain some of her other problems."

After Lowry finished with the news conference, players were interviewed in the locker room.

"What does that sign on the wall in the locker room say?" Jolyn's mother asked.

"Oh, that's a warning about steroids," Stephen responded.

"What about Dexter Curtis and this drug and DUI arrest?" David Knowlton posed. "Will he be suspended?"

"Don't know. I guess we'll find out Tuesday."

"You know, I think I'd like to attend that news conference, Stephen," Jolyn said solemnly.

"I don't know about that. Will you promise to behave?"

Jolyn scowled at him, but then nodded and muttered, "Okay."

"Let me think on it and I'll let you know at the office tomorrow."

"I'm taking a day of vacation tomorrow, remember? And I won't be in until after lunch on Tuesday. You know I have a meeting with Cheryl Bryant, director of NSVRC, in the morning. And I'm going to attend her presentation."

"I'll make you a deal, Jolyn. Not this news conference but the next one. That will give me a little more time to smooth the waters."

"What's NSVRC?" her father asked.

"The National Sexual Violence Resource Center. I'd like to ask Ms. Bryant a few questions about rape shield laws and victim's privacy rights. Research, you know. Perhaps for an article for the paper. Stephen is bugging me about being more prolific."

"I am *not!*" he insisted.

"*Yes*, you *are!*" she snapped back.

"Joey, you shouldn't talk to your boss like that," her father chided.

"Oh yeah, Dad, take your old buddy's side. Well, he may not be my boss much longer. If he doesn't do a Donald Trump act on me first, I think I just might quit!"

With that, Jolyn stormed out of the living room and out the front door. She got into her car and drove off, squealing tires.

No, it wasn't the conversation that troubled her so.

The minister at the service that morning made her cry inside.

He had made an analogy between a marriage between a man and a woman, and the relationship between a believer and Jesus Christ. Reverend Donaldson had developed a sermon from verses in the fifth chapter of Matthew entitled, "What did Jesus say about adultery?"

Thou shalt not commit adultery.

No defense.

***

Ron Kingston's cell phone rang.

He pushed the buxom, scantily dressed young woman off his lap.

After a few minutes of listening without speaking, Kingston said, "Very good, my man. The check is in the mail." Hanging up, he muttered, "More like a big bundle of hundreds in a bag."

Kingston looked menacing at Dexter Curtis pawing another young lady enthusiastically.

"*What*, Ron?"

"Get on a flight back to Pittsburgh. Change of plans—you're not going to be suspended—yet. Looks like maybe you can play this Sunday."

"How the hell did you pull that one off, Ron?"

"Money, Dexter, money—your money. Now get your ass back there and give the Steelers some defense. And *earn* some money instead of spending it."

"Dee-fense!" Curtis growled. He rose and took the young lady who had been the subject of his attention by the hand. "I'll get the first flight out in the morning. You'll see my booty dance when I sack the quarterback on Sunday. But right now I'm gonna git me some booty. Right, honey?"

"Oh yeah," the smiling girl assured him.

CHAPTER 70

Rose saw red.

His significant other, Aldo Martinez, had dressed in Rose's very own Maria Bianca red chiffon top with built-in bra and matching Sateen five-pocket pencil pants.

The nice man had promised Aldo twice the fee for kinky sex.

And the nice man offered dinner at an expensive French restaurant as a prelude to the festivities.

The nice man had initially wanted Rose. But no, Aldo had explained, Rose had an accident recently and couldn't get around real well yet. Or bend over. But Aldo could dress as a passable woman and render all necessary services. Certainly not the first time Aldo had dressed in feminine attire, but he would never be as lovely as Rose.

"I'm *so* glad you decided against a skirt," Rose cooed. "Your legs leave a little to be desired, at least from the 'female' perspective. Now let's find you some appropriate footwear, Aldo," Rose suggested.

Looking in Rose's closet, Aldo gasped, "My God, girl—you have more shoes than Imelda Marcos!"

"Dunno about that, but I do have a nice selection. I gave a lot of head for all these."

Both giggled.

Rose pulled out the Nina satin peep-toe slingbacks, Banana Republic satin mules, and the Andrew Stevens metallic leather sandals with a bows.

Aldo tried them on. And then he tried to walk.

"I *don't think so*, Rose. Can't walk very well in these heels."

"*Practice*, Aldo, it's all about *practice*."

"I have a pair of designer sneakers I'll wear. They'll go okay with the outfit. That's what I wore before whenever I dressed as a woman."

"Just as well. I get chafing on the back of the ankles when I wear the slingbacks, ingrown toenails because of the pointy toes on the mules, and pain in my knees and back because of the sandals' lack of shock absorption. But I love pretty shoes."

"You have lovely legs and feet, Rose."

"Thank you, Aldo."

They kissed affectionately.

"Maybe we could visit the Marikina City Footwear Museum in Manila on our honeymoon? Many of Imelda Marcos' shoes are on display there."

"Whatever you wish, Rose."

Rose fetched his Elizabeth Arden makeup bag and made Aldo look beautiful, at least to the both of them. Then the wig.

"Well, I'm off, Rose. Off to get my new friend off."

They both giggled again.

CHAPTER 71

The last supper.

Aldo and the nice man had agreed to meet in the parking lot of Le Pommier, E. Carson St., South Side. He had said his name was James Smith. They all said their name was something like that.

Aldo got into Redmond's rental car.

"James, would you like me to suck your cock, now? Before we go in?"

The nice man thought about it.

A mouth was a mouth. The excitement of the imminent kill made him horny as hell. Maybe he could just close his eyes and ignore it was a man blowing him. But no, he hated queers. Briefly he thought of his late father, the minister of fire. His rage kindled.

"Let's go inside, my dear," Redmond offered. "What name shall I call you?"

"Oh, how about Sarah?"

"Sarah, let's go inside and have a wonderful dinner."

They did.

The restaurant looked more Paris than Provence to Aldo. The long back wall of the dining room was crimson, reflecting and expanding in the low mirror that stretches along the back of the banquette. White linens on tabletops brightened by a bud vase of fresh blooms and distinguished by attractive tableware, white with a blue bistro band, bearing the "LeP" insignia.

"That wall coordinates quite well with your blouse and pants, my sweet Sarah."

"Actually, the clothes are Rose's. Too bad you couldn't hook up with her. *Quite* the lady."

Oh, I will surely hook up with her, my sweet Sarah. Soon, very soon. Just as soon as I've finished with you.

"Shall I order for you, Sarah?"

"Please do, James."

The nice man spoke to the waiter in French.

"What exactly am I having for dinner, James?"

"Duck breast robed in a rich porcini and roasted garlic jus. A crisped flap of peppery skin capped meat. And for a starter *mouse a trios*—a creamy salmon emulsion, hearty chicken liver pate and a earthy mushroom mouse—to be divinely smeared on crostini."

"Sounds simply scrumptious!"

Soon they ate enthusiastically.

The liver pate brings back delicious memories of Roxanne.

The nice man talked about his love for Mayan culture and art. Aldo had little knowledge of the subject but feigned interest as he ravished the food. His companion spoke of his recent visit to the National Gallery of Art in Washington, D.C., featuring some of the most compelling Maya baubles and artworks ever seen in this country. The exhibit focused on the lifestyles of the Maya elite—kings and consorts, their courts of lords and ladies, their extensive pantheon of gods, the artworks they owned, the costumes they wore, and the wars they fought.

Redmond of course didn't reveal the real purpose of his visit to D.C. that time was to terminate an individual who attempted to extort money from a rather famous congressman, a friend of Ron Kingston's. The assassin wondered what special favors Kingston had garnered from the congressman for that one.

The nice man looked Aldo directly in the eyes and related pensively, "The Mayans practiced anthropophagy—eating human flesh—cannibalism. As did the Aztecs and the Anasazi. They ate their slaves and captured enemies, after ritualistically torturing them."

"James, could we talk about something else, please?"

"Certainly, my sweet Sarah. You talk. I've been rudely dominating the conversation."

Aldo talked about his love for Rose and their desire to be married. He confided they could no longer stand to wait until they had the financial resources for Rose to undergo the sexual reassignment surgery. They just might do it in Vegas one day soon.

"What are the plans for the rest of the evening?" Aldo asked, winking playfully. "I'm up for *anything.*"

"Well, Sarah, I guess we'll head to my place. I have some toys I'm sure you'll like."

"Oh yeah, I *like* toys."

They departed the restaurant. Once they got on I-79 and headed south Redmond began to talk religion, mentioning that he had discussed the subject of homosexuality with a variety of ministers. Aldo remained silent, listening intently.

"I have to urinate," Redmond announced suddenly and pulled over abruptly. "Should have gone before we left. I'll just be a minute."

Fifteen minutes lapsed and Aldo became impatient. He got out of the car and entered the wooded area where the nice man had disappeared.

Redmond appeared from behind a tree. With a revolver in his hand.

"Those ministers, Sarah, told me to live by the latter verses of the first chapter of the book of Romans—those who practice homosexuality are deserving of death. Incidentally, there are no faggots in heaven."

Redmond put a bullet in Aldo's head with the gun that the late Hank Gorton had given him. He wore gloves, being ever so careful not to mar Jolyn Knowlton's fingerprints more than necessary.

"You're off to meet my father in hell," he informed the dying or already dead man dressed as a woman.

CHAPTER 72

Nathan Redmond rang the door bell at the residence of William Garcia and Aldo Martinez.

"Do you want me to get it?" Jolyn asked, as they sat in the kitchen sipping iced tea and eating the buffalo and wild mushroom loaf that Aldo had made Rose for dinner.

"No, I can make it," Ortiz muttered as he got up and limped to get the door.

Ortiz had called Jolyn, crying. She had hurried to his place before he changed his mind. He wanted to "confess" he said. But in the hour since she had arrived they had only made small talk. She didn't want to push him, confident that he'd eventually tell her what was on his mind.

"I'm an attorney," Jolyn heard the voice at the door say. "Aldo Martinez asked me to stop by. Is Aldo here?"

"No, but he should be back soon," Rose responded.

I don't fucking think so. He's dead. Like you will be very soon.

"My name is James Dorchester. Here's my card. Aldo contacted me. May I come in? I can't wait but I have some information I'd like to leave with you—for Aldo. Legal stuff. About gay marriage, Sexual Reassignment Surgery, and that sort of thing."

"Of course, Mr. Dorchester. please do come in."

He did.

"Here's the material."

He handed over a thick folder.

Rose opened it—blank paper.

"What . . . I . . . this is . . ."

Jolyn heard the shot and ran into the living room, without thinking.

204

Rose saw red.

His own blood.

He lay on the floor, bleeding profusely.

Jolyn watched, paralyzed, as the man methodically put another bullet in Rose's head.

Quickly she flipped up her skirt and drew the Glock from the F.L.E.T.C.H. concealment holster strapped to the inside of her left thigh.

But the man had the drop on her.

No chance.

She knew she had little choice but to do as he said. Just as she did when the man whose name she later found out was Gorton pointed the .357 Magnum at her head. And forced her to reveal her breasts and strip off her panties. And do other things. While he filmed her.

"Just throw that little toy on the couch, pretty lady."

Oh my God, he's going to shoot me too.

"What . . . why . . . you . . ."

The man moved closer.

The killings had fueled his lust.

He glared into her eyes. His looked beyond deadly.

"Pretty lady, I'm going to eat you."

CHAPTER 73

Where is she?

Stephen Winslow wondered about Jolyn Knowlton's current whereabouts. Wondering, and beginning to worry. Coach Lowry's weekly Tuesday news conference was scheduled to start shortly. Winslow's staff of reporters began to filter into his office to watch.

"Has anybody heard from Jolyn?" the editor asked the group. They all indicated they had not.

Coach Lowry spoke.

"First, about Dexter Curtis—I'm sure that's what you want to hear about most. He will be practicing this week in pads and may play Sunday against Cincinnati, baring any unforeseen developments. His status at this moment is questionable. Now, these 'legal' issues with respect to him are in the hands of the league and the courts. I have been instructed by our owner, Jeremiah Jones, not to say anything further. So I can't and *don't* ask."

The coach glared out at the crowd and met only silence.

Finally, a local TV sports anchor said, "Okay coach, nobody is asking, please continue."

"We know we are going to play a football team that lost a tough game last week. At 0-2, this becomes a very, very important game for them. They are playing at home and it's my old friend and their new coach Marvin Lane's first game against our football team, of which he served as defensive coordinator a few years back. I know how bad he wants to beat us, and I'll tell you this—they are no longer the doormat of our division. So, this will be a big challenge for us. We are pretty healthy, I think. Jeff Harden has a left ankle, Derron Hayes with a knee, are questionable in addition to Curtis. Mark Higgins with a groin and Spike

Logue with a quad contusion are probable. We got embarrassed by the Chiefs in the second half. This week will be different, I promise you. This week the defense will *not* be missing in action at times."

The media asked various questions about special teams, the play of the secondary, and defensive changes in the red zone. The coach responded to them all patiently. He seemed calmer than usual.

The press conference ended.

"Well, Jolyn certainly wasn't at the press conference," Stephen muttered. "Coach Lowry would have frothed at the mouth at the sight of her. She had expressed an interest in attending, but I persuaded her to wait."

"Hey, she just probably decided to extend her vacation a day, Stephen," one of the staff offered.

"Anybody know what she had planned for yesterday?" the managing editor inquired.

They all just shrugged or shook their heads.

Then one female reporter quipped, "Maybe she has a boyfriend." She and Jolyn had clashed several times, mostly over the latter's refusal to gossip.

Stephen raised his eyebrows sullenly, his affability fading quickly.

"Back to work, people," the editor ordered.

Winslow called David Knowlton.

"David, have you heard from your rebellious daughter lately?"

"I haven't seen her since Sunday evening, when she bolted out of the house. But Jolyn talked to her mother yesterday morning. She said she's not mad at any of us. *Something* has been bothering her."

"Well, she's not at work this afternoon like she said she would be. Didn't call or anything. Not like her."

"On Sunday she said she was going to interview that woman from the National Sexual Violence Center this morning. Got hung up probably."

"Yeah, that meeting with Cheryl Bryant. Probably did get hung up. Hey David, let's get in one more round of golf before the snow flies."

"How about Friday, Stephen? This good weather is supposed to last through the weekend."

"I'll meet you at the club for lunch. See if Ed and Les can make it a foursome."

"Will do. See you then."

Winslow began to wade through a pile of articles ready for editing. He always printed them out and used the blue pencil.

After about an hour of that he decided to try and track down Jolyn.

He found Cheryl Bryant's phone number on Jolyn's Rolodex and left a message on her voice mail.

She got back to him a half hour later.

"Hello, Mr. Winslow. You're Jolyn Knowlton's editor I heard. So where *was* she?"

"What?"

"Your reporter never showed up for our interview this morning."

"That's what I called about. I can't find her. You didn't hear from her at all?"

"No, which surprised me. We talked on the phone several times so she has my cell number. I would have thought she would have called if there was a problem with the appointment."

"Yes, a problem. Must be one. When I find out what it is I'll surely let you know."

"Thank you, Mr. Winslow. I can tell I like Jolyn from our conversations, so whatever the problem is, tell her she can reschedule any time. May not be able to do it in person, though."

"Okay, I'll talk to you again soon, Ms. Bryant."

***

Nathan Redmond had found some rope in the house and bound Jolyn Knowlton securely, hands behind her back and feet at the ankles. He covered her mouth with a piece of duct tape. Removing the holster from her thigh, his fingers lingered, and slipped under the bottom edge of her panties.

"Nice, very nice," he had whispered to her. "I can barely wait to eat you."

His maniacal shrill laugh made her convulse in shivers.

Redmond had carried her to the rental car and put her in the trunk. It was dark and he felt few qualms about being observed. No houses were in sight of the house and very few vehicles passed by. He decided to keep the rental for now and leave his BMW at the airport. Didn't want to taint his beloved car with any evidence. The rental of course had been obtained under one of his aliases. He had worn a disguise, which he discarded shortly before arriving at the residence of Garcia and Martinez. The woman had seen his face. But she wouldn't live to tell about it.

Now he drove to a destination where he would have her, in every way possible.

He smiled smugly.

She will be the best tasting ever.

***

Stephen Winslow called Detective Ed Woods.

"Ed, I can't seem to be able to find Jolyn Knowlton."

"Your star reporter is missing? Now there's a story."

"Not funny, Ed. I'm getting more worried by the minute."

Winslow briefly summarized for the detective the basis for his growing concern.

"I know the super of the apartment building where Jolyn lives," Woods said. "Met him when I investigated the break-in. I'll go over and he'll let me in—just to make sure she's not there. You know, that sicko Gorton who broke into her place and set up the cameras has up and vanished on me. Can't find him in Chicago. I got a pal there who's looking for him."

"You should have arrested him, Ed."

"Maybe, but I found out who hired him."

"Who?"

"I can't disclose that yet, Stephen."

"I wonder why—illegally obtained evidence?"

"Me? If I can't find Jolyn, I'll talk to David Knowlton and obtain her phone records. The companies will give them up quickly if her father and a cop tell them it's an emergency related to her safety."

"Ed, keep me posted."

CHAPTER 74

Stephen Winslow was about to leave the office for dinner around seven when he got a call from Woods.

The detective said he'd pick him up in a few minutes. He had a lead on Jolyn.

"So what's up, Ed?" Winslow asked as he got in the car.

"I know where Jolyn *may* be. At least I know where her cell phone is—the residence of one William Garcia."

"The William Garcia who was shot that night along with Dexter Curtis outside in the parking lot of the bar?"

"The very same. This house is in his name, and another person named Aldo Martinez."

Detective Woods informed Winslow that Jolyn's cell phone is 'E911' capable, which meant it had been embedded with a Global Positioning System chip. He explained how the technology works and a person's location can be pinpointed.

Winslow mentioned that was how the *New York Times* discovered a star reporter's scamming. The cell phone records revealed he was not 'on assignment' but at home."

"There is a call on Jolyn's cell phone at 1:42 PM yesterday from this William Garcia."

The two arrived at the residence.

"That's Jolyn's car," Winslow observed as they parked behind the ten-year-old Chevy Cavalier.

Woods rang the door bell.

No answer.

He tried the door.

Open.

They saw the body and the blood on the living room floor.

"For Chrissakes, don't touch anything, Stephen! Don't even get near the body. In fact, go outside and wait for me."

Winslow did.

Detective Woods searched the house and made a call.

Then he joined Winslow outside.

"Any sign of Jolyn?" her editor asked, his voice shaking.

"Her cell phone is in her purse in the kitchen. No sign of her or anyone else. I called the homicide team and the coroner. They'll be here shortly."

"Jolyn is still missing. Really missing now. In grave danger. She knows who killed that guy."

"That's a definite possibility, Stephen."

"What do we do now?"

"The dead guy is William Garcia. Wallet in his back pocket. Picture on his license matches. I've got somebody tracking down this Aldo Martinez. We'll talk to the neighbors. Check out Jolyn's car. Review all the phone records of Garcia and Jolyn. Look for leads."

"This has something to do with Dexter Curtis, Ed. And that Gorton. Maybe he killed the guy."

"Maybe. What do you know about Garcia and Jolyn?"

"Well, I'm sure the phone records will indicate more calls between the two, whether it be her cell, the office phone, or her home phone. She has been to *this* house before."

Winslow told the detective what he knew. William Garcia—the transvestite prostitute known as Rose—had contacted Jolyn. She came to the house. Aldo Martinez let her in. The two are a couple. Rose had some sort of relationship with Dexter Curtis besides the shootings, but wouldn't tell Jolyn exactly what.

"And," Winslow added, "Aldo Martinez got paid by Gorton for pictures of him and someone from the D.A.'s office engaging in homosexual acts."

The detective looked shocked.

"Damn, Stephen! Why didn't you make me aware of this before?"

"Hearsay."

"Who from the D.A.'s office?"

"Don't know."

"But you might have an idea."

"So might you, Ed."

"Yeah. We both know very well who resigned. I can't frigging believe it."

"Me neither. That's why I didn't tell you. You would have been the first to know if we had any credible corroboration. Like you never heard a false confession."

The homicide team arrived, spoke to Detective Woods briefly, and went to work.

"Take my car, Stephen. You want to talk Jolyn's parents? Normally, I would notify them but—"

"No, let me, Ed. You're immediately putting out an all-points bulletin I assume?"

"Definitely. It will say something like she is wanted as a witness to a homicide and is believed to be an innocent bystander."

"Not armed and dangerous?" Stephen inquired sarcastically."

"No, I don't think so."

"She does have a gun—a small Glock."

"Good. Jolyn may need it. Not in her purse, so she's packing or the perpetrator took it from her."

"Well, I'll go talk to David and Anne Knowlton. You'll catch up with me later?"

"Yeah, I would like my car back sometime."

"How do you tell parents their daughter is missing from the scene of a homicide, Ed?"

"Having done so several times, my only advice is to give them hope."

"Yes, *hope*."

CHAPTER 75

Stephen Winslow and Detective Ed Woods had decided to meet at Sharkey's Café in Latrobe.

A real hot spot during training camp, Winslow estimated today's crowd to be about half of the 325-person capacity. The editor and the detective sat on stools at the horseshoe-shaped bar.

"Easy on the Jack Daniels, Ed," Winslow cautioned. "You'll pass out before the first half ends."

The game between the Bengals and the Steelers at Cincinnati had just begun.

Dexter Curtis blitzed on the first play from scrimmage and sacked the quarterback.

He did his booty dance.

"Yeah, wouldn't want to *miss* anything," Woods vented contemptuously. "How the hell did Curtis get to play today?"

"I hear something is fishy regarding his possible suspension."

"Don't surprise me. He gets off, and he gets off, and he gets off again. What are you drinking, Stephen?" Woods downed the double shot. "I'm buying. My glass is empty."

"Glenmorangie. Crafted by the sixteen men of Tain. The best selling Scotch whiskey, at least in Scotland."

Woods summoned the bartender.

"Mr. Daniels for me and a Glen . . . whatever the hell . . . for my friend here and yeah, I'll take a Bud chaser, too."

"You might want to get something to eat, Ed," Winslow suggested.

"What the hell for? I'm on a diet."

213

"Yeah, a liquid diet. We'll have a couple Creole chicken sandwiches," Winslow said to the bartender. "You'll like these, Ed. Boneless breast of chicken smothered in a Creole sauce, topped with Jack cheese, onion crisps and roasted chili mayonnaise. Served on a toasted multi-grain Kaiser. Oh, and some fries and wings on the side. The fries really soak up the alcohol," he muttered sarcastically for his companion's benefit.

They watched the game intently.

The food soon arrived.

Cincinnati punted. Pittsburgh got a first down on a personal foul flagrant facemask penalty and then stalled after two short runs and an incomplete pass.

Dexter Curtis lusted for head-banging action so much he had begged Coach Lowry to let him play on special teams.

The Steelers punter pooched it toward the sidelines, but it stayed in bounds. The pigskin bounced around erratically, and a Bengals player touched the ball but couldn't control it.

Curtis picked up the football and ran almost untouched into the end zone. The lone potential tackler dove at his heels but to no avail.

A new, improved version of the booty dance ensued.

"Damn, did you see that?" Winslow asked.

"Lucky," Woods responded. "It bounced right to him."

"No, I meant the booty dance, Ed."

"How much is Curtis getting paid to dance?"

"Three million annual salary, provided he plays. His signing bonus is guaranteed money. Rick Louis of the Ravens is making ten million, and he's not even the league's highest paid linebacker."

"That white guy from the Bears must be the highest paid linebacker. I forget his name."

"You seem to forget a lot of things lately, Ed," Winslow commented disapprovingly as he watched Woods down another double shot.

Cincinnati made two first downs after the ensuing kickoff. Then Dexter Curtis tipped a screen pass and intercepted it. Off balance, he stumbled forward. The quarterback tried to stop him, but Curtis knocked him down hard with a straight arm. Several Bengal players gang tackled him at midfield.

The Steelers got three first downs on running plays and short passes. But the drive stalled and they kicked a field goal. The score stood at 10-0 as the first quarter ended.

The veteran Bengal quarterback limped on the sidelines. The rookie came in, the first pick in the draft. Two runs gained three yards. Dropping back to pass, the quarterback dropped the ball. He quickly retrieved it but Dexter Curtis knocked him down roughly before he could get set to pass. Another sack. Another booty dance. Another punt.

"Incidentally, that rookie quarterback who just ate turf is making eleven million," Winslow commented.

Another punt for the Steelers after two penalties for holding.

Coming back into the game, the veteran Bengal quarterback completed a fifty yard pass. Blown coverage. Curtis yelled at the safety responsible for the blunder.

On the next play Curtis blitzed. The quarterback backpedaled and then scrambled for his life to the right as the Steelers ferocious linebacker chased him doggedly. A Bengal offensive tackle attempted to pick up a block on Curtis, but clearly grabbed his jersey. The flags dropped. Curtis shook him off. The quarterback ran out of bounds. But Curtis hit him anyway. More flags.

And then the brawl.

Curtis and two Bengals were ejected.

The Steelers linebacker gave a double-barreled middle finger gesture to the booing enemy crowd.

The first half ended with no other significant developments.

"That is one angry man, that Curtis," Winslow commented.

The detective merely nodded, and downed another double shot.

The two had agreed to meet to watch the game together. They had also agreed beforehand not to discuss the disappearance of Jolyn Knowlton. Because they had discussed her every day for hours since the abduction. No trace. Few clues. No leads. She had simply vanished, along with the person who had killed William Ortiz.

Aldo Martinez's car had been discovered in the parking lot of Le Pommier. But when shown pictures of him, no restaurant personnel could recall seeing him there. Martinez had also disappeared. Detective Woods discounted the possibility that Martinez could be responsible for the murder of his significant other, William Garcia, also known as Rose. Woods also still couldn't locate Hank Gorton, the demented private detective who had victimized Jolyn.

"When do you think you'll get some leads, Ed?" Winslow asked, as they waited for the second half to begin.

"I thought we weren't going to discuss the case today."

"So what about it? What's your prediction?"

"Steelers 20, Bengals 13. Now that Curtis is out of the game, it'll get closer."

"No, I mean about the case. What is it going to take to shed some light?"

"Probably some corpses turning up," the detective responded sardonically.

Corpses.

Woods couldn't help but think of his daughter Amanda. The gang rape. The terror when they ravished a girl who had never known a man. Her suicide. Her corpse. The look on his wife's face.

Winslow shook his head in disapproval at the detective's morbidity.

"Ed, the deceased William Garcia was a transvestite hooker . . ."

"Yeah, so?"

"You might dress up Aldo Garcia in women's clothing, a wig, and that sort of thing."

"What in the hell for, Stephen?"

"I thought you are a detective, Ed. Show the pictures at the restaurant. Maybe someone who didn't recognize *him* as a man will recognize *her* as a woman. I'll even offer to have one of people at the paper do up the pictures."

"It's worth a try, I guess. I'm at my wit's end."

"Yeah, well the booze isn't helping your cognitive capabilities any, I'm sure. If you'd prefer, I'll have the investigator I hired show the pictures at the restaurant."

"Oh, you hired somebody?"

"One of your old friends from the force, Larry Dodd, of Lawrence W. Dodd & Associates, private detective agency."

"Good cop. Thirty years as a Pittsburgh narcotics detective. Then he retired and went to the dark side."

Woods chuckled.

"The dark side?" Winslow asked.

"That's what we call private investigators who were once police officers. It's not a long walk from the left side of the court room, where the prosecution sits during a trial, to the right side, where the defense is seated."

"What about Jolyn's fingerprints on the gun that killed Ortiz? Any new theories on that?"

"I think the killer had some sort of diabolical intent in mind there. To cast suspicion in Jolyn's direction, if even for a brief moment. But then she turned up at the scene of the crime like she did and his plan changed."

The second half began.

Both Winslow and Woods seemed disinterested.

They continued to talk about Jolyn Knowlton.

"So you cancelled your vacation because of all this?" Woods asked, sympathetic.

"Yes, I did. Planned to visit the Princess Grace Rose Garden in Fontvieille, Monaco, among other places. The garden was dedicated in 1984 to the late Princess Grace, known for her love of flowers. Covering some 100 acres, it contains a fragrant collection of over 168 rose cultivars, with 4,000 rose bushes."

"How much do you miss your wife?" Woods asked suddenly, looking very introspective, not inquisitive.

"It's like a piece of my heart was ripped out. I don't know if I'll ever get it back."

"Yeah, I know the feeling."

"Your daughter."

"Yes, Amanda. Jolyn reminds me a little of her. Same kind of fire in her eyes. You seem very fond of Jolyn."

"I am."

The game ended Steelers 17, Bengals 10.

Dexter Curtis was interviewed in the locker room. He had already showered and changed as the other players came in. The reporters flocked to him.

"Dexter, you terrorized the Bengals quarterbacks throughout the game. Well, at least until you got ejected. How did you manage to wreck so much havoc?" an attractive female reporter asked.

"That's me—a holy terror. Too bad I already got dressed, babe, I'd show you my holy tattoo," he said with a wink, "and give you a good look at something else that might interest you. So how did you like my booty dance?"

"I saw the smattering of 'Free Dexter' T-shirts in the crowd. Anything you'd like to say about that? Obviously a reference to your legal difficulties."

"Hell no, I don't want to talk about it. That's what I pay lawyers for. My job is to kick ass and take names, like I did today. Terrorize, like you said. I'm a quarterback's worst nightmare. Did you notice most of those wearing the T-shirts were chicks? I just wish that rookie quarterback would have played more. I wanted another piece of his fucking ass."

"This interview is live, Dexter," she cautioned.

"Just like I want a piece of your fucking ass," he whispered to the woman.

She backed away disgustedly.

Another reporter asked, "Are you going to be able to play next week against Tennessee? There are rumors running rampant you might be suspended for four games because of the NFL's substance abuse policy. You definitely will at least be fined for the altercation on the field and ejection today. And that obscene gesture to the fans."

"I dunno about that. We'll see. But you all saw today what I can do. You think Rick Louis is bad? I'm the baddest motherfucker on the planet."

With that Curtis broke free from the pack of reporters clamoring over him and headed out of the locker room.

The safety who Curtis had chastised after the blown coverage happened to walk past him.

They had words.

Dexter hit him.

The safety fell to the floor, and didn't seem eager to get up.

None of their teammates interceded.

Curtis stormed out.

"I can only imagine how he terrorized Kim McConnell that night," Woods muttered to Winslow. "Every time I talked to her I could feel the fear in her voice when she mentioned his name."

"I can only imagine the terror Jolyn must be experiencing now, if she is still alive," Stephen said softly and sadly.

CHAPTER 76

Love and hate.
Emotions.
Life and death.
Realities.
Jolyn didn't want to think about death as she struggled somewhat to breathe in the trunk of the car.
She blocked death from her mind as best she could.
No, don't think about Zeke.
He reminds me of death.
But also love.
What does Stephen remind me of?
Love—the love he had for his wife.
How about Danny? My first. He told all his friends he had me. I was nothing to him but a trophy.
And Robert?
Oh yes, Robert.
Lies, lies, lies.
Zeke.
Oh my God, how I loved you.
Stephen.
You make me smile.
Laugh.
Cry.
What about this killer?
What makes him laugh?

Cry?
Kill?
Stephen.
I think he loves me.
Do I love him?
Will I even know the love of a man again?
Am I going to die?
I don't want to die.
I want to live.
And love.
What does this man, this killer, want from me?
My sex?
My life?
I don't want to die.
But I'm not afraid to die.
The car stopped.
He shut off the engine.
Why is he evil?
What motivates him to kill?
I want to understand.
I want to live.

CHAPTER 77

Nathan Redmond took Jolyn Knowlton to a summer cottage he owned on a small lake in Ohio.

He had purchased the cottage under one of his aliases several years ago. And he never drove his own car to any of his 'safe houses.' He called the car rental agency and told them he wanted to keep the Ford for another week or so.

Of course he knew her identity. He had rummaged through her purse, although he chose to leave it at the scene of the crime.

Redmond had decided soon after the abduction that he would like to spend some quality time with this beautiful, intelligent woman before he killed her. A little vacation for him. A week of pure terror for her—wondering when the moment of death would come—and how much humiliation and pain would she endure before the final outcome.

Yes, he thought gleefully, *I will torment her until she begs for me to end it.*

As he watched the Steelers vs. Bengals game on television, he fondly reminisced about Lauralee, the Cincinnati Bengals cheerleader he met while attending The Cincinnati College of Mortuary Science.

Oh how she had cried for her life.

But she didn't entertain him for long, just as the latest, Roxanne Peterson, didn't.

Eventually the whining and crying annoyed him more than their bodies and fear delighted him.

He couldn't help but think of the lovely Emily.

Insane at the end.

Driven mad by terror.

RATTRAP

Redmond had taken the Yale Law School student he met at the Lillian Goldman Law Library to the old and dilapidated mansion outside New Haven. He had bought it cheap as a lark with the intention of turning it into a Halloween attraction. Just one of his many seemingly brilliant ideas to make money. But none of them ever seemed to work out. So he turned to contract killing which became quite lucrative. It more than paid the bills and fueled his lust for killing for his own pleasure.

"This one is called the Iron Maiden of Nuremburg," he had lectured Emily. "You can see that it is a tomb sized container in the form of a woman with folding doors. Notice the spikes on the inside of the door. They are not designed to kill instantaneously, but rather to slowly torture to the point of death.

"Here we have the Judas Cradle," he had continued. "Notice the tripod pyramid shape coming to a sharp point. Guess what goes on the point? Right, the anus or vagina. The victim is hoisted up and lowered according to the pleasure of the victimizer, rocking or bobbing the poor soul. I understand this apparatus is still utilized by a few terrorist groups.

"You don't need much of an imagination, Emily, to understand the concept of this one—The Saw. It was used mainly in France on witches who had sex with devils and demons. I'm sure you can visualize how they hung upside down to be sawn in half beginning between the legs.

"This one is the Heretic Fork. Two of the sharp points of the fork are stuck into the throat and the other two are poked into the sternum bone. As you can see, the fork is held in place by a necklace. The forked one could only move his or head and mumble. They were supposed to mumble '*abiuro*' which means 'I recant,' and you will notice that is engraved on one side of the fork. If they didn't recant with that word, at least in the case of the Spanish Inquisition, they were declared an 'impenitent heretic,' dressed in the appropriate attire and led to the stake to be burned. Those overseeing the Roman Inquisition didn't bother with the costume.

Emily soon agreed to do exactly as he wished.

And then he showed her The Pear. It could be used orally, rectally, or vaginally. Inserting the instrument in the appropriate orifice, the screw was expanded, mutilating the inside of the cavity in question.

Poor Emily's heart stopped before The Pear inflicted a fatal wound.

And, of course, there had been Monique.

An older woman, who looked years younger.

He usually liked them young and ripe, but Monique had an arrogance that he drooled about cutting out.

And he did.

The widow had married money.

She spoke seven languages fluently.

Botox injections, microdermabrasion, collagen injections, chemical peels, breast augmentation, upper arm lifts, liposuction, eyelid surgery, a face lift.

Redmond made her watch him take the knife to her.

A different kind of cosmetic surgery.

Redmond now wondered how long this new plaything, Jolyn Knowlton, would hold up under the terror.

The assassin for hire and executioner for kicks smiled knowingly.

Time to shop.

His new pretty woman needed a party dress and accessories.

They had a dinner date.

CHAPTER 78

Booty dance.

It may not have been the Armageddon of the Bible but it did seem to be a war of the worlds—the straight world versus the gay world. The circuit party at a club called Armageddon in Toronto had been advertised as a weekend long bash where anything and everything was readily available. You didn't even have to look for your drug of choice and your sex of choice. It found you.

"Circuit parties," Cassie Forrester informed Kim McConnell, "are the gay alternative to raves."

"I'm not exactly gay, Cassie," she had responded.

Cassie then had placed her hand on Kim's thigh, just above the knee, and whispered, "Sometimes you are." She moved her hand up.

"*Sometimes*," Kim purred.

"Would you like me to make your booty dance, Kim?"

"Yes, I think I would."

Cassie had been Kim's first girl.

They met at cheerleading practice their senior year.

Cassie had transferred from a high school in San Francisco when her family moved to Pittsburgh because of her father's new job.

Kim immediately noticed Cassie's unusual attraction to her, and she herself strangely and surreptitiously fantasized about touching her new, beautiful friend's jet black hair and milky white skin.

Cassie asked Kim to come over to her house one day after cheerleading practice.

"You can help me with some computer stuff, Kim. I can't seem to convert these dang text files into Microsoft Word. We'll jog over. It's only a mile. You can take a shower there."

Kim had gone right to Cassie's computer when they got to her house and began to work with the files.

Cassie began to rub Kim's shoulders expertly and massage her neck as she sat in the chair. Her hands moved off Kim's shoulders. Down her front. She slipped her fingers into Kim's sports bra top. Gently she fondled her breasts. She removed her hands after a few moments and then spun the chair around so she faced Kim.

"Kim, I have a secret," she said softly.

"Well, tell me! Curiosity killed the kitty."

"I like girls."

"Huh?" Kim had responded, confused.

"Girls. I like girls. I like you, Kim. I like to make love to girls. I want to make love to you. I want to lick the sweat off your body. All of your body."

"Um . . ."

"Does my secret surprise you?"

"Well . . . uh . . . yeah . . . I . . . don't know what to say, Cassie."

"You're apprehensive about this? About being made love to by another girl?"

"I . . . I never even thought about being with another girl. That way. I've never even seriously kissed another girl before. Little smooches for my family and girlfriends, but nothing . . . you know."

"Kim, I won't try to persuade you to do anything you don't want to do," Cassie had said sincerely. "Do you think I could kiss you?"

"I guess . . . that would be okay, Cassie," Kim had whispered.

Cassie held Kim's face in her hands. Softly she brushed Kim's lips with hers. And then she really kissed her.

"What did you think about the kiss, Kim?"

"Girls can kiss better than guys," Kim responded frankly.

They both giggled hysterically.

"The 'French Kiss' was first known as *'maraichinage'* which was a term to describe the prolonged, deep tongue kiss practiced by the Maraichins, inhabitants of Brittany, France."

"Is that where you are from, Cassie?"

Kim snickered and stood. They hugged and kissed again. It was even better standing up. Their mouths tasted so sweet to one another.

"When was the first time you had sex with another girl?" Kim asked.

Cassie laughed.

"The first time I had sex with a man," she answered, smirking.

"No, I mean the first time you had sex with a female."

"It happened the same night—the first time I had sex with a female—or a male."

"Huh?" was all Kim could muster.

"When I babysat for this one couple quite regularly back in San Francisco. Quite an attractive couple. One Saturday night when I got there the children were nowhere to be found. It was wonderful. They both made love to me. Ever since that fateful night I have liked to play with both boys and girls, but mostly girls."

After Cassie pleased Kim just as she had done that first time, she gave Kim the lowdown on the bash.

These circuit parties had started with the concept of being fundraisers for AIDS prevention and gay charities. The rampant drug use and uninhibited orgies began to alarm politicians, law enforcement, and the media. But the politicians shut up when their coffers were filled with a substantial percentage of the admission fees and fringe benefits were offered. Some were bribed with the drugs and booze. To others, any variety of sexual perversion that one could possibly imagine had the greater appeal.

The gay community raucously celebrated their culture at these parties, finding safety in numbers. The initial charitable purpose of such parties had become terribly distorted. The dark side of random unprotected sex and widespread drug use ultimately overshadowed any altruistic motives. Organizers of the parties now had medical personnel on the premises to treat drug overdoses.

One major problem always seemed to be that neighbors of the establishments where the circuit parties played complained intensely. Partygoers frequently displayed nudity and lewd behavior. Outraged citizens particularly objected to fellatio being performed right outside the bash, in alleys and along the block.

Cassie persuaded Kim they would have a wild and crazy time.

"It's a real booty dance, girl!"

225

CHAPTER 79

Welcome to Armageddon.

Fire and brimstone.

The club Armageddon had been a hotel at one time, at least the first building. It consisted of two separate buildings that had been connected by what might best be described as a long tunnel of love. The first building contained a large first floor banquet room that could hold about five hundred people where the bands played and people danced.

"Hey, Kim, you can do your booty dance," Cassie joked. "Just like Dexter Curtis did in the game."

"Fuck him. He can't do the booty dance. I'll show you booty dance before this party is over."

The upper floors of the first building provided small rooms that could be had for an hour or all night. The dungeon in the basement was furnished with racks, swings and examination tables complete with stirrups. The other building had a bar, a pool room, a sauna, a movie room with non-stop porno flicks, separate booths like in an adult bookstore for those who like the suspense, and the Maze.

The Maze was just what it sounded like. You walked down a hall and ran into a wall and had to find your way out. Except for one small corner that had a huge waterbed in it, the place did not lend itself well to seeing much of anything. Several times Kim unintentionally brushed up against bodies, and felt a penis or two poking at her. She and Cassie made their way to where the light and the waterbed. It featured two naked girls locked in a hot embrace. Four guys watched with a noteworthy lack of real interest as they amused one another with hands and mouths.

The two girls beckoned Kim and Cassie to join them.

Cassie shed her clothes quickly.

"I'm going for it," she said to Kim. "Me horny. You?"

"No, not yet. I'm going to the bar. Meet me there when . . . you're . . . finished."

Kim made her way out of the Maze and to the bar.

"Hit me with a shot of vodka, make that a double, and a Mountain Dew chaser," Kim requested of the bartender.

The nametag on his shirt said Dave.

When he set the drinks in front of her, Dave smiled with, "Here you go, gorgeous. You look a little upset. Anything wrong?"

"I've been known to be wickedly wild on occasion, but this place is too creepy crazy even for me. And that Maze!"

"Yes, the Maze is one of the favorites here. I like your biker babe outfit. I'll be surprised if you don't win best costume."

"Yeah, my girlfriend and I decided to do the leather thing. She's in the Maze, getting it on with two other girls. I just wasn't in the mood yet. Need a little something to loosen me up first."

Kim toyed with the zipper of her skimpy black leather vest. Full collar, lapels, and front closure so one could show as much cleavage as one wanted. Same one she wore to HOG HEAVEN.

"Do you want something besides the booze?"

"Like what?"

She lowered the zipper.

He could see nipples.

"Ice, Chalk, Crystal, Crank, Fire, Glass—all names for meth. It's all over this place and practically being given away. In fact, here. Swallow it."

She did, with a swig of Dew.

"And this will make me feel . . . like what?"

"Increased alertness, energy, confidence, and stamina. What's your name, anyway? I've seen you somewhere before. Are you some sort of celebrity?"

"Oh hell no—no celebrity—and my name is Denise," she lied. "But maybe I will be a celebrity when this meth kicks in. I talked to the band and they want me to do a couple tunes with them. The drummer suggested *Motor Cycle Girl* by Cruzados. I said I can't sing all that well so some say, and he said just show a little skin and lip sync and I'll be a big hit."

"Honey, I got to say the drummer is right on, from what I can see from here. But I'd rather see you play with yourself than pretend to sing."

"Huh?"

"I could film it and make you a star. This bartending job doesn't do much for the wallet, if you get my drift. I dabble in amateur movies and erotic merchandise on the side. This is the perfect place to do it."

"Erotic merchandise?"

"Here, let me show you." Dave didn't wait for a response. He reached under the bar and pulled out the toys. "This is Charlie the Chimp. Talk about purple passion. The chimp vibrates for clitoral exhilaration. The three AA batteries are installed and it's all ready to light your fire. Just push this button for vibration and rotation."

Kim did.

The buzz startled her momentarily.

"Yeah, I can see how Charlie could make my booty dance."

"Are you religious?" Dave then inquired.

"Funny you should ask. Recently I have been very religious, spending a lot of time on my knees."

"How about some divine intervention?" Dave then suggested lecherously. "You will notice that these silicone dildos have a flared base so you can attach them to a harness."

Dave handed her Jesus, both of them. He had Baby Jesus and Jackhammer Jesus, in addition to Moses and The Devil. And Virgin Mary and Buddha's Delight and the Grim Reaper and Judas.

"Oh my God!" Kim cried.

"Exactly. Would you like me to show you how to accept Jesus as your personal savior? Or perhaps you might like Moses to lead you to the promised land? Baby Jesus goes in the other end."

"Do you sell many of these?" Kim asked. "Seems blasphemous and sacrilegious to me."

"What I don't sell I give away for Christmas. My sister loves these, almost as much as she loves the real thing—my real thing."

"You have sex with your sister?" Kim questioned, a little shocked, and thinking about her stepfather forcing himself on her.

"Of course. There is nothing sexier than tagging your sister, let me tell you. If it were not for incest, how do you suppose we all got here? Just who do you suppose Cain married? His sister don't you think? Close inbreeding was once encourage, and rightly so. The royal prerogative of the Inca rulers was to marry sisters. What about Cleopatra? The Ptolemies married their sisters to keep the money in the family. Oh yeah, and in more modern times Saddam Hussein married his cousin."

"My girlfriend doesn't agree with you about Cain marrying his sister," Kim responded. "And you bleeping your own sister sounds like a *mortal* sin to me. Not as bad as rape, but definitely worth a trip to hell."

Yes, hell, where Dexter Curtis will burn in the lake of fire and brimstone.

Dave spat caustically, "So who is your girlfriend, Oral Roberts? With the emphasis on oral. Excuse me, customers beckoning from the other end of the bar. But hey, Denise, give the toys a little trial run if you like. But if you break it you bought it!"

An attractive, voluptuous young woman in a belly dancing costume took the empty bar stool next to Kim. She looked trashed and immediately began to talk Kim's ear off.

"I dance mostly North American cabaret style . . . to whatever music gets me in the mood. Eat Static is probably my favorite—the *Science of the Gods* album. I can do all the steps from Andulusian Figure 8 to Camel Undulations to the Peacock Stomp and more. I made my own costume including the Turkish-Macedonian vest and Cleopatra headpiece. For the latter I used a doily about the size of a dinner plate and ran crocheted strands around it which hung down to my eyebrows in front and shoulder length elsewhere. I glued beads to the strands. Most important are the bobby pins that hold the thing on your head. Forget them while you are doing the Shimmy or Serpentine Roll and it's goodbye Cleopatra headpiece."

"Yes, I would imagine," Kim responded disinterestedly.

"My name is Samantha, also known as Sam or Sammy."

Kim decided she might as well make conversation. Dave had gotten real busy all of a sudden.

"I'm . . . Denise. You know, Samantha, you remind me a little of the supermodel Frederique; almost six foot tall and big-boned, large hands and feet and a deep voice. Frederique is a native of Holland but has become the quintessential New Yorker. She has done many *Cosmo* covers and *Victoria's Secret* catalogues."

"You think I'm pretty then, Denise?"

"You are very beautiful, Samantha."

"So are you, Denise. I'd jump your bones if women were my thing."

Kim laughed merrily.

"I prefer men myself," she admitted.

"But I do have a secret, Denise—a *big* secret."

"I'd bet just about everybody here has something they'd like to keep hidden away in a closet."

"What I have is extremely difficult to hide."

With that Samantha unclipped her tulip wrap bottom to the belly dancing costume and fully exposed the lace-top thigh-highs. Kim noticed an unusual bulge in her stretch string thong. At first, she could only guess that the bulge in Samantha's crotch might be a Kotex maxi-pad or some such thing.

But soon Kim discovered the real reason for the bulge. Samantha pulled down her thong and revealed quite the nice looking large penis.

Kim felt faint for a moment and could barely speak.

"Oh . . . my . . ." she finally gasped.

"It's real, Denise," Samantha stated solemnly. "You can touch it if you like."

Kim couldn't resist.

It became substantially larger as she fondled it gently.

Big, really big. Only one bigger I've ever held belonged to that fucking nigger who raped me up the ass.

Kim's overwhelming curiosity now demanded that she see what Samantha had on top.

"Please let me see your breasts, Samantha."

Samantha revealed her beautiful melons; very full and firm.

"You like?"

Kim touched them gently. The tips of Samantha's nipples became quite erect.

"I'm beginning to get the picture here, Samantha. You are Sam. And just how in the world did that all happen?"

"Long story, but soon I will no longer have that penis you are holding in your hand."

Sam explained that she wanted to be totally a woman and experience everything that a woman experiences. Her doctor told her that after the sexual reassignment surgery it could be quite possible that she may be able to orgasm just like a normal woman. She knew that sounded incredible but that's what the experts said. Her doctor expounded that he would take sensitive tissue from her penis and use it to create her vagina and clitoris which hopefully would provide a degree of sensation. Exactly what degree of sensation, of course, wouldn't be known until some time after the operation. Some 'new' women had no capacity for orgasm while others got off big time, her doctor cautioned, but made her feel optimistic about a future 'big O.'

"But Sam, how did you become so much *like* a woman? I mean, I never would have guessed."

"Nobody ever suspects until I give them clues, and even then they don't believe it until I show them what I pee with."

Sam said that she had a rather girlish face to begin with and had undergone considerable facial feminization surgery. A male and female skull have basic differences, as any anthropologist will tell you she noted. She had orbital rim contouring to modify her forehead, cheek augmentation utilizing implants, lower jaw surgery, and thyroid cartilage reduction for her Adam's Apple.

"What about your body? Sam, your breasts are fantastic!"

"Yours ain't bad either, honey, from what I can see. You know, just the usual textured saline filled implants. Also a tummy tuck, hip, thigh and leg suctioning, and of course, electrolysis."

"But you even *act* like a woman, Sam. You don't have any prominent male characteristics that I can detect."

"Hey, I read *Creating a Feminine Carriage: Figure, Posture, Walk & Gesture* by Elaine Sagant. She is image and movement consultant to the transgender community. Everything from bending and reaching to getting in and out of cars in a ladylike manner. And I practiced with 'girlfriends' who are also suffering from Gender Dysphoria."

"Well, it's just extraordinary! I can't imagine anyone doubting you are a woman, Sam."

"Yes, Denise, but for one important matter yet to be dispensed with."

Samantha winked at her new friend.

Kim giggled.

"Hey, Sam, you could write a new tune for the Dixie Chicks, a sequel to *Goodbye Earl* entitled *Goodbye Dick*. Are you going to have a funeral or something for your penis? Maybe you should see a taxidermist and get the thing stuffed."

"Great idea! Get it stuffed, and when someone tells me to 'go bleep myself' I'll just pull it out of my purse, lift up my skirt, pull down my panties, and do myself. That or I'll get it pickled and exhibit it at Tate Modern for a million bucks."

"Geez, Sam, I wonder if Hallmark makes a card for this occasion. 'Sorry you lost your dick, but glad you're now a chick' or some such thing."

Both began laughing hysterically and poking each other playfully.

"You know, Denise," Samantha commented ruefully after wiping away the tears, "what concerns me the most about all this is that I'll have to pee sitting down."

"Yes, indeed, the female anatomy is not conducive to peeing standing up. But at least you won't have to stand in front of strangers and pee."

"But I'll miss all the graffiti over the urinals like, 'Don't look up here, the joke's in your hand.' Although I may have to pee sitting down, no PMS for me, unless it's psychosomatic."

"Samantha, I think I can trust you. You told me your big secret. I also have a big secret. My name is not Denise."

"Oh?"

"My name is Kim McConnell."

"The name does sound a little familiar. And you do look a little familiar. But I still—"

"I'm the woman who was viciously anally raped by that football player, Dexter Curtis."

"Oh my God! Why, yes, of course! I saw your picture on the internet. Oh, I'm so sorry, Kim. Do you want to talk about it?"

"No, not really. I want to party now. But I will tell you this. That black buck has a bigger one than yours and he stuck it up my ass after I said 'no.' I never took it that way before. He ripped me wide open."

"Oh my dear God, Kim!"

Samantha reached for Kim and they hugged tightly.

"Yeah, well Sam, I'm going to nail his black ass to the fucking wall. He's going to pay big time, in more ways than one. But let's go dance, shall we? You do your belly dance and I'll do my booty dance."

At that moment a terrific explosion rocked the place.

Plaster fell from the ceiling and pictures and knickknacks dropped off the walls.

Bottles and glasses on the bar shattered.

"Must be the meth lab in the basement of the hotel!" Dave the bartender yelled. "I knew one of these days that damn thing would blow up. We'll have to evacuate!"

People began to panic and look for exits.

Heavy smoke permeated the air.

But the screams couldn't wake the dead.

CHAPTER 80

Dinner and a movie.

Jolyn looked stunning.

Redmond had made a trip to a local boutique and bought her a black flutter dress which she now wore, sitting at the dining room table in the cottage. Amazing lace topped off a romantic flowing silhouette. V-neck and flutter sleeves. Empire seams.

"Black isn't my favorite color," she had remarked snidely when he handed it to her and told her to put it on.

"But you are in mourning, my dear," he responded solemnly. "You are mourning your own imminent death. Besides, that thing you are wearing is all tattered and soiled. Here—shoes also. I didn't think those sneakers on your feet would go well with the dress."

She took the black ribbon high-heel sandals.

"The 'sneakers' are Nike Shox R4. Great cushion and shock absorption. A foam pillar cushions the heel with a traditional air unit in the forefoot. And they didn't come cheap so don't go throwing them away. And my dress is a mess because you stuffed me in the trunk of the car," she snapped sarcastically.

"What do you call that *thing* you are wearing, anyway?"

Jolyn explicated that it was just a plain T-dress. Typical Native American garb and she had made it herself.

"The blue matches my eyes nicely, don't you think?"

"Yes, definitely. Your eyes are incredible blue. Deep blue. Very blue. One gets the feeling that one could fall right into the depths of your eyes and drown. Unless you saved him."

My eyes couldn't save Zeke, she reflected sadly.

"The ancient dye I used to color the dress was only recently rediscovered. According to myth and legend this color dominated the battle garb of female divine warriors and distracted and frightened the enemy."

"Just like your eyes—dangerous."

Jolyn elucidated that the pigment is made by crushing and drying a certain deep water snail the Israelis thought to be extinct. She found out about it while working for the Hebrew University Institute of Archaeology examining Dead Sea Scroll fragments. Her means of employment while studying at the Rothberg International School.

"The Kiowa and Comanche women used calicos for their T-dresses. The Iroquois, my tribe the Seneca a member of the confederation, favored shades of blue and heavier weighted fabrics like satins, silks, and taffetas. But this was only after such material became available from the white eyes."

"You are an Injun then? You don't look it, paleface."

"I have some Native American blood," she replied, revoking her most recent Native American experience—"playing Rambo" with Zeke, and his sharing what he had learned with the Shadow Wolves.

"But the blue eyes . . ."

"Chief Cornplanter had blue eyes."

"Well, my dear, take that old Indian thing off and put on your new dress. It's time to party."

He stared at her, waiting.

"Are you going to watch me?"

"I had planned on it."

"Hey, give me a little privacy to take a shower and change, would you please?" She smiled. "You won't be sorry."

He did.

"You are quite an extraordinary beauty, Jolyn," he now complimented lustfully as she sat at the table.

"Just shows what a shower and makeup can do. But thank you for picking up those items I asked for. Forgot my purse in the rush to leave the scene of the crime. You know my name. What's yours?"

"Call me . . . let's see . . . call me Kurt. Yes, Kurt. Are you hungry, Jolyn?"

"No, I'm starving. All you gave me for nourishment was two cans of Bud Light."

"Hey now, what about the potato chips?"

"Would have just made me thirstier."

"You know, that's how truck stop food makes me—thirsty."

He erupted in laughter.

"What's so funny?" she asked tentatively,

"It makes me thirsty for blood. Ordered up a real delicacy at a truck stop recently—named Roxanne. I ate her. Recollecting the taste of her liver still gives me a hard-on. But then, you give me a bigger hard-on, Jolyn."

"You are one sick puppy."

"Yes, I am. And the one before Roxanne—Maryanne—talk about drumsticks! And I'm going to eat you, Jolyn. But tonight we are doing Japanese. As long as you cooperate we'll postpone cooking you until another day."

"Why don't you just rape me, if that's what you want?"

"No, no. No rape. If you're not willing, neither am I."

"How can you consider me willing if my hands are in cuffs and my legs in irons?"

"But you are not wearing a chastity belt now are you, my dear?"

He served dinner like an experienced waiter at an elite eatery.

"What is all this?" she inquired.

"Horse mackerel sashimi, sea tangle with salty fish roe, smoked Japanese pig liver, teriyaki chicken, Japanese eggplant with soy bean paste, and maki rolls."

She bowed her head.

"What are you doing?"

"Saying grace."

"Oh. Well, don't forget about your last rites. But please say grace aloud. I'd like to hear."

"Heavenly Father, thank you for all the blessings you have bestowed upon us. Lord, we pray that Kurt becomes sober, self-disciplined, and vigilant. Able to think and act rationally and not foolishly in order that he may not fall prey to our adversary, the Devil. He who roams about like a roaring lion seeking whom he may devour. The Lord rebukes you, Satan! Lord, please bless this food to our bodies and we pray that it may sustain us physically as the Holy Spirit sustains us spiritually. All things for our body, soul, and spirit came from You, Lord, and we are ever thankful. We pray in the name of Jesus. Amen."

"Amen! You should have been a preacher."

Jolyn couldn't help herself. She began to ravishingly devour the food.

"Delicious," she complimented. "Even though you're a killer, you're still an excellent chef."

Jolyn thought of Stephen and the dinner he prepared for her. And wondered if she'd ever see him again.

"Drink some of this," the man who called himself Kurt demanded.

"What is it?"

"Sake."

"No sake," she replied demurely. "Do you have holy water?"

"Yes, sake. You drank the beers without protest. Actually, sake is more of a beer than a wine, in that it is fermented from grain, specifically rice."

He explained that it is not carbonated and thus why flavor-wise it is closer to beer than wine, although significantly different in taste than either. Sake had been around since the third century and was originally called *kuchikami no sake*, which meant 'chewing in the mouth' sake. Rice, millet, and chestnuts were chewed up by the members of a particular village and spat into a tub and left to ferment. It became an important ritual in Shinto religious festivals. This particular sake called Sharaku, had been named after a famous ukiyoe painter who mysteriously disappeared one day.

Again, he convulsed in laughter.

"What is *so* amusing? You keep laughing and I don't know why."

"That's what I do, Jolyn—make people mysteriously disappear—and you're next."

She just shook her head, not seeming very upset.

"What's the story with the pornography, Kurt?"

Genitalia adorned every wall.

He elaborated upon the classical Japanese woodblock images originally created by masters such as Katsuhika Hokusai and Kitagawa Utamaro. The scenes portrayed the streets, homes, teahouses, and brothels of Tokyo, then known as Edo, in unique and graphic revelations.

Jolyn stared insidiously at the intricate entanglement of 18th century hair styles, fashions, and body parts.

"Perhaps you know, Kurt, that Edo was known as the city of bachelors because men outnumbered women two to one. This sort of erotic art, as you categorize it, became a popular substitute for the more tangible as has always been the case when demand greatly exceeds supply."

"I never looked at it that way," Redmond replied softly.

"That piece on the far wall, I have seen it before. The work represents symbolically Hojo Masako, also known as the general in the nun's habit. After her husband's death, she became a divine warrior for the Shogunate against their enemies in the thirteenth century. Hojo Masako had an uncommon affinity for the short sword—the *shoto wakizashi*—and believed it to be the soul of her warrior nature."

"You are correct, my dear Jolyn, but that short sword in your hand is merely a butter knife."

"Why all the interest in things Japanese, Kurt?"

"In mid-December, 1937, the Japanese had overrun Nanking. Tanks and mechanized forces came the next day. In the next six weeks 300,000 Chinese suffered torture and slaughter. Over 20,000 women endured gang rape and many were brutally murdered afterwards. The Japanese soldiers cut open the abdomens of many women and squeezed out their intestines. Their genitalia were mutilated with bayonets and other objects."

"Do you have to talk about this while I'm eating dinner?" she complained.

He continued unabashed, "Breasts were cut off. Commanders employed killing contests to boost morale. The winners of the killing games were saluted as the most savage and innovative. But the very favorite sport of some had to be performing cunnilingus and removing the clitoris with their teeth."

Jolyn shivered.

She thought momentarily and despondently of the mutilation of females practiced by the Sunnah of Mohammed. A Muslim female reporter at the paper brought it up on occasion.

Jolyn shuddered.

That reporter, Layla, had told Jolyn what they had done to her. Ablation of the clitoris as well as most of the labia minora. No anesthesia under septic conditions. The *exciseuse*, an elderly village women, did the cutting. Lying on her back, her legs wide apart and restrained by a group of helpers, Layla had been surgically violated. Abscesses and pain from damaged nerve endings long after the wound healed resulted.

"Please stop it," Jolyn demanded futilely.

"That's what I do—cut open the abdomen of a woman—and squeeze out her delicacies—and eat them. Liver is my favorite. I'm looking so forward to enjoying yours, Jolyn."

Jolyn pushed away the food.

She poured another glass of sake for herself.

"So tell me, Kurt, how many men—and women—have you killed?"

He told her.

About some of them of them.

How he murdered Aldo Martinez before he did the same to his significant other William Garcia in Jolyn's presence, and abducted her.

How he smothered to death and then ate the coed at the University of South Carolina. And he told her about the Cincinnati Bengals cheerleader. And again, about his latest, Roxanne Peterson. He critiqued the older widow Monique was a little tough, but Maryanne was quite tender.

"Oh, and that private investigator who clandestinely filmed you?" he offered, eyes gleaming.

"Gorton?"

"Yeah. I put a bullet in his head and he's lying in a shallow grave off an interstate highway."

"Oh my God."

"Exactly."

"Who was the first person you killed, Kurt?"

He told her the story of Elaine, the high school homecoming queen two years his elder. She resisted his juvenile advances and humiliated him.

First, her dog died, after becoming entangled and strangled by its chain. Her cat got hit by a car and Elaine found it in a ditch next to the driveway when she went out to check the mailbox. Elaine drowned in her parent's swimming pool after a skinny-dipping romp. The autopsy revealed she had engaged in sexual intercourse shortly before her demise. The death was ruled accidental.

"Elaine did apologize to me sincerely shortly before she passed away. So all is forgiven. Tell me, Jolyn, did you enjoy the meal?"

She shrugged.

"The food was excellent. I found the conversation somewhat lacking."

"You know, you sure are a spunky one. Under the circumstances. Well, we had dinner. Now time for a movie."

"A movie?"

"Yes, a movie. We'll watch a movie. Would you like to see *Last Cannibal World* or perhaps *Cannibal Holocaust*? I also have *Delicatessen*. Now that one is hilarious. The scenario is post-apocalyptic set entirely in a dank and gloomy building where the landlord operates a delicatessen on the ground floor. But this is a totally meatless world, so the butcher-landlord keeps his customers happy by chopping unsuspecting victims into cutlets, and he's sharpening his knife for a new tenant who has the hots for the butcher's nearsighted daughter."

"Whatever."

"And then we'll make our own movie. I'm going to make you a star."

He showed her the Elura 70 mini DV camcorder.

"Everybody wants to film me lately. I suppose you'll want me to hang up my new dress so it doesn't get wrinkled."

"Indeed. You are so perceptive. I bet you get real wild and crazy. Wouldn't want to mess the dress. But just in case you're not in the mood, I gave you something to perk you up."

"Huh?"

"A speedball. In the sake."

"Speedball—cocaine and heroin. Oh my God! You! Sondra Lewis. You killed her too."

"Yes, so I did."

"Who paid you?"

"Well, for Gorton, those two faggots Garcia and Martinez, and that Lewis whore, yes, I did receive remuneration. The other girls I mentioned I did for me. Like I'm going to do you—for me."

"*Who* paid you?" she repeated.

"Will you smile in the movie?"

"I'll smile."

"Promise?"

"I promise."

"Ron Kingston paid me."

"Dexter Curtis's agent?"

"The one and only."

"Oh my God!"

"I'm hearing an echo. Now, let's go make that movie. The dishes can wait."

"Wait! Do you think I could have dessert?"

"What would you like?"

"Vermeer Dutch Chocolate Cream liqueur over a really big scoop of chocolate-chip ice milk."

"I'd have to go shopping for that. I'm not in the mood for coupons at the moment."

"But you just might if you knew how wild and crazy chocolate makes me. Have you ever been to Martine Leventer Pechenik's boutique in Bloomingdales and had the French bitter cherries marinated in brandy? Ever been to Jacques Torres Chocolate in Brooklyn? Oh my, Confections by Michael Recchiutti in San Francisco—he features a tarragon infused cream with chocolate and butter rolled into a truffle, topped with grapefruit and dipped in bittersweet chocolate."

"Fuck chocolate. I like liver."

Redmond rose from his seat and roughly pulled Jolyn up and dragged her toward the bedroom.

She didn't protest or try to get free.

"And this better be one hell of a movie you and I star in tonight," he said with a huge grin, "or it just might be a snuff flick and you just might be on tomorrow night's menu for dinner."

Jolyn's head spun viciously and she saw multi-colored bright spots that resembled stars. She closed her eyes, thinking she was about to lose consciousness.

Redmond picked her up as if she were a feather and carried her into the bedroom.

He talked while he undressed her.

"With respect to the Aztecs, ritualistic cannibalism began early in the fourteenth century, about two hundred years before Cortez. It became more and more prevalent as the Aztec Empire expanded. Religious ceremonies closed with quite the manly meal. The prisoner walked to the sacrificial stone, a gigantic jasper block with a slightly convex surface. He or she got stretched across the stone as the priests secured his or her head, arms, and legs. Another priest opened the chest of the victim with a razor made of itztli, a flint-like substance, and inserted his hand into the wound and ripped out the still beating heart. The body of the sacrificed person was then dressed up and served banquet style to the warrior who had captured him or her. Incidentally, usually the victims had been sexually ravaged before they were killed and eaten—the captured men violated anally and the women violated in every bodily orifice."

Redmond put in *Cannibal Holocaust.*

"I'm still hungry," he said with a smirk, eyes gleaming.

She showed no fear.

His teeth drew blood.

She didn't flinch.

CHAPTER 81

The witch is dead.
The wicked witch is dead.

Dexter Curtis chanted that to himself over and over as he flipped   back and forth frantically between CNN, ESPN, and other channels trying to find morsels of information.

The news focused this morning on a fire at a night club called Armageddon in Toronto. Over a hundred people had been confirmed dead. Hundreds more had been hospitalized.

One reporter talked about indoor fireworks and dangerous flammable material that had been used as soundproofing around the stage. Another reporter said the club used a highly flammable tar substance to paint hanging ceil tiles black for ambiance. A survivor was interviewed who said the tar burned like gasoline, and dripped, burning, onto anyone underneath, like napalm.

A neighboring business owner said the nightclub was required by law to have sprinklers, but did not. One strange, rather spaced-out looking fellow who claimed he saved five people blamed it on a meth lab on the premises that blew up.

A survivor who identified herself as only Samantha spoke of the stampede to get out of the incredible inferno. The doors marked 'EXIT' had been locked, she claimed. Bodies lay motionless one atop another on the floor as those who could still move trampled on them.

"The place was a rattrap," she sobbed uncontrollably.

"How did you get out?" her interviewer questioned.

"A bartender—a guy named Dave—he knew about a window that had been boarded up. He ripped off the plywood and we climbed out. Others tried to follow, but then the roof caved in . . . and . . ."

The woman fainted.

Discussions ensued about other similar tragic fires. The Coconut Grove nightclub fire in 1942 that killed 491. The fire at the Winecoff Hotel in Atlanta that killed 119 in 1946. A fire at a dance hall in Saint-Laurent-du-Pont, France, in 1970 that killed 146 young people. In 1977 a fire at the Beverly Hills Supper Club in Southgate, Kentucky, left 167 dead. A 1990 arson fire in the illegal Happy Land Social Club in the Bronx killed 87 people. On Christmas in 2000 at least 309 people were killed in a fire at a shopping center. Most of the victims had been attending a Christmas party at an unlicensed disco in the building. And then, the most recent tragedy at The Station nightclub in West Warwick, Rhode Island.

His recognition of Kim McConnell's mother had startled Dexter Curtis.

She had appeared in several news interviews on her daughter's behalf, bashing him.

A reporter by happenstance questioned her outside a school in Toronto being utilized as a make-shift morgue.

The woman ranted hysterically.

Seemingly in shock.

She had just identified her daughter's body.

Yes, certain it was Kim.

Most of her daughter's body had been charred beyond recognition.

But not Kim's right foot with the anklet her mother had given her for her last birthday.

"The wicked witch is dead!" Dexter Curtis blurted.

He pushed the naked girl off him.

"Dexter!" she complained. "You never want to hold me and cuddle, after we do it."

"Not now, honey. The Steelers press conference is on in a few minutes."

He found the local channel.

But Coach Lowry didn't make an appearance.

No, it was the owner, Jeremiah Jones.

"We are not going to have questions today. We won a football game on Sunday. We played well. Dexter Curtis played well. But he stepped over the line. The Steelers are suspending Dexter Curtis for one game because of his part in the altercation, his ejection, and his obscene gesture directed toward the fans. He will be docked one week's pay which is far more money than any league fine would have been. In the NFL collective bargaining agreement's version of double jeopardy, a club and the league can't punish a player for the same offense, unless the NFL decides that a club's discipline is not appropriate and supercedes the club's ruling. That will not be the case in this situation, because I have discussed

241

the matter with the league before announcing this decision. I have no comment on any other matters. Rumors are running rampant as I'm sure you all are aware about other issues pertaining to Dexter Curtis. I have no intention of trying to sort all that out at this time. My deepest sympathy to those who lost loved ones in the fire in Toronto. There *are* more important things in life than football. And this is a warning to Dexter Curtis—get your act together, young man, or you will *not* be playing football for my team."

Jeremiah Jones walked solemnly away from the podium, ignoring the shouts and waving hands.

"Oh fuck him," Curtis muttered to the girl. "He's just saying what's politically correct."

"Huh?" the girl responded.

Dexter began to sing like a munchkin. "Ding dong! The witch is dead. Which old witch? The wicked witch. Ding dong! The wicked witch is dead!"

"I guess you like *The Wizard of Oz*," the girl said irritably.

She had a great body but didn't otherwise impress Dexter. He considered her a real airhead, and she bored the hell out of him except for the great sex.

"Yeah baby, my favorite movie, especially today."

"Oh my, Dexter, you're getting hard again. Something sure turned you on."

"The wicked witch is dead."

He rolled her over on her stomach and propped her behind up.

"Oh Dexter, not *that* again! I told you I don't like that. You hurt me."

"C'mon, baby, it's my lucky day. The wicked witch is dead. I'm a free man."

"What are you talking about, Dexter?"

"Didn't you listen to the news? Your mouth was sure busy but you still got ears to hear. That bitch who ratted me out and said I raped her got burned to a crisp in that nightclub fire in Toronto."

"Oh my God!"

"Yeah. I'm blessed. I'm really blessed. Thank the Lord!"

Dexter inserted the head of his penis in the girl's anus.

She jumped.

"Ouch! No, Dexter! I don't want to."

He held her by the throat with his left hand while he struggled to push his big cock further inside her with his right hand.

"Yes you do, baby, yes you do. Time for the booty dance—bone dancing in your booty. I'll take you shopping later this afternoon. Any place you want to go."

The girl sighed in resignation.

Shopping.

Diamonds. Furs.

Cruises.

Squealing like a stuck pig, she blotted it out with more pleasant thoughts.

RATTRAP

She reminds me of that McConnell bitch, was the singular thought of Dexter Curtis as he pounded away.

So he tried more than usual to hurt the girl.

But the wicked witch is dead.

I'll fuck this bitch to death.

CHAPTER 82

Jolyn woke as the sun rose.

Naked.

Him too.

His arm around her.

He looked wide awake, watching her.

"I've been waiting for your beautiful eyes to open, sleepyhead," he said softly and lovingly.

The bedroom smelled like sex.

"So tell me about your Native American heritage," he asked politely.

"Is this pillow talk?"

"Yeah."

"Okay, I'll talk. But then you talk. Fair? You asked a question. I'll answer. Then I ask a question."

"That's fine, my dear."

Jolyn told him a story. The story of her ancestors, an Irish rogue named John O'Reilly and an Iroquois princess called White Moon by the British. She gave him a Native American history lesson.

"Now you tell me, Kurt."

"Tell you what, my dear?"

"Of all the killings, which one gave you the most pleasure?"

Eerie silence for a few minutes.

"Over 3,000 years ago I was Ehud, the son of Gera, a Benjamite. With a dagger I killed Eglon, King of Moab, and I became judge of Israel. The land had rest for eighty years."

"Why did you kill this Eglon?" she asked, recalling the account in the book of Judges.

"He commanded that there be cultic homosexual prostitution in the temple of the Lord."

"Have you killed many homosexuals, Kurt?"

"Yes, many."

CHAPTER 83

His lust waned after an hour and Dexter Curtis dismissed the girl rudely.

But he did let her borrow a credit card. He laughed at how gingerly she walked.

I hope she brings it back. What the fuck was her name, anyway?"

Dexter called Ron Kingston.

"Guess you heard the good news, Ron—the wicked witch is dead!"

"Yeah, Dex, what a shame. Funny how things work out. Too bad we spent so much of your fucking money on legal and related expenses, though."

"Yeah, funny. I think I might need a second job."

"I've been talking you up for some endorsement deals. Now that you're free and clear of this rape thing, perhaps we can make something work." He laughed. "Maybe a Hummer commercial."

"Oh yeah. But I suppose that reporter bitch Knowlton will still be on my ass, anyway. I don't want any more of that crap."

"What would it be worth to you, Dex, to shut her up—permanently?"

Kingston hadn't talked to Redmond but he knew the killer had abducted Jolyn Knowlton, and if she wasn't dead yet, eventually she would be. He wasn't too pleased with how the terminations of William Garcia and Aldo Martinez had gone down. Too much attention. But everything seemed to be working out. And now he just might collect a little bonus for something Redmond was going to do anyway.

"Oh, about $100,000," Curtis replied, sounding serious.

Kingston laughed again.

"Yeah, that sounds about right. Because she could cost you a lot more than that if her mindless drivel scares off the sponsors I've been talking to. Dexter, you stay out of any more trouble, hear? And when you talk to the press, be sympathetic about the death of Kim McConnell."

"Got it, Ron. Do you think I should go to the funeral? Cry some crocodile tears?"

"Hell no, Dexter. Talk to your buddy at the *Post-Gazette*. Do an interview with him and express your condolences."

"Will do."

"Oh, and give the family some money. You can spare thousands. Considering the fact that you would have had to pay your little ass fuck Kim McConnell millions in a civil suit or settlement, even if you beat the rape rap."

"Yeah, man, I'll toss them a few crumbs. Hey, man, if you're going to put the hit on people, how about Jeremiah Jones? Fuck, he pisses me off with his holier-than-thou shit."

"Rather than have him offed, Dex, maybe I can arrange for you to be traded to the Raiders, 'eh?"

"Right on, man. I hate Pittsburgh. The city sucks. The team sucks. They would have lost to the Bengals if I hadn't kicked ass in the first half. Yeah, get me traded to the Raiders. The further I can get away from this fucking place the better I'll like it."

"One day, Dex, one day. We'll get you to California somewhere or New York. That's where the real money is. Fuck Pittsburgh."

"Yeah, fuck Pittsburgh."

CHAPTER 84

Dexter Curtis met the reporter and a cameraman outside of Emmanuel Christian Church for an interview.

The football player wore an expensive silk suit and a silver cross around his neck.

"I came to church to pray for Kim McConnell's family. May God rest her soul. I am so sorry for any pain caused her family and friends, but I did not cause the pain. I do want the world to know that I did not rape that woman. She bore false witness against me but I have forgiven her. The Lord knows the truth and she is with Him now, for judgment. I also came to pray for the others lost in the tragic fire in Toronto and their loved ones."

Recalling Jeremiah Jones's words, he added after a pause, "This is a tragic reminder that there are more important things in life than football. I sincerely apologize to the Bengals and their fans for my behavior in last Sunday's game. I just got so fired up because it was my first regular season NFL game. I accept my punishment and, again, I'm sorry for my inappropriate actions."

"Dexter, what about the steroids issue that has just surfaced regarding your association with that personal trainer in Miami?"

"Bob, I have never used steroids. I will admit that occasionally in the past I associated with persons that I should have avoided. Live and learn."

"It has been reported you are going to be subpoenaed to testify before a grand jury."

"So be it. I have nothing to hide. I would like to mention that I have taken preliminary steps to establish a scholarship at the University of Pittsburgh in the name of Kim McConnell. Also, my attorney has notified the family to send me the bill for any and all funeral expenses. "

"Dexter, what about—"

"Enough, Bob. I'm going into the church now to pray. I'll be inside for quite some time. Again, my deepest sympathy to all affected by the fire at that nightclub in Toronto."

Burn, baby, burn.

The wicked witch is dead!

Cooked to a crisp.

"Dexter—"

"That's all, Bob. Peace and love to everyone."

Curtis turned around and walked slowly into the church, head down.

Only two elderly women in front.

The reporter and cameraman didn't follow him inside.

He sat in the back.

Soon he reclined on the pew.

No, he didn't count sheep.

In a whispery voice he sang, "Ding dong! The witch is dead. Which old witch? The wicked witch. Ding dong! The wicked witch is dead!"

Soon he snored.

CHAPTER 85

Love is blind.

Nathan Redmond thought he might be in love with Jolyn Knowlton. It had never happened to him before.

But still, she would have to die.

One more night of heaven, he mused.

Yes, and then she must die.

He thrived on their conversations, and found himself hanging on her every word. And the other—the other had been incredible—the best by far he had ever experienced. Just the mere touch of her flesh sent what felt like electrical current surging through his body.

But she must die. Tonight.

Redmond had bought her several more new outfits and accessories. After all, she hadn't had time to pack for the trip in the trunk.

Tonight he asked her to wear the Emma Black beaded silk chiffon asymmetrical dress.

Kurt served the wine.

"Picked this up on my last visit to New York."

To kill Sondra Lewis.

She took a sip.

"Rich blackberry flavor," she observed approvingly. "Soft, silky texture."

"1997 Terrazas de los Andes Gran Malbec. To be paired with grilled red meat. So they told me at The Tasting Room in Long Island where I bought it. Along with a bottle of 2001 Catena Chardonnay. Crisp and fresh, with pear and apple aromas. Recommended with grilled seafood. We'll save that for the halibut tomorrow night. Pine nut crusted halibut served with basil emulsion and roasted fingerling potatoes. "

But you won't be with us tomorrow night, my dear. I'll be dining alone. And it won't be halibut. It will be your liver.

Jolyn didn't see him pour it. He brought two full glasses and the bottle from the kitchen.

"Did you put anything in the wine, Kurt? You don't need to get me stoned. I've done what you wanted."

"No speedballs this time. I do like you better straight."

"What is heroin, exactly? I'm not much of a druggie."

"The poppy seeds of the papaver have been cultivated enthusiastically for at least five thousand years—opium."

Redmond explained that that it was a word derived from the Greek word for 'the juice of a plant.' This highly narcotic milky fluid—opium—is extracted from the plant's ovary. Almost two hundred years ago the different substances in opium began to be isolated. Morphine, named after Morpheus the Greek god of sleep, was extracted by Frederick Serturner in 1806. Then Robiquent gave us codeine in 1832 and Merck gave us paverine in 1848.

He continued enthusiastically and informed Jolyn that when morphine is heated with acetic acid anhydrides in water free conditions, two acetic acid molecules combine with the morphine molecule to form diacetylmorphine. This substance was first synthesized under the name Heroin. Because heroin is more fat soluble than morphine it works faster but for a shorter time. Heroin was originally intended to combat morphine addiction and morphine was originally intended to combat opium addiction.

"Talk about a vicious circle," Jolyn commented repulsively. "So what *did* you put in my drink, Kurt?"

"Just beetle juice."

"Beetle juice?"

"The emerald green blister beetle—Lytta Vesicatoria—more commonly known as Spanish Fly. That was the date rape drug of choice in the old days and the arsenic substitute. The story goes that Livia, the wife of Octavian, used the drug to poison heirs so her son from a previous marriage, Tiberius, would become emperor. Another famous fan of Spanish Fly was the Marquis de Sade. You have heard of him, Jolyn."

So that's how he's going to kill me—poison.

"Now *him* I know. I saw the play *120 Songs for the Marquis de Sade*. It's an opera and opened with a guy strutting across the stage nude except for pink heels and an albino wig. He looked like William Garcia, also known as Rose, who you murdered."

"All in a day's work, Jolyn. But we already discussed that. The Marquis de Sade used the aphrodisiac in question to entice young ladies to participate in his orgies. Unfortunately, he occasionally used a little too much and poisoned his playthings. Cantharidin is the poisonous substance in the pulverized beetles. Normally two grams will result in a fatality within a few hours."

"I don't need an aphrodisiac, now do I, Kurt? Did you put something in my wine? Just tell me the truth, please."

"No, nothing in the wine, Jolyn. Yes, you have been rather . . . *cooperative*, under the circumstances."

But you still must die.

You saw my face.

You saw me kill.

They dined on grilled filet mignon served over a roasted garlic orzo cake topped with a wild mushroom Dunkel sauce. A vegetable medley on the side.

"The filet mignon is delicious, Kurt, though perhaps a tad on the rare side. No red meat delicatessen cannibal jokes this evening?"

He looked pensive.

He's not going to poison me. No, I think he has something far more sinister in mind.

"Maybe I should take you on a trip, Jolyn. You know, a vacation. Would you like that? Perhaps you'd like to go to Hanauma Bay on the Hawaiian island of Oahu? Hanauma Bay is the only beach in the country where you can swim with a multitude of colorful tropical fish in clear, waist-deep water with a fine, white sandy bottom. It's one of the few beaches in the country formed in a volcanic cone, making for incredible scenery."

He's planning to kill me tonight, Jolyn realized at that moment.

"That sounds wonderful, Kurt."

Jolyn thought of some of the beautiful places Stephen had mentioned, and wondered if she would ever get to see them. Keukenhof in Lisa, Holland. Seventy acres of bulbs in bloom featuring hyacinths, squills, daffodils, and of course, tulips by the tens of thousands. Kirstenboch in Cape Town, the National Botanical Garden of South Africa. Ninety acres of lilies, agapanthus, nerines, and thousands of other species.

Will I ever smell the exotic aroma of a beautiful flower again?

Did Stephen go on his vacation to Princess Grace Rose Garden in Monaco?

I don't think so. He's looking for me.

"Or perhaps you'd like to see Michelangelo's *The Last Judgement* at the Sistine Chapel or *Christ Enthroned in Majesty* at the Church of Santa Pudenziana in Rome?"

"Perhaps. I didn't know *you* had a passion for Christ."

"Christianity's most fundamental ritual, the Eucharist, is symbolic endocannibalism; the consumption of the body and blood of 'Our Father's Son.' Is it not?"

Jolyn, about to take one last bite of the filet mignon, set her fork on her plate and pushed it away.

"What is that emblem on your tie?" she asked, attempting to avoid the possibility of another one-sided discussion of cannibalism.

She wanted to prolong conversation, but not on that subject. The more he talked, the longer would be delayed the moment of truth which surely would come soon. But not before he had his way with her one last time.

"The emblem," Redmond explained, "is actually a seal. The figure on the seal can best be described as a lion's whelp with a serpent's tail. It is my family's seal. I was Easamhuin Eamhua, the king of Ireland about two thousand years ago. I married a king's daughter from a foreign land, the one known as Tea Tephi. That comely lass was brought from a foreign land to Ireland by her elderly guardian, who was known as Ollam Folla, the prophet."

"Do you want me to guess who the Ollam Folla was, or should I be quiet?"

"Please be quiet, Jolyn," Redmond requested politely. "Tea Tephi, the name, has Hebrew origins, and means 'little one of fragrant beauty.' The little one, the tender twig of Ezekiel's riddle, perhaps?"

"Perhaps." Jolyn couldn't refrain from speaking tauntingly. "Perhaps Tea Tephi was the prophet Jeremiah's granddaughter and King Zedekiah's daughter. Perhaps. But then, Jeremiah was actually Saint Patrick and drove all the snakes out of Ireland. And I'm the Virgin Mary."

Taken back a bit by her blatant sarcasm, Redmond now sought to change the subject.

"The Virgin Mary? You should have been a preacher instead of a reporter. Well, enough about my family seal, which you, Jolyn, seem to view somewhat skeptically with respect to its reputed historical significance. Obviously you are already familiar with . . . the legend. Let us talk about something else."

"No, Kurt, I want to know about your family. I apologize for being rude."

"Apology accepted, dearest Jolyn. My family?"

"Yes, your family, Kurt."

"Can we save that for pillow talk?"

"I had something else in mind for pillow talk."

Her smile convinced him.

Oh, how I will miss that smile, he bemoaned.

"My father, now deceased, was a charismatic minister and televangelist. Speaking in tongues, healing, exorcizing demons, and that sort of thing. He and the elders of his church put hands on me many times, rebuking the Devil and demanding that the evil spirits depart from me. You don't really want to know how he eventually died, but because of him I became obsessed with death."

"What about death interests you so?" Jolyn prodded.

"Well, let's talk about ancient embalming techniques—now *that* is fascinating."

Redmond gave a discourse. Embalming took place in the mummification process in the necropolis of Alexandria. Natron, a natural salt compound consisting of mainly sodium carbonate and bicarbonate, was the most important substance used to absorb moisture from the corpse. Part of the brain was removed through the nostrils with a crooked iron. They destroyed the rest with caustic acid. Preserving certain internal organs was of utmost concern. More perishable organs such as the lungs, stomach, intestines, and liver were removed and placed in canopic jars.

He howled.

"And what do you find so funny now?" she asked.

"I don't need canopic jars. Roxanne Peterson's perishable organs, at least the most delectable ones, are in the freezer at my place of business. Do you know the story of Sawney Bean?"

"No I don't think so, Kurt."

"Alexander 'Sawney' Bean," he began, "was born near Edinburgh during the time of King James."

Redmond eagerly elucidated that Sawney moved to County Galloway and he and his wife near the shore. They had many children and grandchildren, all the result of incest. He robbed passers-by and the victims became dinner. The family dragged the bodies back to the cave, had a snack, and pickled the rest for later. They had so much meat they threw much of it away in the sea.

He looked for a reaction and Jolyn appeared slightly nauseous.

So he continued, "Severed limbs and body parts that washed up on the shore alarmed the local community and—"

"Stop it, Kurt!" Jolyn demanded.

"Oh, are you giving the orders now?" he responded insolently.

"You promised dessert," she said, hopefully.

They finished dinner off with a deep, dark chocolate sabayon and chocolate sponge cake finished with fresh raspberries he made especially or Jolyn, after hearing her 'complain' about her addiction on several occasions.

"So tell me an amusing story about your Native American heritage, Jolyn. Entertain me."

Yes, entertain you. Give me a brief reprieve from what you have in mind for me soon—Satan, sin, and death.

"Would you like to hear the real story of Thanksgiving, Kurt, from the Native American perspective?"

He nodded.

She informed him that Thanksgiving has been a white man's lie for well over three hundred years. It was murder. In Connecticut in 1637 the colonial militia surrounded a Pequot village and attacked just before dawn. More than 700 Pequot including women and children were slaughtered. The militia celebrated with great joy after the massacre and convinced Governor Bradford to declare by law this deplorable incident a day of celebration and thanksgiving. The story of the Thanksgiving dinner in 1621 with the Pilgrims was hogwash, she concluded.

"Enlightening story, Jolyn. Thank you. Now it's time for the white eyes to have his way with the squaw."

"Squaw is not a nice word. Shame on you, Kurt. The etymology of the word is Algonquin, and has the connotation of whore or female genitalia. Am I a whore?"

Yes, I am a whore—the Devil's whore—tonight.

Redmond didn't answer in words.

He took her to the bedroom.

"Come, Jolyn, it is time for you to please me. You do please me, you know. Very much. More than anyone ever has before. Maybe I'll just keep you around for awhile."

No, I think not, they both ruminated.

Redmond had finally agreed to remove the leg irons. So she could spread her legs wider and wrap them around him, she had suggested. But not the cuffs. No, they would stay on he insisted adamantly.

"Why don't you minister to me, lovely little preacher lady? Then we'll fix your 'Virgin Mary' problem."

He began to remove her dress.

"What message would you like to hear, Kurt? 'Thou shalt not kill,' perhaps? Or 'thou shalt not commit adultery' perhaps?"

"Just give me the naked truth." He guffawed as she willingly let him slip her dress off.

"The peril of adultery. 'For the lips of an immoral woman drip honey, and her mouth is smoother than oil; but in the end she is bitter as wormwood.' Proverbs 5, verses 3 and 4."

"What is wormwood if I may ask?"

"Four varieties of wormwood are found in Palestine. One is Artemisia Nilotica. I can't seem to recall the other three at the moment. No matter. Wormwood is used metaphorically to reflect extreme bitterness, like that of the wormwood plant."

"But you're not bitter to me, Jolyn. No, you are sweet. Sweat meat. I'm going to eat you."

He began to taste her breasts.

"What were the names of the girls you ate, Kurt? Do you remember?"

"Some I remember. The last one, Roxanne Peterson, I remember. I told you about her, didn't I? That's my wife's name—Roxanne."

"Did you kill her too?"

"No. She's still alive. No need to kill her. I married for money. Had to get a grubstake somewhere after I got out of prison. She's older than I am. Much older. But not richer—not any more. My wife is a vegetable in a nursing home. You're my wife tonight, Jolyn. Submit to your husband. Now, *that* is biblical."

Redmond pushed Jolyn on the bed on her back.

Adultery is death.

He took her hard and fast.

Adultery is death.

Missionary position.

Adultery is death.

Afterwards, she cuddled him and gently traced the tattoo on his chest.

"Let me give you a massage, Kurt."

"I'd like that, Jolyn."

"You might un-cuff me. I could do it better."

"No, I don't think so."

Jolyn began smoothing down Redmond's back muscles on both sides, using equal pressure with her fingers and the heels of her hands along his shoulders and neck. She moved along his side, faced him, and repeated the long smoothing strokes, going slightly deeper with each pass. Next she split her index finger and middle finger, placing her hand over his spine, with each of her fingers in the groove between the spine and Erector Spinae muscles, putting her right hand over her left hand and gently manipulating the area.

"Roll over, Kurt." He did. Her fingers traced the tattoo again. "Tell me about the wolf. Have you read *Stewed, Screwed and Tattooed* by Madame Chinchilla?"

"No . . . can't say that I have read that. But it sounds interesting."

Jolyn's fingers moved from his chest to his abdomen.

"Kurt, you're my big bad Wolfie. I like *bad* boys. And you are *very* bad, Wolfie. I could fall in love with you, Wolfie."

"I could fall in love with you, Jolyn. But love is but a fleeting moment. Death, of course, is more of a permanent relationship."

"So tell me about the tattoo, Kurt."

"Tebori. Tebori is the Japanese word for hand tattooing practiced there for more than four centuries. Tattooing has a very long history in Japan dating back to 5,000 BC or older. I won't bore you with all the history, but tattooing in Japan became illegal. The yakuza relished tattooing because it was illegal and enhanced their reputation as outlaws."

He paused.

"And . . . ?" she encouraged.

"I did several murders in prison for the yakuza. In return, they honored me by giving me this tebori—the wolf—the predator."

Her hands moved lower.

His softness became hardness.

She had him in another frenzy in minutes.

"Let me get on top, Kurt," she whispered.

She did.

Just as he seemed ready to explode again, she pulled herself up off him and ministered to him with her mouth.

"Oh my God, oh my God," he moaned over and over.

And then she bit him.

Hard.

Gnawing on him and shaking her head like a tiger ravaging a piece of meat.

Jolyn then, still refusing to let go of his manhood with her teeth, managed to spray the foam contraceptive in his eyes she had begged him to let her use.

She had asked him to buy the product.

He had asked why, in that he planned to kill her.

She replied that maybe he would change his mind.

He laughed, but did as she asked. Only because Jolyn had pleased him, and intrigued him, because she did not seem afraid of death like the others.

Blinded momentarily but still under control, he pulled her hair and punched at her head until she released her grip.

Jolyn jumped and ran.

Naked.

Into the woods behind the cottage.

CHAPTER 86

The lady in red.

The dead lady in red, Detective Ed Woods contemplated, pulling the picture from his jacket pocket.

He ambled into the *Tribune-Review* office to speak with Stephen Winslow. The editor sat in Jolyn Knowlton's cubicle, apparently searching for something.

"Stephen, I have news," the detective greeted, looking morose.

"Concerning Jolyn?"

They had already talked on the phone about the death of Kim McConnell in the tragic fire at the nightclub in Toronto. Woods had lamented that Dexter Curtis received a "get out of jail" free card. Much like those who gang raped his late daughter beat the rap because the body of evidence mysteriously disappeared. The body of evidence in the Dexter Curtis had turned into a charred corpse. Kim McConnell could no longer testify against her rapist.

"The pictures you're having one of your people work up on Aldo Martinez dressed as a woman?"

"Yeah, Ed?"

"Make 'her' outfit red. And long ash blonde hair with bangs. Like this."

Woods handled Winslow the picture.

"Damn," was all the editor could utter.

The detective continued, "Some kids on dirt bikes saw an arm sticking out of the ground. Probably pulled out of the shallow grave by some varmints."

"Where?"

"Just off I-79 between Pittsburgh and the West Virginia line. The bullet in Martinez's head matched the ones in his significant other, Garcia."

"Your theory *is*, Ed?"

"Well, I won't jump the gun until we show the 'new' pictures at Le Pommier, but . . ."

"But . . . ?"

"I'm going to guess that our perp had a dinner date with Martinez. After killing Martinez and burying him, the perp went to the residence and—"

Winslow, interrupting, continued the train of thought with, "And then killed Garcia, an act which Jolyn witnessed. So the perp abducted her."

"Yes."

"I wonder why the perp didn't just kill her at the scene."

"Yes, I wonder."

"But you still have no leads regarding her whereabouts?"

"No, I don't. Do you?"

Winslow shook his head indicating not.

"But I'll tell you this, Ed—*this* is all tied to Dexter Curtis somehow. William Garcia, also known as Rose, was wounded outside that bar where Dexter Curtis also got shot. Jolyn had been pursuing the connection between Garcia and Curtis."

"You know, Stephen, Curtis may have beaten the rape charges because of the victim Kim McConnell's horrific and untimely death. But maybe we can get him on something else—like conspiracy to commit murder. Maybe we can still trap a rat."

"I just hope, Ed, it's not Jolyn's murder."

CHAPTER 87

Cassie Forrester had suffered minor smoke inhalation during the fire and stampede at the Armageddon in Toronto.

She was treated at a hospital overnight and released the next morning.

Cassie sat in the living room of her late friend Kim McConnell's living room. She talked with Kim's mother, stepfather, brother Duane, friend Alyssa Davis, and an attorney representing the family. A dreadful atmosphere to say the least.

Ambulance chasers had contacted many of the victims' families as soon as names of the deceased had been released. Apparently Kim's family intended to at least entertain the possibility of a wrongful death suit. The attorney said that the preliminary body of evidence was overwhelming that the owners of the club are corporate white trash who deserve to suffer for their sins and spend a lifetime trying to atone for the blood on their hands.

Duane McConnell offered to take Cassie home. She had walked the ten blocks to the house and it had begun to rain.

"Did you see my sister's body?" Duane asked on the way.

"No, I couldn't. Your mother identified her remains."

"My poor mother. Poor Kim."

"I loved Kim," Cassie whispered. "I really loved her."

"We all did, Cassie. We all did."

Duane pulled into a parking place in front of Cassie's apartment building.

"You don't have to park, Duane. Just drop me in front."

"I'm coming in with you, Cassie."

"No, Duane, I don't think so. I really—"

He pressed the tip of the knife against the bottom of her chin.

***

Juanita Curtis sat on the porch at her parent's home talking with her mother.

"I'm going to divorce him, Mama. Sooner or later. He cheats, and he cheats, and he cheats. And then he lies, and he lies, and he lies."

"Maybe once you have the baby that will make a difference."

"Yeah, right. I'm going to get his money before he blows it all on dope and legal hassles."

"Well, he doesn't have to worry about that McConnell woman any longer."

"No—now he has to worry about me."

***

Ron Kingston called Jeremiah Jones, majority owner of the Pittsburgh Steelers, to express his disdain for the suspension of Dexter Curtis.

"Jeremiah, the league wouldn't have suspended him. You are really putting the screws to him financially. At a time when he has mounting legal and related expenses."

"His comments in front of that church nauseated me, Kingston. Dexter Curtis nauseates me. The body of evidence brought before me regarding this man is that he is a morally bankrupt apostate."

"What's an apostate, exactly?"

Jones, a devout fundamentalist Christian did not suffer apostates gladly.

"A tare among the wheat. One who breaks the commandments while accusing others of doing so. Curtis is the ultimate hypocrite. The tattoo on his arm of Psalm 27 is blasphemous."

"Why don't you trade him then?"

"I just might, Kingston. I just might."

"The Raiders need a linebacker."

"Maybe I'll trade him to the synagogue of Satan."

Jones hung up on Kingston.

He picked up the article Randy McDougall had written in the *Tribune-Review*. Hector DelMonte, according to a report the newspaper had obtained, told federal investigators he gave steroids to nearly thirty famous athletes. DelMonte had voluntarily given the names of the athletes to an Internal Revenue investigator. DelMonte's lawyers confirmed that in the IRS report, DelMonte was quoted as saying he provided steroids to high-profile athletes. But his lawyers claimed the statements attributed to DelMonte were fabrications and he made no such admissions.

Jones reviewed the list of athletes named again. Two Yankees. Several medal winners at the 2000 Olympics. Four current Oakland Raiders and one of their former players. He was somewhat surprised he didn't see the name Dexter Curtis.

But yes, he reasoned, *Dexter Curtis should wear the silver and black.*

CHAPTER 88

Jeremiah Jones summoned Coach Bill Lowry to his office.

"Bill, I just might get in touch with that maverick owner of the Raiders and attempt to negotiate a trade for Dexter Curtis."

"What? But—"

"We wouldn't get much. Maybe a few low round draft choices."

Jones of course knew he only had a couple weeks until the trade deadline. And he of course knew that if he traded Curtis, his entire pro-rated salary cap number would be charged to the new team immediately, which made making trades during the season so difficult.

"But why, Jeremiah? He had a great game against Cincinnati."

"Yes, until he got ejected just before the end of the first half. I have enough problems, Bill. What with the coercion suit."

A diehard Steelers fan had initiated a lawsuit alleging taxpayers in National Football League cities have been unfairly coerced into paying more than $3.5 billion to build new stadiums. The plaintiff sought $200 million in punitive damages from the NFL and its 32 teams, and triple that amount if antitrust violations were found. The lawsuit cited the case of the Pittsburgh Steelers new stadium. The team contributed less than half the $281 million cost of Heintz Field, but reaps most of the financial benefit from it, the lawsuit charged.

"Jeremiah, we *need* Dexter Curtis. You saw what a difference he can make."

"Okay, Bill—one more chance. If this guy screws up one more time, I'll cut him if I can't find someone who will take him."

"Right, Jeremiah. I'll talk to him."

"You do that. But talk is cheap with that pretend believer. A true Christian is one who fears God. 'The fear of the LORD is to hate evil: pride, and arrogancy,

263

and the evil way, and the froward mouth, do I hate.' Proverbs 8:13. Can you put the fear of God into that man, Bill?"

CHAPTER 89

Coach Lowry hadn't been able to find Dexter Curtis. He left half dozen messages on his voice mail.

Curtis had taken a flight home to Miami when he heard the news of his one game suspension.

Lowry turned on ESPN and began to read a newspaper.

After about fifteen minutes he heard *the* name mentioned.

Dexter Curtis.

Curtis had gone to Lario's restaurant on South Beach and saw his wife having lunch with another man. According to police, Curtis picked up a chair and used it to hit the man over the head, and then turned and kicked and punched his wife. He now sat in Miami-Dade County Jail, charged with battery, aggravated battery, and resisting arrest with violence.

CHAPTER 90

Jolyn Knowlton wouldn't talk.

Not yet.

She had conditions.

"They" had no choice but to play the game by her rules.

After escaping from Redmond and the cottage, Jolyn had made her way through the woods and eventually to the lake.

In nothing but handcuffs.

The father and teenaged son fished off a pier.

Two beautiful golden retrievers lounged in the sun on the bank. They rose and barked as she approached.

"Close your eyes, Ryan," the father insisted as he put a blindfold over his son's eyes with his hands.

The teenager pushed his father's hands away.

Ryan, a strapping seventeen-year-old high school basketball and football star, stood a head above his father.

"I don't think so, Dad. You don't see many heavenly angels these days, except in movies and magazines. This ought to be good."

"But she's—"

"Hey Dad, now you know how Tom Hanks felt in *Splash*."

Jolyn began running toward them frantically.

"I was abducted by a serial killer!" she cried. "He's most likely following me, Do you have any weapons?" she asked, breathless.

"We have fishing poles and filet knives," the father responded, more shocked than she.

"She's telling the truth I think, Dad," Ryan observed. "Let's get her back to the cabin. We got the shotguns and rifles. And my cell phone."

They got her back to the cabin in about fifteen minutes.

"The dogs will alert us if anyone comes close," Ryan noted for Jolyn's benefit.

Ryan and his father loaded the Mossberg shotguns and Ruger 77/22 varmint rifle.

"What's your name?" Ryan had asked her.

"Jolyn Knowlton. Yours?"

"Ryan Hamilton." He pointed. "My dad—please don't call him Daddy unless you put some clothes on—my Mom wouldn't like it—he's Joe."

"Well, Ryan, you could have given me your shirt. It would cover what your father is concerned about you seeing."

"Yes, I could have, Jolyn. But I'm not stupid. Ask my dad. I'm going to be valedictorian of my high school class. Tell me, Jolyn, what beauty pageant did you escape from?"

"Oh, I'm sorry, Jolyn," the father said as he took off his shirt and handed it to her.

She put it on.

"Let me at least split those handcuffs for you, Jolyn," Ryan offered.

He led her outside and put her hands on a large flat rock. His father held the sharp wedge for splitting logs on the middle link between the cuffs and Ryan separated them with one heavy blow from a sledge hammer.

"Thanks, Ryan."

"You're welcome, Jolyn. Here's my cell phone. I didn't take it with me to the pier because the battery needed charged. We know all the local cops. Do you want me to call?"

"I'm going to call a detective in Pittsburgh first. He'll alert the local authorities."

Jolyn made the call.

While they waited the three talked about fishing.

Ryan and Joe talked of their trip to Henry's Fork, near Last Chance, Idaho, considered by many to be America's greatest trout stream. And to Natalilok Bay, Alaska, and the ocean-fresh silver salmon. And to the Au Sable River in Michigan and Armstrong's Spring Creek.

Jolyn mentioned a fishing expedition of her own in Israel, which enthralled the father and son. She and Zeke stayed at a villa near Tel Aviv. They did the Hamei Yoav sulfur spa and the pristine Nitzanim beach. And fished for carp at a small lake adjoining the villa's property.

She didn't tell them all.

The fish were biting.

Fishing seemed to relax her and often she did her best thinking with a pole in the water.

The owner of the villa let them borrow his boat.

Zeke had cast a line there before.

"This is my favorite spot, my honey hole," he told her. "Never have I failed to catch couple big ones here. You'll see. Fishing in the middle of the afternoon on a hot, sunny, windy day is simply the best no matter what the so-called experts say. I'll be darned if I'm getting up at 4:00 A.M., anyway. Besides, we are less likely to be spotted at this time of day. Don't want anyone sharing my honey hole, you know. No one but you, Jolyn."

"Thank you, Zeke, I feel honored," she had beamed. "Why is the fishing better on a day like this?"

He had explained that the wind and the waves break up the water surface and stir up the life and sediment in the water. The wind moves around their food supply and thus the fish are more active. They move from shallow to deeper water when the surface temperature is hot, like in the middle of the afternoon on a day like this was.

"I wouldn't be fishing here at night or early in the morning. You should be much closer to shore then."

"Well, let's fish, Zeke!" She had said. "It's been years for me. What are we fishing for?"

Funny, how I can remember vividly every word of our conversations in the brief time we spent together.

The fishing expedition occurred before she and Zeke had become sexually intimate. But soon afterwards they did. Now she thought about how she had just "willingly" given herself to the first man since Zeke. A man whose real name she didn't know.

Adultery is death.

"We're fishing for carp," Zeke had responded.

Jolyn removed the white T-shirt and jean cutoffs she had been wearing, displaying a red and white striped halter bikini.

"Nice suit!" he had observed, quite appreciatively, looking at her just a little differently than he had before.

"I heard that red and white are the colors that best attract fish. Else why the red and white lures in your tackle box?"

"Actually, we're using doughballs for bait. Yellow cornmeal mixed with water, vanilla, honey, and sugar."

An hour later they had absolutely no bites and they both seemed a little bored.

"I'm going to do a little sunbathing," she had said. "Maybe take a nap."

"Whatever," Zeke had replied nonchalantly, "but don't think you are eating any fish you didn't catch yourself, young lady."

"Whatever yourself, Zeke. I have you wrapped around my little finger and you'll do anything I want. So hurry up and catch some carp, will ya? I'm getting hungry."

Jolyn took the suntan lotion from her bag and applied it to the front of her body as she lay in the back of the boat. Zeke sat on the edge of the boat near the front. He seemed to be paying much more attention to her than he did the water and what might be in it.

About an hour later Jolyn stirred and turned over on her stomach and groggily undid the crossover string that tied in the back of the halter top. Zeke had got quite bug-eyed.

"Zeke, would you please take a break for a few minutes and put some suntan lotion on my back?" she had purred. "I don't want to get burnt to a crisp."

He had dutifully complied, rubbing lotion gently on her long legs also, without being asked. She fell asleep again while he lingered administering the lotion.

When Jolyn woke again she saw that Zeke had caught three carp, each about two foot long.

"Yes!" she had squealed. "I'm starving. Let's eat!"

"Not just yet, my dear. Let's see if we can catch a few more while they are biting. I'm beginning to like this fishing . . . and bikini watching. Why don't you try again?"

"Okay," Jolyn had agreed and jumped up quickly and grabbed her rod.

But she neglected to faster the halter top.

"Jolyn! You forgot something!" Zeke had observed, in shock and admiration."

"Oh well, why bother now?" she had asked coyly. "You've already seen them."

"You did that on purpose!"

"Who, me? Yes, I did do it on purpose."

"Why?"

"I'm not sure. Perhaps I'm making a point. Just don't ask me what that might be."

I am evil.

The dogs barked.

CHAPTER 91

The arrival of the group in three vehicles, one behind the other, had suspended the brief interlude of memories. Now Jolyn had to deal with the more recent horrific episodes.

Now three hours later, Detective Ed Woods, her editor Stephen Winslow, P.I. Larry Dodd, local Police Chief Jim Hamm, and FBI Special Agent Mike Fitzgerald sat around the picnic table in the cabin. Ryan and his father had gone home, asking only that they lock up when they leave.

Jolyn had run to Stephen and embraced him tightly.

Then she had hugged and kissed both Ryan and Joe on the cheek when they departed, saying, "You guys are the best. I'll be calling."

Jolyn had declined any medical treatment or rape crisis counseling.

"I wasn't raped," she stated serenely. "I will say my feet are killing me. Just glad I spend a lot of time barefoot."

She winked at Stephen.

He smiled, recalling when Jolyn kicked off her shoes at her apartment and said she picked up the rugs because she loved the feel of the wood on her bare feet. That's also why she didn't like to wear stockings or pantyhose so she said. Stephen couldn't help but wish he would have been there when she descended on the two fishermen.

Ryan had met the cars in the driveway and told them, "The pretty lady ran through the woods up to us at the pier in nothing but handcuffs. She said a serial killer had kidnapped her and she escaped. I think she's telling the truth!"

"What *did* happen, Jolyn?" Detective Woods asked.

The detective had informed Jolyn before they sat down to talk that her abductor had torched the cottage where she had been held captive and apparently fled. No fingerprints or similar evidence would likely be found.

"I didn't want to tell this story a dozen times. Once, just once."

She grew silent and reflective.

"Have you been drinking, Detective Woods?"

"No." He told the truth. "But I think I need one. To take the edge off us finding you alive. I've been talking with your girlfriend, the addictions counselor. We did make a deal. You did keep Gorton on the line. I just wish I knew what you said."

"How would you like some panties with me in them?"

"Huh?" Stephen uttered.

"That's what I said to Gorton, among other things. Talking sex with that pervert turned out to be worth the effort, now didn't it? Detective Woods caught him with his hand in the cookie jar. Or rather, talking on the phone with me while he played with the panties he pilfered from my apartment."

Jolyn began to cry a little, more out of relief than anything else.

"Well, are you going to tell us what happened?" the FBI agent, Fitzgerald snapped.

"Maybe I'll insist you leave," she retorted calmly. "Do you want to catch this serial killer or not? Maybe without my help you'll find him after a dozen or so more murders."

He scowled, but remained silent.

"Go ahead, Jolyn," Woods encouraged.

Jolyn told all.

Almost.

The sexual aspects she left to their imaginations, although Fitzgerald pressed the issue.

"What about the sex?" he kept asking. "He claimed to have had sex with these other victims, so you said. What about with you?"

She glared at him until he backed off.

"Where would you suggest we start looking for your kidnapper?" Fitzgerald asked.

"He's very careful about disguising his real identity," she responded. "But then, he never thought I would live to tell. You'll just be wasting time trying to trace him on the car and the cottage. I believe he has many aliases. Concentrate on Ron Kingston. You'll find this killer somewhere in Kingston's past."

"You don't know what part of what this guy who called himself Kurt is truth and what part if fiction," the FBI agent observed.

"I know what he looks like. He said he killed Aldo Martinez, in addition to Martinez's significant other, William Garcia, also known as Rose. He—"

"We found Martinez's body, Jolyn," Detective Woods interrupted. Just off I-79 between Pittsburgh and the West Virginia line. An arm stuck out of the shallow grave and some kids on dirt bikes saw it. Same gun as killed Garcia. Your fingerprints on it, incidentally."

"So I'm a suspect?" She raised an eyebrow.

"Of course not," Woods replied. "The killer had some fiendish scheme in mind, but apparently that went haywire when you witnessed the murder of Garcia."

"Yes, back to the murders," she said. "Kurt, or whatever his real name is, said he killed Hank Gorton and dumped his body off an interstate highway. Most likely near Chicago, since Detective Woods said that's where Gorton was last seen. Kurt said he killed Sondra Lewis for which Kingston paid him. He said he killed a young woman named Roxanne Peterson recently. He said he killed a Cincinnati Bengals cheerleader named Lauralee. He said he killed a University of South Carolina coed. Not only did he kill these women, Kurt claimed he ate some of them. Maryanne, the tender one, and Monique, the tough one."

"Cannibalism?" a startled Stephen Winslow blurted.

"That's what he said," Jolyn reaffirmed. "Kurt also said when in high school he killed a popular girl named Elaine who gave him the brush-off."

"What else?" the FBI agent asked.

"Kurt's father is or was a minister and his wife is in a nursing home. He said his wife's name is Roxanne, like one of his victims. Oh, and Kurt has a tattoo of a wolf on his chest."

"Why do you suppose he killed Garcia and Martinez?" Fitzgerald questioned.

"A better question might be why did Ron Kingston pay him to kill those two," Woods spat sarcastically, irritated by the FBI agent's mannerisms and tone of his voice.

"Kurt or whatever his name is killed Garcia and Martinez because of their link to the Dexter Curtis case I do believe," Jolyn rejoined. "He also confessed to me he has killed many homosexuals, but didn't name names."

Stephen added, "The killer had dinner with Aldo Martinez at Le Pommier before he killed him. Martinez dressed as a woman. Larry showed pictures at the restaurant. According to their waiter, the killer referred to Martinez as Sarah and she called him James."

"Yes," Woods continued for him, "and Stephen and I believe Gorton and Martinez engaged in a scheme to blackmail Hawkins, our former district attorney. That's why the D.A. resigned."

Jolyn nodded with, "And Rose, William Garcia, got shot in the parking lot of Reggie's Fat City that night, along with Curtis and the others. Poor Rose never got the chance to tell me exactly what that was all about, but let's guess sex or drugs. Maybe Curtis raped Rose like he did Kim McConnell."

She couldn't quite read the strange looks on their faces.

"We have plenty to start with," Detective Woods observed.

Stephen agreed, "We wanted leads. We got leads."

"Who are you, Larry?" Jolyn asked. "I heard Stephen introduce you, but who are you working for."

"For me," Stephen responded. "I hired him to help find you."

"Thank you, Stephen," she acknowledged. "And I guess you cancelled your vacation."

"Postponed."

Jolyn reached across the table and touched his hand fondly.

"So what's the latest on the Dexter Curtis case?"she inquired.

No one wanted to respond.

Finally, Stephen spoke, but hesitantly.

"There is no longer a 'Dexter Curtis case.' At least not on the rape allegations. Kim McConnell is dead. Killed in a fire at a nightclub in Toronto."

"Oh my God!" she deplored.

Winslow told her what he knew of the matter. About how Kim and her girlfriend Cassie had gone to Niagra Falls to get away. That they decided to go up to Toronto for this big party. How a meth lab in the basement apparently blew up.

Jolyn bowed her head and prayed.

When she lifted her head, Detective Woods added, "I don't suppose you watched much TV or read many newspapers. Dexter Curtis played against Cincinnati, most of the first half anyway. He was ejected for fighting and suspended for a game by the owner of the Steelers. Now he has been arrested for an altercation with some guy he found with his wife. No, not in bed—in a restaurant."

"Curtis did his booty dance in the game, several times," Stephen commented disgustedly.

"I want to go home," Jolyn said softly, and sighed. "I'm tired. All this is catching up with me."

She began to cry again.

"Not to your apartment, Jolyn," Stephen insisted. "The killer could be...uh...you are a witness to crimes he has committed—the only witness."

"Yes—the only witness. Maybe I'm the bait. The bait to trap a rat. You use doughballs to catch carp. Maybe you use me to catch a psychotic serial killer, who murders for both money and pleasure."

Stephen merely shook his head, perplexed.

***

Nathan Redmond knew he couldn't go back to any places linked to his real identity. They would soon know. Jolyn Knowlton had too much information. He had to go totally underground, which wouldn't be that difficult because he had prepared for the possibility. Although he never imagined it would happen like this.

But that woman will pay.
Yes, I will kill her.
And I will devour her flesh.

CHAPTER 92

The late Kim McConnell's friends, Alyssa Davis and Cassie Forrester immediately agreed to meet with Jolyn Knowlton.

Jolyn had told them she wanted to write one last article for the *Tribune-Review*, about Kim, among other things. And she had to write it that day.

They met for a late lunch at The Olive Press, Hyatt Hotel Pittsburgh International Airport. Jolyn wanted to meet near the airport because she planned to take a flight for somewhere after she had written the article and submitted it to her editor Stephen Winslow via Email.

The three selected the Cousine Nouvelle—pan-seared spicy scallops served with a toasted conscous that nicely accented the natural sweetness and subtlety of the fresh scallops.

Conscous. Zeke.

Jolyn didn't eat much, pushing the food around on her plate. She mostly listened.

Alyssa and Cassie talked and talked and talked about Kim.

The discussion drifted to Kim's love for literature such as *Anna Karenina* and *Madame Bovary*.

Adultery is death.

As Kim's two friends reminisced, Jolyn reflected upon what the killer who called himself Kurt had divulged during pillow talk. What he told her that she didn't tell Stephen or Detective Woods and the others at the cabin. She didn't tell them because she thought he may have been hallucinating or merely fabricating. And then, she had been at times under the influence of mind-altering drugs herself. Kurt had told her he had lived previous lives. Reincarnation. He had been Vlad Tepes. He had been Jack the Ripper.

Cassie mentioned Kim's fondness for Byron's *Don Juan*.

Kurt had often quoted Lord Byron, particularly from one work, *The Giaour*, and now the poetry echoed in Jolyn's mind.

> *But first on earth as Vampire sent,*
> *The corpse shall from the tomb be rent:*
> *Then ghastly haunt thy native place,*
> *And suck the blood of all thy race;*
> *There from thy daughter, sister, wife,*
> *At midnight drain the stream of life;*
> *Yet loathe the banquet which perforce*
> *Must feed thy livid living corpse.*
> *Shall know the demon for their sire,*
> *At cursing thee, thou cursing them,*
> *Thy flowers are withered on the stem.*
> *Wet thine own best blood shall drip*
> *Thy gashing tooth and haggard lip;*
> *Then stalking to thy sullen grace,*
> *Go—and with Gouls and Afrits rave;*
> *Till these in horror shrink away*
> *From Spectre more accursed than they!*

But his name wasn't Kurt. No, his name was Nathan Redmond. By the time Jolyn had woke around noon this day after her escape they had his name. And they had found human body parts in his freezer at the funeral home outside Detroit.

> *They won't find him.*
> *No, he will find me*
> *Evil will stalk me.*
> *Fear no evil.*
> *I must understand the nature of evil in order to defeat evil.*

Jolyn reflected on her thoughts about the man who would have killed her, and still might.

Nathan Redmond had sent an Email to the *Pittsburgh Tribune-Review* this morning. It said, "Ha ha ha. Tell them to catch me if they can. It's a jolly nice lark. What a dance I am leading."

Nathan Redmond—a psychopath infatuated with murder, Jolyn deduced. *No remorse. No concept of guilt. No conscience. Incapable of love. No cure. No possibility of rehabilitation. Evil evermore. Until he is stopped. I must . . .*

Jolyn suddenly rose from the table. "I have to go now, Alyssa, Cassie. Thank you for talking with me. I am so sorry for the loss of your dear friend, Kim."

The pair nodded miserably.

276

They had agreed beforehand not to tell Jolyn that Kim's brother Duane had shot Dexter Curtis and the others. The family had suffered enough the two judged. Allysa and Cassie both hoped Duane would go after Dexter again, and they encouraged him to do exactly that. They encouraged him with sex.

"Kim was a wonderful person," Alyssa said softly, "I love her so much."

"Please be nice to her, Jolyn," Cassie urged pleadingly. "Kim's dead now. She can't defend herself."

Jolyn took a room at the Hyatt and began the article on her laptop.

***

Rape turns into murder

By Jolyn Knowlton
Pittsburgh Tribune-Review

PITTSBURGH—McConnell vs. Curtis. The party's over. Dexter Curtis is free at last. But is he? Yes, Kim McConnell is dead. Dexter Curtis had no part in her untimely and tragic passing.

But others are dead as well. Did he play any part in those deaths? Perhaps. Perhaps not. But others have been killed because of him and the rape allegations.

I witnessed the murder of William Garcia. Garcia had been shot outside Reggie's Fat City that night along with Curtis and the others. Curtis and Garcia had some sort of personal relationship prior to the shooting.

A man named Nathan Redmond murdered William Garcia as I watched, helpless. Redmond then kidnapped me. I escaped but not until I learned much about this psychopathic serial killer.

Redmond told me who he has killed, some of them. He will kill again and again and again, until he is apprehended. Not only did he kill—he committed unspeakable atrocities on the bodies of some of his victims. The police and FBI have released what information they want the public to know about this man, labeling him as the latest most dangerous psychopathic serial killer.

Nathan Redmond revealed to me that someone paid him to assassinate certain individuals involved in the Dexter Curtis case. In addition to William Garcia, one of the individuals he terminated was Hank Gorton, whose body has just been found. Gorton, a private investigator, broke into my apartment and set up a hidden camera. He filmed me in various stages of undress and had the pictures published on the internet. He later confronted me and

277

forced me by gunpoint to expose myself and engage in certain sexual acts which he also filmed.

Nathan Redmond revealed to me that someone paid him to murder a woman named Sondra Lewis and make it appear to be a suicide. This same Sondra Lewis confided to me personally that she had a sexual encounter with Dexter Curtis after the alleged rape of Kim McConnell. After Curtis appeared in that news conference holding his wife's hand and admitting adultery.

Ruthless criminals have been major players on Team Curtis. They did "it" to me. They did "it" to Kim McConnell. She suffered far worse than I did throughout this ordeal. May God rest her soul. They did "it" to Sondra Lewis. May God rest her soul. They did "it" to William Garcia and Aldo Martinez. May God rest their souls.

They also did "it" to former district attorney, James Hawkins. I call upon him to speak out on this matter. So God may rest his soul.

A fire took her Kim McConell's life. But Team Curtis took her dignity first. They did rape her.

***

Jolyn transmitted the article and left for the airport.
She had unfinished business.
Where will I go?
Conscous.
Zeke.
Yes, I'll leave this up to the authorities.
Except for Redmond.
They won't find him.
He'll find me.
Evil.
A rattrap.
Fear no evil.

CHAPTER 93

Someone will die tonight.

The thought pervaded Nathan Redmond's mind as he dressed for the evening's entertainment.

He had Jolyn Knowlton. But then he lost her. She slipped from his diabolical grasp just moments before her planned demise. And what a plan. She would have been the main ingredient in one of his favorite liver dishes.

Redmond put on the long black wig and affixed the bushy, drooping mustache. He donned the red suit and black cape and stared in the mirror as he held up the facsimile of the most famous picture of Vlad Tepes, a woodblock print from one of the propaganda pamphlets printed by the Germans on the then recently invented printing press. In the picture Vlad ate his dinner surrounded by impaled bodies. Redmond laughed satanically. He knew what Vlad had for dinner that day—liver.

He walked the short distance from the Hawthorne Hotel on Essex Street in Salem to the Club Crypt. He had been there before. But not to kill.

Redmond strolled down a candlelit alley to the cobblestone patio, illuminated with black and purple lights. The outside walls of the club had cracked from years of wear. The windows had been cemented up. Doorways with iron scroll trellises three stories up had been filled with bricks. A Spanish-tiled fountain on the patio flowed dry ice from many burning candles placed in the water.

No one glanced twice at him. Not around this place. In fact, he thought his dress to be rather conservative in this crowd.

But I'm the only true vampire here tonight.

He entered inside the dark club through a black, shiny hallway draped with white chiffon and brightened only by red lightning.

The old wood bar, twenty-five feet long and eighteen feet high, currently featured devilish dancers dressed in latex, leather, garters, and fishnet stockings. He ordered one drink and took it upstairs to what was called the Dark Playroom. Velvet couches and more candles. The DJs spun everything from old school Goth to the newest industrial electronic.

Redmond sat on a couch and waited.

His thoughts drifted again to *Don Juan*, Byron's brilliant work that to him rivaled Milton's *Paradise Lost*, Wordsworth's *The Prelude*, and Spencer's *The Faerie Queene*.

He then began to recite softly the verses of *The Giaour*.

Lord Byron had compiled shocking verse and notes pertaining to the Nosferatu he had written in Arabic while in Albania in 1808. This material had never been published anywhere, although some of his later poems did touch upon vampires in a quite disturbing manner. The despot of Albania, Ali Pasha, became infatuated with Lord Byron, and fascinated him with unimaginable tales of Nosferatu, endowed with supernatural sexual prowess, seducing women and turning them into zombies. Ali Pasha introduced Byron to the "dark gift" of the Nosferatu.

Mary Shelley conceived *Frankenstein* while in the embrace of Lord Bryon in June, 1816, at Villa Diodati in Geneva, Switzerland. Redmond suspected that she lived a more terrible nightmare than the horror novel she wrote. Lord Byron had seduced her half sister, Fanny Inlay, and also Harriet Westbrook, Percy Shelly's wife. Both committed suicide. Harriet drowned herself and her premature baby fathered by Byron. Mary later married Percy.

She never told her real horror story until on her deathbed in 1851 in London. The nurse who cared for Shelley in those last days wrote an account of the author's seemingly incoherent ramblings of sexual liaisons with a vampire in her youth. The nurse had read *Frankenstein*, and chalked up the diatribe to an overactive imagination, fueled by morphine to combat the pain.

Of particular interest was the nurse's description of Shelley's recollection of an abnormal feeling of being unable to move or talk, as she believed her psyche was being manipulated by the vampire. She claimed he psychically penetrated her mind and whimsically induced in her a state of both incredibly intense fear, and extraordinary, extreme pleasure.

Even perhaps more enlightening was the short story, "The Vampyre," written by Mary Shelley's close friend, Dr. John Polidori. The doctor also happened to be Lord Byron's personal physician. Lord Ruthven, the vampire of the story, was in fact Lord Byron, or so Polidori told Mary Shelley. He also revealed to her that Byron had an obsession with blood, often drinking it from a wine glass, and would ignore questions from whence it came.

The verses from *The Giaour* fueled Redmond's already raging lust. "*But first on earth as Vampire sent, Thy corpse shall from the tomb be rent: The ghastly haunt thy native place. And suck the blood of all thy race; There from thy daughter, sister, wife, At midnight drain the stream of life; Yet loathe the—*"

An attractive and scantily dressed as a witch young woman interrupted Redmond's morbid contemplation.

Her—it will be her!

Thou shalt not suffer a witch to live.

How shalt she die?

Something cryptic.

The dark gift.

CHAPTER 94

The witch wiggled.

In his face. For his benefit he had no doubt.

I'll make her wiggle. Wiggle, wiggle. Die, die.

The witch glanced over her shoulder and smiled seductively.

"Hey," he called.

She turned back and faced him. "Hey, yourself."

"You are a witch," he observed, but a very special witch, I would be willing to wager."

He admired the sheer spider web mesh halter style mini-dress with a low scoop front neckline that had ruffle trim. She wore a witch's hat trimmed with Marabou feathers from which red long red hair dangled in ringlets. Very sensually appealing young lady, although she seemed slightly stoned.

A redhead. I want a redhead. Like Jolyn Knowlton.

"Yes, I am a *special* witch. I read minds, foretell the future, and prepare a variety of magical herbal oils, creams, and powders. I consort with devils and demons and put them under my spell. No, I didn't graduate from Harry Potter's Hogwarts School of Witchcraft. I obtained my Venefica at Hexenshule in Klagenfurt, Austria. But do you know *which* witch I am?"

"A witch from Salem?"

"Exactly! How did you know?"

"Lucky guess."

"So guess my name."

"Please give me a clue."

"Money, money," she almost screamed, as she simulated a violent fit. "Sin and misery."

"No, that doesn't help."

"Elizabeth Knapp—that's me. That's what she roared and screamed while demonically possessed."

"Well, please sit down, Elizabeth, and tell me about this possession of yours."

The one who called herself Elizabeth sat on the otherwise unoccupied couch very close to him. He summoned a waitress and she ordered a Bloody Mary.

He smirked, adrenaline rising.

I'll make her a Bloody Mary. Yes indeed. Very bloody.

Elizabeth told him a long and involved story about how the Devil appeared to her many times over a three year period and proffered to her money, silks, fine clothes, and promised to show her the whole world. So she signed a covenant with Satan to become a witch and gave herself up to him soul and body.

She finished the story, looked at Redmond amusedly, and asked, "So who are you supposed to be?"

"Why don't you guess?"

"I mean, I know you're a vampire. But any particular vampire?"

"You have to guess, Elizabeth."

"Nicholas Cage? Tom Cruise? Two of my fav vampires. I just love *Vampire's Kiss*. Nicholas Cage is a psycho who thinks he's a vampire. I mean, the dude is wacko and it's hilarious. And he eats a live cockroach. Yuk! And everyone loves *Interview with the Vampire* with Tom Cruise and Brad Pitt. I get wet every time I watch that movie. And I'm not talking about a crying jag."

"No, not Cage or Cruise. And if you want vampire movies try *Nosferatu: A Symphony of Horrors*. It first played more than eighty years ago in Germany. Kind of a take on Bram Stoker's novel. Too much of a take, apparently. Stoker's widow sued the maker of the film. She sought to destroy all copies but they continued to surface over the years. A remake entitled *Nosferatu the Vampyre* was released a little over twenty years ago. Then several years after that a restored copy of the original became available."

"Well, I'll have to drop a couple tabs of acid and watch the flick sometime. Sounds scary. So which vampire are you? Bela Lugosi? That dude is scary! You're not scary."

"No, not Bela Lugosi. Go back about six hundred years."

"The real Dracula dude!"

"Very close, Elizabeth. Actually, I'm his son—Radu."

"Really?"

"Oh yes."

"Sweet."

"Speaking of sweet, would you like some candy?" he asked, as he extended his hand that contained little brightly colored pills about the size of an eraser.

"What are they?"

"Ya Ba, also known as Nazi Speed. A stronger and longer lasting high than Ecstasy."

"Hey, I heard about this stuff. Comes from Thailand and Laos they say, and difficult to get." She took several from his hand and swallowed them with a sip of the Bloody Mary. "What's up with that cane you have?"

"Not a cane—a stake. Many hundred years old. As is this emblem hanging from the chain around my neck."

"Well, tell me the story, dude!"

He informed her that the emblem represented the Order of the Dragon, a secret fraternal organization founded in 1387 by the Holy Roman Emperor. The emblem of the order consists of a dragon with its wings extended, hanging on a cross. The same emblem that hung over the door at Curtea Domneasca, Vlad Dracula's palace in Bucharest.

The one who called himself Radu explained that "drac" meant "dragon" in Romanian, with "ul" being the definitive article. Vlad Tepes, or Vlad III, inspired Bram Stoker's novel. His father, Vlad II, had been a member of the Order of the Dragon. The father became known as Vlad the Dragon, or Vlad Dracul. The ending "ula" in Romanian meant "the son of." Thus Vlad III became Vlad Dracula, "the son of the dragon."

He expounded that the surname "Tepes" means "The Impaler" in the Romanian language. Vlad Tepes enforced his self-righteous morality upon his country, expressing violently a particular concern with female chastity. His victims most often experienced torture or death as a result of their indiscretions. Some were impaled through the vagina. Vlad's own unfaithful mistress suffered such a fate.

Elizabeth sighed, looking a little distant.

But he went on. "Vlad the Impaler, the first 'Son of the Dragon,' murdered 100,000 victims by impalement, one of the most gruesome ways of dying one can possibly imagine. He ordered his subordinates to oil the stakes and make sure they were not too sharp, or else the victim might die too quickly from shock. Except for the unfaithful women who got it in the vagina, like I said. And babies were frequently impaled on a stake forced through their mother's chest. But the 'Son of the Dragon' also liked to put nails in heads, burn them alive, scalp and skin, mutilate sexual—"

Elizabeth interrupted, "I dig the group Type O Negative. Tunes like 'Christian Woman' about a chick with a cross on her bedroom wall and the image of a prick burning in her mind and between her thighs. Yeah, and 'Little Miss Scare-All' is another righteous tune. The vamp with the Devil's mark on her neck practices boo bitch craft."

"So which one are you Elizabeth, the X-tian nympho or the horny vamp?"

"Both, dude, both. When I'm in the mood."

He continued, "Nosferatu have the 'dark gift'—the ability to seduce women mentally, and then seduce them physically, over and over and over. Until the women turn into zombies, their bodies satiated with sex, and their brains satiated with remembrances of that sex. Euphoria that they try to relive in their minds again and again. It's all they obsess about. A Nosferatu possesses meta-normal perception, hyper-dimensional consciousness, and extraordinary telepathic powers. A Nosferatu also has superhuman physical ability, which is increased even more dramatically by ingesting human blood. A Nosferatu can maintain a continuous erection, despite multiple ejaculations."

"I know all about that," Elizabeth cooed, "it's called Viagra. You're making me . . . it's midnight . . . do you have a place we could go? I'm in the mood."

"Yes, my dear Elizabeth, I surely do."

CHAPTER 95

"What about the gift?" Elizabeth asked as she teasingly shed her clothing. "Did you take your Viagra, honey?"

Sweet indeed, Redmond observed silently, *but not as sweet as Jolyn.*

"Soon my lovely witch, soon." He produced two glasses and a bottle. "Red Zinfandel. 2000 Montevina Terra d'Orod Old Vines. Hefty and hedonistic. Like blood."

"Well, let's have a glass of blood!"

"To the 'dark gift.' Thank you, Vlad Tepes, my dear father."

They clicked glasses.

"You really play this vampire thing to the hilt," she complimented expectantly. "I like it."

He disrobed and pushed her gently on the bed and lay atop her.

"Elizabeth?"

"Yes, Radu?"

"I don't really want to have sex with you—yet."

"No? It seems to me that you do." She stroked his impressive erection. "It seems to me you *really* do." She began to lick the head of his cock. "What *is* this on your penis? A tattoo?"

"Yes—the sacred name."

Elizabeth attempted to pronounce the word with no vowels.

"A mortal must not say the sacred name aloud."

"Sorry." She giggled.

"*Die Zauberinnem soltu nicht leben lassen.*"

"Say what?"

"German. 'Thou shalt not suffer a witch to live.' Exodus 22:18."

286

"Well, you could eat me before you screw me to death, dude."

"Yes, my dear Elizabeth, I certainly would be honored to eat you. Did you know that the correct word for eating human flesh is anthropophagy?"

"Oh yeah, oh yeah. Do it, dude—anthropophagy—eat me. You got me hot. I am yours, my lord. Bite me, please. Take me to your ethereal world. Take me!"

The one who called himself Radu kissed her tenderly, her face, her lips, her neck. His hands and mouth moved to embrace her breasts. He slowly licked in a circle outside the areola of her left breast, and circled closer toward the nipple as he would an ice cream cone. Teasing her by zeroing in with his tongue, and retreating, he then quickly flicked her nipple, and very delicately bit it. She shivered.

"There is something to be said for a witch's teats," he quipped, as he tried to get as much of one in his mouth as he could, and then the other. He smothered the round curve of her belly with wet kisses. Lower and lower his tongue played with her body. She pushed his head eagerly between her legs. He blew delicately on her clit, which was already exposed.

"Oh my, Radu, you are such a cunning linguist," she moaned.

"Elizabeth, you have a very large clitoris. I think you *are* a witch. Did you know that the word 'clitoris' come from the Greek *kleitoris*, which means a divine, or goddess-like little hill? And I'm going to worship yours. I love that little patch of red hair." He nuzzled it with his nose.

"Hey dude!" she blurted. "Eat a beaver and save a tree, will ya? I'm into ecology, ya know? Damn it! You're torturing me. I'm going to pull your ears right off when you really get going, if you ever do. Now quit talking!"

Radu took her throbbing, eager clit into his mouth and gently sucked on it, at the same time flicking his tongue all around it. She put her hands on his head, pushing him down on her sex as she tugged on his ears playfully. But then he moved his mouth away from her clit, looked up, and made eye contact.

"Can you ascertain for certain if a woman is a witch?" he asked scornfully. "Of course you can," he answered himself.

"Real witches engage in ritualistic sex with the Devil and his fallen angels," she moaned, barely able to speak. "The first written documentation of this is the Toulouse trial of Anne-Marie de Georgel in 1335. Now get to it, you devil!"

"Of course witches do the Devil, my dear Elizabeth. That is well chronicled in the *Malleus Maleficarum*, which was an international best seller and the bible all about witches several hundred years ago. Go back a few centuries ago. Alleged witches were hunted down, strip-searched, tortured, mutilated, and executed. The genital search was a necessary requirement during any witch trial. Back then an enlarged clitoris was today's fingerprint and DNA evidence to prove one undoubtedly a witch."

"Would you please stop talking, dude! Just lick the slit, for Chrissake!"

But he droned on. "The discovery of abnormally large genitalia usually resulted in a death sentence. But not always. Sometimes the woman was shown mercy and the clitoris was amputated instead of her head. In 1595 Nicolas Remy published Daemonolatria which proclaimed no mercy for witches. Like mad dogs, they should not be spared. Dr. Francois Rabelais, in his *Gargantua and Pantagruel*, maintained that an itching clitoris dominates a witch's every thought and action. Is your clitoris itching, Elizabeth?"

"Oh yeah, baby. Do me! Please do me!"

He sucked her clit back into his mouth again. Flicking, sucking, flicking, sucking. Tongue, lips, tongue, lips.

Elizabeth screamed and bucked, pulling him down on her in a frenzy, practically suffocating him. Harder and harder she rocked her pussy back and forth on his mouth. Faster and faster.

"Ohh . . . ahh . . . oh my fucking . . . I . . . oh fuck . . ."

The one who called himself Radu reached up with his hands and manipulated her hard, erect nipples as he sucked her clit relentless and felt her love juice as she wailed like a banshee.

But no, Radu didn't stop, even when she quieted down a bit.

He took her to the peak again.

And then he ate her sex.

Redmond bit off her clitoris viciously and swallowed it quickly. He rose from between her bloody legs to look in the most terrified eyes he had even seen. The blood reminded him of his late father the preacher and the virgin sacrifice of the high priestess. His eyes gleamed like burning coals. He bit her jugular savagely.

Her screams soon turned to a gurgling sound as blood spurted onto both of them like a gusher.

Over and over Redmond chanted, "She walks in beauty, like the night," a verse from Lord Byron's *She Walks in Beauty*.

Finally the woman became silent.

A deadly silence.

"*Now* I want to screw you, my love. Not to death—in death."

He spread her lifeless legs and entered her.

Yes, the 'dark gift.'

For hours he pleasured himself with her corpse.

Finally he ejaculated his semen in a frenzy inside the woman, as he roared, "For you, Jolyn! For you! Until we meet again."

Redmond impaled her on the stake before he left the hotel room.

"I am Radu!" he roared.

He impaled her through the vagina.

"I am a Nosferatu!"

He cut off her tongue.

"I am the son of Vlad Tepes!"

He cut out her liver.

Hotel personnel didn't pay him much attention as he walked out of the lobby, blood dripping from his chin. Just another nut case going over to the Club Crypt to party they speculated.

CHAPTER 96

Jolyn called from Jerusalem.

Stephen informed her that Nathan Redmond had killed again.

He met a young woman at a club in Salem, Massachusetts, took her to his hotel room and mutilated her beyond human comprehension. He left a note. "Ha ha ha. Catch me if you can. It's a jolly nice lark. What a dance I am leading."

"Jack the Ripper," Jolyn murmured.

"He sent a similar note to the paper after your last article appeared."

"I read a very interesting and enlightening book about Jack the Ripper—*Portrait of a Killer* by Patricia Cornwell. The author maintained that there is noticeably less neural activity in a psychopath's frontal lobe than there is in a 'normal' person's. Which suggests that the inhibitions and constraints that keep most of us from engaging in violent acts or giving in to murderous impulses do not register in the frontal lobe of the psychopathic brain. Thoughts and situations that would give most of us pause, cause distress or fear, and inhibit cruel, violent, or illegal impulses don't register in the psychopath's frontal lobe. That it is wrong to steal, rape, assault, lie, murder, or do other evil that degrades, cheats, and dehumanizes others does not compute with the psychopath."

"Yes, does not compute," Stephen agreed.

"The author poses the questions, 'Does an abnormal frontal lobe cause a person to become a psychopath? Or does the frontal lobe become abnormal because the person is a psychopath?' I wonder."

"Yes, I wonder too. Where do you suppose Redmond is headed now, Jolyn?"

"Jerusalem. If he's not here already."

"You mean . . . you—"

"Yes, Stephen. I'm going to stop him."

"But—"

"It's me Redmond wants, more than life itself. He thinks he's in love with me."

"But he would have killed you if you hadn't escaped."

"Yes, he would have."

"This 'game' you are playing is much too dangerous, Jolyn."

"It's the only way, Stephen. The only way to stop him—from killing again . . . and again."

"I also read the book, *Portrait of a Killer*. The author suggests that Jack the Ripper had a deformity of the penis that likely left him disfigured if not mutilated. Probably incapable of an erection and/or not enough of a penis for penetration. He may have had to squat like a woman to urinate. Does Nathan Redmond have a problem with his penis?"

"Not like that."

"Like what, then?"

"The tattoo . . ."

"Yes, you mentioned the tattoo of the wolf on his chest."

"No—the tattoo on his penis—the sacred name."

Jolyn hung up.

"I love you, Jolyn," Stephen said into the dead line.

CHAPTER 97

Bless me father.

During the ten hour El Al flight from New York City to Tel Aviv Redmond remembered his father.

Dr. Jeremiah Redmond had once been a practicing psychiatrist. He authored several books on hypnotism and professed to be an expert on the Benet and Fere Method of Fascination. The patient could be induced into a complete state of automatism under which the subject's personality and short term memory were completely suppressed. This method had been, according to him, clinically proven to be most successful with insane and mentally incapacitated patients where all else had failed.

He also boasted of once having worked for the CIA, involved in mind control research. Brainwashing, narco-hypnosis, electro-convulsive therapy, neuro-linguistics programming, astral projection, and the like. And then he was called by the Lord to become a minister.

Dr. Redmond had his own alternative to the Bar Mitzvah ceremony when a young man reached the age of accountability. Nathan recalled the first one he witnessed at his father's church, Sacred Name Chapel.

The organist stopped playing and Dr. Redmond walked out in a white linen robe. Twelve men in black robes joined him at the altar.

"The twelve disciples," his mother had whispered to him.

"Good morning, our supreme higher power," the congregation greeted in unison.

"We will begin our service today with the table of the Lord," Dr. Redmond announced. "Please come forward and participate."

The pews emptied and the congregation came forward to be served the bread and wine to represent the body and the blood. In later years Nathan discovered there were some hallucinogenic ingredients added to the symbolic body and the blood.

Dr. Redmond then preached his sermon. All about submission. He quoted numerous verses, including Hebrews 13:17, "Obey them that have rule over you, and submit yourselves: for they watch for your souls . . ."

Rhythmic music played softly in the background. The volume was turned up every time the prancing preacher paused to sip from a glass of water.

Nathan's father was incredibly impressive and charismatic. He commanded undivided attention to his words as he paced and flung his hands as he spoke. He kept pointing his finger at the crowd with every "you" and played on their fear and guilt.

Several young men stood and went to the aisles. They began to utter sounds that Nathan could not recognize as any language he was familiar with, and he had been studying several in the church school. Just mumbo-jumbo he thought. A radiance of incandescent light appeared around the bodies of the young men. Their eyes appeared to be aglow. They began to jump up and down, sing, dance, and chant in incoherent tongues. More came to the aisles and engaged in the same behavior. Soon there were a dozen. Two elders brought out some black wreathes.

"What are those things for?" Nathan had asked his mother.

"This is the black crown ceremony," his mother replied as the elders placed the wreathes on the heads of the twelve disciples. "Those are crowns of thorns. The holy men wear them to generate the psychic ability necessary to bring them to spiritual and physical nirvana—the state of perfect blessedness achieved by the absorption of the soul into the supreme spirit. When they do attain nirvana, it can be transferred to other believers via the sacred service. Think of it as communion with the higher power and his disciples."

Nathan wondered what the "sacred service" might be but didn't ask. He would soon see for himself.

The dozen young men came to the altar and got down on their knees in front of the twelve disciples who opened their black robes. Nothing underneath.

"I command you, sinners, to perform sacred service!" Nathan father had roared. "Repent! The acceptance of the holy seed of my disciples will bring you remission of sin and a special communion with the supreme higher power."

One by one the young men brought the disciples to orgasm with their mouths and accepted the holy seed. Each disciple soundlessly ejaculated down the sinner's throat and all over his face.

As the disciples squeezed out the last drops, Dr. Redmond proclaimed, "I anoint you and baptize you in the name of the sacred one. Your seed is now sacred and you must give it to your supreme higher power."

One by one the twelve young men approached the now kneeling Dr. Redmond. He performed fellatio on each one of them.

Afterwards, the preacher said solemnly, "Go my children. Your sins have been forgiven. And now, it is time for the 'hieros gamos.' Who will be the high priestess?"

Every hand raised, but one—a pretty young redheaded girl sitting in the back with her family.

"What is the 'hieros gamos,' Mother?" Nathan had asked.

"The sacred marriage. The supreme higher power receives his full divine power by uniting with the high priestess. In the sacred marriage the man and woman actually become the gods. The high priestess, who must be a virgin, is the holy vessel wherein the supernatural semen of the supreme higher power symbolically impregnates believers with immortality. Not in this world, but in the next."

"What about you?" Dr. Redmond pointed. "You with the red hair in the light blue dress. You are the high priestess. Come up here, young lady!"

The girl didn't move.

Two elders approached her.

She stood in resignation as they took her. The parents didn't protest.

"Your father has the sacred name written in Hebrew on his penis," Nathan's mother advised him knowingly. You won't be able to read it from here, and you should never say the word aloud, anyway. Strictly verboten."

The elders stripped the blue dress from the girl. Then her bra and panties. Dr. Redmond bent her over and entered her from behind as she cried out and grimaced noticeably.

The preacher praised the Lord loudly as he pleased himself with the girl. When he finished and pushed her away, Nathan could see the blood dripping down her legs. She put the blue dress back on, picked up her bra and panties and went back to her seat, a blank expression on her face. Her blue eyes looked so cold and distant. Like ice. Like Jolyn's eyes. The girl never returned to Sacred Name Chapel.

Six months later Nathan's father performed fellatio on his son in front of the entire congregation. After Nathan had performed fellatio on the disciple known as Peter.

No virgin girls were present to participate in 'hieros gamos' that Sabbath. So Dr. Redmond bent his son over and entered him anally.

His first and last homosexual experience. Although after his father passed away he did have the sacred name tattooed on his penis in memory of the man and Nathan practiced his own version of 'hieros gamos' with young women.

But he hated homosexuals.

Jolyn knew he killed Garcia and Martinez. She knew about the marks he killed for money and the young women he killed for lust.

I should tell her about the faggots I offed for fun. And sent to my father's church in Hades.

Nathan Redmond's flight landed in Tel Aviv.

He claimed his baggage and took a Nesher private cab to Jerusalem.

"What are you going to do in Jerusalem?" the Israeli cabbie who drove like a drunken teenager asked.

"Find my high priestess," Redmond muttered incoherently.

"What?"

"Yes, the 'hieros gamos.' And then a burnt offering for my Lord."

The cabbie tried to ignore his passenger's lunatic laughter.

CHAPTER 98

Stephen Winslow gasped in gasped in disgust.

He had turned on the television. ESPN. Tim Grey interviewing Dexter Curtis.

"Dexter, your first season has been nothing but turmoil. You're not playing Sunday against Tennessee. What effect do you think all your off-the-field problems are having on your team?"

"Turmoil? The only *turmoil* that matters is the turmoil I create on the field. Since I won't be on the field Sunday, the Steelers will lose. I'm the man. No booty dance—no chance."

"You don't put much faith in your team, Dexter."

"Faith? I got faith. See this tattoo on my arm?"

"Your owner, Jeremiah Jones, has indicated disgust with your behavior. He—"

"I don't give a damn what that homo says. Like I said, the only thing that matters is what I do *on* the field. And I can't do it on the field if he suspends me. Screw him."

"Dexter, what are your feelings about the dead woman, Kim McConnell?"

"Feelings? She did bear false witness against me. A mortal sin, 'eh? 'Thou shalt not bear false witness against thy neighbor.' The ninth commandment."

"A newspaper reporter in Pittsburgh wrote an article about you that attributed her kidnapping and certain murders to—"

"Fuck that stupid bitch! I told you to stick to football in this interview. Fuck you too, asshole."

The profanity was bleeped but what Curtis said was obvious if one is a lip reader. Tim Grey, a devout man, thanked the Lord that the interview did not take place in person because Dexter Curtis looked very, very angry.

After Curtis disappeared off camera, Grey stated morosely, "Dexter Curtis is out of control—a catastrophe looking for a place to happen."

Stephen recalled what Jolyn had said about Curtis being a fatal distraction to the Pittsburgh Steelers in his office the day after his DUI arrest. They had watched Coach Lowry's press conference. Jolyn said she would have asked Lowry, "Hey coach, are you sorry yet you drafted this fatal distraction?"

Stephens cracked a small smile.

Such a precocious child, he mused.

Then his face turned wry.

And he prayed for Jolyn's safety.

CHAPTER 99

On Tuesday Dexter Curtis showed up for practice, late. The other players, except Kevin Jones, gave him the cold shoulder.

It didn't take long for Curtis to tussle with his own teammates, particularly the offensive linemen. He and Gary Randazzo, the center, exchanged a flurry of punches.

Coach Lowry ignored the altercations. He thought a little spirited play might well motivate the team.

Contact with the quarterback was prohibited in practice. Ronny Masters, first string quarterback, dropped back to pass. Curtis hit him helmet-to-helmet from the blind side just as Masters turned to look for a receiver on the other side of the field. The quarterback crumpled like a rag dog into a fetal position on the turf. The team stood in shock as an ambulance pulled up. Masters was put on a stretcher and rushed to a hospital.

Jeremiah Jones watched the practice. He ordered security personnel to escort Dexter Curtis from the field.

"He's done!" Jones screamed at Coach Lowry. "He'll never wear the black and gold again. And you might think seriously about politics, Bill. Next year we're drafting a quarterback. The one we have now may never play again—thanks to Dexter Curtis."

CHAPTER 100

The reporter from the *Pittsburgh Post-Gazette* who interviewed Dexter Curtis at Emmanuel Christian Church after the death of Kim McConnell tracked him down.

The Steelers player waited at Pittsburgh International Airport waiting for a departing flight, ticket in hand.

"Dexter, you really put the big hurt on Tommy Masters."

"Bob, I didn't mean to hit him. Going all out like that, I couldn't stop on a dime, ya know? I can't play at half speed. Not my style."

"Masters had some rather derogatory things to say about you lately, Dexter. How you disrupt and adversely affect the team."

"Who cares what that pansy says. I don't much care for fancy fruits."

"Are you implying Tommy is gay?"

"Like my home boys tell me: If it looks like a rat and smells like a rat, by golly, it is a rat."

"But he has a girlfriend, that model. How could you miss her at practice on numerous occasions?"

"Yeah, well, our senator who just came out of the closet and resigned has a wife and kids don't he? And he's being sued by some dude who worked for him for sexual harassment." Curtis stopped his foot dramatically. "Splat! All I did was stomp a rat."

"Dexter, do you think you'll ever play a down for the Steelers again?"

"Hell no. I'll be wearing different colors soon. Maybe the Raiders. Big bad Dexter Curtis and the black and silver has to be a match made in heaven. 'And we know that things work together for good to them that love God, to them who are the called according to his purpose.' Romans 8:28. I gotta go. My flight is boarding."

"Do you have any parting words for the Steelers or the fans?"

"Fuck Pittsburgh."

CHAPTER 101

Dexter Curtis flew to Miami.

He went home, angry, very angry.

Tommy Masters suffered paralysis. Much like Darryl Stingley of the New England Patriots had been paralyzed after a hit in a preseason game in August, 1978. The Oakland Raiders defensive back Jack Tatum crushed Stingley as he ran a crossing pattern. Darryl Stingley severed his fourth and fifth vertebrae and he became a quadriplegic who gets around in a wheelchair. Tatum, known as "the Assassin," never displayed remorse for the results of his actions.

Likewise, Dexter Curtis showed no remorse.

***

Stephen Winslow turned on the television. ESPN. Tim Grey reporting. "Dexter Curtis was involved in an incident involving his wife last night. He allegedly beat her and she is in serious condition at Jackson Memorial Hospital. Juanita Curtis has suffered a miscarriage. The police indicate Curtis will be arraigned this afternoon, and will possibly be charged with murder, among other things. I also have spoken with Jeremiah Jones, owner of the Pittsburgh Steelers. Curtis may be charged in connection with the Ronny Masters tragedy. True, it was a football-related injury, but Curtis purposefully, so Jones maintained, violated the prohibition against contact with the quarterback in practice which the owner witnessed. 'Curtis intentionally caused grievous bodily harm with an illegal helmet-to-helmet hit,' so Jones says. The owner is also taking legal action to declare Curtis's contract null and void. That means the player will be asked to return millions of dollars."

Stephen just shook his head in disgust and horror.

CHAPTER 102

Hall of the names.

Where Jolyn had first met Ezekiel.

She had told Kurt about Zeke. Or rather, she had told Nathan Redmond, psychopathic serial killer and assassin for hire.

He had asked about her past lovers.

Jolyn told him. She told him the truth. To keep him talking about his past lovers. The ones he had murdered. And eaten.

Yad Vashem on the Mount of Remembrance in the western part of Jerusalem. Jolyn had walked down the Avenue of the Righteous Among the Nations with trees planted in honor of non-Jews who saved Jews during the Holocaust. She then entered the Children's Memorial. Inside this cave-like structure, the light of candles is reflected by a system of mirrors, so that millions of flames shine in the darkness, in commemoration of the million-and-a-half children who perished.

Now she stood at the symbolic gravestones at The Hall of Names. The gravestones that recorded names and biographical data of millions of martyrs, as submitted by family members and friends.

A stooped and elderly grey-bearded man stood next to her examining the names. He wore a long blue robe under a multicolored ephod. The robe was much longer than the ephod and the bottom of it was ornamented with bells alternating with pomegranates. He wore a gold, purple, and scarlet breastplate above the ephod.

"Hello, Kurt."

He gasped noticeably, and then laughed.

"How did you recognize me?"

The stench of death. The eyes of a killer.

"Do you mind if I call you Nathan?"

"No, not at all. I didn't like that article you wrote about me, Jolyn. I'm going to punish you."

"Like you did the last woman you murdered?"

"Maybe. I bit off her clitoris, you know. I didn't see that in the papers or on the news. I scalped her. Would you like to see her beautiful red hair?"

"No thank you, Nathan."

"I skinned her. I ate her liver."

"Are you going to kill me, Nathan?"

"No, not if I don't have to. I want you to come with me. You are the most lovely and exotic woman I have ever had the pleasure of knowing. Your flaming red hair is like I picture the fires of hell. But being intimate with you is like I visualize heaven. I want you, Jolyn. I must have you. It's your destiny, don't you see? I want to possess you—in every way. It's God's will, you see."

"It may be your god's will, but it's not my God's will. I can't come with you, Nathan."

"No?"

"No."

"Why not, my love? Pray tell me."

"You are surrounded, Nathan. Mossad agents. This is a trap. I knew you would be compelled to come after me. No matter how dangerous. You don't want to be caught. But you want me more than life itself. You are totally obsessed with me. You want to totally possess me. And then you want to kill me. Don't you, Nathan?"

He laughed again, more like a growl.

"Yes, Jolyn. I don't believe you about the trap."

She raised her hand in a signal.

A dozen female agents revealed themselves by drawing weapons. They masqueraded as a group of American college students, all wearing the same university sweatshirt.

"I never would have guessed. Brilliant, Jolyn. I cased this place before I approached you."

"You're surrounded, Nathan. You can't possibly escape."

"No, I suppose not. But I'm not afraid to die. After all, I'll be born again."

"Who next time?"

"Well, I do like Jerusalem. I shall perhaps return to the earth as the abomination of desolation and stand in the holy place."

"The antichrist."

"Yes. My father will turn and twist in his grave."

"How did your father die, Nathan?"

An ominous, hateful look crossed his face.

"An accident. In the shower. I smashed his head against the edge of the tub."

Jolyn slowly backed away from him.

He began to sing.

Redmond drew the pistol quickly from underneath his robe and shot Jolyn in the chest.

She fell to the ground.

"You are evil," Jolyn gasped. "You *are* evil."

He put the pistol in his mouth and pulled the trigger.

CHAPTER 103

Super Bowl.

That's what the majority of pundits had predicted for the Pittsburgh Steelers in July.

No way. No how. Not now.

Stephen Winslow and Ed Woods both knew it as they watched the game against Tennessee at The Church Brew Works.

"I wanted to come here because this place reminds me of Jolyn," Stephen confided to Ed. "I care a great deal for her."

"Yes, so do I."

"I love her."

"You're old enough to be her father."

They both chuckled.

"Her father is my best friend. Maybe I'll ask him to be best man, Ed."

Woods began to howl. Winslow now frowned.

"What's so funny? Jolyn once said I look like Michael Douglas. He's twenty-five years older than his wife."

"Jolyn looks more like Catherine Zeta Jones, except for the hair color, than you look like Michael Douglas. She told me I look like Karl Malden. Douglas and Malden starred in that TV series, *The Streets of San Francisco.* Remember?"

"I remember. Jolyn loves that movie, *The American President*, starring Douglas. She said I look presidential."

"And she criticized me for being a drunk. I just pray she makes it back from Jerusalem safely," Ed said softly, turning serious.

"And Redmond is apprehended," Stephen added. "She should be safe. *Ha-Mossad le-Modiin ule-Tafkidim Meyuhadim* is protecting her."

"Ah yes, Mossad. She told me she might stay in Israel and work for the LAP Department."

"*Lohamah Psichologit*? Psychological warfare, propaganda, and deception operations. I hear they have quite a few young and attractive females in that department."

"Somehow I think Jolyn would be very good at that. She did escape from Redmond's clutches. That's a first."

"Well, Ed, sure hope she can do it a second time."

"You said you told her to wear that damn bulletproof vest, even to bed."

"Jolyn promised she would. I recommended a Maxsell Model 'Sherman' specifically designed for women. Individual cup size allows a more natural fit, you know."

"So I heard, Stephen. That model even comes in a bunch of colors. Which did Jolyn select?"

"I suggested light blue but she chose desert camouflage. That nut case Redmond thinks he's a vampire, Ed. I've heard all kinds of theories about how to kill vampires. The old stake screwed through the heart, a nail through the temple, remove the vampire's heart and cut it in two, cut off their toes, cut off the head and boil it in vinegar, bury them face downwards, expose them to direct sunlight. So what works?"

Woods sprinkled more garlic powder on his pizza. "In some areas of Romania they still today smear garlic on the windows and doors of their homes, stuff it in the bodily orifices of corpses to prevent the evil ones from entering the dead body, and things like that."

Winslow pushed his pizza away. "You ruined my appetite, Ed. The French occultist Robert Amelian claimed it was arsenic not garlic that foiled vampires. Somewhere along the line garlic, which smells somewhat similar was substituted because it was cheaper."

A substitute linebacker named Rocky who claimed Metallica as his favorite group rocked the Steelers. He sacked the quarterback for a safety and returned an interception sixty yards for a touchdown. The game ended 30-13 in favor of the Titans.

The only amusing note of the entire afternoon for Steelers fans happened in the post-game press conference. Asked about the play of the Steelers rookie cornerback, Ike Baylor, Coach Lowry gushed, "I like Ike!" Most of the reporters guffawed. Lowry didn't get it. He thought they laughed at him.

"He'll make a great senator," Winslow quipped. "He's got all the right stuff."

"Do you think those Republican Party officials are serious? Begging him to run to replace Gary McGarvey?"

"Look what Arnold and Jesse accomplished. Not to mention our late former actor turned president."

"We found some evidence that Hank Gorton had an uncommon interest in Senator McGarvey."

"All sorts of rumors about corruption have begun to surface since he resigned," Stephen said. "Ed, thanks for putting pressure on that webmaster to remove the pictures of Jolyn. That last batch under the caption 'Kidnapped woman gets off' was far beyond the boundaries of human decency."

"The webmaster fessed up that last group of pictures from the incident with Gorton in the parking lot came from Ron Kingston. We got him, Stephen. Kingston is going down."

"Hell is too good for him."

"And Coach Lowry should make a career change. The Steelers are done," Woods concluded, disgusted. "Stick a fork in 'em. This season is over."

"I'm afraid you're right, Ed. They won't even finish at five hundred, let alone make the playoffs."

"Dexter Curtis sent this season right down the drain," Woods grumbled.

"He ruined a lot more than the season, Ed. He ruined lives."

CHAPTER 104

"This is the end."

That's what cannibalistic serial killer Nathan Redmond sang just before he put the barrel of the gun is his mouth, pulled the trigger, and assassinated himself. But not before he believed he had killed Jolyn Knowlton.

"This is the end, beautiful friend. It hurts to set you free, but you'll never follow me. The end of laughter and soft lies. The end of nights we tried to die. This is the . . . end."

Jolyn had heard somewhere that Jim Morrison of The Doors took the name of the group from Aldous Huxley's book on mescaline, *The Doors of Perception.* That book quoted a William Blake poem. "If the doors of perception were cleansed/All things would appear infinite."

She contemplated her own fascination with Blake's work.

Satan, Sin, and Death.

Jolyn called Stephen from Jerusalem.

"Nathan Redmond is dead. I didn't kill him—he killed himself."

She told him everything.

"Lucky for you he shot you in the chest, Jolyn."

"Oh really? You should see the nasty bruise between my breasts."

"I'd love to."

Stephen told her about Dexter Curtis's latest dilemmas. How Curtis beat his pregnant wife and killed his unborn child. How Curtis paralyzed his own team's quarterback with a cheap shot. Stephen told her that enough evidence had already been obtained to charge Ron Kingston with conspiracy to commit murder and several other crimes.

"One other thing, Jolyn . . ."

"Yes, Stephen?"

"Robert Earl Stone. He—"

"How . . . how . . . did you . . . know about him?" she interrupted, jolted.

"I hired a private investigator, remember? Larry stumbled across your Mr. Stone while going through the late Hank Gorton's belongings looking for evidence and leads. Gorton had written in a notebook that you had married one Robert Earl Stone. Larry tracked down this guy. You never married him. It was a fraud. He's a fraud. He played this 'fake marriage' game with several other unsuspecting young women. The credentials he utilized to obtain a professorship—fraudulent. In fact, Stone is now in prison in England. He had been teaching at Oxford and supplemented his income via the sale and distribution of large amounts of cocaine."

Silence on the other end of the line.

Finally Jolyn said softly, "So I was never married. I did suspect Robert occasionally did cocaine, but never caught him, and he denied it."

"No, never married. One more thing." He paused.

"Yes, Stephen?"

"I am the anonymous voice who called you and gave you the tips. Told you about Sondra Lewis . . . and Gorton . . . and gave you the money."

Silence on the other end of the line again.

"But—" she finally blurted.

"It was me, Jolyn."

"So you used me to trap a rat."

"Not exactly. You took that upon yourself in the face of grave danger. I'm very proud of you. But why?"

"*Satan, Sin, and Death.* In order to defeat evil, you must understand the nature of evil."

"Of course, I should have known. Oh, and one more thing."

"What else, Stephen?" she snapped.

"I love you."

Silence once more.

"Will you marry me?"

Silence.

"Is this another fraudulent proposal?" she asked in a much gentler tone.

"No, Jolyn. I love you."

"Maybe I love you, Stephen. But I'm not telling—yet. I'll be home soon. Let's discuss it. Dinner? Your house?"

"There will be a ring in the double chocolate mousse cake. Chew carefully. What do you think your father will say about you marrying a black man?"

"Oh, how about, "Well, you *do* love chocolate, Joey." That's what he'll probably say."

They both laughed.

"I love that sound, Jolyn."

"I can't remember the last time I laughed, Stephen. Why don't you reschedule your vacation to Monaco and the Princess Grace Rose Garden? Make it in about a month. I just might go with you."

"Oh, I didn't know *your* interest in 168 rose cultivars and 4,000 rose bushes rivaled my own."

"But Stephen, I loved the dozen white, pink, red, and yellow roses you gave me on our first date. And . . . somehow I don't think you'll be spending all that much time worshipping the roses."

"You can have all the roses you want, Jolyn. But please, no more guns."

"No more guns, Stephen."

"Promise?"

"I do."

"Till death do us part, Jolyn?"

"No guns. Just roses. Oh . . . and you can call me Joey."

Printed in the United States
41718LVS00007B/14

9 780976 451044